KEPT WOMAN

"Tear my dress off me. That's what you want to do. Tear it off me!"

He shook his head and she knew he saw through her desire to demean him. It angered her that he should find her so transparent, so she undid her buttons as slowly as possible, watching his face, tempting him to push aside her fingers in a frenzy of the passion he held on such a tight leash. Finally she stood beside him naked, her eyes sullen.

"I've never stood like this before a man."

His voice was husky. "You've the most beautiful body I've ever seen. Beautiful . . . You're as I thought you'd be. Lillith reborn. From the first time I saw you I felt a sympathy for Adam."

Zula ran her hands through his hair. "Lillith? Is that another name for Eve?"

He laughed. "She was before Eve and infinitely evil. But Adam found her very desirable—and very destructive."

"I could never hurt you. You've given me everything I could want."

He closed his eyes. "For how long, *ma belle*? I'm afraid the day will come when this cottage will seem very small and I'll appear incredibly ancient." His grave eyes probed into hers. "Zulu, when that day comes, I'll either kill you or myself."

She laughed softly. "I've everything I could want," she assured him. "Everything . . ."

THE PASSION STONE

Harriette deJarnette

Book Margins, Inc.

A BMI Edition

Published by special arrangement with Dorchester Publishing

Printed in the United States of America.

Prelude

It had been a long time since they had heard the dogs, and as they paused for breath, Jules voiced the thought Zulu had been trying to suppress.

"They've called them back. They know even a hound couldn't find its way out of here."

Zulu's hair had fallen loose. Gray fragments of moss clung to the long, tawny strands she tossed back over her shoulders. Defiance was in the gesture and in her eyes. "There's a path," she said. "We'll find it."

Jules smiled down at her, but his voice was grave. "Will we?" He stared out at the lonely stretches of wilderness. "I'd like to believe we'll find it. I'd like to leave more to show for my work than a few runaway slaves hiding in the marshes."

He reached for her hands and held them tightly between his own. Love and compassion reflected in his clear, intelligent eyes. "It's even worse for you, Zulu, you have your Writ. You didn't have to do this."

Zulu looked at their hands. Strange, for the half light of the place darkened the paleness of her skin and lightened his fingers almost to a tan. Still, the contrast was apparent, and it was hard to believe that through their veins ran an equal percentage of Caucasian blood.

That trickle of Africa, that remaining eighth of a darker heritage showed itself so differently in the two of them. Her entire appearance belied it, but it was there, deep inside her. It was there to blame. A whipping boy.

In Jules it was on the outside. In his soft, dark eyes, in the etched, sharp planes of his cheekbones, and in the richness of his voice. Yet, his mind was no battleground of two races. Why, then, did hers have to be?

Would it have been the same, she wondered, if she had been reared differently? Or were the seeds sown and ready, no matter the soil?

Jules had begun to gather wood. "We can shelter here for the night," he told her. "I'll build a fire and tomorrow we'll find the path."

Build a fire to keep away the animals—or the swamp? But of course, Jules wouldn't know. This place wasn't an evil entity to him.

Most of her life, Zulu reflected, she'd been running from the swamp, running from all it meant, all that was buried deep at the very roots of her being. Now there was no hiding place. Now it was all around . . . waiting.

It was silent, too. Silent except for the far away splash of a 'gator and the little furtive swamp noises. Cypresses twisted their tormented knees out of the water and from their branches the gray streamers of Spanish moss trailed—stiff, tattered shrouds.

"It's not fair," she protested softly. "It's not fair for you, Jules. You've at least tried to do right."

He paused, still squatting over the pile of dead wood and brush. "And you?" he asked. There was an intentness about him, as if the answer mattered very much.

She spoke bitterly. The more bitter because it was true and neither he nor she could deny it.

"I've never done anything but destroy."

He continued to regard her, but she could not meet his eyes. She, who had unfalteringly met far more critical gazes, and lied without a qualm of nerve or conscience. Strange that facing the truth at last, her voice thickened and there was no brazenness left.

The fire finally flickered into flames and Jules sat

6

down beside her. He pulled her head onto his shoulder and his fingers ran through the tangled waves of her hair. His touch was tender, soothing, as if she were a child to be comforted.

"It's true, Jules," she persisted. "I've done nothing but destroy. Even you. I wanted to see them hang you."

He shook his head. "It's time to rest now," he said gently.

"I don't want to rest." Zulu pulled away before the nearness of him robbed her of her resolutions. "You know we'll neither sleep with all that out there—so let me talk. I want to tell you everything, Jules. Right from the beginning, through when I met you—and even after."

His eyes told her how sorry he felt, but his touch told her he understood the growing necessity of the thing.

"You don't have to," he said. "It doesn't matter to me. It never has."

She looked at him wonderingly. "I believe you, Jules, still—"

Still, she had to go over it, even if only in her own mind. She had to go back and piece it together, find its beginning, its middle and, maybe, that way she could understand what the end might bring. Maybe, that way, she could understand about herself.

Chapter One

As near as anyone could figure, Zulu was three months old when she came to Elmside. She arrived clasped tightly in the strong arms of the big fieldwoman, Mala.

The plantation was new, then. Clay Haldfar had only come to Alabama four years before, in 1816. The row of elm trees that lined the avenue were still saplings, and though the main house had been completed in the spring, it still had an air of rawness about it.

Miss Ginny Haldfar had been sitting on the veranda when the pair were brought to the house for her brother's approval. It had been two months since she had come to Alabama for her sister-in-law's funeral, and she was still not reconciled to the heat.

Two months, she reflected, as she rocked, hoping to catch a breeze. Two months and it might well be forever, what with her brother's two motherless children to raise. She leaned forward, thinking of her tiny niece.

"Clay," she called, "if that's a female, we might consider taking her into the house for Rosalie."

"It's a female," he assured her, and led Mala up the stairs. He motioned for the woman to hold out the baby.

"Just about the right age, too!" Miss Ginny exclaimed, delighted. "What a bright looking 'ninny!"

"Ninny?" her brother repeated. "She's so light we'll have to put a mark on her so Esmeralda can tell the difference."

Miss Ginny had never been noted for her sense of humor, and now she stared at her brother with indignation. "Nonsense! They're mostly all light at that age. No one in their right mind could mistake her for our little girl."

For all her words, her voice had an uncertain note. Had she not detected the overseer's obvious amusement, the baby might well have been relegated to the quarters at that point. Somehow Blandin always had a stultifying effect upon her. She didn't like him and she didn't like his superior English accent that always seemed to hint at condescension.

Of course Clay's increasing property and prosperity had made it essential that he take on an overseer, but somehow she couldn't quite consider him the God-send

8

her brother thought him. To Clay his only flaw was his occasional bout of fever, but they both agreed that except for this, he never would have left his more profitable trade on Africa's Gold Coast.

It had been his idea to purchase blackbirded merchandise. She reflected on the conversation.

"A man would be a fool to pay the prices they ask hereabouts for field hands. What you need are raw blacks right off the boat."

"But with the slave trade outlawed—" Clay began, only to be interrupted by Blandin's hoot of laughter.

"Blackbirders are still chancing it, Mr. Haldfar. "The *Drusella* was hanging offshore when I left Sierra Leone, and Layton's barracoons were overflowing with top stock. I hear she made it through the Middle Passage with almost half her cargo and they're coming up for auction. I'd be glad to go look them over and see if I can't get what you need."

"I understand they're pretty puny right off the boat."

"True," Blandin agreed, "but fed good food and properly trained you'll have yourself fine stock without spending any more than you want to."

He had been as good as his word, Miss Ginny reflected. The blacks he'd brought back the night before seemed healthy enough, though it would certainly take a pile of victuals to fill out their frames. This woman, Mala, already showed the benefit of wholesome food.

Blandin bowed slightly to Miss Ginny, who, as usual, pretended she didn't notice the gesture.

"The woman's a Kru," he said. "She never bore that child."

Miss Ginny leaned forward. "And why are you so positive?" she inquired.

"Her color, for one thing. I'd say she might not have more than an eighth black blood."

Clay shook his head. "Hells bells, man, how could an octoroon be born on a blackbirder? Besides, by law, she'd be free.''

"Only if someone could prove it." Blandin hesitated. "As for how she happened on the *Drusella*, I have a theory. Kru is a common dialect and I got enough of a story out of Mala to make a fair surmise."

Miss Ginny fanned herself and perked up her ears at the prospect of a story. "What was it you fancied, Mr. Blandin?"

"I think her mother could have been Dave Layton's woman. There's always a scattering of breeds around the posts, but she was the best looking I'd ever seen. He was sending her inland to her people."

"Why?" Drat the man, Miss Ginny thought. He was deliberately baiting her curiosity.

Blandin made a show of reluctance. "Because, if you'll pardon my, er, indelicacy, Madame, she was breeding and Layton was too new on the coast to care to see his off-colored bastards running around."

"Mr. Blandin!" Clay stormed.

"Never you mind, Brother, I asked," Miss Ginny said. She turned her attention back to the overseer who seemed to be enjoying the little scene. "And if she was being sent inland what would that have to do with your story?"

"Madame, when I saw her as I left that morning, she was holding a *loa* stone her mother had given her. It wasn't a good *loa*."

"A conjur?" Clay asked.

"You mght call it that—only more so. A *loa* is a spirit and a *loa* stone is a stone that holds a spirit. But only a strong *juju* woman could hold a stone like the girl had. And her mother was one of the strongest. The *Drusella* was supposed to sail with the evening tide. I have a feeling there was good reason for Layton's woman to leave with the cargo."

Clay scowled. "I don't like the sound of all this," he said, "anymore'n I hold with any hoodoo howling and carrying on. We're God fearing church people and I

10

don't think I'd care to have that offspring of tarnation near my little girl.''

"Now, Brother," Miss Ginny admonished, but there was doubt in her voice.

"I ain't letting her near Rosalie," Clay continued. "When my girl grows big enough, I ain't going to let her ride a horse with a bad bloodline, and I won't anymore give her a body servant who had a *juju* woman for a grandma!''

Miss Ginny's fierce sense of justice came to the fore. She waved her knitting needle at her brother.

"Stuff!" she exclaimed. "We can't hold that mite responsible for her grandma. As I recollect, grandpa was a—''

"All right!" Clay shouted. "Have your way. But don't say I didn't warn you!''

Mala fought to keep the baby. It took the two men to subdue her.

"With what they go through getting here you'd think they'd of learned to respect a white man," Clay muttered. He held the woman's arms so Blandin could take the child.

The overseer stared down at the infant. "Damned if her features aren't as clear as Zulu's," he said.

Miss Ginny remained aloof. "Mr. Blandin, I'll thank you to see that the—Zulu—is taken to Esmeralda." She used her haughtiest voice, unaware that she had given the baby a name.

She resumed her knitting and promptly lost a stitch. "Stuff!" she said for the second time, but she spoke without conviction.

Chapter Two

From the first, Esmeralda predicted dire things about the baby selected for the young miss. Miss Ginny suspected that she resented an outsider given the honor, and Clay questioned whether Mala had spread stories about the child's grandmother. Faced with these accusations, Esmeralda only shook her head.

"She ain't neber goin' know her place. I sees it in her eyes. I sees it in de way she snatches de sugar tit frum Miss Rosalie."

"I'll not have that kind of talk!" Miss Ginny exclaimed, glancing hastily at her brother. "A baby doesn't know the difference. And don't you let me see her getting puny. You feed her all she wants."

Esmeralda glanced down at her heavy breasts and grunted. "I'll feed her all right. But she ain't neber goin' git all she wants. Not dat chile."

Miss Ginny read trouble lines deep in Esmeralda's face, and for a second she was aware of an uneasiness. "I'll watch the girl," she promised Clay at dinner. "But we at least should give her a chance."

Miss Ginny firmly intended to keep her word, but as Elmside grew in the next few years, and as Clay took on more land and more slaves, her responsibilities increased until it was all she could do to attend to the household and arrange entertainment for the friends Clay constantly invited for a stay. The children were healthy and handsome and wasn't that enough? Even Esmeralda finally ceased to voice her forebodings. What was the use, when no one listened?

Still, all the signs were there, and Esmeralda missed none of them. There was Zulu's pride that could not be spanked into submission, the sudden narrowing of eyes that marked the first flickering sparks of rebellion. And Esmeralda muttered dolefully to herself when she noted how often it was the body servant who decided on the game to be played.

"Ain't good fur a nigger not to know her place," she warned Zulu. "You jus' mak fur misery."

Zulu's reponse justified Esmeralda's worst fears. "I'm not a nigger!" The small chin lifted and the six-year-old body was taut with rebellion. "I'm not, and you can't call me one!"

"Neber knowed white folk to git thimselfs birthed on a slave boat," Esmeralda told her. She swept on to her duties making little disapproving noises.

Yet, she tucked Zulu in at night as tenderly as she tucked the young miss, and she sang as soft a lullaby to her. She cuddled them both against her, one under each arm, when she told them stories about the spirits that lived in the spring house, way down in the cool depths of the well.

"You wanna listen careful in de dawn to de singin' when dey brings up de food," she instructed them. "Dese spirrits, dey likes to git sing to, and when dey takes de notion, dey makes omen songs."

These were important things, and Esmeralda was generous with her great store of knowledge.

It was Esmeralda who shielded them both from Miss Ginny's wrath when they exchanged frocks, pretending that Zulu was the young miss, the day the new preacher called. It was also Esmeralda who administered spankings when Miss Ginny's patience had been pressed too far.

When they were seven, Clay hired a governess. Esmeralda mumbled, torn between bereavement and relief. But she knew her reign was over.

Chapter Three

Miss Lejon had been selected because of her native ability to speak French. She was a sharp eyed maiden lady, and she found it easier to teach Rosalie and Zulu separate from young Len Haldfar and his boy, Lance, but she could not find the courage to explain the reason to Miss Ginny.

"Young Len is a bright enough boy," she wrote to her sister back north, "and he's only a year older, but when he's in the same room as the girls, he can do nothing but stare at his sister's body servant. He's an absolute dolt at such times! I'm really concerned, but it's not my place to speak.

"About Rosalie's girl, Zulu. I have the most peculiar feeling that she regards me as a sponge. It's as if she's squeezing every possible bit of knowledge out of me. Sometimes she asks so many questions that I actually feel mentally bruised.

"I'm still not reconciled to the situation here. But all the planters seem to do the same thing. I think they feel the law against educating blacks doesn't apply to their children's body servants. And really, they are more companion than slave."

Even her letters failed to convey how troubled she actually felt. No matter her efforts at justification, educating a slave was still contrary to the law, and she was innately a law abiding person.

If only, she reflected, Zulu—what a name for a child—were more like Lance. It was dubious whether he ever heard a word or opened a book, and his eyes took on a far away expression the minute lessons began. It wasn't that he was stupid, but rather that he had resigned himself to the fact that education would do him little good. Once she had come on him as he was softly singing a spiritual. The sheer, haunting beauty of his voice had brought tears to her eyes, and she could not help but wonder at the depth of sadness felt, rather than heard. He could have been one of a chained line of blacks, this boy who was nearly white.

But there was no resignation in Zulu. From the first she drained knowledge from each book with an avidity that was indecent in a female, and certainly not to be expected of one who was merely permitted to sit in at the classes. Miss Lejon knew something should be done, but what? Speak to Miss Ginny? Miss Ginny had enough worries. Besides, Rosalie was so much easier to teach when Zulu shared the book with her.

Still, even that presented problems she could not, in conscience, ignore. For instance, when she gave Rosalie tests, she need only leave the room for the results to be excellent. There was no doubt about it, Rosalie was not nearly so brilliant when she stayed in the room while the papers were being written.

Premonitions and doubts aside, it wasn't until they were nearly ten that Miss Lejon faced what Esmeralda had known from the beginning.

It happened during a French lesson. Suddenly she realized that for the last fifteen minutes conversation had deteriorated to a duet between herself and Zulu.

"You simply must hold your tongue!" she exclaimed, reverting to English in her annoyance. "This class isn't being held for you. I want to test Rosalie's accent." Despite her words, she had tried to keep her manner gentle, but Zulu's reaction left her stunned.

The girl's golden eyes flashed and she shoved back her chair. "You're just afraid I'll know as much as you," she retorted heatedly. "You don't want me to learn!"

It was a minute before Miss Lejon was able to speak.

15

"Zulu," she finally admonished, "aren't you forgetting your place? Aren't you forgetting you're only a—"

Zulu took advantage of the brief hesitation to interrupt. "Only a what, Miss Lejon? I'm only a what?" Her voice was too quiet.

Miss Lejon was aware of a reasonless panic, an atavistic sort of fear, but no such emotion touched the young mistress of Elmside.

"A nigger, silly!" Rosalie laughed, and then, tardily, even she realized this was not in the usual course of things.

"Rosalie, you've been taught better manners." Miss Lejon took on her most authorative stance, grateful for Rosalie's interruption. "I was about to remind Zulu of her position in life, not her blood." Then she added, her voice finally under control, "Zulu, I must instruct you to leave the room."

Zulu made no move to leave. "I'm not." She spoke distinctly, looking straight at Rosalie. "I'm almost as white as you. You got no call to say those things."

"You've got black blood and pa bought you," Rosalie said matter of factly. She glanced a bit anxiously at her governess. "You'd best leave or she'll be calling Aunt Ginny."

Zulu's fists were clenched and Miss Lejon could almost feel the hurt that welled up inside her. "My blood's red, just like yours." Then she slammed the door behind her.

Dear Lord, Miss Lejon wondered, what have I awakened?

Zulu stood very still out in the hall. She held out her arm and looked at it. The only difference between her skin and Rosalie's, was that hers was a warmer tone, as if the sun had touched it a bit. It was true that her eyes weren't blue, but they weren't black, either. They were like her hair, the same shade as Miss Ginny's amber necklace. She brushed away the beginning of tears, angry at her weakness.

I'll run away, she thought. I'll run away and they'll never find me.

But where could she run? Where could she hide when she had never been beyond the orchard or even into the pine forest near the swamp? Then she thought of the white man, Blandin, who had been overseer before the sickness took hold of him.

She'd heard that now he lived in a cabin out in the pinewoods that surrounded the useless marshland. The kitchen help feared him, and a big black fieldwoman had to come for his meals each day. She never seemed to mind that sometimes he shouted wildly at what no one could see.

"I'm not afraid of him, either," Zulu assured herself. Of everyone on the plantation, only Blandin had ever treated her as if she were a person, not just Miss Rosalie's shadow. Why, he had even ignored Elmside's young mistress that day he paused by them as they played in the garden. But of course, that was long before the sickness. "You're a beauty," he had said, looking at Zulu. "But then, I knew you'd be."

Rosalie sulked for almost an hour.

It wasn't hard to find the cabin. Zulu had only to follow the path from the cookhouse through the trees. But the swamp was more than she'd expected. She'd heard of the green, life-taking waters, but no one had told her there was beauty here, too. She sat on a stump and slowly her hurt and anger washed away under the unfamiliar music of the place and the knowledge that for the first time in her life she was free. For the first time she had a sense of kinship. It wasn't only that there was no Miss Rosalie to call her, nor Esmeralda to scold. It was something much more vital.

She closed her eyes and slipped into a wonderful, imaginary world. She was a princess. Her mother had been a queen sold into captivity by traitors, just like some of the stories Miss Lejon gave them to read. She stood up and pulled the swamp odors into her nostrils.

Here she had come into her own. This was Africa, her kingdom. The mud curled around her toes and the plants leaned forward to caress her cheeks and hands. They knew she belonged, and they loved her.

This was her kingdom, and it was beautiful. Treacherous, but not to those who knew the path. Its treachery was her protection. She listened to the rustle of insects moving the leaves, of birds murmuring above her, of a small animal pushing through the reeds and the honking of a duck. There was a loud splash and she sensed the thrill of danger.

Her clothes felt stiff and awkward. She wanted to strip naked and feel the fecund air sweep over her, claiming her as part of the place. All of this was hers, and she loved it. Never before had she loved anything, and it was a glorious sensation. It wasn't an outside feeling, but something that spread all through her, inside.

An awareness of silence brought her back to the present. The insects had stopped buzzing and the birds were still and suspicious. She waited, not daring to stir.

The tall grasses parted at the edge of the pines and a bone thin man advanced toward her. In all of him, only his eyes were alive.

"Go away!" she screamed. She wasn't a princess now. She was Zulu, frightened and only ten.

The man laughed and it was a good sound. "I saw you come in here, so I followed. This isn't the best place to wander."

He didn't look crazy, and besides, princesses were never frightened. She regained her regal air and moved closer, aware that he was studying her face.

"It's there," he said. "You could pass, but still it's all there." He shook his head. "You've got your grandmother's eyes. Hers were black and yours are the color of a lion, but the looks are the same."

"You knew my grandmother? My mother was a queen, wasn't she?"

It was just as she had thought, and she couldn't wait to tell Rosalie.

Blandin laughed. "Hardly. Though you might say your grandmother was held as something just as important out there."

"But my mother? My mother was—"

"She was a girl. A beautiful girl, but not like you. She was gentle."

His voice changed, retreated into the past, and his eyes took on a fixed stare. Zulu knew he no longer saw her, but she wasn't frightened, for his gaze was blind rather than wild. The blindness of one who sees another time and another place.

"I could have told them when I first saw you and heard what Mala had to say. But it wouldn't have done. . . Not then."

He sat on the stump she had vacated. "I didn't want to think of the last cargo I brought out. Fever . . . the worst yet. Two carriers ran away in the night with provisions. It was plain hell and I knew that if ever I made it to the coast, I'd never go back in. Then that damn chief wanted a *bungee* worth more'n the trade. I was glad to see a white man again. Even a snobby son of a bitch like Dave Layton."

Zulu sat beside him, waiting for his mind to return. There was so much still to ask. But not now. Not until the present came back into his eyes. . . .

Chapter Four

Davis Layton wasn't really a bad sort. A woman would have thought him handsome, with his blond hair and newly sunburned face. It was just that he was so insufferably proud of his lineage. Most likely a defense—something to hold himself above the dirty work he did. Blandin often wondered which was worse, the men like himself who tramped the jungle trails with long, chained gangs of prisoners bought or stolen from the native chiefs, or the men who packed them into enclosures, stripping and branding them, readying them for the first stinking blackbirder that put into shore.

To say the best for him, he was probably a younger son out of favor with his family back in England. He's got company aplenty there, Blandin reflected, trying not to think of the home he'd never see again.

But it wasn't Layton that made the visit memorable to Blandin. It was the girl who took care of him until the fever subsided. Leil, Layton called her, and she was beautiful. Probably the most beautiful girl he'd seen on the Coast. Still, it wasn't her beauty, but rather her gentleness that impressed him. Docility he'd seen, in fact it was the rule, but not gentleness.

He remarked on this fact when he was once more on his feet and able to linger over drinks with his host. To his surprise, Layton laughed. "Do you know I was warned I'd do better to sleep with a boa? She's the daughter of our local *juju* woman."

Blandin stared at the girl, incredulous. He'd only seen Feig once, but it had left an enduring impression. She was a handsome mulatto with long, heavy lidded eyes, and an imperious manner.

"There was this mission fellow," Layton was saying, "Went out to show the native that *juju* was all bosh. Set out to show Feig the error of her ways. The next thing he was living with her, right in her hut. Some other chap came out from the mission to see why they hadn't heard from him, and they shipped him back home."

"That girl was their child?"

"Nothing to worry about there. She takes after her father."

Blandin studied the girl. "Her baby'll be only an

eighth black," he speculated. "Probably won't even show the tar brush. In the states she'd be free by law."

Layton stared at her. "God Almighty, she's not breeding?"

Leil was bending over the cookfire and he turned on her with unrestrained fury. "Straighten up! Come closer, damn it! Let me get a look at you."

It was there, the first rounding, the undefinable ripeness. Leil's eyes betrayed her fright, but she held her head up, her long hair tumbling down her back like a badge of honor.

"I'll send you inland to your mother tomorrow," Layton told her. "Damned if I'm going to have off-colored bastards running around this place. You go inland tomorrow, and if you sneak back I'll sell you to the Arabs."

"Aren't you being a bit rough?" Blandin asked.

"Who the hell's here to care?"

"I care," Davis Layton replied. "Keeping a woman to stop you from going crazy is one thing. I draw the line at bastards."

Christ, you'd think he was a Crown Prince, Blandin thought, his lips quirking in amusement. Anyway, he'd shed the fever and it was certain he'd be happy to shed Layton's company as well. He stretched.

"I'm starting out tomorrow," he said. "Got to get things in order. Made up my mind back in there that this would be the last. That damned fever's got me worse each time."

Blandin nodded. "I keep telling myself I'm a fool to stay. With those damned government clippers like bloody lice on a dog and the captains getting nervous about even a prime cargo—I can't see how the bottom's not going to drop out of the whole business."

But he wasn't leaving. Blandin had seen his type before. He saw the chance to make a fortune and he wasn't going to let anything turn him aside. Not the damned law and not even the government clippers waiting to catch the blackbirders. Even if the captain had to throw his chained cargo overboard, Layton would be safe here, in this hut, with the money paid per head.

And where's the money I was going to take home? Blandin reflected. Gambled, lost in giant carousals, and some even sent home to help those in that big house he'd never see again. I've money, he decided, maybe enough to last until the fever takes its final hold. But what did it really matter? It was enough that he had the courage to leave while he was still alive.

He set out early the next morning. Layton was still asleep when he left the hut, but Leil was standing by the path with her possessions gathered in a bundle. When he came up to her, he saw that she was opening the strings of a small bag.

He paused to watch as she reached in and took out a stone. She held it in her palm, watching as it clouded in the air. She rubbed the surface in an attempt to wipe it clear, and she shuddered.

A *loa* stone, Blandin thought. From the look of her this was the first time she'd touched it.

"I see Feig gave you a dowry," he remarked, but his attempt at humor fell flat.

"She told me it would help in trouble," the girl said. She dropped the stone. "I do not like *juju*!" She looked at the hut, and the love that shone in her eyes was naked. "I do not want that kind of help."

Blandin picked up the stone, replaced it in its bag and dropped it into his pocket. All the time he was wondering if he should turn back and warn Layton. There was more than love in those eyes that were like a lion's. . . .

No, by God! They'd been soft and dark. They hadn't been like a lion's. That was someone else. Some other place and some other time. . . .

"Tell me about my mother . . ." The words came to him dimly at first. It was hard to decide which was real,

22

his memories or the voice. No! Damned, if he hadn't been treading the past again. Zulu represented reality. Zulu asking what she had a right to know.

He studied the girl as she emerged from the haze. She was frightened, but only her quickened breath told him that he'd been raving again. There was pride here, and there was always danger when pride was born to slavery.

He reflected on what Mala had told him about the stinking hold of the blackbirder. Here Mala had lost her own son toward the end of the voyage, only to have this strange child thrust into her arms. How had Leil come onto the *Drusella*? All Mala could tell him was that the night before sailing Layton's woman had bribed the guards and slipped into the barracoons where the wailing blacks were packed like hounds. At dawn she'd been loaded abroad the converted whaler with the rest of the cargo. No one noticed, not with her hair clipped and soot rubbed into her skin. She had even branded herself with the "D" that marked the cargo for shipment.

He had long suspected that Dave Layton wasn't alive to see the *Drusella* set sail that morning. Leil was her father's daughter, but Feig was still her mother.

"I don't know what happened to your mother," he told the child. "Mala wasn't very clear about that." Why tell her how the soot had come off when Leil was hosed clean with the rest of the shipment? About the captain taking her out of the hold, and how the baby, with the birth soil barely washed off, was one day forced on Mala.

He stood up. Mala would want to see the girl. He scowled as he tried to remember if it was the time Mala brought food and cleaned the cabin. It was hard to keep things straight these days. Everything had an annoying habit of merging into the past.

But of course it was time. Why else would he be wandering by the edge of the swamp? It was easier to go outside than to be chased with mop and broom.

"Mala must see you," he told her and motioned for her to follow.

Zulu moved slowly. She was reluctant to leave the marsh, and the immensity of her disobedience had settled heavily on her.

"Thank God for Mala," Blandin said as they neared the cabin. "She's more afraid of never hearing the *Kru* dialect again, then she is of evil spirits."

Then they were there, at the shack everyone avoided. A huge black woman stood in the doorway. Zulu was aware of a gaze that devoured her every feature, searching as if afraid of finding something strange and different.

"*Dju-prubwe Ku.*" The words were almost a caress, and the woman came forward. She touched Zulu's hair.

Zulu pulled away. "What's she calling me?" she asked Blandin.

"Devil's baby." He smiled, "but she doesn't seem to mind."

The black woman spoke to Blandin in a language unintelligible to Zulu, and he nodded. She went into the cabin and came out with a dust covered bag.

She held it out to Zulu. "*Siwnyi,*" she said, her eyes searching the girl's face.

Blandin took the bag and opened it. A small stone fell out onto his palm. "It's yours," he told Zulu. He turned the stone in his fingers, watching it cloud and his eyes took on that strange, far away look. "I think it would be better if you threw it out into the swamp."

"Is it a *conjur*?" Zulu asked, fascinated. She had heard of *juju* and charms, but only in hints and murmurs. Such talk was forbidden at Elmside.

"In the West Indies they call it a *pierre loa*, but in Africa they've an older name."

"Is it as old as the pearl ring Miss Rosalie's mother left her?"

Blandin smiled that death head smile of his. "Older than anything you can imagine."

24

Zulu took the pebble and she was swept with a strange exhileration. It was akin to the sensation that had engulfed her by the swamp, yet it was different. There was the feeling of freedom, but more than that. A defiance. Suddenly and surely she knew she hated Rosalie and all like her. And she knew such would never again have the power to hurt her.

"Put it in your pocket if you must keep it." Blandin's voice came from a distance, but Zulu found herself obeying him. Reality returned then, forced back the more swiftly by the sight of Clay Haldfar riding up to the cabin porch.

"What the devil's she doing here?" he demanded as he reined in his horse. "You git up to the house, you little vixen. Go tell Miss Ginny where I found you. She'll see to you!"

Blandin watched Zulu run up the path to the orchard. "Right now might not be a good time to punish her," he said quietly.

"Bullshit!" Clay snorted. "You'd think, what with having my Rosalie for an example, it'd be different, but my sister tells me Zulu's overdue for a thrashing."

Miss Ginny harbored broader ideas for Zulu's punishment. "From now on," she told her brother, "Rosalie will take her lessons alone. No good can possibly come from educating a slave. Besides, Miss Lejon is upset because it's against the law."

"If we're going to be so almighty pure, Ginny, we'll have to stop Lance, too. You know they both do better when they have company."

Zulu's lessons were stopped briefly, but Rosalie grew sullen and resentful. If being quality meant a body had to spend the best part of the day over dull old books while others got to play, then she wanted no part of being quality.

As usual, Rosalie wore down all attempts at resistance, and, within a few days, Zulu was back in the classroom.

It was a different Zulu who bent over her books, now. A Zulu who had learned a truth. White folks set great store by education, therefore, it was important. No longer were books an intriguing challenge. Now they were survival. She resolved to shame Rosalie in every lesson, but not so obviously that she'd be sent out of the room again.

She'd take everything they could give her at Elmside. Then, maybe someday— Lord God, someday things would be different!

Chapter Five

Zulu preferred to believe it was the *loa* stone that changed her way of thinking, that her feeling toward Rosalie wouldn't have been more than a casual resentment, if she had never held it.

When she tried to explain this to Blandin, he only laughed at her. "It was always there," he assured her. "Holding a stone's not going to change a person's thinking."

"Why shouldn't I hate belonging to someone—like I was a dog or a horse? Why shouldn't I want to belong to myself?"

"None of us belong to ourself," he told her. "It took me a lifetime to learn that. I doubt you'll learn it any sooner."

"What if I had my papers," she persisted. "What kind of place would there be for me? I could pass and nobody'd know the difference, but where would I go?"

He frowned as he thought over the question. "If

you'd been born in New Orleans there might have been a life for you. The French and Spanish take a different look at a bit of the tar brush. Why, when I stopped there before I went out to Africa, I saw quadroons dressed like queens, sitting in special rows in the Opera House. But they were born free—if you can call being a rich white man's mistress, free."

She considered the thought. "I could be Len's mistress," she said gravely. "But that wouldn't get me fine clothes and a place at the Opera House."

Blandin laughed. "I could guess what it could get you. I can guess even better what it'll get you right now when they find you've come out here again."

"I'll be back before they even know," Zulu said. "Rosalie's got friends visiting." She reflected bitterly on the huddle of heads with their bouncing curls. All they ever did was whisper about boys and giggle over their lemonade. But then, if it weren't for the distraction of visitors, she'd never be able to come out to the cabin and talk to Blandin.

His head wasn't always as clear as it was today, but even when he was raving, she'd crouch in a corner and listen, torn between wonder and fright, as he lived in Africa again, as he fought fever and extinction. She was with him by the night fires with drums beating and talk of things a white man could never really understand. These times she no longer was at Elmside. Miss Rosalie didn't even exist.

Yes, it was worth the chance of being caught. Sometime she felt she was only really alive out here in the cabin by the swamp.

Then, when she was fourteen, Blandin died. Mala came running to the cook house early one morning, wailing and screaming. Zulu knew without being told. Now there'd be no one she could talk to—no one who cared what she thought. She felt a terrible sense of loss, and she had to bite her lips to keep from joining the loud laments.

They buried Blandin that same afternoon and the next morning Zulu arose before daybreak to visit his cabin.

Already the door was ajar, and already it seemed the marsh grasses were creeping toward the door stoop. The swamp was reaching for the dwelling as surely as it reached out for her. It would smother the cabin in time, just as it would smother her, should she permit it.

Yes, it would possess the cabin, but she could make certain it would never possess her.

Suddenly she was frightened. She had loved the swampland when first she saw it, reveled in a sense of belonging. But no more. . . .

And Blandin—Blandin had been her only friend, but now she found herself fearful of his restless spirit, of his soon to be devoured cabin.

Why should he be different now just because he was dead? But the last of her courage deserted her and she ran blindly through the orchard, not stopping until she was on the knoll above the spring house.

She paused, breathing hard. For the first time she was aware of a sense of gratitude just to have people around her. Only among the living could she shake off that terrible aloneness. She tried to forget the new grave and the empty cabin as she listened to the creak of the cable that lowered the bucket down into the well. Already, Lucy from the kitchen house had lifted her voice in a plaintive wail to appease the well dwellers.

It would be an omen song today, Zulu thought. With a newly dead spirit, still restless on earth, it had to be an omen song.

A big Gullah woman broke into a spiritual, and Zulu turned away, disappointed. There would be no omen after all. Blandin was dead and buried, and it was as if he'd never been.

She hadn't heard Len come up beside her. "You're crying," he said. There was concern in his expression.

"I'm not!" Zulu denied, even though she was newly

28

aware of the tears on her cheeks. "I don't cry."

Len looked back at the orchard path. "I'll miss him too," he confessed. "He used to tell me about Africa . . . I'm glad I'll be going off to school. It won't be the same here without him."

What right had Len to talk of Blandin? What right had he to visit out by the swamp? Jealousy mingled with grief as she met Len's gaze.

At sixteen, he was tall and thin, with sandy hair that was constantly falling over his forehead. And he still looked at her as if there were no one else on earth.

"I'll miss you, too," he said. "I'll miss you more than anything."

Zulu refused to dignify his words. She turned her back on him, knowing she could be as rude as she wished, and he'd never tell Miss Ginny.

He caught her arm. "Aren't you even going to say goodbye?

"Of course," she replied bitterly. "I'll stand out there with all of the rest of the house slaves, and wave as you leave. I'd be thrashed if I didn't."

She watched him walk back up the path, wondering why there wasn't more satisfaction in hurting Len. If only he'd been like his sister, she'd have found pleasure in lashing out at him, but not when he just turned pale and clamped his mouth tight. Why did he keep after her when he could have his pick of the house girls? Or of Miss Rosalie's friends, for that matter. She'd seen the way they looked at him.

Miss Rosalie had her parties, and even the kitchen girls whispered in giggling snatches about "meetin' their friends." What did she have? She closed her eyes and tried to think what it would be like . . . Blandin had fulfilled her desire for companionship, but that was gone now—and she needed more. She was a woman grown, by house servant standards.

The smell of smoke filled her nostrils. Lord God, the cookhouse fires were going full blast, and it was past time to rouse Miss Rosalie. Miss Ginny always threw a fit, even if she was a little late.

Zulu ran to the side of the house and up the stairs that led to the second floor gallery, that way she avoided going through the house and encountering Esmeralda. Now, if she could only get past Miss Ginny.

Miss Ginny's windows were opened, but her back was turned. Zulu scuttled by, undetected, and eased herself over the sill into Rosalie's room. Her feet still on the window seat, she paused to study the place. What must it be, she reflected, to sleep behind those fine bed curtains, knowing a freshly starched, spriggled muslin was laid out, with pink hair ribbons? Miss Rosalie didn't care that Blandin was dead. She didn't care that the swamp would soon have his cabin and that it would be hungry and reach for more. Maybe she cared a little that young Mister Norm Peltier from Peltier Acres had singled her out, but that someday she might be mistress of a plantation three times the size of Elmside, seemed to matter very little. Why should it? Wasn't this all her due? Part of her heritage, along with her blue eyes and those soft features that could be so willful?

From behind the bed curtains there was a rustle of sheets as Rosalie sat up.

"Zulu, for heaven's sake, you make me nervous when you stare like that! It gives me the chills clear through. And you're late again. What with the picnic today and the party this evening, you know there's lots to do!"

Lots to do. Zulu mulled the words scornfully. Miss Rosalie's idea of a lot to do was to stand around giving orders. She'd see her favorite pieces were played and that the decorations were to her liking. It didn't matter that all this fuss was supposed to be for Len who was going away. Rosalie would see that she was the center of attention.

Zulu climbed down onto the carpet and pulled aside the netting as Rosalie swung her legs over the edge of the bed. Rosalie's hair was touseled down her back, and her cheeks were still pink with sleep. With a touch of envy, Zulu realized how very pretty Elmside's mistress really was. Far prettier than any of her friends, even when she pouted. Petulance became her.

"You'll have all afternoon just to do nothing," Rosalie went on. "A body'd think you could at least have been on time!"

The words still rankled, long after Rosalie had left, settled in her buggy admidst well-laden picnic baskets. Zulu watched out the window at the young men galloping down the road after the girls, shouting and laughing. Then she turned to survey the turmoil in which the room had been left. Somehow, Miss Rosalie never was satisfied with the dress she'd instructed be laid out. She always had to try two or three frocks, only to leave them strewn across the floor while she moved back and forth in front of the long mirror.

Zulu picked the dresses up, one by one, replacing them in the wardrobe and smoothing out rumpled ruffles. If she took them downstairs to be pressed again, Alice was like to throw the flat iron at her.

When the room was finally in a condition that would pass Miss Ginny's inspection, Zulu closed the door behind her and stood, leaning against the wall, aware again of the new emptiness in her life. She descended the stairs slowly and crossed to the kitchen house where she knew lunch would be left out for her.

As she picked at her food, she listened to the girls. She had never made friends with any of them, but they gossiped freely around her, confident that she paid no attention to their talk.

Lord God, didn't they think of anything but sneaking out to meet a man? But then, that's all Miss Rosalie's friends talked about, too. Maybe that was why she felt so alone. But who was there? Lance? That would never do, not when he was Master Len's shadow. There was the gardener's helper, but he was always so muddy.

There was Caleb at the stable. The thought of his

muscles bulging under smooth, tan skin, stirred a response. But why should he even look at her, a barely grown girl, when the women from the house and field alike were after him like bees after honey? Besides, what with Miss Rosalie always having her fetch and carry, what time was there to attract his attention?

But there was time now. Everyone except Clay Haldfar was at the picnic, and he'd be out in the fields.

She left her food and went to the door. The old gardener was crooning to himself as he set in young plants, and through the branches of the wisteria she could see out to the field nearest the house. The blacks had slowed in their work and the driver had his back to them, his eyes on the horizon, his arms hanging loosely at his sides.

There was no harm in just walking by the stable. Besides, there'd be no one there except Caleb. Sam and the older men would be driving the buggies.

Caleb was out in the paddock exercising a gelding when she drew near the open stable door. She climbed up into the loft. What harm was there in pretending she was his girl, waiting for him to finish his work so he could join her?

He was singing softly when he came through the doorway. Digging her elbows into the straw, she managed to find a place where she could look down on him as he worked.

It was much hotter in the stable than it had been in Rosalie's room, and as Caleb shoveled the manure into a cart, damp, dark spots grew on his shirt, spreading down his spine. She could smell the rank, pungent odor of him, and she wondered why, instead of repelling her, it sent a strange sensation, like a warm ache, through her body.

Caleb dropped his shovel and wiped his forehead with his arm. Then, with a sudden upward motion, he caught hold of a low hanging beam and swung himself up into the loft. Zulu dodged backward, barely in time to escape being struck by one of his feet.

There wasn't room to stand, so on her hands and knees she scampered for the ladder, her cheeks burning with the shame of being caught. Caleb caught her by her ankle and yanked her back as she fought to pull loose. Finally, he held her, pinned to the straw, and he grinned down at her.

"Knowed sumone up heah," he told her. "But look heah what we got! You ain't frum de kitchin and you din't cum heah to look at no horse."

"Let me go!" Zulu panted. "Let me go or I'll tell Miss Ginny."

He shook his head and his grin widened. "You ain't goin' tell nobody." Close up he was even handsomer than Zulu had thought. His black hair kinked like a cap over his scalp. "You miss's girl. I know who you is."

She lay still, staring up at him, liking the feel of his nearness, shivering under the touch of his hand. He released his tight hold on her so he could undo the string that held his pants, and sudden realization came to her.

What was she doing? All that fine book learning wouldn't make her any more than a kitchen slut or a field woman if she rutted out here in the hay like she was one of them!

She jerked herself free before he realized her intentions. She threw herself down from the loft and landed in a bale of straw. She jumped to her feet and before he could even start after her, she was running toward the house, sobbing and shamed. Wanting to go back, but knowing she couldn't.

She stopped running in the safety of the garden, and she reached into her pocket. For one frantic moment she thought she'd lost the *loa* stone, but there it was, tucked into a corner. She held it against her hot cheek and its coolness soothed her.

There was no place for a stable boy in her life. When

33

she gave her body, the price would be high. Blandin had said she wasn't born to be a slave, and Blandin had known.

Chapter Six

It wasn't the usual thing for a healthy young house servant to remain unattached until she was seventeen, and several times Clay haltingly suggested they "marry" Zulu, but Miss Ginny only shook her head.

"Leave her be," she said. "Zulu won't be happy forced into a match."

"It ain't right," Esmeralda told Zulu. "A girl lak you shud have a man."

"Miss Rosalie's not married yet," was Zulu's ready answer, but Esmeralda would only shake her head.

"You jus wait till she cum bak frum dat school. Der'll be big doings, den. And fore you knows it, you'll be livin' over at de Acres."

The entire plantation, household and field hands alike, began to anticipate that big day. Everyone was agreed that it was bound to occur soon after Rosalie's return from the school in Virginia, where, as Miss Ginny put it, she was being "polished."

Len returned from college a week before Rosalie was expected, but it was a different Len from the boy who had pleaded with Zulu. Now when he looked at her, it was with the determined air of a man who knew what he was about. She made a point never to find herself alone with him.

Then, finally, it was the day before Rosalie was due home. Zulu spent the morning putting the bedroom in order, and when her work was finished, she paused by the window that looked out over the front path. Down below, on the gallery, Clay Haldfar was arguing with Mace Telt, a distant relative, who was from Virginia.

"This is 1837, Mace. Things like that ain't likely to happen nowadays."

"Clay, I tell you it for a fact!" Mace's voice was a deep rumble. "If we don't watch out, we're going to have an uprising of slaves like they had in Santo Domingo! Cousin, the situation's serious."

Clay laughed. "Years ago they might of made trouble, but now they know they're well off. Up north there's white folks starving, but our darkies get plenty food and they got warm clothes for their backs. Why, who'd take care of them if it wasn't for us? Just because a few bad niggers scared some poor whites don't mean the world's going to end."

Zulu shut the front window and went to the garden side. It was a still, sultry morning. The sort of morning that always sent chills chasing up and down her spine. The air was sweet with flower fragrances, moist and heavy, alive with clouds of insects.

She turned away, vaguely discontent. Her eyes swept over the room again. Rosalie might as well be a princess royal, the fuss they'd made over redoing everything!

She went out into the hall as Prissy came out of Miss Ginny's room with a tray of empty dishes. Two cups, Zulu noticed. That meant Mrs. Telt was in there, too.

Mrs. Telt's high voice came through the half open door, confirming the fact.

"Rosalie wanted to come back with us, but there were so many affairs planned for her last month, I couldn't see taking her away. She sent her love to everyone, and—" Mrs. Telt giggled, "her regards to that young Norman Peltier."

"Has school and Virginia changed her?" Miss Ginny's voice, always low, sounded oddly gentle by contrast.

35

Mrs. Telt readjusted her bulk, and even in the hall Zulu could hear the swish of her fan. "Frankly, Ginny, I'd say it was for the better. I always felt she was a bit spoiled, not that I blame you, honey. But she did seem spoiled and I'm glad she's gotten over it. She'll remind you of her mother."

"She always did take after Saline," Miss Ginny replied.

"They both look as if they was put together with glass, but I've a notion Rosalie's robust enough. Stronger then she'd like you to think."

"The Haldfars are sturdy stock," Miss Ginny agreed reluctantly, "but I always did admire that flyaway look of Saline. She was such a beauty!"

"Rosalie will fair take your breath," Mrs. Telt affirmed.

Zulu turned away. Always Rosalie! Why did the entire world have to revolve around her? What right had she to all that adulation? She tossed her head, defying the two on the other side of the door, and it was then she became aware of Len standing near.

"Toss your mane like that again," he grinned. "I want to see if you really will spit out fire." His hand closed on her arm.

"Let go of me! You think I like to be grabbed like a field woman?"

"That's the only way I can keep you from running away." With his free hand he reached into his vest pocket and brought out a small box. Zulu watched as he lifted the lid. She even drew a little closer, but it was a cautious movement.

In spite of herself she could not help but pull in her breath at the sight of the glittering ear bobs that nestled, green as spring grass, on their black velvet pad.

"I bought these for Rosalie," Len said, watching her expression. "If you let me put them on you, I'll give them to you."

Zulu returned his steady gaze, then, slowly, she drew

back her heavy hair. As soon as she felt the last ear bob tighten, she pulled out of his way.

Len's face was white and his hand shook a little. "You've got me in such a state I can't even call on a girl without thinking of you!" His mouth tightened. "I wish to hell they did things here like in New Orleans."

New Orleans. . . . The name brought Zulu to a standstill, Blandin's words in her ears.

"What do you know about New Orleans?" she asked. "Blandin told me—"

Len's voice was soft. "You'd be a woman of color if you'd been born there. Not like it is here. I spent a vacation on a plantation out in the Bayous with some Creole friends. If Elmside was in Louisiana all I'd have to do was tell pa how I felt about you. And later, when I had to marry, it wouldn't make any difference. I'd get you one of those cottages down by the ramparts. I could see you any time I wanted."

Zulu stared at him, hardly daring to believe. "A cottage of my own? With no one to tend to?"

He grinned. "Just me. Why, I saw quadroons at the theater wearing jewels that'd make Aunt Ginny's diamonds look like pebbles."

Just as Blandin had told her, though she hadn't really believed it could be true.

"And you'd be called by my name, just as if you were my wife—Madame Haldfar. No man thinks anything of giving his *placee* better jewels than his real wife. After all, he took his *placee* because he loved her and most likely he only married his wife because it was a good thing for his and her family. All this damn prudery we have here!"

"But won't Master Clay let you pick out your own wife?"

"Me, maybe," Len replied scornfully. "But do you think it's all Rosalie's idea to marry Norm? Don't you think the fact that our plantations adjoin might have something to do with Norm being pushed at her all her

37

life?" He lowered his voice. "You could even have a maid in that cottage. You'd like that, wouldn't you?"

"I'd like it," she admitted. Then she realized that Len was drawing her closer with this talk. Behind her back, she tightened her fingers on the knob to Rosalie's door. "Yes, I'd like it, but you're not one of those Creoles, and besides, I'd want a man to go with that cottage."

She twisted the knob and stepped backwards into the doorway. Before he had realized her intentions, she had the door shut and the lock snapped.

She turned to the mirror and admired the sparkling ear bobs. Then she closed her eyes and in their place she imagined emeralds, emeralds glowing like green fire against the tawny masses of her hair. Blandin had been right. Her place was in New Orleans. What if she hadn't been born there? She'd find a way.

Even now a boat was loading down at the dock. It would be pushing off to travel the tortuous chain of waterways that finally ended at New Orleans' wharves. Why couldn't she be on it when it set out? She'd be far down the river before anyone would miss her. No one would ever think of her getting on a boat!

She took the *loa* stone out of her pocket and felt a fresh surge of assurance. How did a person decide what to believe? Could Miss Lejon be ignorant, after all, in certain essential matters? Could Esmeralda, in her illiteracy, know more than Miss Lejon with all of her books?

This stone, now. To Miss Lejon it was a stone, and no more. To Esmeralda it was a conjur. It held a captured spirit, and it was the slave of its holder.

She closed her fingers over the smooth surface. "You get me to New Orleans," she said. "I don't care how, just get me there."

She dressed hurriedly the next morning. As the first streaks of dawn filtered through her window, she could hear stirrings downstairs in the cook house. Rosalie was due by noon, and the next evening there was to be a big celebration of her homecoming. All of Elmside was in a state bordering on hysteria.

As she ran down the stairs, she could hear them out in the springhouse.

"Praise de Lawd

Oh chillums, praise de Lawd. . . ."

Esmeralda wouldn't like that. The voices were happy as they began the song and that was a bad sign on a day when omens were important.

She stepped off the path to pick a speckled iris that grew by the fishpond, and pushed it into her hair. Then she paused to look at the garden, still shimmering in a morning dress of dew. It stretched all about her as far as she could see, the huge magnolias, the oleanders and the wisteria that clung to the stairway under Rosalie's window.

As she resumed her way toward the house, she wondered what it would be to ride up the avenue of elms, knowing that the big white house with its cool verandas and the stretches of smooth lawn were one's natural possessions. But then, she reflected, those that had it, never gave it a thought. It could never even occur to Rosalie that things could be any other way.

Miss Ginny passed on her way to the cookhouse. She swished her wide skirts, swaying the flower heads, and her high piled curls were only recently free of wrapping papers. Miss Ginny always gave the impression that she was being pulled forward by her ample bosom.

As she passed the clearing where she could see down into the quarters, Zulu noticed that the picaninnies were playing on the stoops of their cabins. That meant that this day would be like Sundays and holidays. No cotton picking, no weaving, an extra ration of molasses to every adult, and a half ration to the ninnies.

She started up the stairs leading to the back of the house, but paused as she heard the sound of a horse trotting up the path. She wasn't surprised to see it was Norman Peltier, but where, she wondered, was Miss

Thalia? Miss Thalia had come from Virginia about the time Rosalie had left for school, and already the month's stay had extended into a year. It was becoming difficult to picture Peltier Acres without including Miss Thalia as part of the household.

He must have set out well before daylight, Zulu reflected. What must it be to know the owner of Peltier Acres was just waiting the proper time to speak? And, except for his mother, Rosalie would have full say over the household. Not that old Mrs. Peltier would be in any position to interfere—she'd been confined to her room two years now, and no one expected she'd last much longer.

As the time for Rosalie's anticipated arrival neared, field hands and house servants alike, took their places along the avenue. Zulu knew that she was expected downstairs, but for the present nobody'd miss her. There was no real reason she couldn't sit by the gallery window and listen to the talk below.

There was the steady swish of a big overhead fan pulled back and forth to keep off flies. Miss Ginny was clicking her knitting needles, and Norman's voice rose above the other sounds.

"I'm sorry I've got to leave before dinner," he was saying, and Zulu pictured him as clearly as if she, too, were privileged to sit on the vine shaded gallery. Norman would run his hand through his wavy, light hair as he spoke, and his cleft chin would be held at the precise angle he favored.

"The truth is," he continued, "we're expecting my cousin Breel. We just got word last night. That's why Cousin Thalia stayed at The Acres."

There was the thump of a chair brought down to all four legs, and then Len's excited voice. "Breel Luton? I heard you were kin, but I didn't know you were cousins."

"I don't boast about it." Norman's voice was grim.

"When I was visiting in New Orleans there was a lot

of talk about him. He was in some sort of a scrape."

Norman said drily, "When isn't he?" Then he added, as if in explanation, "His mother was French."

"I should think he'd find The Acres dull after New Orleans."

"He will if I have my say," Norman promised.

But Zulu was no longer listening. There it was again! That magic city. Surely, it was an omen they should speak of it on this, of all days.

Once again the voices intruded on her thoughts. Len's chair creaked as he leaned back again. "I saw Miss Donna Moulton in her box at the Orleans Theater. Is he really betrothed to her?" Len paused to clear his throat and Zulu recognized the man-of-the-world voice he'd brought back from college.

"One thing you've got to admit about those Creole women. They've a charm none of our girls here can come up to."

"I'd like to believe it's her charm and not her money that's attracted my cousin," Norman said. "I—"

He was interrupted by the shouting down at the gate, and Zulu hurried down the side stairs to a place near the front porch as the carriage rolled up to the coach block.

Even Norman forgot his usual dignity as he bounded across the front of the house to be the first to open the door. Clay Haldfar galloped up from the field. The groom had to wave his whip threateningly to clear the way of house servants who ran right up to the horses.

Th first thing Zulu noticed as Rosalie came out of the carriage, her hand resting lightly on Norman's extended arm, was the pale blue dress she wore. It flounced about her in tier upon tier of stiff ruffles, and her waist was laced a good two inches smaller than it had been when she left Elmside. Under her shirred bonnet, her features seemed softer, more piquant. She smiled up at Norman, then moved to her brother.

"I thought you'd still be at college," she said as she kissed his cheek.

41

"Pa wants me to go back," Len explained, "but I think it would do me more good to stay here and learn to run the plantation."

By then Miss Ginny had reached Rosalie. They clung to each other, laughing and crying until Clay dismounted and crushed Rosalie against his dusty vest. Then she turned her attention back to Norman.

"It's so kind of you to be here," she said, and Norman blushed from the cleft in his chin to his hairline. He took the hand she held out to him and he carried it to his lips.

"My, hasn't school made us grand!" Zulu muttered to herself. Almost at the same moment, Rosalie caught sight of her.

"Oh, Zulu! You'd never believe what a clumsy girl I had at school." She threw her arms around Zulu. "Wait till you see my hair. It's a fright!"

"I've missed you, too, Miss Rosalie." Missed her? A year of not having to fetch and carry at her every whim? Yes, she'd missed her!

Rosalie turned back to her aunt and they went back up the stairs, their arms linked together.

"I'm sorry we're so late," Rosalie was saying. "There's a boat loading down by the landing and we had to wait until a cart got off the road—"

Norman had turned to Clay, his face still flushed and his voice a little less precise than usual.

"I'd like a word in private with you, if I may, sir."

That'll take care of Miss Thalia for once and all, Zulu reflected.

Rosalie spent the afternoon resting, and when Zulu was certain she was asleep, she slipped out the window onto the balcony. It was the hottest part of the day, and even the old gardener was nowhere in sight. Of course, being a holiday made everything much easier.

There was no one to question her as she climbed the stairs to her room, She gathered together the few things she might want, the green ear bobs, a change of clothes. The *pierre-loa* she pinned tight to her dress, and then she paused. There was so little that was really worth taking.

She hurried down the road that led to the levee, and as she neared the landing a feeling of exhileration came over her. Whenever she'd considered escape, it had been a nightmare of hiding in ditches with howling dogs pursuing, not this mere act of walking down a road that led to the river on a sunny May afternoon.

The cart that had slowed Rosalie's carriage must have been the last load, for now Zulu saw that the barge was nearly ready to shove off. On the deck a huge, redbearded man was shouting at a black roustabout, and Zulu waited until he finished. Then she called out.

He turned, an annoyed scowl drawing his bushy eyebrows together, but he grinned when his eyes fell on her. He took hold of a stanchion and pulled himself up on the landing.

Zulu sat on a stump by the bank. The roustabout had turned back to his work, his rich voice rising in a lilting tune sung in a barbaric French.

"Ah Suzette, chere to pas L'aimain moin, chere
Ah Suzette, Z'amie to pas L'aimain moin!
Si to te zozo z'amie
Et mo meme no té fizi
Mo sré tchoué toiboum!
Mo sré tchoue toi raide!"

Zulu smiled. That was the way to live. Like that big Creole negro, lamenting the lost love of his faithless Suzette.

"If you were a bird, Suzette
And I was a gun, my Suzette
I would shoot you down, sho!
I would shoot you down dead!"

It wasn't exactly Miss Lejon's sort of French, but with a little imagination, it could be understood. She knew, then, that she was certain to like New Orleans. A place that nurtured that sort of song was a place that understood how to love—and how to live. No gloomy Gullah spiritual, that.

"Captain Gram at your pleasure, girl." The red bearded man towered over her. bigger and rougher even

43

then he had appeared on the barge.

Zulu stood, deliberately letting him stare his full before she looked up into the little red rimmed eyes.

"I want to go to New Orleans," she said.

His eyes were still taking in details, and his whisky-heavy breath blew down on her.

"Ain't anyone I'd ruther take."

For the first time Zulu was aware of a feeling of apprehension, but this was no time to weaken. She held out her ear bobs and tried to keep her voice steady.

"I don't have any money, but I'll let you have these."

He laughed and took them from her. "Come closer," he said.

She hesitated only a second. She wanted to go to New Orleans. No matter the cost, she must get to New Orleans. She moved close, so close that her dress brushed against him.

He pulled out the bodice of her gown and dropped the ear bobs inside. "You don't need money," he told her, "and you can keep your baubles."

"Then you'll take me?" Lord God, was it going to be that easy?

"I'll take ye providin' ye can show me your papers. I ain't takin' no chances on gettin' me neck stretched for runnin' slaves. I ain't been loadin' cotton on this levee for ten years without knowin' the Elmside frock."

"But nobody need know," Zulu pleaded. "Nobody'd ever suspect I'd go to New Orleans—"

He shook his head. "You show me a proper Writ of Freedom, girl, and I'll take ye to Halifax and back, if that be what ye want."

Zulu turned away, and she felt his eyes follow her as she moved up the road. She was trapped. She had been trapped from the moment of her birth. Trying to run away on foot would be foolish. They'd send out dogs and men and she'd be dragged back with no human dignity left. As long as she was without a Writ, she was an animal, and even the *pierre-loa* could not help her.

As she neared the house she saw Len riding across the field. She was aware of annoyance when he turned his horse's head and trotted toward her. But as she watched him, an idea grew in her mind.

She stood squarely in his path as he reined in his mount.

"What are you doing out here? Aren't you supposed to be with Rosalie?" It was obvious that he still smoldered under yesterday's insults.

Zulu stroked the chestnut's neck. "She's sleeping. I'm sorry I acted so pert yesterday." She looked up at him. "Those earbobs are the prettiest things I've ever seen. But—"

He leaned down, his face eager. "Why don't you like me?" he asked.

Zulu lowered her eyes. "It's not that I don't like you. I don't expect you'd understand, but if I went to you—if I even let you hold me—it'd be because I'm a slave. It wouldn't be as if I was free to give myself."

"But you've everything you could want here at Elmside. You're not out in the fields working under a driver."

"I'm a slave." Zulu permitted a sullen note to creep into her voice. "I don't want to go to you as a slave."

"Hells bells!" Len exclaimed, his face red, "you drive a man crazy." He stared out over the horse's head. "I remember how clever you always were," his eyes returned to her, "I'm not really a fool, you know. I'd wager a bet you've already figured how I could help get your papers."

"You could tell Miss Rosalie you were giving Lance his Writ on your birthday."

Only she and Len really knew Rosalie and he caught her implication at once. "You figure she'd up and say she'd already planned to give you yours? Just so she could be first?" He was quiet a minute, then he shook his head. "It might work at that, but damn it, Zulu, I don't want to ask pa for Lance's Writ. He just might take it into his fool head to leave, and I'd never find another boy like him.''

"Rosalie's birthday comes before yours."

He laughed. "You almost had me fooled. If you had your papers what's to keep you from going away? You think I want that?''

Zulu met his eyes again, and the desire she saw there was a painful, living thing.

"I'll never go to you while I'm a slave." Then she added slowly, watching its effect on him, "I've never been with a man yet."

Len nudged his horse and Zulu watched as he galloped across the field, barely clearing a fence she'd never seen him take before.

She pulled the *loa* from its bag and held it. Suddenly she realized she was praying to it. Praying as if it were a powerful deity instead of a bit of stone.

But now it was time to return to Rosalie. Rosalie in her shirred bonnet and ruffled dress who owned her as surely as the bitch hounds out in the kennels.

Chapter Seven

When Zulu opened the bedroom door, Rosalie was up and staring out into the garden.

"Pa sent for me," she explained. "Prissy woke me up and said pa wanted to see me down in the library."

She moved over to the dressing table and loosened her hair so Zulu could brush and arrange it for dinner. There was an air of mystery in her eyes as she settled back, her fingers tapping the inlaid surface of the vanity.

The room was reflected in the huge, carved mirror,

46

and Zulu saw that Rosalie was taking in the changes. Well, she ought to be pleased! The carved furniture had been her mother's, and Miss Ginny had sent it to be polished and recovered. Each piece had been imported from France when Elmside was first built.

Then there was the great hand-carved bed with its netting and crisp new tester the same shade as the deep piled rose rug. Through the windows came the all prevading perfume of wisteria. What more could she ask?

Rosalie drew a deep breath. "They've made it so beautiful here." She fell to studying her fingernails. "How do you think you'd like Peltier Acres, Zulu? It's a much finer house."

Zulu continued to brush Rosalie's hair. It was long and honey-blonde, with just enough curl to make it easy to arrange.

"Pa gave Norman his consent. I know it's all wonderful and what I always wanted. But I just can't seem to feel excited about it."

Zulu swirled the hair high on Rosalie's head, leaving the ringlets to fall free from behind her left ear to her shoulder. Rosalie studied the effect in her ivory hand mirror.

"You're the only one who's ever been able to do my hair that way," she said as she put down the mirror. "I think I'll wear my new lavender gown."

They were spread on the bed, her new frocks, and they still smelled faintly of their recent pressing. Zulu's fingers lingered on the crisp material as she reached for the lavender silk with its tiny pink floral print. Someday I'll wear dresses like that, she told herself.

Rosalie was quiet as Zulu fastened the hooks, but when she was ready to leave the room, she paused, her hand on the door knob.

"Remember how we used to sit in the garden and talk? Let's forget we're grown up and do that now."

Zulu shook her head. If there was anything worse

47

than an uppity white person, it was a condescending one.

"I've got to hang these clothes before they get wrinkled again. Then there's your bags to unpack. Miss Ginny'll have a fit if I don't get to them."

Rosalie sighed. "It seemed such a good idea," she said as she went out.

As soon as she was alone, Zulu returned to the dresses. Suppose they really were hers, she thought as she placed them on hangers. They'd fit about right, and how different she'd look. She picked up Rosalie's brush and arranged her hair high on her head. The curls fell lower because her hair was longer.

"I look just like a lady!" she whispered to the mirror. She held a ball gown in front of her uniform, pulling it in at the waist. Fixed up like that, there was no doubt but she'd pass, why her skin was even fairer that the O'Shay girls, for all their talk of having a Spanish grandmother.

She swirled about the room, dancing with an imaginary partner until she heard Esmeralda's heavy footsteps in the hall. She hung up the dress and yanked the pins out of her hair.

But in New Orleans. . . .

It took longer to unpack than she had anticipated. She was just finishing when the dinner bell sounded out in the quarters. Downstairs there was the rattle of china as the table was being laid, and Miss Ginny was in her room dressing. Through the open window Zulu could hear Esmeralda scold the little boy who was supposed to keep the lawns clear of leaves. Where had the day gone?

And Grant's boat would even now be on its way to New Orleans. If she had her Writ, she'd be on her way down river, too. . . .

She stepped out onto the balcony, grateful for the freshness of the air. A soothing breeze had swept away the day's heat. It swayed the elms up and down the avenue, pausing to play with some leaves that had

48

become detatched. It was a sweet, gentle wind, without a trace of dust.

And it was a breeze full of scents and sounds. The drone of voices as the field hands left their cabins to get their dinner rations, the yelp of a dog out in the kennels, and the tinkle of the glass prisms down on the gallery.

Yet, Zulu was hardly aware of the breeze. It was the smell of growing things she inhaled. The dank, earthy rankness of roots and newly watered soil, heavy on the moist air. It was a good smell, rich and full of purpose.

A big red roan galloped through the gates as she started toward the cookhouse. She recognized it as belonging to the Peltier stables, but she knew at once that it was not Norman astride. He rode well, but never that hard or with that flamboyant elegance.

The stranger reined in, raising the roan off its front legs. Lord God! There was a man who didn't care how he treated someone else's horseflesh. If Clay Haldfar had been around, there'd have been a scene, sure. All his natural hospitable instincts left Clay when it was a matter of a horse or a slave being mistreated.

The stranger dismounted and his long, Spanish spurs caught the late sunlight in blinding flashes. Zulu heard him laugh as he tossed the reins to the stable boy.

"Not bad for an Alabama raised horse," he said.

The stableboy mumbled, his black hands passing soothingly over the roan's sweat soaked neck. As he led the horse away, it tossed its head, throwing froth flecks into the air.

Zulu could not take her eyes from the stranger. Dark and slim, he moved with a lithe grace she'd never seen before in a white man. He flicked his whip against his boots and surveyed the place. There was a man to know, she decided. A man who could send a woman through heaven and hell and all within a minute.

A twig cracked back by the balcony. Rosalie was standing under its shadow, her eyes on the stranger's back.

She'd never looked better, Zulu thought. Her pale beauty against the green shrubbery made one think of the first columbine against the spring grass. Fragile and startling. Her arms were filled with newly gathered blossoms and a damp wave brushed her cheek.

The stranger gave his whip a parting flick and turned around. He saw Rosalie immediately, his dark eyes darting over her. Amusement touched his lips as he saw the flowers. He took off his hat and approached her.

"What a shame. The scene's all set for Cousin Norman and I had to come along first."

Still Rosalie did not move, but the color rose in her cheeks and for a moment Zulu thought she'd drop the flowers. There was vexation in her slight frown, but Zulu's eyes passed that over as she noted her mistress's quickened breathing. Well, here was a man with a confident maleness that even her elegant Virginia schooling hadn't prepared her to meet!

Norman Peltier rode up the path, but neither the clack of his horse's shoes, nor the patter of the stableboy running to take his mount, was heard by the two below the balcony. He stood still a moment, scowling, then he squared his shoulders and went up to them.

"I thought you'd be late, Cousin Breel." He brushed past the stranger and took Rosalie's hand. "My cousin Breel Luton. Most likely you've heard me mention my Louisiana kinfolk."

The spell was shattered. Rosalie smiled at Norman and nodded to his cousin.

"I should have known!" she exclaimed. "Len said that Norman went back to The Acres because he was expecting you. I'm so glad he brought you to meet me before the party tomorrow night."

"To tell the truth," Norman said wryly, "I all but had to hogtie him to get him over here, even though he did arrive before me. I had to stop at The Birches, and Breel said he wanted to ride a bit."

Ride a bit, Zulu thought. Wait till Mister Norman sees that horse!

Breel laughed. "Norman thought you should know the worst about his family before the announcement is made."

Norman reddened. "That was hardly the purpose. You—"

"Tut, tut," Breel murmured, "I've embarrassed him again." Then he focussed his full attention once again on Rosalie. "As a matter of truth, I did come somewhat unwillingly. I hardly expected Norman to show such taste. I thought I could wait a day to see you, but now—"

Norman laughed uneasily. "Slowly, Cousin Breel. She's promised, you know."

A flicker lightened Breel's dark eyes. Norman might as well have thrown a flame at tinder, Zulu reflected.

Len joined the three. His clothes were disheveled and there was straw clinging to his boots.

"I've got a sick colt, Norm," he said. "I'd like your opinion."

Norman glanced uncertainly at Rosalie and his cousin, but Len had already started down the path, too absorbed to even wait for an introduction.

Breel's teeth flashed. "Go right ahead, cousin," he invited. "Miss Rosalie can show me the gardens."

Norman's lips grew thinner, but he followed Len.

Breel turned back to Rosalie. He took both her hands in his and drew her closer.

"You're actually real?"

Rosalie lowered her lashes and made a motion as if to free herself of his grip. "Isn't this a little too cousinly?" she suggested. "After all, I'm not even married to Norman yet."

"Thank God for that!" Breel said fervently.

Zulu repressed a gasp. Why, he wasn't treating her with any more respect then he might show a house wench who'd caught his eye. And Rosalie, way up on her pedestal, didn't even know the difference.

Rosalie made a more determined effort to free her hands. "Please," she begged, "I'm afraid Norman might not understand if he saw us like this."

Breel's grin deepened. "On the contrary, I'm certain he'd understand very well. You know, he really doesn't like me very much."

"If this is an example!" Rosalie's voice was sharp, but the face raised to his, was flushed.

"It's mainly impulses," Breel went on. "I'm not known for resisting them." He pulled her even closer, but not so close as to make it mandatory for her to struggle. "Right now, for instance, I've an impulse that centers around your lips."

"Mr. Luton!" There was coquetery in her voice, "I've hardly known you for ten minutes!"

He laughed and released her. "You definitely should be annoyed with me," he agreed. "Maybe your brother should call me out?"

"But you didn't even try to kiss me." There was a petulant note to Rosalie's protest that brought to mind a little girl refused a sweet.

Breel raised an eyebrow. "Should I have?"

The pink in Rosalie's cheeks deepened to a bright stain and she turned away. Breel caught her arm easily.

"Lead on," he said. "This tour of the garden has me breathless."

Zulu watched until Rosalie's skirts disappeared around the hedge. Rosalie as mistress of Peltier Acres would be pampered and spoiled, but as Breel Luton's wife, it would be another story. Lord God, you could almost feel sorry for her.

But, as Breel Luton's wife, Rosalie just might take her to New Orleans. . . .

Chapter Eight

It was not Zulu's nature to feel remorse, yet in later years she often wondered how much of the blame was hers. Surely, hadn't at least a part of Rosalie's fate been sealed when she watched Breel gallop up the path?

Yet, the germ of the idea was her own, and as she set about her work that evening, she could not free herself of the possibilities that presented themselves. Certainly Rosalie did nothing to deter them.

Even from a distance she could sense her mistress's mood. Norman Peltier had always been considered handsome, but next to his cousin he was colorless. His precise voice sounded prim set against Breel's easy banter.

When Rosalie burst into the bedroom that night, her eyes were sparkling and her voice had a lilt. Zulu stood back while the girl threw herself into the window seat to stare out at the moonlit night.

"Zulu, have you ever thought about how fascinating New Orleans must be?" she finally asked, her voice soft and pensive.

Since when had she thought about anything else? Still, Zulu had a quixotic impulse to warn Rosalie. Maybe it was because the *pierre-loa* wasn't in her pocket that night. Or, more likely, it was the last feeble protest of a diminishing conscience.

"I've heard Master Breel doesn't have anything of his own," she said.

Rosalie turned and the defiance in her eyes revealed that she had already considered this possibility.

"Why should that matter?" she demanded. "Why should property be so important? To hear pa talk you'd think it was the Peltier Acres and house I'll marry instead of Norman. After all, the man counts for something, too!"

She flung herself in front of the dressing table and Zulu began to unpin her hair.

"If anyone supposes I'm going to snub Breel Luton just because he doesn't own a passel of slaves!"

No arguments were necessary, Zulu reflected. Rosalie was attending to those, herself.

The next day Rosalie was quick tempered and nervous. Zulu stayed out of her way as much as possible, as the girl wandered from the ballroom where decorations were being hung, to the balcony where she spent long minutes staring down the Elm avenue to the gate. Even Miss Ginny noticed.

"Land," she teased, "You can't expect Norman to spend every minute here. Don't forget, he's got a big place to manage.

"I wasn't looking for Norman," Rosalie snapped. Then she flushed and Miss Ginny went away, still chuckling. After all, some degree of modesty was to be expected.

When the time came to dress for the evening, Rosalie was impatient to go downstairs, yet Zulu had to do her hair three times before she was satisfied. Still, she managed to join her aunt in the hall before the first guest had arrived. Zulu, following at a little distance, noticed Miss Ginny frown slightly as she glanced at her niece.

"Don't you think that flower pulls your gown a little too low? You're showing quite a lot of bosom."

There had been a scarf designed to wear over the shoulders, but as Rosalie reached for it, Zulu came forward with a single rose instead.

"I don't think Norman will approve," Rosalie had said as she looked in the mirror.

"A man likes to see just a shadow," Zulu reassured her, knowing that was what she wished. "I hear they show a lot more in New Orleans. . . ."

Now, under Miss Ginny's concerned eyes, Rosalie shrugged. "We're so country here!" she told her aunt. "In Virginia they showed much more bosom."

"If you say so, honey," Miss Ginny murmured. "Still—"

Zulu joined the others who were already pressed close to the windows that looked in on the ballroom. If Breel had any idea of relinquishing the chase, Zulu reflected, that low draped bodice would be an invitation a man of his type was not likely to ignore. And there was always the challenge of taking from Norman. Smug Norman, with his negroes and acres. In a way there was a parallel there. The thought brought a smile to her lips.

The Peltier carriage was the first to arrive. Norman assisted Miss Thalia to ascend and Zulu noted that with each visit, her clothes seemed to become less prim.

"Soon as Miss Rosalie take over at de Acres, she git rid o' dat one," Prissy observed from Zulu's side.

Miss Thalia had taken Len's arm, but her eyes were on Norman as she was greeted by Rosalie.

"It may take some doing," Zulu observed. Just then Breel rode up on another of the Peltier horses. He threw the reins to a stable boy and went directly to Miss Ginny. He stood there, until the next carriage arrived, conversing warmly with the older woman. He acknowledged Rosalie with the barest of nods.

So, he had read the imperious light in Rosalie's eyes. No open pursuit there, but he could overdo the act and Zulu watched with growing concern as the dancing started.

New men were always at a premium and Breel quickly became the most popular guest. He danced with an easy grace and during the intermissions he could scarcely be seen for the crinolines that surrounded him. He ignored Rosalie almost to the point of rudeness.

Maybe he really wasn't playing cat and mouse, Zulu thought, alarmed. Maybe Rosalie had never really interested him. Was the dipping neckline too obvious? A man like Breel would relish the chase as much as the capture.

Even as those fears ran through her mind, Breel stopped by Rosalie almost as if in accident. They were in clear view from outside the window and though she could not hear what was said, she could see in Rosalie's lifted chin, the sharp retort to Breel's invitation.

Now was the deciding moment. Breel could lose the ground he'd gained. But it was apparent he had no intention of abjecting himself. Zulu breathed easier as he shrugged and started to move away.

"Lord God, he may as well have slapped her!" Zulu muttered to Prissy.

Rosalie caught his arm and he turned back to her, a brow raised quizzically. Not to be outdone, Rosalie raised a hand to her forehead and glanced toward the open French doors.

The music started again and in the flury of dancing couples, Zulu lost sight of them. She waited for them to whirl by, but the waltz neared an end, and there was still no sight of them.

When the music stopped, Clay climbed up on the musicians' platform and Norman joined him.

"Where's Rosalie?" Clay called out.

So Breel had accepted her invitation to step out into the garden. What a moment to choose!

Clay grinned. "You all must have guessed by now," he said, "but the announcement can keep till after refreshments."

The musicians picked up the strain of another waltz and Norman went out the French doors, oblivious, even, of Miss Thalia, who started after him.

Zulu pushed her way out of the crowding house servants and ran down the path to the summer house.

Rosalie was bound to be there and Mister Norman would most likely look for her first in the formal garden where the other couples strolled. That would give her a few minutes.

She heard their voices as she turned the corner. Illuminated as they were by the moonlight, she could plainly distinguish them sitting on the bench under the honeysuckle trellis, but the shadow of a flowering tree concealed her from them.

She started to call out to Rosalie, but stopped as Breel took her mistress into his arms. Rosalie made only token resistence, then with a little sob she strained against him, her arms pulling his head down to her lips.

After what seemed to Zulu an endless passage of time, the kiss ended and Breel laughed softly. "That was very wicked of me," he said, his voice carrying in the still air.

Rosalie drew back. "Is that all it meant to you? Can you kiss a woman like that and laugh about it?"

Zulu waited for the answer, almost as eagerly as her mistress, but Breel only shrugged.

"When the woman's my cousin's fianceé, I'd damned well better laugh. Certainly, it wouldn't help to think any other way about it."

"Then it did mean something to you?" Rosalie's voice was eager. "Oh Breel, it—"

Footsteps on gravel brought her words to a standstill, and Zulu drew even further into the shadows.

"We'd better go back," Breel said. "That's probably Norman out looking for us."

Rosalie caught his arm. "But I've got to talk to you," she begged. "We can't just go back there as if nothing had happened—"

"We've no choice." His voice softened, "But I do find this spot enchanting. I think I might ride back after the dance tonight. I'm certain it wouldn't have the same charm in daylight—not with Cousin Norman near."

He rose to his feet and assisted her up. "No, Miss Rosalie," he said, hardly changing his tone, "I don't think you'd like New Orleans—say in February—that's when the fever usually hits. Why, one year it was so bad there wasn't even time for funerals. Just carts to—"

"Hardly a pleasant subject for a lady," Norman remarked coldly as he met them at the turn of the path. "Tell me, Cousin, have you been wasting this moonlight to talk about the plague times in New Orleans? It scarcely seems in character."

"What else should I discuss with your intended?"

Norman ignored Breel as he turned his attention to Rosalie.

"Your father started to make the announcement, but you weren't there."

"Oh!" Rosalie's hand flew to her throat, then she put her other hand to her head. "I felt so faint, Norman. Breel was kind enough to take me out for some air."

"You might of asked me."

"But you were dancing with Thalia, and it would be dreadful if she thought I was jealous." Rosalie accepted his arm and rested her weight on it. "Please don't be cross. I've such a headache . . ."

The two of them went down the path and Breel stood alone, watching them. He sat down on the bench and leaned back, hands behind his head, a curious, half speculative smile on his lips.

Again Zulu was struck by the lack of respect he displayed toward Rosalie. Was he seriously attracted, or was this just an amusement? Could it be that there were white men with the temerity to claim the favors of the young miss as casually as they'd bed a colored wench? If that was true, there would be no point in encouraging Rosalie in this flirtation. As the wife of Breel Luton she'd go to New Orleans, but if he only intended to seduce her out of spite for Norman, then there'd be nothing in it to further her own plans.

As she went back to the house, Zulu tried to ponder the thing to a decision. There was definitely more than one way to look at it, and one could not underestimate Rosalie. Perhaps it had really started out of spite, but Rosalie was both pretty and willing and Breel did act as if she more than interested him. In any case, it was a gamble that must be taken.

Zulu climbed up the back stairs and settled in Rosalie's window seat to wait. She drew her feet up onto the cushions and rested her chin her knees as she continued to speculate on what lay ahead. Even now she could stop Rosalie. But should she?

New Orleans . . . New Orleans and the theater. Jewels that would make even Miss Ginny's diamonds look like pebbles. A white cottage with maybe even a maid to tend her. . . .

Whatever happened, Rosalie would land on her feet. Her very position and birth would protect her, no matter what she might do.

"But it'd be different with me," Zulu murmured. Startled at the sound of her own voice, she moved across the room to the wardrobe where the new dresses hung in rows. This was her chance, perhaps the only chance that might present itself. She had to hold to it, no matter what.

Downstairs the carriages had begun to pull away. From out in the hall came the sound of Miss Ginny's voice as she saw to the comfort of the house guests who were staying through the night. Rosalie came through the door, her mouth set in the old, familiar pout.

"You'd of thought I'd disgraced the family for generations!" she stormed. "What with the way Pa carried on, and Aunt Ginny stood by with a handkerchief to her eyes. Just because I went out into the garden with a man who'll be my cousin. Just because I felt faint and needed air!"

Zulu waited by the dressing table. "You want me to take down your hair now?" she asked.

Rosalie turned, her eyes flashing. "I'm tired of never doing what I want to do! It'll be even worse after I've married Norman. I'll be expected to spend hours reading to old Mrs. Peltier like Thalia does—and you know I've never liked to read. And Norman—all

59

Norman can talk about is how much cotton he expects to get out of this or that field. And Thalia—I'll have to get rid of her. You should have seen the prissy way she stood by while Pa scolded me for being out in the' garden!''

"You'll feel better after I've brushed your hair and unlaced you."

Rosalie went back to the window. "I wouldn't even dream of meeting him out there tonight if everyone hadn't carried on the way they did. I'm so mad now, I don't even care. It'll serve them right."

She turned around. "Yes, get me out of this dress. And you can find me something dark that doesn't rustle every move."

Did she realize what she was asking for? Just how much did she know about men? All that talking and giggling—did those silly girls really know enough to say anything?

"Miss Rosalie, I think—"

"I don't care what you think!" Rosalie stormed. "I don't care what anyone thinks. Norman kissed me goodbye and I thought I was going to be sick, I'm not going to marry him. I'm going to marry Breel."

"But suppose Master Breel doesn't want to marry you?"

Rosalie's eyes softened. "He wants to, Zulu. He kissed me out there tonight, and I know he wants to."

Zulu leaned over to pick up the slippers Rosalie had kicked across the room and the *pierre-loa* rolled from her pocket. It stopped by Rosalie's feet and the girl picked it up.

Zulu watched, wondering. In all their life together, she'd never known Rosalie to stoop to pick up anything.

"What a strange stone." Rosalie held it on her palm. "Where did you get it?"

"I found it out by the marsh." Zulu reached for it, but Rosalie made no move to return it. She pressed it against her cheek.

"It's cool," she said, surprised. "Yet, it's hot, too—all at the same time." She opened her fingers and let it fall. "I don't think I like it!"

She watched while Zulu retrieved the stone. Then she shook her head, as if to clear it. She remained silent while Zulu helped her out of her ballgown.

When the last hook was fastened on the dark, blue cotton, her eyes darted toward the darkness outside the balcony.

"When I was out there with Breel nothing else really mattered. I just wanted to stay close to him." Her eyes grew dreamy. "He'd never have kissed me that way, Zulu, if he didn't feel the same."

Lord God! If Rosalie only knew the times she'd been caught on the stairs of the cookhouse and kissed till her mouth was bruised—of how she had to avoid being caught alone in the hallway by the butler—of how she didn't dare go near the stable. Love? She felt something close to pity for Rosalie's ignorance.

Rosalie handed her the dark cloak. "Put this on and go down to the summer house," she said. "If Aunt Ginny sees you on the path she'll think you're a house guest. Soon as he gets there hurry back as fast as you can to tell me."

As Zulu started out the window, she added plaintively, "Do hurry! I'm scared half to death."

The moon had moved across the sky and the white, revealing rays no longer fell on the bench. Thanks for that, anyway, Zulu thought as she settled down to wait.

Nearly an hour passed and the shadows spread. She got up from the bench and moved restlessly to the bend of the path. Maybe Breel never intended to return, after all. What a comeuppance that would be for Rosalie.

There was no warning crunch of gravel—or perhaps she was so preoccupied with the thoughts of Rosalie's chagrin, that she failed to hear him approach, but suddenly he was behind her. Strong arms turned her around and his lips covered hers.

61

She knew, then, why Rosalie had surrendered so quickly. This man knew how to kiss, how to draw forth latent passion, sending her blood pounding through veins that felt as if they must burst, if denied. The very breath went out of her as she clung to him, returning his kisses with parted lips her body pliant and arched against him, her nails digging into his shoulders.

He raised his head, finally, and his voice was husky. "Good God . . ." he muttered. Then, again, "Good God, I wouldn't have believed it."

This was the part of herself she had fought down that morning so long ago, outside the stables. New Orleans, the white cottages—all would fade into insignificance if she permitted it to rule her. She pulled out of his arms.

"You've got the wrong girl." Even to her own ears her voice sounded strange, choked.

"I wouldn't say that." He laughed softly and pulled her out into the light. With a rough hand he jerked off the hood of the cloak and her hair tumbled onto his wrist.

"How could I have missed you earlier?"

Zulu met his eyes steadily. She pulled her arm free and with slow deliberation, opened her cloak, revealing the Elmside house servant uniform.

"I'd have sworn you were white," he muttered, then he shrugged. "God Almighty, you throw out heat like a bitch in season." He continued to stare at her, his eyes warm and appreciative. "When I go back to New Orleans, how'd you like to come along?"

"Can you buy me?" Zulu knew the answer.

He grinned. "Not at the moment."

"I thought you were calling on Miss Rosalie. I'm supposed to fetch her now that you're here."

If she'd wondered before, she knew the answer now. If it hadn't been Rosalie, it might have been any other girl. Just something to break the monotony of country life. Still, Rosalie was pretty and she was clever. She could change that.

"Stay," he invited. "I liked the sample."

Zulu laughed back at him, and then ran toward the house.

Rosalie was at the foot of the stairs, her eyes bright with impatience. She snatched the concealing cloak off Zulu's shoulders and threw it around her own.

"I thought you'd never get back!" she snapped. Then the temper went out of her and was replaced by uncertainty. "Maybe . . . I shouldn't meet him after all—"

Zulu's fingers tightened around the stone in her pocket. "He's out there," she said. "I promised to tell you."

Rosalie raised her chin. "I said I'd meet him. Still. . . ." she caught Zulu's hand. "You follow, but don't let him know. Just stay near in case I call you."

Zulu waited until Rosalie was out of sight, then she followed. Breel was certainly not in the mood for talk, she reflected. If Rosalie really meant what she said, she'd be calling out soon. But did she mean it? Rosalie was accustomed to getting what she wanted, and right now that list was headed with Breel's name.

Her answer was apparent. Already Rosalie was in Breel's arms, clinging to him as if she'd run the last part of the way. The cloak lay where it had slid off her shoulders, and her face was turned up to him.

"I shouldn't have come out here," she was whispering, but there was more yearning than fear in her voice. "Oh Breel, I shouldn't of. . . ."

He didn't kiss her until he had her up in his arms, then, with his face bent over hers, he carried her blindly through the door into the summer house.

Zulu heard him stumble over the settee, where Miss Ginny often rested after gardening.

She hesitated. But wasn't this what she had planned? Now he'd have to marry Rosalie, and New Orleans was certain.

Why, then, this sick feeling? As if at last she'd

stepped firmly onto the path she'd known would be hers, even that morning long ago by the swamp. As if up to now, she'd been two persons, instead of one.

She turned back, taking no care to walk only on the grass. Neither Breel nor Rosalie would hear the gravel crunch under her feet.

Chapter Nine

The early morning light flickered through the leaves of the wisteria, painting small, fantastic patches of sun and shadow on Rosalie's face. She was huddled in the window seat and Zulu looked at her, worried. She had come quietly through the window when the first signs of day streaked the sky, and now she refused to go to bed. Instead, she stared out to the misty dawn dimness of the garden below.

"If you get into bed now, you'll have a few hours sleep," Zulu reasoned. She, herself, was heavy with weariness, though she had dozed during the hours she waited for Rosalie.

For the first time since her return, Rosalie looked at Zulu and spoke. There was a wondering note in her voice.

"When he left me this morning, he said I was the cleanest thing that had ever come into his life, and he wasn't smiling when he said that, either. I don't think I ever saw him look so serious."

Maybe it would be all right after all. Maybe everything would work out the way she'd planned. New Orleans had never seemed so near!

The chant of mellow voices drifted through the window, accompanied by the jangle of the chains that held the buckets deep inside the well. Was it that late already?

"You've got to get to bed," Zulu insisted, but Rosalie motioned her to silence. When the final, long wail of the chant shrilled through the air, she shivered.

"I wish it had ended differently this morning. . . ." Her eyes sought out the window again. "Remember what Esmeralda used to say?"

As if either of the two of them could ever throw off those superstitions! Somehow they imprinted themselves on the mind with far greater permanence than anything Miss Lejon might have taught. "When de singin' start happy dese spirrits git jealous, you watch, de song end bad. But when he song starts bad, dat's good."

What could Rosalie really know of the forces that conceived and birthed that song? Rosalie who could not even stand the feel of the *pierre-loa* in her hand?

"As if there really were spirits down there that gave a thought to whether happiness comes too easily!" Rosalie laughed without conviction. "Aunt Ginny calls that nigger talk and she used to scold me for listening."

The sun had crept higher into the sky and the dawn mists cleared before the impact of the new day. A bird sang from a nearby limb, and downstairs someone raised a window to let the sweet, garden air into the house. In the next room Prissy was opening Miss Ginny's blinds.

The last bucket was being drawn up from the well, and a deep, rich voice had started the first verse of a spiritual. Zulu watched Rosalie's face as the words drifted up to them.

"What shall I do for a hidin' place?
And a-heav'n bell a-ring and praise God.
I run to de sea, but de sea run dry
And a-heav'n bell a-ring and praise God
I run to de gate, but de gate shut fast
And a-heav'n bell a-ring and praise God

65

No hidin' place for sinners dere
And a-heav'n bell a-ring and praise God—"

Rosalie's face paled, as if for the first time she fully comprehended how far she had stepped.

"Does it show so clearly?" she whispered. "You knew. You knew the minute I came back." Suddenly she started to cry. "I want to die," she said. "I want to die!"

Zulu helped her to her feet and unfastened her dress. "You'll feel differently after you've had a sleep." She spoke coaxingly, as if to a weary child.

Rosalie nodded, half convinced, and Zulu worked quickly, unpinning the girl's hair and helping her into a nightdress. When finally she was in bed with a light cover pulled under her arms, Rosalie began to relax. She smiled unexpectedly, a glowing softness in her face.

"He was so sweet, Zulu. I didn't know a man could be so sweet."

In the next room Prissy had taken up the spiritual as she worked. Her rich, mellow voice came through the wall.

"Remember me, poor fallen soul
And heav'n bell a-ring and praise God
Your righteous Lord shall find you out
And heav'n bell a-ring and praise God—"

Rosalie's smile dimmed and she caught Zulu's hand. "Do you think God minds so terribly?" she asked.

Did it matter more to God when it was a white girl instead of a black girl? Zulu was aware of a sudden anger as she pulled her arm free.

"Go to sleep," she advised. "I'll tell Miss Ginny you've a headache."

It was early afternoon when Zulu awakened her mistress with the news of Norman's arrival.

"Tell him I still have a headache," Rosalie murmured without opening her eyes.

Zulu kept her voice carefully casual.

"Mr. Breel will be mighty sorry to hear that," she said.

Rosalie opened her eyes and sat up. It was hot in the room and her forehead glistened. She threw back her cover and was out of her nightdress before Zulu could select a gown from the wardrobe.

The window was opened over the front gallery and Miss Thalia's voice drifted up through the quiet air. Rosalie frowned.

"She would have to come!" She pulled in her breath clinging to the back of a chair as Zulu deftly laced her corset. When she was again able to exhale she went to the window and pulled it shut.

"I've got to talk to Breel without everybody fussing around," she told Zulu. "I want you to stand by in the hall. If we get a chance to be alone I can watch the stairs, but I wouldn't know if anyone was inside the door."

Zulu lowered the dress over Rosalie's head and fastened the broad pink sash. The flowered voile had been a fortunate choice, and the skirts flounced over the starched petticoats. She brushed Rosalie's hair so it fell down her back in soft waves and tied it with a ribbon. It was a soft effect, calculated to draw attention from the fact that her eyes were not their usual clear blue.

Rosalie studied her reflection. "Do I look different?" she asked anxiously.

"You'll look the same," Zulu assured her, "to everyone but Mister Breel."

Zulu waited until Rosalie had left the room and was well down the stairs before she followed. She paused to pick up a bottle of smelling salts. What better an excuse for lingering near her mistress? Miss Ginny already knew Rosalie was not well, so there should be no awkward dismissal.

Rosalie had apparently hesitated before stepping out the door, because she still was being greeted when Zulu took up her position. There was a clatter of chairs as the men resumed their seats and Zulu moved to where she could see through the half open entranceway.

Len leaned toward his sister. "I was about to tell Norm I'm thinking of giving Lance his papers," he announced. "Of course, I wouldn't want him chasing off, but I'd give him his Writ—say on my birthday—and after that he'd know he was free, and I'd know it, even though everything stayed the same."

Lord God, he sure wasn't taking much in the way of chances! But then, what did it matter now that she was sure of another way to get to New Orleans?

Breel stretched out his long, booted legs.

"Can't see how that'll do him much good," he remarked, amusement in his eyes.

"Well, he—well, he wouldn't have to get a ticket everytime he went to The Birches to see his girl."

"My cousin in Virginia has a body servant who was free till he was twelve," Miss Thalia said. "His father was a white man—a professor and one of those dreadful abolitionists. He was caught smuggling slaves up north, and—" Thalia made an expressive face. "He had some children by a colored woman and they were sold when she was returned to her owner. Personally, I always felt my uncle made a terrible mistake when he bought Jules for my cousin. A little freedom's bound to go to a darky's head."

"What's he done?" Len demanded. "Killed his master while he slept?"

Thalia's lips thinned. "Of course not! But he's been caught teaching the ninnies to read. When my uncle was alive he put a stop to it, but I'm afraid my cousin just looks the other way."

"What so bad about teaching a ninny to read?" Len bristled. "Lance can and so can Rosalie's Zulu."

"Well, for one thing, it's against the law!" Thalia snapped.

"I'd hate to see all the planters who'd be jailed for

breaking that particular law," Breel laughed.

"I think that if Len wants to give Lance his Writ, it's his own affair," Rosalie said, her eyes on Thalia.

Len grinned. "Now you folks just watch Rosalie. Her birthday's only two months away and I'll wager she beats me to it."

Lord God, need he be so obvious? Zulu held her breath, half expecting Rosalie to turn on her brother, but instead, Norman Peltier brought his chair down on its front legs with a crash.

"I don't think I'd care to have free niggers at The Acres," he said. "I'll have to ask you to forget this nonsense, Rosalie."

The scorn Rosalie had been about to unleash on her brother, turned full force upon her fiancé.

"Zulu doesn't belong to you yet, Norman!" she exclaimed. There was an ominous note of rebellion in her voice.

Norman flushed. "I didn't mean any offense, Rosalie, I—"

Clay Haldfar had ridden up to the porch while they were talking. He dismounted and handed over the reins.

Len didn't wait for him to get up the stairs before he turned to his sister. "Now would be a good time to take it up with pa," he urged and from her vantage point Zulu watched anxiously. Rosalie pouted, her expression a combination of indecision and defiance.

"I think Cousin Norman is right!" Thalia persisted. "After all, he has his own darkies to consider."

"Oh?" Rosalie asked. She went up to her father and he smiled down at her, kissing her cheek.

"Feeling better, honey?" he asked.

Rosalie nodded. "Pa," she said clearly, "I've just decided what I want for my birthday."

"Anything you say," he promised absently and went into the house.

Len laughed, the relief was plain on his face. "He'll be bound to his word, now!"

"Of course," Rosalie retorted. "He's not stuffy."

Breel covered his mouth and coughed, Norman started to speak, but changed his mind. Even Len became aware of the tension.

"You haven't seen the new gelding," he said to Norman. "I'd like for you to come down to the stable and give your opinion."

Norman stood up, visibly relieved. "I'd be glad to."

Thalia's eyes were on her cousin's face and she arose, shaking her skirts in Rosalie's direction. "I've yet to see an Alabama horse that can match our Virginia line."

Norman hesitated by Rosalie's chair. "Are you coming with us?"

She shook her head. "I've seen it, and besides I feel far too faint to go out in the heat."

Breel tilted back his chair and crossed his legs. "I'll take a look at it later," he said.

"My cousin spent half the night riding around the country side," Norman told the others. "I was surprised he even rode over with me today."

Rosalie's color deepened and Zulu saw Breel glance at her through lowered lids, but neither spoke until the others were well on their way down the path.

"I hope," Breel said, "that we won't have to spend every visit hoping for a horse as an excuse to be alone."

Rosalie ran across the gallery and dropped down at Breel's feet.

"I didn't think we'd get a chance to talk." Her eyes searched up into his face.

He brushed the hair back from her forehead and she smiled. "Everything seems so right when I'm with you." She carried his hand down to her cheek and held it there.

"Do you know you're a pretty little thing?" he asked her.

She laughed. "When Norman got so pompous about Zulu, I felt like telling him right there that it'd never be his affair."

"Won't it be?" Breel's voice was soft.

Rosalie pouted. "Why do you tease me? Can't we tell Norman and everyone when they come back?"

"Tell Norman—?"

"That I'm going to marry you."

Breel's eyebrow jerked upward.

"I am, of course," Rosalie went on complacently. "After last night there can't be any question."

Breel kissed her lightly on her forehead and she wrapped her arms around his neck.

"I'm glad, Breel. I'm glad, because I love you so much."

Gently he disengaged her arms and sat back. "We've got to give this more time. There's a lot to be considered. I think your father will have some mighty strong objections."

"Then we won't have to tell him. We'll run away to Montgomery and get married there. Or in New Orleans."

"Rosalie," he said quietly, "surely it's no secret my family cut me off without a penny? What do you think we'd live on?"

"There's nothing to worry about. If you couldn't find something in New Orleans, well, we'd come right back here. After Pa got over being mad everything will be all right."

He stood and raised her to her feet. "Meanwhile, I'm my cousin's guest. "This is hardly the time—"

"But when?" she persisted. "When?"

The others were returning from the stable and he placed a finger lightly on her lips. "We'll talk about it later. Now that I know which is your window."

Rosalie refused to get into bed that night. Zulu shrugged and settled down to wait.

The hours passed slowly, but there was no sound from the darkness outside. Rosalie moved restlessly about the room, once even sending Zulu to the summer house in case she had misunderstood.

"Probably company stopped by," she decided. "He'd have to stay if there were guests."

Zulu nodded, fervently hoping in her own mind that this was true, but Rosalie's face was white and strained when she finally climbed into bed. She did not speak, even when Zulu drew the net and wished her goodnight from the doorway.

No one rode over from The Acres the next day and Rosalie was so subdued that even Miss Ginny glanced sharply at her.

"I think you need a tonic," she decided and glancing at Zulu, she nodded her head. "I think I'll have Esmeralda give the both of you a tonic . . ."

That night Rosalie permitted herself to be helped into her bed things without a protest.

There'll be a reason, Zulu told herself, but she couldn't help the feeling of apprehension. What if he'd left The Acres already? Rosalie should have known better then to talk about marriage right away. Even a kitchen girl would know better how to handle her man!

She went to the window to draw the curtains, and there was Breel grinning at her and motioning for her to undo the latch. Again she was aware of the way his eyes swept over her. It was almost a physical contact.

"Miss Rosalie," she said softly, "Mr. Breel is right outside the window."

Rosalie leapd out of her bed, snatching a robe. "Let him in, Zulu. For heaven sakes, let him in!"

Still Zulu hesitated. This wasn't a man who was going to be pushed. This was no Norman or Len. There was a ruthlessness under that pose of indolence. She'd been wrong to think everything would fall into place.

"Hurry!" Rosalie whispered. "If Aunt Ginny should happen to look out her window—"

Zulu threw the latch and stood aside as Rosalie threw herself into Breel's arms.

"It's dark out there," he assured her. "No one could see me." He paused, searching her face. "I promised myself I wouldn't come back."

Rosalie laughed triumphantly and once again she was the Rosalie who got what she wanted.

"You couldn't stay away. Not anymore than I could tell you to stay outside the window."

"But you should have," he said. "You should have."

Zulu eased the door shut and went on silent, naked feet down the hall. Why, she wondered, should she feel as if all the responsibility was hers? As if, when she held the *loa* in her hand and wished for Breel to come she had irrevocably drawn him?

She paused on the stairs before climbing up to her room over the cookhouse. The air was fresh and sweet in her lungs but it failed to blow away the heavy sense of foreboding.

Chapter Ten

The foreboding was still with her, but it was a vague thing, rendered less than a ghost by each week that passed. Every sign was good. Breel postponed leaving The Acres week after week, and even in the kitchen the girls were snickering about how he was becoming as much a fixture as Miss Thalia.

Why, it was two months, Zulu reflected as she hurried through the garden fragrant with summer's blossoms. Nearly two months since Breel had ridden through the gates, and now, at last, it was Rosalie's birthday.

Surely Breel couldn't put Rosalie off much longer? Maybe, today, on her birthday—Yes, that was the way it should be. She would get her Writ and Rosalie would get Breel. All on the same day.

She felt like dancing as she went through the house and up to Rosalie's room. Maybe, later, Breel might not

73

be too good a husband, but at least Rosalie would live more in a few months than a lifetime with Mister Norman. She smiled to herself. How could Esmeralda say it had been evil to wish for these things when she held the *loa*? How could good come out of bad?

She opened the door quietly, but Rosalie was already awake and up. Zulu looked at her critically.

"You've been sick again?"

Rosalie nodded. She hesitated a second, then she drew a pipe out of her robe pocket.

"Breel left this on the table by my bed. It'd been terrible if I hadn't seen it before Harmony came in to sweep up."

Zulu laughed. "She'd have been mighty impressed with Mister Norman. This is the one he favors, isn't it?"

Rosalie managed a smile. "I'm afraid property rights don't impress Breel much. Why isn't he more careful? Doesn't it matter to him?"

Zulu took the pipe from her and dropped it in her pocket. "I think you'd better talk to him tonight. With it being your birthday and all—"

Now was the time Rosalie should make her announcement about the Writ. Zulu waited, but Rosalie turned petulantly to the window.

"It doesn't seem a bit like a birthday. I feel so terrible I don't know how I'll ever be up to the folks Aunt Ginny has invited. And even the mare Pa promised me hasn't got here yet."

It was plain she'd forgotten all about the Writ. A paper that spelled the difference between being an animal and a free human meant so little to her. So little that she must be reminded!

"Remember," Zulu ventured, "how on your birthday we used to pretend it was both ours because we never knew mine?"

Some of the petulance left Rosalie's face. "Oh, I almost forgot." She opened a drawer and took out her jewel case.

Zulu stared, stunned, at the golden link bracelet her mistress held out to her.

"I bought this when Aunt Ginny and I were in Montgomery buying my trousseau. I knew you'd like it the instant I saw it."

A chain. A golden chain, but a chain. Zulu was barely able to mumble her thanks.

"Can you imagine," Rosalie went on, "For awhile I thought I'd give you your Writ just to spite Norman. Why I even had Pa get it. But spiting Norman doesn't matter anymore. Besides, how would I manage without you?"

A spasm of mixed fury and frustration left Zulu trembling. She turned to the wardrobe, pretending to be busy arranging the clothes. "I wish I was old Winnie out in the quarters so I could put a curse on you!" she thought wildly. "Or that I really was like my grandmother. I'd hate and hate!"

"Anyway," Rosalie went on complacently, "I took the Writ from Pa and—" she giggled, "if the sky fell on me or something, you'd be free."

How could she be so stupid? So utterly incapable of understanding that even a body servant was made up of hopes and desires just like anyone else? Lord God, she was asking for everything she'd get!

And she'd get it. There was no longer any doubt in Zulu's mind. It had all seemed a wonderful plan. Like a fairy tale ending. Rosalie would marry Breel and they'd all go to New Orleans. With her Writ in her hands, no one could stop her from leaving, once they got to the city.

But in New Orleans without her Writ, there'd be no escape. They'd find her in no time if she tried to get away. Now it was just as important that Rosalie stay in Alabama as it had been that she go to Louisiana.

With some semblance of calm returned, Zulu mulled over the remaining possibilities. It was back to the way it had been before Breel arrived. She could still escape to

75

New Orleans from Alabama, no one would ever think to look for her there.

"You do like the bracelet, don't you? I thought it was so pretty."

"You shouldn't have done it, Miss Rosalie. You really shouldn't have done it."

After Rosalie went downstairs Zulu made no move to leave for her breakfast in the cookhouse. There were plans to be made, and no time to waste.

When Rosalie came up to be dressed for dinner, even as unperceptive as she usually was, she sensed the change.

"Zulu, you're so quiet tonight. If it's about me—it'll be all right. Just as soon as I tell Breel, he'll make arrangements and we'll go to New Orleans. We can lie about dates, and no one will ever guess."

Yes, it would have been easy. Just as everything had always been easy for Rosalie. Only this time. . . .

While Rosalie waited on the gallery for Breel, Zulu took up a position outside the gateway. She waited in the shadows of the orchard, where she could take cover if, by some mischance, Norman Peltier came first.

It was over an hour before a horse and rider came into view. Zulu had been certain it would be Breel, yet she felt relief when she recognized the dark head. Of course, Norman always rode beside the carriage that brought Miss Thalia. Nobody could deny he was the perfect host.

She touched the *loa* stone as she stepped out onto the road.

Breel reined in his horse. "What are you doing here? Is something wrong?" Inadvertently he glanced back down the road.

"I wanted to talk to you alone," Zulu said. She stepped back into the orchard and waited while he turned his horse's head to follow.

"Did Rosalie send you?" he persisted. "Have they—is there trouble?"

She'd have to be bold. That was the only language he'd understand.

"Do you love Miss Rosalie?"

He frowned. "Aren't you being a bit impertinent? What business is it of yours, anyway?"

"She expects to marry you."

"And maybe she should. But what's this got to do with you?"

"I'm Miss Rosalie's body servant," Zulu said. "There's nobody knows her the way I do. She's always had everything she could want and she's used to the sort of life Mister Norman could give her. How long do you think she'd be happy living around as a poor relation?"

For a second, Zulu expected Breel to bring his crop down on her, but instead he slapped at his boot.

"She said she has money of her own. Her mother left her something."

"Enough for a year, maybe. But after that?"

Breel swore softly at her. He started to turn his horse away and for a second Zulu thought she'd lost her gamble, but he pulled up on the reins.

"Why do you think I've put her off so long? Hell, don't you think I've been over all of that?"

It was strange, Breel Luton talking to her as if she were a white woman. She hastened to reap the full advantage.

"I heard there's a girl in New Orleans promised to you."

There was a reflective note to his voice. "Next month. Donna Moulton and all the Moulton holdings . . ."

She knew then that she had won. He had only needed to find justification. To set one possibility against another.

"It'd be better if you didn't say goodbye. That way she'd turn to Mister Norman quicker."

"Suppose I told Rosalie about this?" His eyes studied her face, trying to read her thoughts. "Aren't you taking a chance?"

She returned his look. "I'm not taking a chance," she said with certainty. "No chance at all."

She watched Breel go back down the road, wondering what explanation he would give to his cousin and Miss Thalia when he passed by them. She felt a twinge of pity for Rosalie as she reflected on how easy he had been to convince.

A twig cracked and she turned to find Len standing behind her, blocking the way. His face was white and there was an ugly twist to his lips. Gentle Len! Even in a nightmare she couldn't have imagined him looking at her like this.

He caught her arm. "So this is why Breel comes over here every chance! And all the time I thought he was after one of the kitchen girls. I didn't expect to find you sneaking out to meet him. You, who wouldn't even let me put a hand on you!"

Zulu jerked her arm free. "I haven't been meeting him. I haven't been meeting with anyone."

But Len was in no mood to listen. She doubted he even heard her. He caught her arm again, and pulled her against him. She struggled, kicking, biting and scratching, but his embrace only tightened. She knew she wasn't going to escape this time, no matter how hard she tried.

"I kept my word," he panted. "You made a promise."

Zulu twisted her head away from his mouth and he laughed as she tried to bite through the jacket to his shoulder.

"Rosalie's keeping the Writ," she gasped. "I told you I had to be free."

"You're free whenever she takes the notion. I didn't promise you anything else."

Then there were no more words possible. His mouth was hard on hers, hungry and beyond control. She continued to struggle as he dragged her to the ground, but he was insensible to the bite of her teeth and the tearing of her nails.

"You're going to keep your word," his voice rasped in her ear. "No matter what, you're going to keep your word."

He was contrite as he helped her to her feet. The sun had finally left the orchard and the early evening rustling of birds was all around them, but she heard none of it as she tried to repair her torn clothes.

"I'm sorry," Len's voice was unsteady. He ran his hand over his forehead, pushing the hair away from his face. "You know I didn't want it to be like that. But when I saw you and Breel together, I thought—"

"You know, now." Zulu spoke without emotion, but the bitterness was heavy inside her. If Rosalie had left any little fragment of compassion, her brother had ripped it away. Now she didn't need to touch the *pierre-loa* to experience hatred. Now it was a part of every breath she drew. There were no more thoughts about turning back. Now there was only one person who mattered. Herself.

"It's not right I should feel the way I do about you," Len was saying. "I thought once I had you it would be different, but it's not like that."

"Suppose I told Rosalie?" Strange, almost the same words Breel had used what seemed centuries ago.

Len shook his head, the shamed look left his eyes. He took up the stance of a white man with a colored woman. "I'd just say you were lying." But he was trying too hard. Zulu knew by the way he avoided looking at her.

"Don't worry," she said scornfully. "I won't tell her—or anyone else."

"I'd marry you," his voice was wistful. "I'd marry you if you were white."

"If I were white," Zulu assured him, "I wouldn't have you!"

She left him standing there, his own clothes disheveled. She didn't run until the trees hid her from

79

his view.

In the shadow of the springhouse she worked feverishly to draw up a bucket of water, and she splashed it in her haste to carry it up the stairs to her room.

Maybe if she scrubbed every inch of her skin, she could erase the memory of Len. Erase the realization—the realization that even if a baby resulted no one would think twice about it. Just another ninny to train for the house. Lord God what a coming down they'd all have when they found it wasn't only colored wenches that got themselves in that fix! She'd see they found out—and just let Rosalie try to say she was raped!

It would take more than water to clean away Len holding her helpless while he thrust savagely into her unwilling body. More than water to banish the aching soreness.

Her eyes fell on the pipe where it had fallen from her pocket when she stripped off her uniform. Let them feel some of the shame they had no hesitation to inflict!

Rosalie's eyes were frightened when she came up to bed that night.

"Breel's left. He's gone back to Louisiana."

"Did he leave a letter?" Zulu asked, knowing the answer.

Rosalie shook her head. "He'll be back. I know he'll be back even though Norman said—" She raised her chin. "I'm not even worried."

Zulu unpinned the long, fair hair and as she brushed it, she found herself softly singing.

"I run to de gate, but de gate shut fast. . . ."

Rosalie dropped her mirror and they both stared at the broken fragments.

Chapter Eleven

Zulu slipped through the side entrance of the house. Outside the last glimmering of twilight was fading into night. It made a soft, glowing light, like the smoldering embers of a fire. A warm, moist quiet hung over the treetops, and the elms up and down the avenue were as still as an audience listening to a beautiful aria.

It was dark inside the doorway. Zulu paused until her eyes adjusted and then she hurried up the stairs to where the night candelabrum had already been lighted. She passed it and went into Rosalie's room.

Rosalie was looking over the heap of newly unpacked gowns and petticoats that had been delivered only that morning. The name of the Montgomery dressmaker was still on the crumpled wrappings.

"It really was funny," she told Zulu. "Aunt Ginny kept pointing out patterns she thought Norman would like and all the time I was looking at the same things, deciding whether they would please Breel."

Zulu closed the door. "It's been over a month, Miss Rosalie."

"He'll be back. I know he'll be back."

"I've just come from the levee. The boat from New Orleans is taking on cotton."

Rosalie's face drained of color.

"I talked to the captain," Zulu continued, relentlessly.

"You've still got to have your papers," Gram had said. . . .

"I asked if he'd heard anything about a Mister Breel Luton, and he said the only Luton he knew of was the young gentleman who'd just married the Moulton money. He said it was one of the biggest weddings he could remember hearing about."

"Go away. . . ." Rosalie's voice was barely above a whisper. "Go away. I've got to think."

Zulu moved to the door, but she did not open it. Once she would have felt sorry for Rosalie. But that was before the withheld Writ. Before Len in the orchard. . . .

"I'll have to marry Norman." Rosalie's face was white and set. "I'll have to marry him real soon."

No tears for Breel. Only a quick, practical grab for the obvious way out. Only this time it wasn't going to be that easy. This time she would learn what it felt like to be trapped!

"I'll send you to The Acres with a note in the morning." Rosalie swept the pile of frocks onto the floor. "You can get me ready for bed and pack away those things. I. . . . don't think I could face anyone downstairs tonight."

It would be so easy, Zulu thought as she folded the clothes, so easy to stand by and watch you get your way like always. But this time the uneven scales would be put into balance.

You fool, Rosalie. You made it have to be this way!

She drew the bed curtains and bent over the candle that still flickered on the dressing table. Unexpectedly, she caught her reflection in the mirror, and it was a stranger she saw there. The shadowy light played around narrowed eyes that were murky instead of golden, it etched provocative hollows under her cheekbones and she felt herself possessed by this foreign face. She pulled in the air and pursed her lips letting it escape slowly, so that the flame did not die a merciful death, but flickered and begged, sparking up, then failing until finally it went out altogether, leaving the room in darkness.

Chapter Twelve

Zulu went to Rosalie's room at the first stirring of the kitchen help in the cookhouse, but already the note was written and Elmside's mistress was tapping her fingers impatiently.

"I told you to be early! You know Norman always rides out to the fields right after breakfast. If you hurry you'll get there in time to catch him by his stables. I wouldn't want Thalia to see you."

Zulu accepted the note in silence. She found herself unable to look at Rosalie directly or to speak. Lord God, where was her spirit? Why should she feel guilt? Did Rosalie show guilt when she deprived her of her freedom?

Still, it was with a mounting heaviness that she hurried down the road. The morning was sweet with the fragrance of the last flowers. It wasn't the sort of day that lent itself to her plans.

She was waiting by the stables when Norman came down the path. At the sight of her his face showed alarm.

"Is something wrong?" Again, almost Breel's words. But it had been easier with Breel. Then there had been Norman. That was before Len and her rape in the orchard. Before the *loa* had ceased to disturb her.

When she handed Norman the note, he hesitated to accept it at first as if afraid of what it might say, but as he read his face brightened.

She could have recited the words. She had opened the note on the way. Rosalie had been clever. One line in particular. . . .

"I do so hate the fuss of a big wedding, though I know Aunt Ginny will be disappointed. But with your mother too ill to attend, I do believe it would be nicer if we rode into Montgomery just quietly and got married. It's not as if we didn't have Pa's consent. . . ."

That, when he had expected a note breaking their engagement, when she had barely been civil to him on his last visit. No wonder he looked as if he wanted to throw his hat into the air.

She knew, then that she had no choice. That she had really never had a choice at all.

"We heard about Mr. Breel getting married. We just got word last night."

Norman's expression sobered a little. "Oh?" His eyes softened again as he glanced down at the note. "You can tell Miss Rosalie I'll be by for her in about two hours. Just as soon as I can make arrangements here."

It was as if she could look into his mind, feel acceptance of the fact of Rosalie's infatuation for Breel, realize how it was inevitable she would turn to him once Breel was out of reach.

Never had the *loa* felt stronger. It fanned up the mounting hatred; it made her body ache again with its violation. It carried Rosalie's voice denying her freedom.

For a second she thought she would faint from the suffocating power that made her own voice strange and far away. And purposely, a little stupid.

"I almost forgot. Miss Rosalie never can seem to remember to give this back to you, so I brought it along."

The smile left his lips as he stared down at the pipe she held.

"How did Rosalie get this? It was one Breel lost . . . on one of his night rides."

Zulu shrugged. "I picked it up by her bed one morning. I guess she just kept forgetting to give it back to you."

Norman's face was ashen, but Zulu continued, unperturbed. "I knew you held it special because I used

84

to see you with it a lot." She moved as if to leave, "I'd best hurry. Miss Rosalie wasn't feeling very well this morning and she'll be waiting."

"She's ill again?" Norman's voice was cold and his mouth hardened. "Of course that wouldn't have anything to do with this note?" He tore the paper to shreds and watched the breeze pick up the fragments. He was silent for several minutes and when he looked again at Zulu there was fury in his eyes but he spoke flatly, without emotion. "Give your mistress my best wishes. There's nothing else to tell her."

As Zulu started down the path, he called softly after her, "And thank you for returning my pipe. My cousin had an unfortunate way of making himself free with what I particularly favored."

Rosalie was waiting on the gallery, her eyes bright with excitement. If there had been any lingering grief at losing Breel, Zulu reflected, it was gone now. Maybe Breel was luckier than he realized.

"What did Norman say? When will he be by for me? I've put some things in a bag and I want you to take it through the orchard to the road. I got everything ready all by myself!"

Rosalie who never bothered to lift a finger!

"Mister Norman sent his best wishes," Zulu said.

"Yes! But what time will he be by for me?"

Zulu shook her head. "He just sent his best wishes."

Rosalie stared at her. "But that's not like Norman. You must not have understood. . . . Or do you think he could have guessed?" She lifted her chin, the old imperiousness back. "But that's stupid. He's just in a snit because I haven't been very civil to him and he's teaching me a lesson. . . . Only there isn't time."

Rosalie's delayed birthday present was led to the foot of the gallery stairs for her inspection almost at the same time a Peltier house servant arrived with Norman's reply.

Rosalie glanced at the mare and snatched at the note.

When she finished reading she looked up at her father who still held the mare by its halter. Her face was carefully composed and there was no note of distress in her voice.

"What a surprise, Pa! Can you imagine! Norman's gone off to Montgomery to marry Thalia. I declare, she worked hard enough to get him."

Clay's face reddened. "I'll call him out!" he stormed. "He can't treat my daughter like that!"

"Oh, Pa!" Rosalie laughed. "I sent him a note this morning. I told him I wasn't going to marry him."

It was the first time Zulu had experienced anything close to admiration for her mistress. There wasn't even a hint of the fright her face had shown earlier as she went down the stairs to inspect her present.

"She's a beauty, Pa. I guess she was worth waiting for. I'm going right up and change into my riding things."

"We'll have to work her over first, honey. I don't think she's used to a side saddle." He hesitated. "You're sure, Rosalie? You're not just saying that about Peltier?"

"You think I want to live over at The Acres with that old woman always talking about how sick she is in that old, musty room? And Thalia settled in as if she owns the place? And Norman acting like an old man already—or—or like a prim old maid?" She stroked the mare's neck, "And I am going to ride her. She's my present, isn't she? You know I can ride anything we have in the stable!"

For a minute father and daughter locked glances in a silent battle, but as usual Rosalie won.

"You'll be careful? She's got a lot of spirit, honey."

"You're hardly any bigger," Zulu observed as she helped Rosalie into her habit. "I'd expect you'd be showing a little."

Rosalie laughed bitterly. "I just about stopped eating. I figured I could keep on that way till Breel came and took me to New Orleans. I've been dreaming of what a hog I'd make of myself then.''

"Keep that up and you'll be fainting all over the place. Then everyone will guess.''

Rosalie paused by the door. "Does it matter anymore?'' Her eyes sparkled and Zulu wasn't certain whether it was with anger or defiance. "I'm going to ride where everyone can see me. No one's going to be able to say I took to my room grieving over Norman!''

The filly shuddered when Rosalie settled into the saddle. A breeze blew her skirt against its shivering flank and without warning it took off down the avenue and out the gate. Rosalie held a firm seat, letting it play out its fright, and her laughter floated back to them.

Miss Ginny ran out onto the gallery. "Clay!'' she screamed, "Clay, do something!''

Her brother looked up at his sister with scorn. "My girl'll take the frolic out of that horseflesh,'' he assured her. "She's doing just fine.''

They came into view again, galloping across the field, Rosalie's skirts flowing out behind, her head high and her hand firm. Then, without warning, her body slumped in the saddle and she tumbled onto the ground, her head striking a rock.

She was still unconscious when old Doctor Hayward arrived late in the afternoon. He touched the place where Miss Ginny had shaved back the hair to clean the wound, and frowned.

"You did about all that can be done, Ginny,'' he said. "It was a bad cut but she should be coming out of it soon. Still, you can't always tell—something like this—''

"She'll be all right,'' Clay insisted subbornly. "The Haldfars are strong stock. Why, when I was a boy—'' But his face was gray with worry and his hand shook when he reached out to brush a curl off his daughter's forehead.

Zulu stood at the back of the room. This wasn't in her

plans. That fool, Rosalie! Going without enough food for a bird and then letting the horse gallop away with her. There was a lot she could say, but Lord God, they sure wouldn't thank her for it. And, after all, what good would it do? Everything was out of her hands now. Just when she thought she had full control.

Miss Ginny settled the doctor in a room nearby, and by common consent, Zulu was allowed to remain. A cot was placed for her near Rosalie's bed.

Toward morning Rosalie stirred for the first time. She moaned as consciousness returned and Zulu pulled aside the bed curtains, tilting a candle so she could see the girl's face.

Rosalie's eyes fluttered open and she caught Zulu's arm.

"See, it didn't matter after all," she whispered. Zulu moved to call the doctor, but Rosalie held tightly. "I wanted to tell you—the song had a last verse. I thought of it just now. . ." Her face drained of color and her grip went lax only to tighten again as she twisted in a spasm of pain. Her shriek brought the doctor running, before Zulu was able to free herself and reach the door.

"Don't call Miss Ginny," Zulu said, and the doctor nodded, after a quick look at the pain gripped girl and the growing stains on her nightdress.

At first he worked with the confidence of one who expected the flow of blood to cease when it had accomplished its mission, but finally his shaking old hands and grim expression acknowledged what Zulu had somehow known from the beginning. The hemorrhage was not to be staunched while there was still life in the slight body.

Together they worked to change the bedding and Rosalie's night clothes. The doctor pulled the clean sheet over the girl's face.

"Do you think I should have said something?" Zulu asked. It was a question that had filled her mind in the hours they labored together.

He shook his head. "I can't say. Maybe if I'd known. . . ."

"Would it have saved her?" Somehow, it was vital to know.

"I don't think so." His old voice was kind. "Now get those things into the trash fire in the cookhouse. They've got to be burned before anyone comes down to start breakfast."

He had treated her along with Rosalie for childhood ills and he paused, his keen eyes on her face, "Still, I'm trying very hard to tell myself you did a good thing to protect her."

But had Rosalie really wanted it this way? And back in the dim unacceptable part of her mind hadn't she herself, been aware that this was a way to freedom?

She knew the answer. Both she and Rosalie had known the only real problem was telling Miss Ginny. There'd have been a trip somewhere—Norman's marriage would have furnished an excellent excuse. And when they returned Rosalie would have been her old self again. Ready for parties and picnics.

She had barely finished burning bedding, towels and nightclothes into an unrecognizable heap before the kitchen help started to appear. When she went back into Rosalie's room it was to find that Esmeralda and Miss Ginny had already laid out the girl's body.

"I looked in on her before I went to bed," Miss Ginny was tearfully telling the doctor. "I'd of swore her face had more color."

"Ginny, it was a harder fall then we thought. She might never have been right if she'd lived. A blow on the head like that—sometimes things are for the best. . . ."

Zulu moved to the open window as the sound of Esmeralda's renewed wailing merged with Miss Ginny's hysterical weeping.

Below, the old gardener sang softly, almost longingly;

"I know moonlight, I know starlight
I'm walking troo de starlight

89

Lay dis body down. . .''

Zulu closed the windows, but still the strains of the familiar old spiritual ran through her mind.

"I lay in de grave and stretch out my arms
I lay in de grave and stretch out my arms
When I lay dis body down. . . .''

Chapter Thirteen

She stood alone, looking out at the swamp. There was nothing but a few sagging timbers to mark where Blandin's cabin had been.

"I'm free!" she whispered to them and to all the lushness around her, to all the rank vegetation, to the hum and vibration that was the life throb of the place. Maybe Blandin was somewhere out there. Maybe he'd hear and be glad.

By why wasn't she, herself, glad? Why was there still that gnawing inside? The restlessness that smoldered and burned?

"For what?" she asked, and her words came back to her. Tossed back by the emptiness and fullness that was all about.

Then she was no longer alone. She sensed someone near. Someone who moved as silently as the swamp creatures. She turned and faced Mala.

"You followed me?" It came to her that Mala knew the answer. Mala who had nursed her and carried her to Elmside.

"I watch you," Mala nodded. "I watch you always. I see when you hold the stone and make *juju* in your heart."

Zulu laughed, but there was no laughter inside.

"You are like Feig. *Nyene we!* You bring evil where you walk. And always you will want, like now. Always, unless—"

"Unless? Mala, unless—?"

Mala looked out at the swamp.

"Feig inside you," she said, "is sick for home."

Chapter Fourteen

Zulu crossed the road to the levee, carrying three of Rosalie's portmanteaux one in each hand and one under her left arm.

There were no slaves bending over the crop. It might as well be Sunday or a Saturday afternoon, she reflected. Except there were no shouts or laughter echoing from the deserted slave quarters. Everyone was at the burying ground.

She had worked hard that morning. Miss Ginny had told her she could take some of Rosalie's clothes should she decide to leave, and Zulu knew the offer was intended to include only some of Rosalie's day frocks and maybe a simple bonnet or two. Still, she had not said as much, and it was very improbable that she would get around to sorting her niece's things until a few weeks had dimmed the hurt. Most likely she'd still shy away from the folding and packing, and the melancholy task would fall to Prissy.

It was not the finery packed into the bulging bags that brought a frown to Zulu's face. It was money. Though she'd emptied all of Rosalie's purses, there had been little more than change. She'd need money in New

Orleans. A lot of money.

She rounded the turn, and there was the barge, still tied to the dock, just as she'd expected. The last bales were being strapped to the deck and there was no doubt they'd be casting off soon. Still she hesitated.

Could she go through with this? The memory of Gram's lustful little eyes and the loose mouth under his ragged red beard, sent a wave of revulsion through her.

But what other way was there? If she tried to get to New Orleans over land there could be worse. There was white trash and runaway slaves in the swamps. There was weather to contend with, and aching feet. Most likely her bags would be stolen the first day. There simply was no other choice. There was nothing she could do but accept Gram, and be grateful it wasn't worse.

She cupped her hands to her mouth and called. The black roustabout glanced up, and then went back to his work. Zulu called again, and this time a tow headed young man came up to the shore side.

Lord God, had Gram sold the boat? She stared at the stranger in consternation. His sun browned features were clean cut, but his mouth was thin and there was a disconcerting sterness to his eyes.

"We don't carry passengers," he stated. "We've a full cargo and the water's too low at the mouth of the Rigolets to risk extra weight."

To think she'd hesitated about accepting Gram's offer. Now it was the most important thing in the world.

"Where is Captain Gram? I've made arrangements with him."

"Captain?" he repeated, his voice thick with scorn. "Madame, I think I should tell you that Gram and I are full partners and I hold him to the agreement that no women are permitted aboard."

The flap of the tent-like cabin was tossed back and Gram poked out his head.

"Damn it to hell! Can't a man sleep around here

without this infernal shouting? God Almighty, Bill, if ye wants to fight with the wench, go ashore to do it.''

The younger man's annoyance increased visibly. ''Anyone who spends the night brawling can be expected to be disturbed by decent folks living natural lives in the daylight!''

Gram stumbled out onto the deck. Still half asleep, he presented a disorderly sight. His chest was bare of all but his sweaty red hair, and his trousers were wrinkled and splotched. He knotted his two great fists and started toward his partner, roaring out river threats as he stumbled over the gear that littered the deck. Even from a distance it was obvious that he still was not entirely sober.

A gun flashed in Bill's hand, and it brought Gram to a sudden halt.

''Christ, but I'll be glad to be rid of this stinking mess!'' Bill patted the purse that hung from his belt. ''After this trip you can take this crap ridden dingy and go to hell with it.''

''Gram!'' Zulu called from the bank. ''Gram, I've got my papers!''

Gram turned slowly, aware of her presence for the first time. His face lit with pleasure. ''Well, I'll be a gin soaked alligator! If it ain't me little sweetheart!'' He glared back at his partner. ''What's holding ye? Can't you see the lady's of a mind to board?''

''Lady?'' Bill shoved his gun back into its holster. ''More likely some bawd you've picked up. Damn it to hell, Gram, my wife almost left me the last time you packed one of your harlots down river. You know the agreement if I was to finish the year.''

Gram laughed. ''Zulu ain't from any fancy house. She's right respectable.'' He jerked his head toward one of the staring roustabouts. ''See that lady's helped aboard. Ain't there anyone with manners around?''

Zulu expected Bill to protest, but he remained silent as she was helped onto the barge. Gram directed one of the blacks to put her bags in the cabin, then he winked at her.

"Don't ye be minding Billy-boy here. He's just itching to get hisself a pretty piece. He was a right good bully until that black eyed little—"

"Shut your filthy mouth!" Bill roared, his face livid. "You ain't fit to mention my wife."

"Till that black eyed little Mississippi woman ate into his guts." Gram shrugged. "Any reasonable female would know it ain't natural for a man to go four or five months without some kind of woman. But not Miss Nancy."

The gun was back in Bill's hand and his mouth was ugly. "The next time you mention my wife, Gram, as sure as—" he wheeled around without finishing and bellowed shove off orders at the roustabouts.

Gram grinned, then he turned his attention back to Zulu.

"First off, show me them papers."

Zulu had them ready in a hand bag. Gram examined them carefully before returning them to her. His small eyes darted the length of her.

"Those are mighty fine trappings," he observed. "Didn't steal them, did ye?"

Zulu shook her head.

The dubious look remained in his eyes for a few seconds, then he laughed. "Let them catch up with you and strip them off if you did," he decided. "But for now there's more important things. I'll show ye into your new lodgings . . ."

Despite her resolutions, Zulu found herself stepping backward, but he caught her by the arm and pulled her through the flap that served as a door. Inside it stank of sweat, tobacco and whisky.

Lord God, if only there were some other way to get to New Orleans.

"I've some money and after I'm in New Orleans I'll have more. If you take my word, I'll pay you as soon as

94

I can.''

Gram snorted. "I don't give a horse's ass end for your money. Talk to Bill about that ye must, but there's no need."

Now that it was too late, Zulu decided that any way to New Orleans would be better than to have this pig routing over her. She snatched up her bags and started to back out of the cabin.

"I didn't know there'd be trouble. I don't want to make bad feelings between you and your partner. Just let me get back on the bank. I don't have to go this trip—"

Gram laughed with delight. "Now I got ye here ye think I'd let ye go? Besides, can't ye hear we're pushing off?"

She was aware then of the movement and the clanking of the mooring chains. Her suitcases went tumbling across the cabin as Gram caught her, pushing her down onto the smelly heap of blankets. His groping mouth and beard would have smothered any cries, but she knew the uselessness of any struggle. Hadn't she known from the beginning what the price would be? Still, when he started to rip down the front of her dress, she caught his hand and undid the buttons herself. She twisted her head and his hot breath was in her ears. Despite her revulsion, she knew her body was reacting. This was no inexperienced Len. Dirty and odorous though Gram was, he knew women. She felt her nails biting deep into his flesh.

Somewhere, in another dimension, Bill was shouting orders, but his voice was indistinct, without reality. Nothing was real but Gram and the reek of sweat and whisky. He had released her and lay panting at her side. She buried her face in a blanket as a spasm of nausea seized her.

This time she found no joy in the voice of the roustabout as he sang of his faithless Suzette.

"Ah Suzette, chere to pas l'aimain moin chere

95

Ah Suzette, Z'amie to pas l'aimain moin!
M'allais la montagne z'amie
M'allais coupé cannes chere amie
Ma'allais fait l'argent plein
Pou porté donne toi!''

Gram was snoring, his mouth open, and Zulu pulled away. She tried not to look at him as she sat up.

If this was the price she had to pay to get to New Orleans, she'd pay it in full. But God help anyone who tried to interfere when the time came for her to collect!

Chapter Fifteen

Zulu never liked to reflect back on that trip downriver. The memory of the tent-cabin was enough to choke her with revulsion. Except when he was needed to guide the barge through the shallow spots in the stream, Gram snored through the daylight hours, storing his energy for the night.

He was part of a way of life that was stumbling to extinction. In 1820, when he had first started working the flatboats, he had been in his element, and he still wore the red turkey feather of a river champion. He lived hard, drank prodigiously, and made love like a great, fumbling animal.

When the barge finally left the shallow streams and floated in the broad river, they occasionally passed one of the gilded steamboats that were fast devouring the river man's way of life. At such times Gram would shake his fists at them and shout curses in their wake.

The nights were a horror and the days endless. Often

Zulu and Bill found themselves together in the limited living quarters and at such times he acted as if she were non-existent. It was only when she taunted him about his money bag that he gave any acknowledgement of her presence.

"Why do you carry that purse where everyone can see it?" she finally asked. Aren't you afraid of being robbed and killed while you're sleeping?"

"Who'd do that? You?"

She laughed. "I'd find other ways if I wanted it enough."

He regarded her thoughtfully. "You're a funny piece," he finally admitted. "Gram says you're colored, but you could of fooled me, and you talk as if you've had some learning. You're not his usual whore."

"I'm not a whore and you haven't answered my question. Why do you carry that purse right out in the open?"

"So I can keep my eyes on it." He patted his holster. "I'm known to be a light sleeper and a damned good shot." He looked out at the sweep of river ahead. "It's going to take me out of this life. The barge and the keelboat died on the Mississippi, and it's dying here. How can a keel boat compete against steam? It's as if those shallow, twisting streams we left back there tried to stake themselves against the river. I live in 1837, not the past."

He turned his eyes back to her. "I'm going to buy me a half interest in a steamboat, and on the Mississippi I'll be able to see my wife and live as God intended a man should."

"You love your wife?"

Bill spat over the side aiming at a rock that showed above a shallow spot in the stream.

"How would you understand? How soft and clean she is—how her voice sounds in my ears like a prayer inside a church, and how when she laughs . . . Oh hell!" He turned abruptly, leaving Zulu to stare after

97

him.

Gram was right. He needed a woman. And she needed the money dangling right out in plain sight. But why even think about it? Bill would never part with that purse as long as he was alive or conscious. . . .And she wasn't a thief.

"M'allais fait l'argent plein
Pou porte donne toi!"

That was what the roustabout had been singing the morning the barge pulled away from the Elmside levee. . . .

"Make a heap of dollars
And bring them all to you!"

Wasn't it enough just to be a white woman and loved? What real need did Bill's wife have of that money pouch?

She narrowed her eyes against the sun, trying better to see the position of the purse, of the knife stuck in his belt and of his gun, but most of all the way his two hands hung down at his side, clenched into fists.

Chapter Sixteen

It was early morning when the barge tied up at the levee in New Orleans. Gram's excitement had increased visibly from the moment the first dim crescent of the docks came into view. He bellowed out river songs as he helped to secure the boat, then he ran a whisky bottle up a pole.

The big roustabout who constantly sang of Suzette, grinned at Zulu.

"Dat mean he ready do business."

Zulu nodded, but her eyes had left Gram to sweep over her surroundings. Lord God, she'd never dreamed there was that much dock in the whole world. Nothing she'd ever been told prepared her for the bedlam of sound that came from all sides. A short distance away three drunken bargemen leaned against some crates shouting combined insults and invitations to two weary looking girls who had just emerged from a nearby saloon. Hurrying back to whatever oblivion hid them during the day, they barely glanced back at the men. Overhead the gull swooped low, screeching and fighting.

The bargemen joined arms and started on their unsteady way.

"We're looking for the bully
The bully of the town
We're looking for the bully, boys
The bully must be found. . . ."

The old river song faded out as they rounded a stack of kegs, and Zulu became aware of another sound that had been steadily increasing in volume, but so naturally, so insidiously, that she was hardly congnizant of it, even as it caught and gripped her emotions. It was the steady, mournful throb of melody that came from the throats of the black stevedores who were loading further down the wharf.

The sound was alien to the spirituals of Elmside. Alien and infinitely more melancholy. Underlying was a gripping rhythm, the heartthrob of a people, the yearning of a race.

Unexpectedly she became aware of a deep, satisfying pride. That melody was her heritage, also. The dignity, the beauty—and most of all, the compelling simplicity.

Gram crossed the deck and shoved the roustabout. "Get back to work, you black bastard!" he roared.

The black's gleaming muscles knotted and his eyes flashed. Then a mask of submission fell over his features. "Yas, Mast' Gram," he muttered and slunk away.

Pain and disgust merged. Where was the dignity she'd imagined? The beauty?

Gram caught her by the shoulders and pulled her around to him. He scratched her cheek with his beard.

"Looking at the old Crescent City, eh? Can't see much from here, but ye've got the bully can show ye like nobody else. First I got to go into the town and see to supplies and sellin' the cargo."

On the way down river he had boasted about the time they'd have once the barge was docked, but always with the warning that first supplies must be purchased for the next trip so there'd be no chance of squandering the money on his binge. All of this Zulu knew and on it she had based her plan. But now she pretended dismay.

"You're not going to leave me here alone with Bill?"

Gram laughed. "You ain't afraid of Bill? God knows no female need be afraid of him anymore!"

Zulu spoke slowly, hesitating over the words. "He's got a look about him—"

"If I was him, so would I!" Gram mussed her hair. "Don't ye worry. If Bill wanted a wench, he'd be a damn sight smarter then to mess with my woman. There ain't the man can stand against me and Bill knows it."

Zulu watched Gram go ashore. The seeds were planted, she reflected as he disappeared from sight. She went into the cabin and dressed carefully. She had selected Rosalie's best traveling suit and it fit as if it had been made to her measurements. She set her hat on a box near the entrance and placed her portmanteaux near by.

Now there was only to wait and to hope Bill would stay on the barge until Gram returned. Still, there was small chance he'd leave, what with the cargo that had to be guarded, and the bales to be checked against the ledger.

When Bill finally went into the cabin carrying a pan

of water heated on the cook stove, she knew it must be nearing the time of Gram's expected return. She could hear him whistling as he stropped his razor. She watched the wharf anxiously. If he was fully dressed before Gram returned it might make her ruse seem less believable. Still, it was in Bill's way of doing things to wait until it was almost time for Gram before he readied himself for his visit home. While he was busy his mind was distracted, but once shaved and dressed, waiting would be intolerable.

Finally Gram strutted in sight. There was no mistaking that cocksure air, nor the red turkey feather. Zulu breathed a silent invocation to the stone that hung heavy in its bag between her breasts, then she pulled aside the canvas drop and went into the makeshift cabin.

Bill had not finished dressing and a quick glance at the interior reassured her. The plan would work. His money bag lay on the stand near the wash basin and his belt with gun and knife were out of his immediate reach.

Zulu leaned against the framework, aware that Bill could see her reflected in the cracked mirror.

"You're getting yourself mighty pretty for that wife of yours," she remarked.

He continued to trim his sideburns, but his back stiffened slightly.

The barge lurched as Gram stepped onto it. His voice boomed out an order to a roustabout.

Bill set down his scissors and patted at his face with a clean rag.

"Gram says she's a slut, you know. That she's been with a different man each night."

She moved closer as he turned on her. The fury in his eyes betrayed a fear that had festered deep inside. Zulu screamed as he struck out at her. If his fist had caught the side of her face as intended, it would have smashed the bone. She screamed again and caught at him as she fell backward. He landed heavily on her, his fingers at her neck. There was a terrible second when she thought Gram wouldn't reach them in time. Flashes of light and dark flickered before her eyes.

From somewhere there came a roar and she was free, with Bill's body wrenched from her. She crawled on her knees to the door opening as Gram's great fist sent his partner against the canvas wall. Part of the structure collapsed and the wash pan clattered to the floor. Zulu pulled her skirts free of the soapy water and snatched up the leather pouch. She dropped it into her handbag and then turned quickly, her eyes searching for a way past the fighting men.

"He went after me, Gram!" she screamed. "He went after me just like I said he would!"

Bill tried to regain his feet, but Gram caught him by the collar and threw him out onto the deck. He leaped after him and Zulu couldn't repress a shudder as Gram landed on his partner's back. Somehow Bill struggled free and he was almost on his feet when Gram let out a shout of pure joy as he threw him back against the rail.

Zulu felt a sick sensation gathering in her chest, but this was not the time to weaken. Now was the time to escape. Now when neither man remembered she existed.

She pinned on her hat and snatched up her bags. There was no need to hurry, Gram was fighting the way he made love, with a lust for bloodshed that would not be sated until he had exhausted himself.

She made her way onto the dock, pushing her way through the crowd that had gathered.

"They'll kill each other!" she screamed, but the riverman nearest her shook his head, his eyes not missing a blow. "Ain't our concern. It's their fight."

No one turned to look after her. A fight superseded a woman any day in a bargeman's world. Women could be bought anywhere, but a good fight didn't come cheap.

She hurried down the levee, not pausing until she could no longer hear the jeers and shouts of the mob.

Then she set down her traveling bags and drew a deep breath. The harsh smell of strange spices filled the air.

She picked up her bags and started on again. Should she continue on the wharf or turn toward the city, she wondered. And how was she to know what street to take?

She side stepped some rough looking men who stopped their work to stare at her and then her nostrils were assailed with the smell of freshly caught fish. She moved past the oyster boats and ahead a line of blacks were bent double under gigantic stalks of green bananas. Out on the crest of the Mississippi two fine steamboats were racing toward the levee, their stacks erupting in huge billows of smoke. Another steamer was leaving the dock and the coffee colored water frothed at its bow. She could plainly make out the gilt decorations and carvings. Surely, it must be the most magnificent boat on the river! On the deck she could see the fashionable folks who could afford to travel in such style, and a pang of envy gripped her. Someday she'd be there, too. Someday she'd be one of them chatting as if—

She shook away the delusion. Were women of color permitted on the promenade deck? For after all, she was still Zulu, despite Rosalie's clothes.

She glanced down at herself and was reassured. She was dressed as well as any of those ladies on the boat out there. The plum colored suit had been an excellent choice, she decided, noticing how discreetly the skirts flared over the horsehair petticoat. The tight bodice was tan and the plum colored vest fitted snugly when she fastened the dainty buttons that ran down the front.

Still, her hands were damp inside the tan gloves and the unfamiliar ostrich plume that swooped over the side of her hat tickled her cheek. Could folks look at her and know this was the first time she'd worn such clothing? Did they seem strange on her?

A deafening explosion shook the boards under her

feet. Stacked bales tumbled down and flying debris filled the air over the river. Someone screamed continuously on the steamboat pulling out and part of a bulkhead splashed into the water, sending up a spray. As the smoke lessened she realized that where there had been two steamboats racing for the port there was now only one. Where the other had been was only a mass of flame and rubbish. What remained of the hulk became dimly visible for a second then disappeared in a fresh outburst of fire.

She wasn't even aware of dropping her bags as she stared out at the river, unable to move. People were scurrying in all directions, jumping out of carriages, running from behind bales and out of warehouses.

"Which one was it?" someone shouted.

"Boiler bust?"

"Mon Dieu! Andre, regardez!"

"Dat de secon' one dis month. Lawd, what's to do?"

"Oh my God, was it The Belle? My wife and son are on The Belle!"

"Quel dommage!"

Esmeralda would have held it was a bad omen that a thing like that should occur at the beginning of the new life she'd hoped to find. And it wasn't easy to cast aside Esmeralda's teachings.

Able to move once again, she picked up her bags. Suddenly she was running. Running as fast as she could for the city. Voices rang in her ears as if she were involved in some terrible dream. She knew she must get away from the stench of burned flesh and steam or she'd be sick all over Rosalie's best suit. She had to get away from the memory of men beating each other, away from Rosalie with the sheet pulled over her face. Once in the city all those things would belong to the past. They had to be forgotten because there was no room for them in the life she planned.

She was far from the wharf when finally she paused. Her breath came in hard gasps and her throat was raw, her chest tight with the pain of breathing, but the hubbub was far behind. The hubbub and Bill and Gram. Not that she need fear Bill. If he still lived it would be days before he would be in any condition to realize his money was gone. And it never would occur to Gram.

She rested her bags on the raised banquette. Under the wood planks the filth of the gutter lay torpid and stinking. But then one never expected all to be beauty, even in this fabled city.

She looked around, wondering how long she must remain lost in this strange place. Nearby was a half completed structure and a sign proclaimed it was to be the St. Louis Hotel. Ahead was a street called Royal, if she was to believe the marker. None of it meant anything to her.

For the first time she permitted herself to realize that all might not be as easy as it had seemed back at Elmside. Here she was, in a strange city with foreign ways, she who had never even been as far from home as Montgomery. How should one go about finding a place to stay? Surely a colored woman couldn't walk into a hotel and sign her name the way she would if she were white? Where, then, did her sort find lodgings?

She watched the well dressed people go past, so secure, all so intent on their errands. Finally a well-dressed mulattress sauntered past and paused to gaze at the men working on the new structure. She was clad in bright green, but the material was good and the cut of her gown reminded Zulu of sketches she'd seen in Miss Ginny's "Godey" book, back at Elmside.

She approached the girl, trying to conceal her sudden timidity. "Could you tell me a good place to find lodgings?" she asked.

The mulattress turned and Zulu was startled to see thick paint on her lips. Still, she had heard that some of the fashionable ladies used paint. Surely, this must be one of the women Len had talked about.

105

"Fresh from the country?" The girl spoke with a Mississippi accent.

Zulu nodded, aware of the critical eyes that swept the length of her. What use was there in denying it when the appraisal had already been made? Was it possible Rosalie had felt as awkward around the Richmond ladies?

The mulattress reached into her reticule and took out a card. "Go down Royal until you come to Ursuline Street," she directed. "The address is on Gallatin. It's between the market and the new mint."

Zulu held the card uncertainly. "They take colored women?"

The girl grinned. "They'll take you all right. Be sure to tell them Cassandre sent you."

Zulu hurried down Royal Street. There was the temptation to pause and relish the strangeness of her surroundings; the balconies with lacing of iron, the grillwork on the great gates that closed off entrances to court yards and, most of all, the gowns worn by ladies sitting in their open carriages, but first of all she must find lodging. Only then would she be free to wander about the city and see all there was to see.

Even the colored folks were different from the negroes at Elmside. There was a huge brown man who moved lazily down the street singing a song he made up about the strawberries he had to sell; a shining black washerwoman—blanchisseuse—glided past with a basket of laundry balanced on her turbaned head. She swayed as she walked, not unlike an elephant dancing to a slow beat.

Carriages clattered down over the cobbles and the landaus proceeded at a more leisurely pace, some stopping in front of the stores that set under the monogrammed balconies of fine houses. One carriage turned into the porte-cochere of a mansion and Zulu stared, unabashed, at the palm shaded patio she could see through the opened gate.

At the corner of Royal and Orleans, in front of St. Anthony Gardens, the rains started. There were no warning drops, only a sudden, torrential deluge. She hurried on down the street, half running. Once she slipped and nearly fell on the wooden banquette.

Lord God, was this Gallatin Street on the other side of the earth? Her shoulders ached with the awkward weight of the three bags, and her boa was sodden.

The shower had spent itself by the time she turned up Ursuline Street and there was a cleaner look to the stucco buildings. Still, it was nothing like the fresh look of Elmside's lawns after a rain. Nothing like the rich smell of growing things and sweet earth.

The voice of the vendors carried from the French Market, two blocks away, and Zulu realized she was hungry.

Later. There would be plenty of time later.

Then, finally, the sign proclaimed Gallatin Street. Zulu felt a twinge of apprehension. It was no more than an alley lined with tightly shuttered houses and saloons. Still, lodgings for the colored certainly wouldn't be in the best part of the city. Besides, this was only a temporary measure. Only a room to stay in until she knew the place well enough to search out better quarters. Until—

Again she was assailed by the uneasy realization that nothing was as simple as it had appeared at Elmside. Some of the women she passed were truly beautiful. Not only the white ladies in their landaus, but girls like herself, on foot. Exquisite girls with soft, dusky eyes and tawny skins. She remembered there was a law against women of color riding alone in a carriage, but still they managed to look elegant as they shopped, followed by a black maid. Their fingers flashed with jewels and their dresses were of the finest fabric. One in particular stayed in her mind. They had almost collided and the girl had whispered a soft, "Pardonnez-moi!"

Decidedly, this was not Elmside!

She stopped in front of the address shown on the card. The house had a secretive air, it was reminiscent of an aged bawd masquerading under plain clothes, but ready to throw them off at the first sign of dusk.

Zulu shrugged and lifted the knocker. This was not the time to indulge in fancies.

To her surprise it was a heavily powdered white woman who answered the door and invited her inside when she displayed the card. Zulu entered, and at once she felt stifled by the strange smelling air in the hall. She hesitated a second before following the woman into a side parlor.

"I would like a room," Zulu said. Then she added a little uncertainly. "I was told it didn't matter here that I'm colored."

The woman laughed. "With a body like yours, you could be purple with pink dots!" She narrowed her eyes thoughtfully. "You could even pass—don't get me wrong, I'm not suggesting it."

Zulu stared. A white woman suggesting that she pass? This was wrong. Everything was wrong.

"Do you have a room?" she persisted.

The woman buffed at her nails with a tiny brush. "Depends," she parried. The nasal quality of her voice lent it a bargaining note, and Zulu didn't need the pictures of eastern cities that hung on the wall to realize that she was neither creole or southern born.

"Depends?" Zulu repeated, puzzled.

The woman set aside her buffer. "If you're as lively as you appear I've damn well got a room for you. We always put a new girl on trial the first week to see how good she goes over."

"I didn't ask for work!" Zulu exclaimed. "I've the money to pay for my rent."

"That isn't the way we do business." The woman held her nails up to the light and examined them critically. "Some houses, maybe, but I advertise my girls and spend good money building up their names. I take only the best and they pay me percentage."

Lord God! Once she'd heard Len talking to a friend about a place where women could be bought by the hour or the night, but she'd never really stopped to think about it. How, out of all New Orleans, did she manage to stumble on such a house?

Still, she should have known. Cassandre hadn't looked like the girls she'd seen in the perfume shops. As soon as she saw the difference, she should have suspected.

"Of course," the madame continued, "if you're new to town, we can advertise you as a virgin. There'd be good money for a month or so selling your virginity. New girls in from the country are always good money makers."

She arose to her feet and yawned. "I make it a rule for Raoul to look over the new girls. Wait here while I go get him."

As soon as the hallway was clear, Zulu snatched up her portmanteau and ran to the door. She hurried out onto the street and didn't stop to rest until she'd reached the outskirts of the French Market.

She paused to rub her aching fingers. Was she fated to spend every moment in this city running from something? It was time she sat down and thought out a plan.

She had been leaning against a poster that announced the appearance of Madame Julie Calvé at the Orleans Theater, and the sight of the glamorously attired lady in the picture gave her new heart. She straightened her hat and found her boa was almost dry and the rain had not watermarked her suit. After all, matters could be worse.

She turned her attention to the babble of sound that assailed her from all sides. Surely, she reflected, all of New Orleans must be here. Certainly all classes were represented from black cooks buying green groceries for their master's table to the elite sitting over café au lait in the best stalls. The bedlam of noise was at such a continuous pitch that after the first few minutes one ceased to be aware of it unless an outstandingly raucous or melodic voice sent up a new chant.

She moved uncertainly toward the place, but no one seemed to single her out for attention. White and black all brushed past her, intent on their own errands. Somehow, that gave her courage. She purchased copies of two newspapers and found an empty stall. After ordering coffee, she unfolded the papers, grateful for Miss Lejon.

The waiter appeared with a black brew that in no way resembled coffee at Elmside. She watched while he lightened it with cream, and after he left she hesitated, regarding it with a dubious eye. Still, it was something to revive the spirit and now was not too soon to start cultivating the tastes of the society she had chosen.

She sipped the mixture, trying to accustom herself to the bitterness then she settled back to read. She selected the "Picayune" over "L'Abeille." Both papers featured the breaking up of a band of fugitive slaves who had been hiding in the cypress swamp near the city. She read the account avidly.

What courage those hunted creatures must possess. They had dared to run away, knowing all the while that the price of their freedom would most likely be their life. Would she have had as much nerve? She pondered deeply, weighing the possibilities.

She turned the page and an editorial caught her eye. A lecturer from up north had announced that the negro brain capacity was equal to that of a white. She read the scathing comments on this statement and found that the Creole attitude toward the negro was not very different from what she'd observed at Elmside.

However, there did remain one difference. At least here a mixed blood was not irrevocably negro. The café au lait lost some of its bitterness with the thought.

She turned to the ads for which she'd purchased the papers, and she ran her fingers down the columns.

"Six prime negroes, strong, of cheerful disposition . . ."

"Clean rooms for young gentlemen with good references . . ."

"Thanks to St. Ann for prayers granted . . ."

There they were, rows of ads. Clean rooms, good food, large rooms—and all for young gentlemen.

She folded the papers with the advertising section outward. Who would better be able to advise her where she might find a room than those who dealt in lodgings?

She had no luck at the first address. The mistress of the lodging house was a lady whose darker blood was only faintly discernable, and about her there was an air of disdain. She only shook her head and shrugged in reply to Zulu's queries.

Zulu paused outside the second house on her list. It would take courage to face another rebuff. Still, when one was desperate . . .

A little girl danced up to her and her great, solemn eyes admired the boa. Her tightly kinked curls offered an amusing contrast to her golden skin. In her starched ruffles and dainty pantalettes, she was as well attired as any little white girl Zulu had seen in Alabama.

"You live here?" Zulu asked.

The little girl nodded. "*Oui*!" Impulsively, she caught Zulu's hand and led her up the stairs. "Maman," she called through the open door.

A light brown woman appeared in the hallway. She wore a spotless apron and the tignon that bound her head was a dazzling white.

"Milissy, *Z'amie*, must you shout like the common gutter *negrillion*?" All the time she scolded, her eyes appraised Zulu, the smart cut of her suit and the stylish hat with its plume.

Zulu decided to use her knowledge of French. Perhaps that might create a better impression. "I'm looking for a room, madame," she said in that language. "I'm willing to pay well."

111

The woman shook her head. "My rooms are only for young gentlemen."

There was sympathy in her voice. Perhaps . . . Why, she'd do what Rosalie would have done in such a situation! Zulu dropped her reticule and put a hand to her forehead.

"I'm so terribly tired and frightened," she murmured before collapsing gently to the floor.

"Quick, Milissy! A glass of water!" The woman made soft, clucking sounds as she bent over Zulu.

Zulu waited until her head had been gently raised and the water was at her lips, before she permitted her lashes to flutter. She gasped delicately and allowed a few drops of water to pass into her mouth. The woman helped her to her feet and took her to a small, neat room at the back of the house. The main piece of furniture was a large, four poster bed with a huge feather mattress. Zulu allowed herself to be assisted onto it.

"*Eh bien*," the women explained, "it is true I have this one small room, but it would not be the place for a young lady."

Suddenly Zulu realized the problem.

"But I'm colored."

The woman smiled her relief. "I couldn't be certain. A white lady it is true would be with her parents at a hotel, still, sometimes they will go to any extent to spy on some young gentleman. Such things are embarrassing and one cannot be too careful."

Zulu sat up. "You'll let me stay? I won't be any trouble."

The woman nodded. "I'm Eugenie LaFrome," she said. "You are just from the country?"

"This morning. I came by boat."

"Perhaps you have the intention of keeping a dress shop?"

Zulu looked at her steadily. "I want a cottage. Down by the ramparts."

"But that's not possible!" Eugenie exclaimed. Then

she added more gently, "A country girl wouldn't even be permitted to attend the Quadroon Ball. You must understand, there is a certain etiquette. Certain rules."

Lord God! Had she planned and schemed all these years only to meet defeat practically at the threshold? But there must be a way. There had to be.

"Why? I have the clothes and I can dance."

"*Certainement*, but the Quadroon Ball is not a bordello! First, one must have a chaperone who is known and respected."

"I'll find a chaperone, then."

Eugenie studied Zulu as she stripped off her gloves and paced restlessly across the room. "I have never heard of such a thing happening. Still, there is an air about you—"

Zulu faced her eagerly. "You know someone? You would help me?"

Eugenie hesitated. "There's Ferne. We had the same mother, though she's a quadroon, while I—" she grinned. "Ferne lived near the ramparts once, but—" she shook her head. "No, Ferne is too independent. She would refuse."

"But I can pay. I can pay her well!"

"Your money wouldn't matter. In any event a settlement would be made should you be taken as a *placee*. But Ferne does not need money." Milissy joined them and Eugenie stroked the child's head. Zulu smiled.

"I'll buy Milissy a new dress and slippers if you'll take me to your sister so I can talk to her."

Milissy's eyes shone beseechingly at her mother.

Eugenie spread her hands. "*Eh bien*, I would be a beast to fight such an argument. When my sister's father made a settlement on my mother she married a freedman and bought this house, and my husband was a freedman, also. I did not have a sponsor to shower me with jewels as did Ferne."

She paused, looking down at her child. "It might be that my half sister is bored and would like a change, but

I doubt it very much.''

She took Milissy's hand and started out into the hall. She paused before closing the door. "I'll try, but you must understand Ferne might take a dislike to you, then there is nothing I could say. She's a very strange woman, *ma soeur*.''

Chapter Seventeen

Ferne was very light of skin. Her hair was thick and black and there was knowledge in her large, dark eyes. Zulu was aware of an uneasiness under her scrutiny.

"This is foolishness," the woman finally said. "Eugenie knows I am not for hire.''

Zulu closed the door and followed her into the room. She waited until her visitor had seated herself, which Ferne did with an elegance that made Miss Ginny, by comparison, a field woman.

"I'm willing to pay well.''

Ferne shrugged her disdain. "Money is so important to the Kaintuck. Always they think it will buy anything.''

Obviously there was nothing to be gained by pleading. Zulu moved to the window and stood with her back to Ferne. She felt as if each one of her imperfections were being laid open by those shrewd eyes.

"If you won't help me, you must know someone who will," she blurted. "Lord God, I'd give everything I have!''

"The Quadroon Ball is not for the Kaintuck.''

Zulu dumped the entire contents of Bill's purse on the table. On top of the coins and silver she tossed the earbobs Len had given her, the chain of golden links and finally, in desperation, she even tore the *loa* stone out of its bag and threw it with the rest.

Ferne laughed. "There is nothing there to tempt one who could be *chaperon*. Nor would you be permitted to wear such trash should—" Suddenly she paused, her eyes on the stone. She reached out and touched it and quickly withdrew her hand.

"*Sacre nom!*" Her voice was not more than a whisper. "How do you have a *pierre-loa*?"

Zulu picked up the stone. "I was told it came from Africa. That it belonged to my grandmother."

"Only a *mamaloi* would dare own such a stone. Do you know the power of it?"

Zulu looked at the stone, hardly daring to believe the change it had brought about in Ferne's attitude. For all her great show of superiority the woman was as superstitious as a field hand! Her face had paled and her breath was uneven. Only a fool would hesitate to make the most of it.

"Has it enough power to make you help me?"

Ferne hesitated. "I can make a *gris-gris* more powerful than any of Marie Laveau's. But nothing I might conjure could protect me against the anger of that *loa*."

Perhaps, after all, this woman was merely having a joke. Trying to find how gullible she might be.

"Lord God, why should a pebble—"

"A pebble!" Ferne shuddered. "Did Eugenie tell you our mother was of Santo Domingo? She brought with her a *loa* in a stone, but it was a good *loa* and sometimes it gave luck."

Zulu held the stone up to the light. Just a pebble that gathered the moisture out of the air. Yet Mala had been anxious to get rid of it and Blandin had advised her to toss it into the swamp. And had not she, herself, felt the strangeness of it?

"When I was a girl," she said, as if to herself, "I used to wish on it."

"You wished?" Ferne snorted. "You wished what it desired you should wish. If it were mine I would destroy it before it possessed me entirely."

Zulu laughed and pinned it back into the bodice of her dress, then she gathered up the silver and returned it to Bill's purse.

Ferne sighed. "*Tres bien*. Let me see what you have in your *armoire*."

Zulu opened the wardrobe door and Ferne examined each gown, feeling the texture of the material and narrowing her eyes as she studied the style. Finally she held up a black velvet ballgown, her steady gaze measuring the effect of it against warm skin and the tawny gold of Zulu's hair. "This will do for the introduction."

She hung the dress back in its place, then she motioned for Zulu to walk across the room. She nodded approval.

"You've a beauty," she admitted unexpectedly, "and a natural grace. But were I a man I'd not want a woman with the eyes of a tigress half asleep. I would not want to be near when the tigress awakens." She shrugged. "Thank *Le Bon Dieu* I am not a man."

She sat down and stripped off her gloves. "Now there is much you will have to learn. You do not know how to walk and how to sit. You don't know how to talk nor even how to wear your clothes. It will be weeks—maybe even months before I can take you into society. How long will depend on you."

Chapter Eighteen

In the weeks that followed Zulu found Ferne's instructions every bit as absorbing as the lessons she learned from Rosalie's tutors. Several times she surprised on Ferne's face the expression that had been so often in Miss Lejon's eyes.

"You would take from me every shred of knowledge," Ferne told her once. "It is well that you learn so quickly, yet I do not like it. It's as if you will leave me empty, a *zombie* that can move and talk yet has nothing inside."

Even so, it was months before Ferne decided she was ready and Zulu found her nervousness increasing as the night of her debut drew near. At Elmside it had seemed so easy. She had merely to attend the ball and everyone in New Orleans would be at her feet, but Ferne had pointed out her rivals as they shopped or chatted over *café noir* in the French Market. Not one of Rosalie's friends could have attracted a second glance against those exotic beauties.

"Visitors from Europe say they are the most accomplished and beautiful women in the world," Ferne told her. "Also the most faithful. Perhaps if a sponsor makes a settlement a *placee* might eventually marry a freedman as did my mother, but only after waiting a long time. Men sometimes change their mind."

Now, as she dressed, Zulu felt the need of Milissy's constant "*Tres jolie.*" Even the knowledge that the black velvet with its narrow edging of white fur suited her far more than Rosalie, gave scant assurance.

Ferne had chosen well because already there was a

winter chill in the air. The dress was just right she reflected as she watched the sweep of the skirt with its sprinkling of red velvet roses.

She moved back and forth in front of the long mirror Ferne had provided. Yes, her walk had just the proper hint of promise and restraint. Why, then should she be nervous? Certainly Rosalie with her pale pink and white beauty could never have looked so elegant.

Ferne entered the room, her eyes critical as ever. "One rose in front of the ear, but no more," she said as she picked up the cloak that had hung over a chair. "I've hired escorts so put on your oldest shoes and give me those slippers. I have a boy to run ahead with them."

"Lord God," Zulu retorted, forgetting, "I've enough money to hire a carriage!"

Ferne raised an eyebrow. *"Pourquoi? Gens de couleur* aren't permitted that unless they're with white folks. And how many times is it necessary to remind you that to speak of money marks you as a Kaintuck?"

What good was a Writ of Freedom when on all sides one still was enslaved? What must it be for a full blooded negress? Let them step on her now! Let them trample her—as long as it got her what she wanted.

"'I have a feeling," Ferne said slowly, "that I'll always regret tonight."

Two big blacks waited outside. At Ferne's signal they lit their lanterns and trotted ahead to light the way through the dark streets. There was no other illumination.

A landau drove past, its wheels sucking at the mires and Ferne drew her out of splashing radius.

"All arrangements must be left to me. Above all, you must conduct yourself as a lady. This is a respectable place, not a brawl on Gallatin Street."

Then, finally, they stood in the doorway to the Orleans Ballroom. After the darkness outside, the place seemed to glisten—as a bubble glistens at its fullest, just before it bursts. The floors reflected the grace of the dancers who moved to soft music. There was none of the clamor that had marked the balls at Elmside. Even the music was different, gay, yet restrained and sweet. The mirrors that lined the walls reflected dark, liquid eyes and the soft fire of jewels. Zulu felt shabby in Rosalie's best black velvet—and surely only the handsomest, richest men in all of New Orleans were here! Rosalie's homecoming ball was a shout meeting compared to this.

Though the windows were open to the breeze from Lake Pontchatrain, the air was heavy with perfume. While they stood in the entranceway watching, the bells from the nearby Orleans Cathedral sounded over the music.

Ferne waited until intermission so they could proceed across a cleared floor. Zulu felt the eyes turned on her and her heart beat like a great, suffocating hammer.

"I told you this was not a *fais-dodo*," Ferne taunted softly.

The music started once again and dancers filled the floor. Several nodded at Ferne, but no one approached.

"Why don't you arrange introductions?" Here she'd expected to turn the men on their ears and no one had even appeared more than mildly interested!

Ferne shrugged. "*Eh bien*, you make so pretty a wall flower. A *bredouille* beyond compare."

Zulu bit back a retort as her eyes rested on a gentleman who was on his way past them. One could still be a lady and manage these things. Many a time back at Elmside when she watched through the windows she'd seen more than the white gentry realized.

At just the right instant she turned her head as if intent on conversation with Ferne, and stepped forward. The man collided with her even more violently than she had anticipted, and his arm went around her bare shoulders to keep her from falling. Zulu gave a little cry and looked down at her foot as if she expected

119

to find it crushed.

"I've hurt you!" he exclaimed. His fine, dark eyes showed his distress.

Zulu smiled bravely. "It was an accident. It doesn't matter."

"But it does." He took her arm and helped her to a chair. After she had arranged her skirts Zulu looked up into his face. He was not young, his hair and neatly trimmed mustache were iron grey, but he moved with the lithe grace of an accomplished swordsman and his features were finely cut.

"Good Lord, but you're beautiful!" he said.

Ferne drew up to them and though she darted Zulu a dark look, there was deference in her manner when she turned to the man.

"M'sieur Randolph."

He smiled. "I'd consider myself honored if you introduced me to your protegé, Ferne." He spoke a clear, precise English that somehow went with his clipped mustache.

There was a shadow in Ferne's eyes, but she nodded.

"Zulu, M'sieur Shadney Randolph."

"Do you think we can dance?" There was a touch of laughter in his tone. "Or—have I really broken your foot?"

What if she hadn't deceived him after all? But at least she had a partner, and no thanks to Ferne. She looked downward, letting her lashes sweep her cheeks.

"Your flattery has healed it." Ferne couldn't fault her on that!

It was a pleasure to dance with Randolph. He held her gently, yet with a firmness that made it easy to follow his steps. She felt a vague sense of loss when the music stopped.

"I can't remember when I've enjoyed a waltz more," he told her as he led her back to Ferne.

"And I don't remember dancing with a man who waltzed so well." She smiled, wondering what he'd say if she told the truth. That she'd never danced with a man before.

Her eyes rested on the bespectacled young man who waited by Ferne.

"Lord God!" she exclaimed. She gasped and put her hand to her mouth.

Shadney laughed. "I won't tell Ferne," he promised.

Ferne rose to her feet and smiled at Randolph before turning to Zulu. "M'sieur LaFruge has honored you with a request for the next dance."

When LaFruge returned Zulu to her chaperone there were several young Creoles waiting. Zulu acknowledged the introductions with a smile only to have Ferne shoot a warning glance at her. She must not appear triumphant. She must act as if this were an occurrence to be expected.

She frowned and laughed at the men, as if trying to decide among them, only to again accept Shadney Randolph's arm. They would be all the more anxious when she returned.

"You're upsetting the regime," Shadney told her as he led her away. His eyes twinkled. "Look at Helene over there, she'd like to tear out your hair. And Antoinette Soulier—" He nodded toward a copper colored girl, "she'll be seeing Marie Laveau or Ferne for a *gris-gris* tomorrow if you dance with LaFruge again."

Zulu made a face. "I think I'll not begrudge her M'sieur LaFruge."

"But Naida—" Randolph indicated an exquisite girl who was smiling up at a tall, slim Creole, "Naida is the one who concerns me. Don't look too often at her Ramon. She suffers enough because of him."

"And what of your *placee*?" Zulu spoke softly. "Is she watching me also?"

Randolph regarded her with an expression of mingled amusement and gravity. "Suppose I tell you I've never taken a *placee*?" It was impossible to know whether he was serious or teasing.

121

Ramon waited by Ferne when the dance was over and Zulu accepted his arm. She felt Naida's soft eyes watching, and she moved a little closer than the dance warranted. Let these women with their superior airs learn that a Kaintuck was not to be dismissed so lightly!

She sensed Ferne's anger as soon as Ramon led her back. There were men waiting an introduction, but Ferne murmured an apology and drew her aside.

"You're causing trouble. Remember you will be living among these women. Leave their men alone or you'll have only enemies."

"At least they won't be able to say I was neglected."

"Did you expect to be? Even with what I have taught you, and with your face and your body? Tomorrow, wherever men gather you'll be toasted." Then her eyes lit up with satisfaction. "But where there are only women you will be slandered. That's inevitable. You are from another world and you don't belong here, taking what is theirs."

"It's not theirs if they can't hold it."

She awakened early the next morning, far too early to leave her bed. She clasped her fingers behind her head, lashes half veiling her eyes as she relived the wonders of the proceeding night.

The sun began to send its shafts of light through the window and even the single quilt became too much. She tossed it aside and stripped off her nightdress. Then she lay back on the soft bed studying the round circles of her breasts, the gentle curve of her hips and the long lithe lines of her thighs. She moved her fingers lightly over the smooth skin of her flat abdomen, noting the faint hint of golden tones. She had a good body, she reflected, and it was important to make the most of it while it was still young and firm.

How wonderful it was to just laze away the morning, knowing there wasn't a Rosalie awaiting her ministrations and that there wouldn't be the ordeal of a hasty breakfast in the cookhouse, hemmed in on either side by the gossiping, giggling house servants.

She yawned and stretched again. As she pulled herself up to rest on an elbow Ferne's voice sounded out in the hall.

"Come in!" she called out.

Ferne could not see her through the mosquito bar. She closed the door and looked around the room.

Zulu laughed and pulled aside the mesh. "I'm still in bed."

Ferne snorted. "So I see. You lie there like some shameless animal while New Orleans shouts about you." She tossed Zulu a robe. "For the love of God, cover yourself!"

The primness of Ferne's manner amused Zulu. She swung her feet over the edge of the bed and admired her reflection in the mirror.

"If all women looked as well naked we'd have no clothes."

"Please yourself. I didn't come here to discuss your lack of modesty."

For the first time Zulu noted the sparkle in Ferne's eyes.

"Is it so unusual for a girl to be noticed at her first ball?"

"How can you remain so calm?" Ferne's voice was almost shrill. "You, a girl from the country. A Kaintuck! With just a few month's training! I knew you would not pass unnoticed. But this!"

"Must a girl have training to know what pleases a man?"

"But a country girl!"

Zulu frowned. "Will you please stop calling me a country girl. It makes me feel like a heifer."

"But this has never before happened. Even Europe has none such as the New Orleans quadroon, yet you—"

"The important thing," Zulu interrupted, "is whether anyone's made an offer."

"What have I been telling you?"

"Nothing. Nothing that I wanted to hear. Who made this offer?"

"This? These. I knew you had something—something more than beauty, I expected you'd turn a few heads, but—"

Zulu leaned forward. "Shadney Randolph? Was he one of them?"

"Next, I suppose, you'll expect the governor himself! No, M'sieur Randolph did not make an offer."

Here was that deference again. Zulu had not particularly cared whether or not Randolph had made an offer, but now it became a challenge.

"Why shouldn't he? He seemed interested."

"M'sieur Randolph comes often to the Ball, but he has never taken a *placee*. Not even when he was young."

Zulu felt her interest quicken. "Is something wrong with him?"

"I've never heard it said that he wasn't a man, and no one wields a finer sword. It's just that some men—" she spread her hands deprecattingly, "seem satisfied with their wives."

Zulu put on her robe, frowning as she knotted the cord. "I'd be tempted to test that if he were younger."

"Younger! What is a young man but a greater nuisance than an old one? A young man nearly always has a mother and sisters to influence him, and later there will be a wife."

"But he has a wife."

"*Oui*, and that is the difference. It is better to become *placee* to a man who already has his life settled. There isn't the risk he will marry a woman who will make him give you up."

"And this Ramon Vauregard, did he come to you?"

"Ramon belongs to Naida," Ferne snapped. "Besides, he's to be married very soon."

"He's very handsome," Zulu said, picking up her

brush.

"LaFruge made a good offer. He would like permission to court you. You could do worse. He has a generous allowance and I understand his father is concerned because he has not yet taken a mistress."

"He's only a boy! Besides, he has no chin and he looks like an owl." Ferne may as well understand she hadn't come all the way to New Orleans for that.

"It will probably be some time before he marries."

"I should hope so!" Zulu continued to brush her hair. "What is Shadney's wife like?"

"Madame Randolph? Like any white lady. She's a Creole, but M'sieur is neither Spanish or French. They live outside town on the Bayou St. John."

"How has she kept him from taking a mistress?"

"Perhaps it is because he is not a Creole. She's a very handsome woman and one always reads of them entertaining important people. *Eh bien*, I suppose it is not in some men to be unfaithful."

"It's in any man." Zulu set down the brush and experimented with various hair styles, tilting her head to one side and holding up the hand mirror. "Tell me, Ferne, what will happen to Naida when Ramon marries?"

"Naida refuses to believe he'll permit the marriage." Ferne made an expressive gesture. "If he does, he'll make her a settlement—after awhile he might even start visiting her again. He's already bought a good property out of the city for their son though, of course, he will manage it till the boy is of age."

"And will Naida find another man?"

Ferne's eyes widened in horror. "She might buy a boarding house such as this, but she'll never take another white man. She might even kill herself. The boy will be cared for."

"But there are always other men."

"*Oui*, but a woman has only one heart."

"Unless she's like me. And has none."

125

"You think that?" There was something malicious in Ferne's smile. "It's those who think that who often suffer most." Then she settled down to the business at hand. "Of course you mustn't accept any of these offers yet, but you may permit one of them to pay you court. Now there was—" She rattled off the names of those who had called on her. "You will be valued more highly if you show reluctance to make your decision. It is important now that you be seen at the right places. Tonight it will be the theater."

Zulu sighed, knowing that she'd have to settle down to another day of being told what to do.

Chapter Nineteen

Had she really given it any thought, she would have realized that sooner or later she would inevitably meet Breel Luton in New Orleans. But somehow it didn't seem fair that she should encounter him so soon.

It was certain she had no thought of him as she sat beside Ferne conscious only that she was the focus of attention from the gentlemen in the dress circle. This even exceeded her wildest dreams back at Elmside.

It was difficult not to stare back at the men with their white gloves and at the quietly dressed women by their sides.

"They're as different from folks at Elmside as country niggers are from city."

"Turn your head to the stage," Ferne hissed. "It's in bad taste to gawk at the audience."

"Some of the men were at the Ball last night," Zulu

remarked as she obediently watched the performance.

"Such stupidity! You know no man down there. When a man is with his wife you don't know him. Not even if he is your protector and he left your bed not an hour since." She paused. "Your dress has slipped too low. Another inch and you will have no decency left."

"I want them to see I'm not padded."

"Push your straps a litt'; higher. Only a blind man could have any doubts left.

Zulu stifled a smile as she obeyed. She tried once again to concentrate on the play, but the glamour of her surroundings so outshone the performance on the stage, that Ferne had to constantly poke her in warning.

Finally the intermission came and at last she was free to look about. Ferne escourted her about the restricted area and she pointed out the loges across the theater where the curtains were drawn.

"That's where the pregnant women sit. And the families in mourning." She led the way back to their seat. "You must not be away too long. You must show you are not afraid to be viewed under the stronger light."

The minute she sat down, she felt his eyes. "There's someone watching me," she whispered to Ferne.

"Naturally!" Ferne snapped. "Isn't that the purpose?"

"No! This is different." How could she explain the cold sensation of fear? Something was about to happen. Something that was not good.

Despite Ferne's hisses she turned and stared out into the dress circle. It was then that she saw him.

"Lord God!" she gasped. "Lord God, Ferne, it's Breel!"

Ferne followed the direction of her eyes. "M'sieur Luton? But he hasn't been at the Balls lately. How can you know him?"

Zulu sat frozen with panic as Breel stared up at her, a puzzled scowl on his face. It was true she must present a

127

different picture in the flame of her gown, and with her hair piled high. Maybe he might not recognize her after all. But even as she drew comfort from this thought he grinned and nodded at her.

"M'sieur Luton is very handsome," Ferne was saying, "But he has no money."

Breel had beckoned to an usher and Ferne drew in her breath as she watched him scribble a note.

"Most likely he is asking that you meet him in the lobby when the act begins. You must not."

"Why?" Zulu demanded, though she was not at all certain she wished to see Breel alone.

"When a woman looks at a man as you have just looked at M'sieur Luton, it's a chaperon's duty to watch closely."

"Chaperon! What do you care about my morals?"

"Nothing!" Ferne snapped. "For your morals I care not a particle. But your reputation is another thing. While I am your chaperon your reputation must be impeccable."

"And meeting Breel in the lobby would ruin my reputation?"

"If it became known it could." Ferne stopped speaking as the usher approached them. She accepted the note and nodded. Not until the lights were dimmed and the curtains parted did she unfold the paper.

"It's as I thought." She gave Zulu the note. "I can see you will ignore my advice. At least, then, be discreet."

Down in the dress circle Breel was whispering something to the woman who sat beside him. Zulu had not been aware of her before, but now she strained her eyes trying to see her better, but only a blurred white outline was distinguishable.

"If you must meet him, leave before he does!" Ferne whispered.

Zulu got up hastily, but she paused at the back of the box. Surely she should avoid this. Surely this was not the time—

Sooner or later she would have to face him. Better now. Better to have it in the past.

He was already waiting in the lobby when she descended the stairs. He had his back turned and did not hear the sound of her slippers, muffled in the high piled carpet. She paused a second, trying to get a grip on her courage.

"Really," she said softly to his back, "you could have chosen a better moment. I was enjoying the play."

He jerked around. "So it is you." His voice was full of wonder. "I was certain there couldn't be two women with hair like yours."

Zulu laughed. Better to keep the conversation on herself. "Was it my hair you were looking at?"

"Do you think I'm gelded?" Then his black eyes became serious. "So you did find someone with the money to buy you?"

"I'm free!" Zulu felt a wave of anger that even rose above her fear of his questions. "I've got my papers."

"Oh? Was that why Brother Len was so all fired anxious to free his boy? I thought he was cooking something. I'll wager you're the only body servant at Elmside that got a Writ."

His mind was too quick. Ferne had been right. She should have avoided this meeting. She snapped her fan shut and started to turn away, but he caught her arm.

"Well?"

"Don't you think you're being presumptuous?"

"No, not a damned bit. But tell me, how could Len let you go after collecting the payment? And don't tell me Len would have gone to that much trouble for any other reason."

Almost without realizing her intention, Zulu struck his face with her closed fan. She caught her breath sharply in horror of her own act. Breel raised his fingers to the red streak on his cheek, his face white.

"I could have you jailed for that. I could have you

beaten until that smooth skin of yours was covered with welts."

"You've no right to insult me!"

"Is that possible? I plan to discuss the matter in a more fitting place."

"I don't want to see you again. Not ever!"

"You've no choice." Breel smiled. "Do you actually think, Zulu, that I intend to let you get away with what you have done? But I really wouldn't enjoy seeing you jailed and publicly whipped. I can think of other things far more appealing."

She watched him walk across the lobby, and then she slowly went up the stairs to the second tier. Lord God, she'd have to learn to control her temper. Here there was no Rosalie to stand between her and Esmeralda's wrath. This was a white man's world and as long as she had those few drops of black blood in her veins, she was as subject to punishment as any full blooded negro.

She had hardly resumed her seat when the lights were turned up.

"It's about time," Ferne hissed. "Look at you! Your hair is disarranged."

Zulu tucked in the offending curl, but her eyes were on Breel. He glanced up at her and nodded.

"*Mon Dieu*! That is the second time. You might as well be leaning out a bordello window."

Now, in the brighter light, she could see the woman beside him. She was a slim girl with a sensitive mouth, and her white satin gown fell low over pale, sloping shoulders. Where the faint shadows hinted at the swell of her breasts there was the glow of a beautifully set ruby. In her luxuriant black hair she wore a single creamy camellia.

As usual Ferne was alert to the direction of Zulu's eyes. "You'd do well to study her. There's always that restrained elegance to Madame Luton's toilette."

So this was the woman Breel left Rosalie to marry.

"Madame Luton's very rich. I've heard she is out of

130

her mind about M'sieur.'' Ferne shook her head. "What such a woman can see in that worthlessness."

The girl was looking up at Breel now and her face glowed with her happiness. She reached out and almost shyly took his hand. He raised it briefly to his lips, then his eyes found their way up to Zulu again.

"A woman thinks of other things when she's with Breel," Zulu told Ferne.

The realization that she was bound to confront Breel again preyed on Zulu's mind throughout the following week and even as she dressed for the Ball. It robbed the occasion of the joyous anticipation that should have been with her as she drew in her breath so Eugenie could draw the laces to their tightest point, it robbed her of the delight that should have been hers as she looked at herself in the mirror. But somehow, a part of the fear was a restlessness. A hunger that could not be satisfied by food.

Ferne regarded her through narrowed eyes. "It will be well not to wait too long before choosing your protector. There are some women who only cause trouble when they are without a man."

"What trouble have I caused?" Zulu demanded, yet she was aware of the flush on her cheeks and the uncertainty of her mood. Did she really, underneath her fear, look forward to seeing Breel again?

But Breel was not at the Orleans Ballroom that night. Surely he must have known she'd be there. Perhaps, after all, he'd decided to forget her. Perhaps he realized she could be as dangerous to him as he was to her.

Shadney arrived soon after the first dance, but by then her success was assured. The first night her success might have been attributed to the fact that she was new, but now there was no one who could question that she was the most sought after woman on the dance floor. Even Ferne was pleased.

It was not until the following week that Breel made an entrance. It was as if he had deliberately waited until she

131

felt secure again, and then, there he was, his eyes following her.

He was waiting by Ferne when the music stopped and he stepped between her and the man promised the next dance.

He nodded politely to the Creole and then took Zulu's hand. "I'm afraid she's forgotten, but she promised me this dance a very long time ago." Before anyone could object he had led her to the dance floor.

Zulu was furious. "You had no right to do that!"

Breel laughed. Was it possible he had forgotten the fan dashed against his face?

"You don't really want to dance with Jean. He's much too fat to hold you the way you should be held."

"Why didn't you stay home with your wife? I told you I didn't want to see you again!"

"I must say that scowl doesn't become you. I'm certain Ferne is displeased. Really, Zulu, you must learn to make your emotions less transparent. People have their eyes on us, you know."

"If you don't let me go I'll scream. I can name at least six men who will give you their glove."

He raised an eyebrow. "So? Start naming them."

"There's LaFruge."

Breel laughed.

"There's Jean Sonet."

"I told you he was too fat."

Her voice grew a little desperate. "Etienne Grande, Shadney Randolph—"

"Oh?" he interrupted. "Have you really been honored? Frankly, if it's true I'm a bit disappointed in Shad."

"Disappointed! Does it indicate such bad taste to show interest in me?"

"Only bad judgement and Randolph's a shrewd man. Too shrewd to have anything to do with a woman like you."

"Suppose I told you he has asked me to become his

placee?'' The words were out before she had time to consider the boast.

He laughed.

"Do you think I'd lie?"

"As long as you ask—yes."

She tried again to pull free. "Let me go. Let me go this instant!"

"And smudge my reputation? I refuse to be left stranded in the middle of the Orleans Ballroom. Besides, there are things I want to ask. Has Rosalie married Cousin Norman yet? Did—"

Zulu caught Shadney's eyes, beseeching him. The older man's face tightened and he picked his way across the dance floor. Slowly others became aware of what was happening and they drew away.

Breel glanced around, then his eyes rested on Randolph. He pulled Zulu's arm tight against his side and waited.

"It's obvious your company is not welcome," Randolph said as he joined them. "I suggest you leave Zulu to finish this dance with me."

"Suppose I'm not open to your suggestion?" Breel's voice was soft and there was a slight smile on his lips.

"How am I to interpret that?"

"Any way you damn well please."

Shadney started to strip off his glove, but Breel shrugged.

"Don't bother. I haven't the least intention of meeting you under the oaks." He jerked Zulu's hand forward. "The gentleman would like to finish this dance with you, Zulu. We mustn't disappoint him." He turned and strode away.

Just as if she weren't worth fighting for! As if—

The slight pressure of Shadney's arm on her waist reminded her of where she was. She managed to smile up at him as they moved to the music.

"Breel Luton is a particularly objectionable young man, *ma belle*, I wouldn't want to see you make a

133

mistake."

"I hate him!

"I saw you watching him at the theater. I think everyone saw you watching him."

A new note had entered his voice and she looked up at him, Breel forgotten for the moment. "Did you mind?"

He frowned. "I'm afraid I did. I'm afraid I find myself minding everything you do, and I'm not certain I like that."

"But I'm flattered!"

He shook his head, his eyes were grave. "You're neither flattered nor surprised. You expected it would happen. You could destroy a man, Zulu."

"You needn't worry. I've about decided to accept Andre Dumont's request to call. After tonight I've decided I need a protector."

Shadney remained silent for the balance of the dance, then he led her out into the courtyard.

"I don't think Ferne will mind," he told her. "I need to talk to you."

He settled her at a table and ordered wine. He was silent until they were served, content to watch Zulu as her eyes wandered about the moonlit enclosure. It was unseasonably warm and though the great bushes of night blooming flowers bore few blossoms they still shed a fragrance grouped as they were around the tables, screening each couple from the others.

"Now tell me about yourself. Where do you come from?"

Zulu sipped her wine. "Is that so important?"

Shadney shrugged. "I suppose not. But you're not native here. That tawny hair is natural and you'll not often find it in your New Orleans quadroon. Also, your French is too pure."

"Does this matter to you?" She leaned close to him, her moist lips parted, the moonlight golden in her eyes.

He took her hand and held it against his lips. "It matters a great deal. There's something about you that

134

reaches out and snatches at a man's soul. I want to know what it is."

"I'm not the first woman you've met here. Certainly there's no mystery."

"I enjoy watching all of the beautiful women just as I enjoy a play at the theater and I've been a friend to many of them. I took Yvonne in my carriage to see young LeSieur off for France. I helped Ramon select the land for Naida's son—but I've never found myself hurrying here so that I might hold one of them in a waltz. I've never found myself thinking of them in a way I didn't want to think of any but one woman."

Zulu knew the candlelight was all she could wish with its misty aura and she made the most of it. She looked downward at the hand he had released.

"Is it you or is it my time of life? I've watched other men make fools of themselves when they reach my age. It's a bad time, Zulu, when a man knows himself to still be a man, yet feel the years crowding in on him—"

"You're not a fool." She caressed his cheek with her finger tips. Then she leaned forward so that her lips lightly touched his, the more tantalizing for the will-o-the-wisp quality of the kiss.

He stood up, his chair falling backward. "I'm going to make arrangements with Ferne—God help me!" He accepted the righted chair from a waiter and sat down again. For a minute he leaned on the table, his hands over his face, but when he looked up again his expression was under control and his voice so calm as to almost be cold.

"I want you to accept me knowing it will be final. There are younger and more attractive men all around us, but my *placee* must forget them. I'd have no fear if you were like the others—faithfulness is their life's breath. But you're different."

He studied her face as if hoping to find reassurance before he continued. "There are certain advantages I can offer you. I'm not likely to marry you and

135

leave . . . that part of my life is settled. Financially I'm in a position to provide well for you and I'll see that provision is made for you in case of my death."

"You make this sound like a business transaction." Lord God! Wait till Breel hears. Wait till New Orleans hears!

"A business transaction? Isn't that the way you regard it, *ma belle*?" Again his eyes searched into hers. "I wonder if there really is a heart inside that tantalizing body?"

Zulu smiled, remembering Ferne's words. "*Il n'y a rien d'impossible.*"

"You're right. Nothing is impossible. Still . . . I wonder . . ."

Chapter Twenty

Ferne burst into the room in the early part of the morning and startled Zulu out of a sound sleep.

She jerked aside the mesh. "Look at you! Sleeping as if you hadn't disgraced us all. I've a mind to wash my hands of you."

Zulu yawned. "Are you still in a state because I danced with Breel?"

Ferne threw up her hands. "You not only dance with him but you choose the middle of the ballroom to have a fight. I was concerned about Naida and didn't notice what you were doing until I saw M'sieur Sonet's distress. I hadn't realized it was necessary to watch your every movement."

Zulu clasped her hands behind her head. "Perhaps," she suggested, "when you're my chaperon your attention should be on me, not Naida."

Ferne went to the window and took a chair. "This is the second time Ramon's failed to meet her as he promised."

"That's Naida's worry. If she were half a woman and gave him something to worry about maybe he wouldn't find that white girl so interesting." She snapped a finger. "I could have Ramon like that!"

"You'll have no one with another exhibition like last night's."

"What does it matter? I've decided I'll accept Shadney Randolph."

"*Eh bien*, wait all of your life if you must be stubborn. But you will be without a protector when your hair is gray."

Zulu regarded her lazily. "Better get out of your *gabrielle*," she advised. "He's coming to see you this morning."

Ferne stared at her. "*Sacre Mère!*" She shook her head. "It's the *loa*."

Zulu laughed. "Lord God, I'd forgotten I even had that pebble! No, Ferne, it's me. What I want I work and plan to get."

"Are you really so blind?" Ferne askes softly. "Can you look in the mirror and not see a fire blazing in a jungle? Voodoo as we have it in New Orleans is an ancient evil but it is *rien* next to your stone. And you were born to hold that *loa*. I can see now that it is not by accident you possess it."

"You're worse than our Alabama field niggers screaming out about hoodoo! Do you really believe such stuff, Ferne?"

Ferne shrugged. "Maybe it's as well you remain ignorant." She opened the door to leave.

"And I must have the biggest cottage he can get!" Zulu called after her.

Ferne paused. For a moment she appeared pleased. "The biggest cottage by the ramparts belongs to Naida. It's not for sale."

"I can wait, Ferne. I needn't have it right away."

Zulu dressed carefully, choosing the gown she thought would most meet with Shadney's approval, then she sat by the window to wait.

The afternoon passed with no words from him, nor from Ferne. She remained up long past her usual bedtime, but still there was no sign of him. When she finally slipped into her nightclothes some drunken roustabouts were shouting down in the street and a group of young Creoles were laughing and talking on their way home from a party.

Zulu frowned into the darkness. Maybe in the morning there would be a message saying that he had changed his mind . . . And Breel would laugh. How Breel would laugh!

She pounded her pillow. He wouldn't get away with it! She'd see to that!

But then, again, Shadney had a wife. Maybe he had to wait until she slept. Maybe she was entertaining and there were guests to see to the door. . . .

That could well be it. It might be that he'd come to her in the early hours of the morning. She smiled and closed her eyes.

The rain had started again, gently but persistently it splashed off the eves onto the wooden banquettes. It lulled her to sleep.

When she awakened the sun was shining brightly through the lattices. She sat up, shaking the sleep out of her head, then she ran to the door.

Milissy was playing in the hallway and she looked up. "*Bon jour*," she murmured.

"Go tell Ferne I want to see her at once!" Zulu slammed the door and then threw open her *armoire* for a dress. When Ferne arrived she was thrusting the last pin into her hair.

"Well?" Ferne said from the doorway.

Zulu whirled away from the mirror. "Where is he? Have you bungled everything?"

"Bungled?"

"Where's Shadney? Why hasn't he been here?"

"Oh, that. How should I know? Perhaps you expected me to follow him to his house?"

"Then he did call on you!"

"Didn't you say he would? He's completed the settlement with me. My work is done."

"But he's not been near me! An entire day and night's passed and he's not even called!"

"M'sieur Randolph is a gentleman, not a stallion at stud. He'll complete arrangements before he sees you again. Did you expect him to break open your door and fall on you as if this were a common amour? Remember, you will be called Madame Randolph, and to you this must be like a marriage."

"I never thought that being a gentleman would stop a man from acting like a man," Zulu muttered, but she felt chastised.

"Now I'm through with you. I've done what I promised to do. M'sieur Randolph is your choice and I find it hard to believe you should show such judgement. I do not expect to be sent for again as if I were a common charwoman. If you do send for me, don't expect me to come."

It was late in the following afternoon before Shadney came for Zulu. Eugenie brought him to the room and then closed the door quietly behind him.

Shadney stood very still and his dark eyes traveled over her as if he had never really seen her before. Zulu was suddenly conscious of her simple, full skirted frock and the fact that her hair fell loosely over her shoulders, tied back with a narrow velvet band. She hadn't expected Shadney until evening and she'd been sitting in a chair reading the *Picayune*.

"I hadn't realized how very young you are," he finally said. He crossed to her side and picked up the paper, glancing at the heading.

"I see you are interested in the problem of our

139

maroon bands—the runaway blacks hiding out in the cypress swamps. We'll clean those places out yet!'' He rumpled the paper and tossed it back into the chair. "You mustn't identify yourself with them, Zulu. That could be dangerous."

She put her hands on his chest, her face turned up to his.

"I expected to see you much sooner," she said softly.

He smiled down on her, but made no move to touch her. "It wasn't too easy for my agent to find a suitable cottage. I wish I could offer you better, but it's the best to be had for the present. Building takes time, and to tell the truth, *ma belle*, I'm an impatient man. Later, perhaps, we can find something more appropriate."

"I can wait." She raised her face for his kiss, but he moved away and opened the door. At his signal a young negress appeared.

Her large, round eyes swept over the furnishings, then rested with approval on Zulu. She grinned and moved forward. Her walk was impudent and her skin a rich brown.

"I'll tend to yore packin', Miz Zulu."

"I've already told Letty she'll have the most beautiful mistress in New Orleans," Shadney said as he watched the maid's deft movements. "She's from Georgia. I thought you'd be more easy with her than a Creole negress for your personal maid. I did get a girl from Santo Domingo for the cooking and house cleaning, though. I've become fond of Creole dishes. Annette's at the cottage getting it ready for us."

Two slaves of her own! Back at Elmside even her most far fetched dreams had never dared this far!

"You're a thousand miles away, Zulu."

She nodded, honest with him for once. "Back in Alabama at the Spring House." She threw off the mood quickly, laughing. "Oh Shad, I didn't expect you'd get all this so soon!"

"Remember, I go with it."

They left Letty to do the packing and went on ahead. The rain had stopped the day before, but a high wind tore at them as they went up the street.

"We're in for some bad storms this winter," Shad remarked. "This wind's off the gulf."

At the Place d'Armes the wind renewed its onslaught and they had to bend forward to walk against it. Shadney helped her across the muddy street and she paused in front of the Presbytere to secure her hat more tightly. When she took Randolph's arm again she saw he was staring ahead at the Orleans Cathedral.

"I was married there," he said. Then he smiled down at Zulu. "I'd hate to say how many years ago."

They turned up Pirate's Alley and came out on Royal Street. At St. Anthony's Garden they crossed to go up Orleans. Once again he paused to look back, his eyes on the spires that stood sharply against the sky.

Four blocks up Orleans and Zulu had her first glimpse of Rampart Street. Before them stretched rows of white cottages and Shadney tightened his grip on her arm as they moved toward them.

He stopped in front of a newly painted house. Two steps led off the banquette to a closed *jalousie*. Shadney took her up the steps and pulled the blinds open so she could enter the enclosed porch. He drew two keys from his pocket, one he gave her and the other he inserted into the lock. The latch clicked open and he withdrew the key, attaching it to his chain. It was a ceremony in itself.

He opened the door, waiting for her to step inside.

"Do you like it?" His voice was anxious.

Zulu looked around the room, at the soft, mauve carpet, the new, comfortable furniture and the wide fireplace. Shadney's pipes were already on the mantle.

This is my house, she thought. A real house with tables and chairs.

"There's a small patio and the rooms are large. It's more than I expected to get on such short notice." He left her standing in the middle of the room and disappeared down the hall. She heard him open a door, then the sputter of frying food. "Annette, I want you to come out and greet your mistress."

From the kitchen came an answer in a dialect that was not quite the *gumbo* Zulu had heard spoken among the blacks in the New Orleans streets. Yet it was similar.

"*M'ap vini.*"

Shadney reappeared with the sound of feet behind him. "I told you Annette's from West Indies, and while she can understand English I find she doesn't care to speak it. But wait until you taste her *jambalaya!*"

Annette entered the room, a ladle still in her hand. She was a large woman and very black. She wore a blue tignon around her head and it gave her face the appearance of a great, round moon.

She looked at Randolph, affection in her eyes. "*Comment now yé,*" she grinned.

"Those couldn't have been grillades I smelled cooking?" he asked.

She nodded her head, delighted.

"Turn them low. We won't want them for a while, and I wouldn't have anything spoil them. Greet your mistress and you can go back to them."

Zulu was aware of the critical scrutiny of the black eyes as Annette nodded her head.

"Madame Randolph," she acknowledged.

Zulu felt Shadney stir slightly by her side and she realized he hadn't touched her yet, except to take her arm.

There was a small jeweler's box on the table and he picked it up. His hand trembled a little as he lifted the lid.

"Let me try this on your finger," he said, but when Zulu held out her left hand he shook his head. "The right, *ma belle*. It would be better there."

He slid the opal onto her finger and Zulu held her hand up, mute with triumph. Her first real gem. It glowed softly, set in a nest of dainty diamonds.

"Shad!" she exclaimed. He had come very near and she threw her arms around his neck, her lips hard on his and her body tight against him. She felt him shudder and he drew away.

"Not here," he whispered. "Not here." He drew her to the door that had remained closed and when he opened it she saw a bedroom almost as luxurious as Rosalie's back at Elmside. There was a nightdress and robe that looked as if they had been made of woven moonbeams, and by the bed, velvet slippers.

Shadney closed the door and she saw that his eyes were dark with passion but his face was pale. Haunted, almost. Then he was holding her, his hands fumbling with her clothes.

"Take them off," he whispered. "Hurry!"

"Back in my room you wouldn't even touch me." Somehow it pleased her to hold him off, to watch the dignity leave him and see the desire for her blot out the memory that had been in his eyes when he looked back at the Cathedral.

"If I'd so much as touched your finger, I'd have had you right there. For God's sake, don't keep me waiting."

"Tear my dress off me. That's what you want to do. Tear it off me."

He shook his head and she knew he saw through her desire to demean him. It angered her that he should find her so transparent, so she undid her buttons as slowly as possible, watching his face, tempting him to push aside her fingers in a frenzy of the passion he held on such a tight leash. Finally she stood before him, naked, her eyes sullen.

"I've never stood like this before a man."

His voice was husky. "You've the most beautiful body I've ever seen. Beautiful. . . ."

Then he held her in his arms and she felt herself responding to the caress of his seeking hands and his lips

143

were stoking up fires that had nothing to do with him, but only with the act of sex that was, somehow, apart from him.

She let out a little cry and pulled him toward the bed.

"Wait," he said unsteadily and disengaged her arms so he could undress. He had restrained himself while she disrobed but his control was all but gone as he threw off his clothes.

She lay on the bed waiting. "Hurry. . . ." she whispered as he lay down beside her, then he crushed her to him and she smiled as he took her as urgently as Len or Gram. The dividing line between a lusty riverman and a gentleman was: more easily breached than either realized, she reflected before her own needs blotted out all but the pulsating, aching demands of her own body. She held tightly to him, catering to his needs until once again he was seeking her, though his breath was short and his hands shaking. Finally, white and spent he lay with his face pressed into the softness of her breasts.

"You're as I thought you'd be. Lillith reborn. From first I saw you I felt a sympathy for Adam."

Zulu ran her fingers through his hair. "Lillith? Is that another name for Eve?"

He laughed and looked up at her. "She was before Eve and infinitely evil. But Adam found her very desirable—and very destructive."

"I could never hurt you. You've given me everything I could want."

He closed his eyes. "For how long, *ma belle*? Right now I'm afraid the day will come when this cottage will seem very small and I'll appear incredibly ancient." He leaned on his elbow and his grave eyes probed into hers.

"Zulu, when that day comes I'll either kill you or myself."

But she laughed softly and pulled him back to her.

"I've everything I could want," she assured him over and over. "Everything."

Chapter Twenty-One

The rains came in earnest the next few weeks. The streets were a mire and carriages could no longer negotiate many of them. It was impossible to visit the shops in such weather and Zulu moved restlessly through the rooms of her cottage. Even the delight of having a house of her own began to pall under the monotony of this enforced inactivity.

There were few evenings that Shadney did not call on her and he fell into the habit of remaining late, not always for love making but often for her company alone. There would be dinner set by the fireside, and after Annette had removed the dishes, he would relax back in his easy chair, smoking and talking to her, though he was sometimes content to spend long hours reading from the supply of books he had brought.

Zulu fell on those volumes when he was away, and she read all of them, regardless of the subject. Her mind hungered for more, but she hesitated to let Shadney know and her pride wouldn't let her ask him for others. That was a part of herself she didn't have to share with him. It belonged to herself alone, and she clung jealously to it.

Late at night, after Shad had left, she would often be awakened by the sounds of others returning from the Orleans Ballroom. The flicker of torches would light her room momentarily and then the laughter would trail off and she'd be alone again. Had she come to New Orleans to be shut away from the very gaiety that had drawn her?

"Why don't you ever take me to the Ball?" she finally asked Randolph as he smoked by her fireside. "Are you ashamed of me?"

He set down his pipe. "Ashamed of you, *ma belle?*" His voice was thoughtful. "Not of you, but of myself, perhaps. And it is true. I have neglected your social life."

She knelt beside him and he cupped her face in his hands. "Do any of the women call on you during the day?"

Zulu lowered her lashes to hide the resentment she felt.

"Naida has. But no one else."

"It would be Naida." He sighed deeply. "I've been selfish. At home there's so much of balls and entertainment that I've looked forward to this as a refuge—and why should I go to the Orleans Ballroom to watch beautiful women when I've captured the most beautiful?"

Zulu's eyes grew sullen and he laughed. "You've a right to complain. You were never meant to be caged. I'll arrange for Ferne to chaperon you to the theater, and maybe a waltz or two might keep me from settling into my dotage."

"Ferne won't chaperon me," Zulu predicted. "She'll refuse."

Nevertheless, it was Ferne who appeared on her porch the next day.

"M'sieur Randolph called on me this morning," she announced. "I told him I'd had enough of you, but he wouldn't listen. *Eh bien,* he has a way with him. I told him you would need clothes and he said we were to call on Madame Volante this afternoon. Arrangements will be made."

A modiste, and the most fashionable in New Orleans! It was almost more than Zulu could believe. To actually wear clothes that had been made for herself alone. Not to put on a little memory of Rosalie with each petticoat and frock. She tried to hide her excitement behind a yawn. "I suppose I could find the time this afternoon."

Ferne laughed. "Are the others perhaps giving you a

soiree? And is your house so full of callers that you have not time for yourself?'' She settled herself into a chair. "And now there is the matter of jewels. What has he given you?''

Zulu held out her hand proudly, but Ferne was not impressed.

"An opal! And what is an opal besides bad luck? Have you no necklaces, no brooches? Hasn't he even presented you with earrings? Do he value you so low?

As Ferne spoke, Zulu felt a growing anger. Lord God, had she sold herself too cheaply? How dare he to place her in a position where Ferne could jeer? She yanked off her ring and threw it across the floor.

"He'll give me jewels! He'll give me jewels better then any you've seen!''

Ferne retrieved the ring. "Don't be a fool. If you're not afraid of opals this isn't a bad one. Wear it and at least you will have something.'' She frowned thoughtfully. "Maybe you haven't made it clear you admire such things?''

In the days that followed Zulu made every attempt to clarify that point, but Shadney appeared deaf to all hints. Even when she mentioned Naida's new pendant or admired the jewels worn by some passing *placee,* he only nodded and smiled. Yet there were times when she suspected there was a twinkle in his eyes and a waiting look about him.

Finally the new gowns were delivered by the modiste and she selected a cream satin to wear to the theater. It was cut low, displaying much of her bosom, and it left her shoulders quite naked. She drew her hair back and piled it in curls high on her head, leaving her ears and neck exposed.

When Shadney arrived she turned and swirled so that her wide skirts founced away from the layers of petticoats and flew about her in a shimmering circle. In the doorway Shadney leaned on his walking stick and smiled his appreciation.

"But I must keep on my wrap at the theater," she told him as she went into his arms. "Then no one will know I don't even own a necklace."

"Your neck has beauty enough of its own." A smile twitched his lips.

She pulled free of his arms. "Lord God! Do you think I want everyone saying you're not generous?"

He laughed. "Are you trying to say you want a necklace?"

She turned on him, furious and shamed. "Must I ask? Why must you make me beg?"

"Because of the pride in you." He spoke slowly. "Only when I can break through it a little do I really believe you belong to me."

He took a key from his vest pocket and opened the lid of the desk he kept in the corner. With still another key he opened a compartment and took out a small casket.

"I've been buying you jewelry. When I see something that belongs on you, I can't stop myself."

She snatched for the box, but he held it out of her reach. "Not all at once. With half of New Orleans facing bankruptcy this year, it wold be in bad taste for you to be seen with too many jewels." He selected a pair of jade earrings and watched while she put them on. "Besides, my Lillith—"

She looked away from the mirror. "Besides, what?"

He fastened a carved jade necklace around her throat and caressed the nape of her neck with his lips. "I don't flatter myself that I—or any other man can hold you. But I think jewels you can't have all at once, might."

But she hardly heard him. Her fingers touched the jade with wonder. Each piece an art work in itself and the incense of the East still clinging to the stones.

"It must have cost you a fortune, Shad... And you had it for me all of the time!"

He locked the desk. "Don't forget, there's more. Each piece waiting for the right time."

"And must I beg each time?"

"I think, perhaps," he said, "you must."

Breel had been far from her mind. Part of another world, as far distant from the present as Elmside. Yet the fear of him returned in all of its fullness as she took her seat beside Ferne in her theater box.

A quick glance told her that Breel was not down in the Dress Circle and she relaxed back against the cushion, weak with relief. She was conscious of eyes on her, and of the whispered comments. Certainly it was not everyday that a man such as Shadney Randolph took a *placee* and it was important that she do him proud.

She sat straight, with her chin high, a soft smile of pleasure on her lips. It was good to be admired. Good to know she disappointed no one. This was the life intended for her.

The sense of security was still with her when she passed through the door of the Orleans Ballroom, her finger tips resting lightly on Shadney's arm. Breel wouldn't have the nerve to show his face here after refusing a challenge on the very floor. Yet her eyes darted quickly over the dancers.

Shadney paused to watch two men who were arguing. A very young girl stood a little apart from them, a gleam of pride in her eyes.

"There are more duels fought over the women here than over our wives and sisters," he remarked. There was a wry bitterness in his eyes. "There's a ballroom for white folks down the street, but I'll wager half the men on this floor have escaped from there. Right now their wives are standing by the wall wishing their husbands didn't spend so much time in the gaming room. That's New Orleans, Zulu. Sometimes I can see black men in chains, dead these many years—and ancestors of these girls. I can hear them laugh."

I hope so! She was surprised by the violence of the thought. I hope so!

Shadney's attention had turned to the ballroom as they waited for the dance to end. "There's Ramon. I

149

wonder how he finds time to be here when his betrothal is to be announced tonight."

"Tonight?" Zulu wondered briefly how Naida must feel. Still, Naida wouldn't be left in difficult circumstances.

"Naida invited me for lunch yesterday. After seeing her cottage mine seemed hardly big enough to breathe in."

"So soon, Zulu?" His eyes followed the girl as Ramon led her to the courtyard. "I'm glad she'll at least have that. Naida's one of the greatest ladies I've ever known."

Zulu started at him. "But she's got more black blood than I have. A lot more!"

"Should that make a difference? Being a lady is more complicated than race—or clothes."

"You'd get yourself a mess of trouble if anyone heard you say that," Zulu muttered. She frowned. "When you think of a lady, Shad, what do you think of first?"

"Graciousness. True graciousness." He took her arm. "Would you like to dance now?"

Zulu glanced toward the door to the courtyard. She must study Naida more closely, she decided. Try to find what it was that brought out that protective instinct in men and women alike.

"I think I'd like refreshment first," she said.

As if by accident, she chose the table nearest to where Ramon sat with his *placee*. It was early as yet, so they were the only two couples in the moonlit enclosure. They nodded a greeting, but once seated the shrubs gave them each privacy from the other.

Zulu shivered. "There's a chill out here." She glanced down at her bare shoulders. "Would you fetch me my wrap?"

After Shadney left, Zulu moved to the chair closest to the bush. She had noticed as they passed that Naida's wine was untouched and the glow of happiness had left her face. Now her voice was distinct in the night air,

150

though she spoke in soft, sibilant French.

"But Ramon, you did promise you'd stay tonight... I've been so happy all day, just thinking about it!"

Ramon's voice was low, but underlying it was the hint of impatience. "I didn't say I wouldn't be back. I just said I had to leave for a while. When my mother entertains she expects me to at least show myself."

"You won't forget?"

"Haven't I promised?"

"But you've forgotten so often, lately. The bed's so big and empty when I'm alone. All night I keep reaching for you, but you're not there. Sometimes I even cry a little because I'm lonely. Last night I took the baby to bed with me and he—" she laughed, "he has no conscience, that one! Then he kicked his feet and smiled at me the way you do when you've had too much to drink."

"I've got to leave now. I should have left half an hour ago."

Naida's dress rustled to her quick movement. "Is it that white girl?" Her whisper barely carried to Zulu's ear. "I've heard she's pretty. Tell me the truth, Ramon, have you given your word?"

Ramon's voice was gentle with a tenderness that stirred a vague envy inside Zulu. "How many times must I tell you that the baby and you are all that matter to me, Naida?"

"Ne m'en voulez pas," Naida begged.

Ramon laughed. He bent to kiss her and started to leave as Shadney returned with Zulu's wrap. He stopped by the table to greet Randolph, poking him playfully.

"I didn't believe Naida at first! Then I heard it was Zulu and it became understandable."

"One look at Zulu and a man's young again."

Ramon nodded appreciatively and went on his way. There was only silence at the next table, but somehow Zulu knew Naida was crying.

If I had her house I wouldn't care whether the man

151

left or not! Zulu thought. Shad could afford to build me one as big. There's no reason why he shouldn't.

But when she mentioned it later, he only shook his head. "I know I promised you a bigger place—but not for a while. These are bad times and there are rich men facing ruin. I've told you before it would be in bad taste to make a big display of spending money on my *placee*. But this depression won't last forever. You just have to be patient."

"Then buy Naida's!"

"In some ways you think like a child. Naida wouldn't part with her house—not while she can still breathe. Not with anything Ramon gave her. Money isn't as important to her as it is to you, Zulu."

Zulu was sitting in front of her mirror practicing ways to do her hair the next morning when Letty announced visitors.

"Madame Vauregard and another lady." She spoke triumphantly, as if it was as much to her credit as her mistress's that finally someone had joined Naida in a call.

Zulu was aware of more excitement than she cared to admit. She arranged her hair quickly and went out to them. Naida's friend was a tall, fair skinned woman whose strong features were a lovely but striking contract to Naida's flower-like beauty.

"Zulu, I want you to meet Yvonne LeSieur. She lives only next door."

"I've often thought I should call on you," Yvonne said. "Already our cooks are friends and M'sieur Randolph has been very good to M'sieur LeSicur and myself. Only yesterday I found Naida knew you."

"I can't remember seeing you at one of the Balls. I'm certain I would have remembered your face."

Yvonne laughed. "That is a compliment, I hope? No, I haven't attended one for a very long time. M'sieur LeSieur has been in France for over a year."

"But surely there are others who would be glad to

take you!''

Yvonne frowned, but Naida broke in quickly. "Zulu's new here and she doesn't understand." She turned to Zulu, her voice gentle, "*Oui*, there are other men, but they are not the man Yvonne loves. She has selected her protector."

Zulu motioned them be seated. "It's hard to understand—everything is different here. Your men are white and you know you can never be their wife. Yet you set so much store by faithfulness."

"*Cela va sans dire!*" Yvonne exclaimed, falling out of her precise English. "He is the only marriage I'll ever know. Even if it's ten more years, I will wait still."

"Ramon says ours is marriage to him," Naida said. "He tells me a priest's sanction is not important when two are as close as we." Her eyes clouded. "If he left me I'd kill myself."

Yvonne touched Naida's hand gently.

"But why?" Zulu asked. "I've heard of some who married after their protector left."

"Marriage is only possible with men of color. I have a friend who married a man who was only an eighth black—he had a farm out in the country."

"A man of color!" Naida shuddered. "That's for the mulattos—or the *griffes*, but not us."

"My friend's very happy," Yvonne persisted. "We are great snobs, Naida. We turn our backs on our own kind."

Zulu studied her visitor more closely. Here was a person who thought beyond the precise society that bred her.

"How do you know your man will come back?"

Yvonne opened her reticule and took out several small, odd shaped sacks. "These are strong *gris-gris*. Each one of them by itself should bring him back." She unbuttoned her basque and pulled out the medals pinned to an undergarment. "I wear these sacred things next to my heart. Each morning when I pin them there I

153

say a prayer for him to come back, and each evening I remind them of the prayer. Every afternoon I light a candle in the church. He'll come back.''

Zulu took one of the sacks in her hand and her nostrils dialated to the pungent odor. She turned it over and something that was almost a memory stirred within her.

"In Alabama the field niggers made *cunjuhs* and talked about avoiding a plat eye—that's the worst kind of a ghost. But voodoo? Is that the same sort of thing? Ferne talked about it the first time I met her. She's no field nigger.''

Yvonne laughed. "That is for certain. But she made the *gris-gris* you hold. I think she has more power than Madame Dédé ever had, and I think if she wished it, she could take Maria Laveau's place as Voodoo Queen. Ferne's power comes from within, not from *tafia*—"

"*Tafia?*" Zulu repeated.

"It's rum made from sugar cane. Enough and one can see anything. Besides, Marie Laveau brings the Virgin and the Saints and places them right beside Le Grand Zombi. I think she doesn't know which she believes.''

"Isn't that the same as your medals and *gris-gris*?"

Yvonne shook her head firmly. "That is different. But I'm not alone in thinking it should be Ferne, not Marie Laveau who sits on the throne—except, maybe, Ferne is a little afraid of her power. Would you like to go with me to the meeting tonight?"

"No, Zulu!" Naida exclaimed. "And Yvonne, I wish you'd stay away from them. Ramon laughs at me for being so terrified of Voodoo, but the priests say it's evil.''

"The priests say the way we live is evil, also," Yvonne reminded her. "But in your heart do you feel you are sinning?"

Naida looked down at her hands. "I don't know. My mother lived this way and she was a good woman—the

154

only man she knew was my father. Her own mother lived like we do, and people said she had the heart of a saint. When my grandfather died she devoted her life to raising my mother. Maybe it is wrong, but how can it be evil?"

Yvonne stood up. "Evil or not, I'm going to the meeting tonight and I'll stop by for you, Zulu, if you decide to go." She picked up her wrap. "My maid's outside with the market basket. I have to leave now or everthing will be picked over."

Naida remained after Yvonne had left. "Your house is so comfortable," she said. "M'sieur Randolph showed great taste when he selected the furnishings.

"It's a quarters cabin next to yours," Zulu retorted. She hesitated. "Shad would give you a good price for your cottage."

Naida laughed. "Sell my house? Each little inch has a thought of Ramon in it. I'd never sell my house."

She paused by the door. "And please don't go with Yvonne tonight. I have fear of it for you. It's foolish, perhaps, but when Yvonne invited you I felt a coldness inside."

After Naida left, Zulu found herself staring at the wall and not seeing it. Some far off portion of her mind was deep in thoughts that simmered but refused to surface. She was aware of only a blankness, as if she were asleep and awake at the same time.

She called to Annette. It was past time to do her own marketing, a chore she enjoyed. In fact, she reflected, her only chore. She had learned that other household purchasing was better left to Annette and the vendors who made daily calls.

Chapter Twenty-Two

Yvonne was dressed in black and she wore a lace scarf over her head when she called on Zulu that night.

"I brought you a white *tignon*," she said, taking a kerchief out of a pocket. "Your maids will only have blue ones—Annette might own one that's white, but she'd never admit it."

"And why shouldn't she?" Zulu wanted to know.

Yvonne shrugged. "You must know these meetings are forbidden—but that makes very little difference. You'll see white folks there and not just the poor ones, either. In fact, it's usually one of them who is asking a special favor and pays for the wine and *tafia*."

Zulu looked with disdain at the *tignon*, but submitted to the indignity of having her hair bound up. Yvonne tied the kerchief expertly, careful that all seven points should be upturned.

"Now put a scarf over your head. Anyone seeing your *tignon* would suspect where you're going."

"Do they hold these meetings often?" Zulu asked.

"When enough people have requests—or a rich enough person. Of course, the big festival is on St. John's Eve in June, that's the one time the Voodoo queen must lead the worship. Tonight it could be anyone she might choose."

Zulu frowned, trying to understand the mixture of symbolisms.

"You said Marie Laveau puts your saints right alongside of your Voodoo gods—"

"Le Grand Zombi?" Yvonne smiled. "She has a great regard for the power of the saints, but each Voodoo queen is permitted to make any changes in the ritual that might please her so long as the snake is the pivot. There are men who have power, also, and we call them doctors. But it's the queen who is important."

They stepped out into the cold December night. There was no need for torches, the moon was full and round.

"I'd have been here sooner," Yvonne said, "but I found Naida had read of Ramon's betrothal in *L'Abeille*. I must have been guided there. I stayed with her until he came and now she's happy. *Le Bon Dieu* knows what sort of a story he gave her. She believes he won't marry."

"Maybe he won't."

Yvonne snorted. "That one? Why do you think the wedding is set so soon after the betrothal? It'll be before Lent! He has to marry—and soon. He's gambled away everything. Even what belonged to his mother and sisters. Only this announcement will hold off the creditors."

"The white woman is rich?"

"*Naturellement!* He'll probably wait until after the wedding and then write Naida a letter. I try not to think of it."

"Naida's a fool!" Zulu said. Then she noticed with some alarm that Yvonne seemed to be heading in the direction of a brickyard.

"We're not going in there, are we?" she asked.

"In the old days they used to have meetings right out on Congo Plains," Yvonne told her, "but that was divided for buildings and meetings were outlawed, so now they're held in lonely places. Sometimes here, and sometimes by Lake Pontchatrain."

They turned into the entrance of the yard, holding their skirts clear of the debris. Yvonne knocked on the door of a long, low shed. From inside they could hear the muffled throbbing of drums. Yvonne knocked a second time, and a woman answered.

Until the door opened and the onslaught of drums and discordant music blasted out at them, Zulu had

157

actually not given much thought to what the meeting might involve. Up until then it had only been something unusual to relieve the boredom of a night when she knew Shadney's wife was entertaining.

But this was something else. There was danger here. Danger far more subtle than the pull of the swamp or the pull of the *loa*. A reluctant fear that was beyond reason brought her to a standstill.

Yvonne caught her hand and pulled her inside. Behind them she heard the bolt drop into place. A red, smoke filled haze almost blinded her at first, then she was able to make out the source, three great brick rimmed fires blazed at each end of the shed and near the platform in the center of the building. The flames twisted and crackled, throwing strange shadows over the two stuffed black cats that glared from their perches on either side of a long table. Between them a malevolent doll leered at her.

She found herself trembling to the vibrations of ancient evil that seemed to reach for her from all sides. She fought to keep her senses, to resist what she could feel, but not see.

Naida had been right. This was not for her. Not the rising rhythm of the goatskin drums Yvonne called *tamtams*. Not the steady tempo that mounted and climbed until it reached a frenzied peak of insanity, then slowly subsided to a hearbeat, a dull, steady pulsation.

"Yvonne," she whispered. "I'm leaving. I shouldn't have come."

"You can't leave now!" Yvonne exclaimed. "Once you're inside you've no choice."

Zulu clutched Yvonne's arm and moved with her toward the platform. She felt a dizziness that had nothing to do with the stifling, smoke filled air. The stench of sweating bodies grew stronger with each step toward the central platform where a frail, yellow skinned man was leaping into the air, shaking a huge, seed filled gourd.

"*Voudou Magnian!*" he screamed. "*Ai! Ai!*"

"The *kanzo*," Yvonnne explained, using what Zulu realized was the Haitian term. Around him old women were clattering bones together, a light skinned man was twanging off key on a strange, stringed instrument. Somewhere in the background was the eerie keening of a flute.

There was only one chair in the building and that was on the platform. A handsome mulattress sat on it with the dignity of a queen on her throne. Just below her was an ancient woman. Her *tignon* was half off her head and kinky white hair stuck out from the sides. Her glazed eyes were fixed on the fire and her toothless mouth moved to constant incantations.

A low table had been spread below the platform. Wine and what Zulu realized must be *tafia,* the rum Yvonne had mentioned, was passed from person to person as clay containers were filled and drained.

Then, at a signal from the woman on her throne, the table was pulled aside and a girl sprang into the center of the circle. Slowly at first, she swayed to the rhythm of the drumbeat. One by one men and women joined her, swaying in snake-like undulations until the drums increased in frenzy and the dancers whirled and screamed, ripping off their clothing, tearing at their hair, screaming and mouthing strange words as their ecstacy mounted.

The *kanzo* had put aside the gourds and now he held a snake, waving it above the dancers. The mulattress had left her throne and sprinkled water from a container over the dancers, chanting and swaying.

"*Voudou Magnian!*" the *kanzo* shouted. "*Voudou Magnian!*"

The pear shaped gourd rolled to Zulu's feet. She stepped back.

"Don't touch the *asson,*" Yvonne warned her. "It has the backbone of a sacred snake as well as seeds. It's not permitted that everyone hold it."

"Hold it!" Zulu felt a hysterical desire to laugh. "I'd sooner hold a cottonmouth!"

A howl welled up and the drums raced to a new fury. The old man wailed a loud, screeching cry and the dancers continued to shout and twist. A woman writhed on the floor, moans coming from her foaming mouth, and a man straddled her, his body moving rhythmatically.

"*Houm!*" the *kanzo* shouted. "*Ai! Ai!*"

Zulu could feel the pull. As if part of her responded and strained to be free. She found herself swaying and she had no memory of when her body had started to throb with the drumbeat.

"Your eyes!" Yvonne laughed nervously. "The firelight makes your eyes look strange."

The old woman turned her glittering gaze on them. Her nostrils twitched as she stared into Zulu's face.

She knows what's inside me, Zulu thought. She knows what this is doing to me...

"My *conjur*," Yvonne said to the woman. "You said it would be ready tonight."

The woman took her eyes from Zulu and waved an orange colored sack over Yvonne's head.

Again the throbbing surged through Zulu's body. A restless hunger grew like a drunkeness and she was aware of a heat more urgent than the overpowering warmth of the fire. She had to leave. Another minute and nothing would matter. Another minute and she would know more than she wished to know of the powers released by this hysterical worship of evil.

She closed her eyes, and against her will the memory swept through her...

A fire was leaping up to a black sky-- a woman-- was it herself? danced naked while the heat beat at her golden limbs, while the flames enfolded her like the arms of a lover. And there were trees, strange trees, thicker than those in the cypress swamps... Some jungle animal yelped beyond the clearing and a drum beat

160

steadily. It beat for her...

She opened her eyes, willing the ancient memory away. She was aware that sounds were coming from her mouth. Words that had no meaning to her. Words such as the *kanzo* shouted. Words that had been conceived by jungle fires long ago—that had been handed through the generations until they had evolved into a Haitian chant.

"Dambala Wédo mandé tête cabrit,
C'est sang li mandé
Damballa Wédo C'est sang mandé pou allé
C'est sang li mandé..."

The memory inside Zulu repeated the phrases. The meaning was the same, but the phrases different from the garbled Haitian French.

"Damballa Wédo asks for the head of a goat
It is blood he asks for
Damballa Wédo it is blood he wants before he leaves
It is blood he asks for!"

Only it wasn't to the Haitian Damballa Wédo to whom Feig had chanted. Feig! Were her grandmother's memories to haunt her? The thought drew itself out of her, and once released it was as if a cork had been pulled from a bottle of ancient evil.

What was it that big black women—Mala—had said? "Feig inside you is sick for home... Let Feig go home, then." She wanted no part of her or her memories...

But that was her voice calling out— "I am *Nyené We*! I hold *Ku* in a stone I carry next to my heart!" And the memories continued to flood her consciousness...

A bird was screaming in back of the clearing, the fire leapt to a new height over the jungle, straight up to the African sky...

A huge *Congo* sprang up onto the platform facing her.

"*Nyené We!*"! he shouted. "*Kru!*"

How was she to explain that she did not know the *Kru* dialect? That those words belonged to a past that was not her own?

A negro leaped up onto the platform. He carried a small black coffin.

"Le Grand Zombi!" The roar filled the air, swelled in volume—a shriek in a void.

"L'appé vinie le Grand Zombi
L'appé vinie pau fe gris-gris . . ."

The dancing had degenerated into an orgy of leaping, whirling and falling in fits. Men and women coupled, taking their rhythm from the drum beat. A few had sunk to their knees, hands clasped and glazed eyes fastened on the coffin. The old woman split a pigeon in two and celebrants surged forward, fighting to touch the blood so they could smear it on their chests and faces.

The man holding the coffin raised the lid and a snake slithered out. A huge snake, twice the size of the one the *kanzo* had waved.

The noise ceased, but the silence hung like a suspended shriek... And the memory was there, waiting...

There was silence in the jungle, too. The flames were folding themselves into a tiny stone. Into the pierre loa that even now hung between her breasts. The trees whirled and crashed and a voice, her voice, broke the silence...

"I hold *Ku* in a stone. I am Feig and I hold the devil in a stone!"

"Nedyipwe!" the *Congo* shouted

The snake slithered across the platform and curled at her feet. There were words she should say. Incantations on the tip of her tongue. The memory inside her stirred and screamed out her lips, but the words were wrong. The memory was losing its strength...

The *kanzo* was staring at her.

"En bas caille là c'est nous hounfor legba!
Damballa Wédo c'est nous gros coulève
M'ape marré pouin moin, c'est pou'm tuye yo frête!
M'ape sonnin asson'm pou'm ca ba yo gross pouin!

162

Abobo! Abobo! Abobo! Bobobobo!''

The last two verses ran through her brain.

"I am tying my pouin, it is to kill someone

I am sounding my rattle to make strong magic for someone!''

It was the words he would chant to someone who had asked for a death charm. He was making the death charm for her, but she hadn't asked for a death charm. Who was there she could wish to die? Maybe, once, Rosalie, but that was long ago and almost forgotten. Yet the *kanzo* saw her wishing a death wish. He saw what she hid even from herself.

A white chicken was brought to the platform and the queen left her throne. She held it by the neck and drew a knife down its squirming mid section. Blood splattered in a wide spray and feathers adhered to her bloody fingers.

"Le Grand Zombi!

L'appé le Grand Zombi!''

Zulu felt weak, her hand trembled as she tried to wipe the perspiration from her forehead and her stomach churned. She must get away. Already it might be too late!''

"Yvonne...'' she whispered. "Help me!''

But Yvonne was staring ahead, her eyes glazed.

A firm hand took Zulu's arm, and she leaned on it, grateful for the guidance. She could hear herself sobbing as she permitted herself to be led away from the throne, away from the pulsating heat of the fire. A blast of air struck her face as she passed through the doorway, but still she held hard to the arm that supported her.

She was leaning against a tree outside the brickyard when awareness slowly returned. She was very sick for a few minutes, gagging and choking. She took the handkerchief that was handed her and used it.

Finally she was able to draw in the clean air, though the throbbing of drums echoed inside her head and sent warmth through her body. Only then did she realize it was Ferne who stood beside her, but somehow she felt no surprise.

"So you've finally learned what I knew from the beginning," Ferne said.

"They're like animals," Zulu whispered. "Worse than animals."

"But it reached out to you. I watched your face from the time you came through the door." Ferne frowned. "What was there in you that pulled away? Why did you become ill instead of accepting le Grand Zombi when he crawled to your very feet? Not even Marie Laveau nor Madame Dédé have been shown such favor."

"I hope I never hear a drum again," Zulu said, but all of the time it was there, throbbing with each beat of her heart.

"Can it be that there is both in you?" Ferne shook her head. "If that's so, I could feel sorry for you. It's better to be one or the other, not a battleground. It's not easy, that."

But Zulu had turned away and she moved rapidly toward the entrance of the brickyard. It took all of her control to refrain from breaking into a run when she saw the gates. Still the drums pursued her. They followed her down the quiet, moonlit streets. They were with her when she stepped onto her own doorstoop and went into her cottage. She threw herself onto the divan, her nails digging into the cushions.

"So now it's Voodoo?" came a derisive voice from Shadney's chair. "Did you get a *gris-gris* to keep me away? Or to bring me to you?"

Zulu lifted herself onto her elbow and looked into Breel's face. His eyes were on her white *tignon*.

"It's too early for the rites to be over. Did you have to run home to see if the *gris-gris* worked?"

"You've no right here." She spoke dully. There was no will in her to fight. Only the all consuming heat the drums had awakened.

He smiled slightly, as if the rise and fall of her breasts told him what he wanted to know. He jerked the tignon from her head and ran his fingers roughly through the heavy waves that fell about her shoulders and down her back.

Her arms pulled him down to her and the tam-tams beat loud in her brain as she strained against him.

His voice was husky. "Do you realize you're making me part of the voodoo rites?" He laughed. "Not that I mind."

Later, with the drum beat gone from her brain, she pulled away from Breel. It was as if she were sobering after a drunkeness. She looked down at her torn gown and brushed back her disheveled hair.

"Lord God!" she exclaimed. "Suppose Shadney had come! How did you get into the house?"

He grinned, his hands clasped behind his head. "If you read your society news you'd know the Randolphs are entertaining tonight. If Shad gets here at all it'll be very late." His eyes took on a reflective look. "I'm afraid I didn't make a very good impression on your cook."

"Annette let you in?" Why couldn't it have been Letty? "Annette's bound to tell Shad!"

Breel got up and filled one of Randolph's pipes. "You'll find a way to stop her. I've infinite faith in your resourcefulness."

"Not always. You said I couldn't get Shad."

He raised an eyebrow. "How else could I make certain you'd try? He suited my purposes far better than any other candidate."

Of course. It should have been obvious. She felt a fury at both her own blindness and Breel's deviousness. With it was a masochistic desire to hurt them both and she found herself broaching the very subject she wanted most to avoid.

"Aren't you going to ask about Rosalie?"

His face tightened and he set down the pipe.

"You've a very powerful effect upon a man, Zulu. Here I've been planning this little *viellé* for a long time, and the first question I intended to ask was about Rosalie—and then I leave it for you to bring up. No doubt she and Cousin Norman are happily keeping house at The Acres. I do wonder if she's managed to get rid of Miss Thalia yet."

"Rosalie's dead. It happened right after we heard about your marriage."

"What?" It was the first time she had ever seen Breel shaken. He started at her a moment, then his eyes hardened. "If this is your idea of a joke—"

"Miss Thalia is married to your cousin. Rosalie died when she lost your baby."

For a moment she thought he would throw her across the room, but he pulled himself under control, his hands cutting into her shoulders.

"You knew she was pregnant when you sent me away. You had to know! Why did you do it to her, Zulu? Was that the price of your freedom? Did you hate her so much?"

"You were the one who gave her the baby. You were the one who had the heiress waiting for you."

"And you wanted to be free." He released his grip, but his eyes were still dark with fury. "If I knew for sure—"

He caught up his clothes and slammed out of the house.

Zulu remained in bed long past her usual rising time the next morning. She felt restless and irritable. Angry at herself and at Breel.

He'll be back, she thought. He'll always be back.

She thought back to the night before. Certainly Breel was an accomplished lover, physically he was all a woman could want. But why this restlessness when she should be content? Was it to be always like that, hungry even when sated? Was there always to be this gnawing need inside, this search for what couldn't be found?

As she pulled on her slippers she heard Letty greeting someone at the door. She recognized Yvonne's voice and when Letty poked her head into the room, she nodded.

"You can bring Madame LeSieur in here."

Yvonne came quickly into the bedroom. Her face was strained and there were dark shadows under her eyes.

"I want to apologize for last night. You asked me to help you, but I was powerless. It was as if you were talking from a great distance."

"It didn't matter. I found my way out."

Yvonne's eyes rested on the torn gown where it hung flung over a chair. Barely perceptibly her eyebrow went up the slightest bit. She arose from the seat by the door to leave.

"I just wanted to make certain you were home and safe. I'll not further interrupt your toilette."

After she left, Letty came into the room. As she passed the chair she, too, noticed the torn gown. She grinned as she picked it up.

"Reckon I can mend this today," she said.

At least there would be no trouble from that angle. But Annette—

"Letty, send Annette to me."

Annette's eyes were defiant. She stood in the doorway, wiping her hands on her apron. When Zulu nodded for her to come into the room she entered with a great show of reluctance.

"I had a guest last night." Zulu spoke slowly, watching the black face, wondering how it could show such animation when Shad was around. Certainly it had nothing but grudging obedience where she was concerned.

Annette nodded.

"He was an old friend. It's natural he should call on me, but I'd rather you didn't mention him to M'sieur

Randolph."

Annette remained silent.

Zulu opened her fingers and waited while Annette stared at the stone.

"Do you know what this is?" Zulu asked.

Annette started to draw away, but Zulu extended her hand toward the cook.

"Hold it. Feel the power of it." There was a direct command in her voice.

Reluctantly Annette touched the *loa*. She pulled her hand away as if her fingers had touched a flame.

"*Adie!*" she exclaimed, her eyes wide.

What was it Ferne had said? Zulu searched her memory for the exact words and she repeated them softly.

"Only a *mamaloi* would dare command so powerful a *loa*."

There was fear in Annette's manner, but the dislike was still behind her glance.

"I think," Zulu said, "that you will forget I had a caller."

When Shadney called that night Annette busied herself as usual in the kitchen, but as if by accident she left the door ajar. Her throaty voice carried down the hall to them, punctuated occasionally by the rattle of a pot.

> "Mandé belle, belle femme
> Qui moune té entré la caille là?
> C'est soir m'pas wevis yo
> Minuit tout pres, li so 'ti
> Mandé belle ti femme
> Combien maris li gagnin?"

Shadney regarded Zulu strangely. "Do you understand what she's singing?"

"Only parts of it." Zulu knew she was trembling.

Shadney translated softly:

"Ask the beautiful woman
Who is the man who entered her hut there?
It is dark, I cannot see his face
It is almost midnight, he goes away.
Ask the beautiful little woman
How many husbands has she?"

Zulu couldn't meet his eyes. She smiled and leaned lazily back in her chair.

"I think Annette could show more taste in what she sings," she remarked. "If a man were inclined toward jealousy—" she shrugged.

"You said Yvonne LeSieur called?"

Zulu nodded and went into details of what the quadroon had worn, hardly hearing her own words. Lord God! She could breathe again!

It was through Yvonne that one by one the other women began to accept Zulu. It didn't take her long to discover that her accounts of country life fascinated the city-bred quadroons. She wracked her brain and imagination for stories to tell them, and it gave her a feeling of importance to sit on her divan surrounded by an audience as she related how the field hands lived in quarters back of the house.

Sometimes it happened that Shadney called when the women were visiting. At first they all made quick, polite excuses to leave when he came through the door, but soon he convinced them that he enjoyed sitting back, listening to their conversation.

"You're very fortunate to have a man such as M'sieur Randolph," Yvonne remarked once when they were alone. "He's a fine gentleman—not like M'sieur Luton."

"M'sieur Luton?" So Yvonne knew! It was a wonder

169

everyone didn't know about Breel's visits.

"I live next door to you, Zulu. I am no more blind than M'sieur Luton is discreet."

Zulu sat down heavily. Discreet? Only the night before he had lingered until almost the moment Shadney was expected. And when she asked him to leave he only laughed and flicked ashes on the carpet. It was as if he were inviting trouble, she had thought as she opened all the windows.

"I'd have known there was another man even if I hadn't seen him," Yvonne was saying. "That morning after the meeting your gown was ripped. M'sieur Randolph was not in town that night."

"Does everyone know?"

Yvonne shook her head. "But if you're wise you'll see that M'sieur Luton is a bit more careful."

"It's no one's business." Zulu snapped out the words, but fear was tight in her chest.

"Immorality," Yvonne said softly, "is something the women around here would never understand."

"Immorality! None of them are any better than a harlot. Ask any white lady."

"Sometimes I wonder which is the harlot. The white lady who lives with her husband because her family arranged a loveless marriage—or we who live with that same man because of love."

"Is it love when you take a protector?"

Yvonne nodded. "We can refuse whom we will. I refused three men before I chose M'sieur LeSieur."

"Is he married?"

"No. He has refused arrangements his family tried to make. He's not the oldest son so it isn't so important."

"How do you know he hasn't married by now? France is a long way from New Orleans."

Yvonne's eyes were shadowed. "I never felt he would

marry."

"You're blind. Just like Naida."

"*C'est très possible.*" she admitted. "Sometimes it's easier to be blind."

Zulu moved across the room, her skirts swishing. She ran her fingers over Shadney's pipe rack. "I'll never have to worry. If anything happened to Shad, I'd still have Breel."

"Perhaps we're foolish." Yvonne's voice softened, "but we've a happiness you'll never know."

"Why shouldn't I be happy?" Zulu demanded. "I've everything I could want. Except, maybe, a bigger house."

Despite the realization that in due time Shadney would arrange it for her, the desire for a bigger cottage grew within her until there was seldom a moment when the thought was not in the back of her mind.

In a way it was Yvonne who gave her the idea. Yvonne told her that Ramon had made Naida promise not to read the papers. Every day Zulu searched the society columns for the announcement that must soon be there.

"Before Lent," Yvonne had said, and it was barely before Lent when it appeared. Long paragraphs were devoted to the event and Zulu read each word avidly. When she finally set aside the paper, it was to tell Annette to prepare refreshments. She sent Letty to deliver invitations for coffee, to the closest of her group.

She hadn't expected that Ferne would arrive with Yvonne, but she managed to smile a welcome. After all, she had an announcement to make that should soften even Ferne's suspicions of her.

It was a clear day, warm enough to sit in the courtyard when the sun reached its height. The promise of spring was in the air.

Zulu waited until there was a pause in the conversation.

"I haven't even told M'sieur Randolph yet, but I am *enceinte*!"

Even those who still remembered earlier resentments let down their barriers. From all sides she was offered congratulations and advice.

Ferne instructed her in the things that must be avoided so the baby would be a daughter. For a daughter it must be. Through a daughter a woman could live again when she was old. That way there would still be an excuse to attend the theater and balls.

Naida glanced down at her own baby who was playing on the patio flagstones.

"If your man should leave you will still have a part of him that will never belong to his wife. A part that is yours alone."

Both Ferne and Yvonne turned apprehensive eyes on the quadroon. So they knew. But then, Zulu reflected, probably everyone except Naida knew. Wasn't that why they had been so quick to respond to her news? Grateful for something to relieve the tension?

"Has Ramon said anything yet?" Yvonne asked quietly and abruptly all small talk and gossip was still.

Naida shook her head. "He'll put off the wedding until she tires of waiting." There was a firm confidence in her voice.

"Even if he should marry," Yvonne ventured, "he'll be back. A man gets weary of a woman he must keep on a pedestal."

Naida's eyes flashed. "I tell you he will not marry! *Je suis en sur*!" She took up her baby and moved to the other side of the courtyard where a saffron skinned girl was strumming on a guitar.

Yvonne spoke to Zulu with sudden contempt. "He's a weakling, that one! Last night he slept with his bride while Naida waited on her doorstep. There's not a one of us here that have it in our heart to tell her."

"She'll have to learn sooner or later," Zulu said. "What a fool to let herself get that way over a man!"

"And what kind of a woman are you?" Yvonne asked. "Don't you feel it a sin to carry a baby when you're never known love?"

Zulu laughed. "We always end up talking about sin. You think I should run into the church each day like you do, and cower there in the darkness where I'm not even wanted?"

"We're cut off from the church," Yvonne agreed, "but it doesn't mean we can't go there and pray for understanding."

"And Madame Dédé, she gives you understanding? Have the candles you lit and the *gris-gris* you've bought, brought back your man?"

Yvonne stood up. "You're full of hate and you're not happy unless you are infecting someone else with it! Be careful or your child will be born spitting at the world."

From the other side of the patio Naida watched Yvonne leave. She set her baby down and came back to Zulu.

"Sometimes," she said as she settled onto a bench, "Yvonne makes me feel very impatient."

Zulu planned her words very carefully. "Yvonne was only trying to give you hope. Why do you try to hide it from us, Naida? We've all read about the wedding. And it is true a large house seems far more empty than a small one. M'sieur Shadney will be glad to—"

Naida's soft eyes were large and dark in her pale face. Even her full lips had lost their color. "You would say things like that just to get a house? You would try to frighten me that terrible way?''

"I think you should face what has happened. You can't lie to yourself forever. It was in the paper yesterday—that's why I thought this would be the time to tell you M'sieur Randolph would make arrangements.''

"Yesterday?'' Naida whispered.

"In the Cathedral. There was a big reception afterwards—''

"*Merci*,'' Naida whispered. "*Merci bien*.''

She took up the baby and went out the door.

Zulu selected an orange and dug her nail into it. Wasn't it really a kindness to let Naida know? To stop her from acting the trusting fool? After all this time if she hadn't prepared herself for what had to be, well, then she deserved the shock!

Zulu had finished the orange and was gathering together the rind when Ferne sat down beside her.

"Naida left in such a hurry she forgot her hat,'' Ferne remarked.

Zulu wiped her fingers. Somehow the orange didn't set too well. But of course it was her condition. And that made a larger cottage all the more important.

"Was it something you said to her?''

It was impossible to ignore the suspicion in Ferne's tone and Zulu shrugged. "I told her what none of you had the courage to say. I also said M'sieur Randolph would buy her cottage. A big house only seems more empty—''

"You put it that way?''

"It had to be told—you women were letting her act the fool.''

"But there were other ways of telling her. You know what she's threatened.''

174

"She wouldn't be that stupid?"

"You think not? You with the *loa* whispering in your ear?" Ferne caught up Naida's hat and hurried out of the courtyard.

Zulu looked down at the peelings, still sticky and damp in her hands.

". . .I am tying my *pouin*, it is to kill someone. . . ."

Strange the *kanzo* should have chanted those words to her.

In the corner, under a palm, the girl with the guitar had started to strum a verse of "*Dansez Calinda*" that had become so popular in Congo Square.

"Michié Préval li don main grand bal
Li fé nég paye pou sauté in pe
Dansez Calinda, boudjoum, boudjoum!
Dansez Calinda, boudjoum, boudjoum!"

Ferne came through the courtyard door. There was blood on her hands and on the hem of her skirts.

"Come with me." She spoke softly. Only Zulu had noticed her, the others were singing along with the guitar, their attention on the musician.

Zulu rose and followed. The command in her voice left no room for protest.

As they went through the hall Letty ran to Zulu, her eyes wide, only to be brushed aside by Ferne's arm. Zulu was aware of the slam of the *jalouise* as they stepped out onto the street, but all else was unreal.

The baby was screaming in his cradle when they entered Naida's cottage, but Ferne went on past him without a glance. She opened the kitchen door and stepped aside so Zulu would have an unobstructed view.

"There's Naida," Ferne said. "Thank her for the cottage."

Naida lay on the floor of her neat kitchen. The tiles were bright with the blood that flowed from her severed wrists. Zulu drew back, holding up her skirts.

"It's not good for my baby to see this. . . ." she whispered.

A strange expression drove the fury from Ferne's face. She gripped Zulu's shoulders and forced her to bend over Naida. "Part your lips," she commanded, "Breathe in deeply and maybe her soul will be caught as it passes. Maybe that way you can save your child. One does not die quickly this way, so there is still the chance. . ."

Zulu tried to wrench away, but there was no strength to fight the tight fingers that held her, nor strength to fight the hypnotic chant that repeated words over and over. Strange, foreign words of garbled Santo Domingan French mixed with the old African phrases. There was no fighting the lethargy that dulled will and spirit, not even when the overwhelming tide swept through her entire being until she felt as if she were miles away from the kitchen with its stained tiles. Miles away, but still able to look down on herself as if at the edge of a great pit. A great pit with a still deeper chasm inside, and within that still another and another. And underlying it all a swamp. A rank, lush swamp that waited patiently, as it had always waited.

Through it all was the cry of something very young. Something that rushed past her, whirling and seething and changing form.

The whirling stopped and there was a silence. Even Ferne's chant had ceased. Sharp fingers dug into her arm now, not her shoulders, and a pungant odor set her to choking.

She opened her eyes and pushed aside the salts. She looked up into Breel's face, and over his head, at Ferne.

"Voodoo!" he muttered. "Between voodoo and the fever it's a wonder there's a human left to rot in this place!"

He knelt beside Naida's body, his face dark and angry. "So it's the mistress of my good friend Vauregard. God help the fool!"

He rose to his feet and turned to Ferne. "Get your priest and let him clean up this mess."

Then he took Zulu by the arm. "When I come to see you," he said, "I expect to find you home."

Chapter Twenty-Three

As soon as they were alone, Zulu told him about the baby.

"I suppose," he said, "it would be ridiculous to ask if you know who the father is?"

"You know very well! This wouldn't have happened if you'd left me alone."

He narrowed his eyes. "So you think it's mine?"

"Shad's never had any children, he's told me that a dozen times. You must know that. You seem to know everything else about him."

Breel sat back in Shad's chair and laughed. "You could be right," he admitted. "I'd like to see his face when you tell him! There's nothing like a man of his age who suddenly finds himself potent."

"I'm glad you find it amusing."

Breel regarded her thoughtfully. "What a hell of a combination. You and me. If there's anything to heritage we should have a monster." He went to her and took her face between his hands. He kissed her eyes, mocking. "What are you complaining about? You know you'll have Shad right where you want him."

She pulled away. "Get out," she said. "Get out and let me think."

"About Rosalie? About the baby she and I might have had? Do you ever think about that, Zulu? About how you sent me away?"

"It didn't take much to make you go," she retorted contemptuously.

When Shadney called Zulu was wearing a lavender voile gown that had belonged to Rosalie. It was not her best shade, but she wore nothing to relieve the pallor it cast on her skin. She had settled herself among the divan cushions holding a handkerchief that reeked of smelling salts.

Shadney kissed her lightly, then stood back, a smile on his face.

"It really won't work, *ma belle*. I doubt you've ever been ill a day in your life. Why don't you just come out and tell me what you want? Does your new dress need a clip? Haven't I been taking you to the Balls enough? Or has Ferne refused to accompany you to the theater again?"

Zulu turned her face away. "Those things. They aren't important."

"Oh?" He sat down beside her. "I'm sorry, but that's my repertoire. What have I missed?"

"There's hardly room in this cottage for the two of us . . ." She felt him tense, so she went on more hastily than planned. "When the baby's born where will we put it? And its nurse?"

He caught her hand. "You're certain?" his voice was unsteady with emotion. "You wouldn't joke about such a thing?"

She lowered her lashes. "Think, Shad. You should know."

He got up and stood staring at the fire. When he

turned back to her his eyes were sparkling.

"I'd given up hope of ever seeing my own flesh and blood! At my age to have this happen! It makes me feel young again, just as you always have made me feel young."

He took her into his arms gently, as if he feared to touch her.

"I'll get your bigger house even if I have to build it. And I'll start asking about a likely wet nurse. What else will we need, Zulu? I want to do everything I can."

What else would they need? White blood, maybe. A baby who would never have to face a white man's world and bow its head because generations before it had a black ancestor.

"The baby will only have a sixteenth black blood—but what difference will that make? It might as well be all black."

Shadney looked at her in surprise and she regretted her outburst. She knew better. A white man didn't like those reminders. She should be happy for what she had.

"A sixteenth . . ." he repeated and she realized that this was different. This was his child and that changed everything. His eyes regarded her with an understanding she had never seen in them before. "Don't worry, Zulu, it won't grow up here. When it's old enough I'll send it to France—it's different there. I'll make every provision. Boy or girl it'll never have to face what you've had to face."

Somehow, that night as she lay beside Shad, it was different. She felt at peace with herself.

But at Naida's funeral the strange, lost sensation she'd experienced when Ferne held her over the body, returned. It was a tense ceremony, but Zulu resolutely followed the procession from the church to the cemetery and stood by while the coffin was slipped into a niche in a long brick wall.

It was only then that something of herself began to

creep back. Together she and Yvonne picked their way around the graves, the shells crackling under their feet.

"I understand M'sieur Randolph's agent has already contacted the Vauregard lawyers," Yvonne remarked.

But Zulu had paused to stare back at the long wall of niches that would house a body only until climate and time had reduced it to nothing when it would be replaced by another.

"When it's time for me to die I don't want to be here," she said. "The dead should go back to the earth."

Yvonne shrugged. "The ground's a marsh. A grave would be filled with water before a coffin could be lowered."

Zulu shuddered.

Shadney was waiting at the cottage, but she was too immersed in the thought of death to notice his expression.

"A woman in your condition shouldn't attend a funeral," he told her.

Zulu took off her hat and set it on the table. "When I die I want to lie in good, solid ground with earthy smells. Not one of those things they call ovens—and not in a marsh, either."

Shadney went into the kitchen and she heard him instruct Annette to make coffee. Then he came back and stood behind her.

"My agent is making an offer to buy Naida's cottage."

"I know." For the moment even the cottage was unimportant. "Shad, always when I have a nightmare, there's a swamp. Today Yvonne told me what it would be like to die here. It was like having a nightmare while I was awake."

He turned her to face him. "You wanted this cottage, Zulu. You've kept after me, God knows. Doesn't it mean anything to you now? Is it that things come too easily to you?''

Her eyes widened with fear. ''Why do you say that?''

He shrugged and turned away. For the first time she realized something was wrong. He looked old and she'd never thought of him as looking old before, distinguished, but not old—and tired.

She gave Letty her scarf and then drew an ottoman up to his chair. She sat on it, her head against his knee.

''There's something wrong, Shad. You were so happy when you left last night. But now you're different.''

Shadney pushed her away and went to the window.

''What does Breel Luton mean to you?'' he asked, his back still turned to her.

Zulu felt the color leave her face. She had expected, at the worst, that Ferne had accused her to him of Naida's death. But not this.

''Why do you ask?'' She hoped her voice was steady.

He turned on her, his face hard and white. ''Because I must know. I warned you about other men, Zulu.''

''Who has said anything about Mr. Luton?''

''I was told he brought you back here after you found Naida.''

Zulu tried not to display her relief. She moved to the table and flicked at a bit of dust.

''Was it my fault he was visiting someone and heard my scream? Ferne was with me and she'll tell you I hadn't been with him.'' She turned, her eyes flashing. ''Why my house was full of guests—until they heard about Naida. Would I be entertaining a lover with a patio full of gossiping women?''

Shadney drew a deep breath. He went to her and took her into his arms.

''I've hated that man ever since the night at the theater when I saw you looking down at him.''

''I was admiring his wife's jewels.''

Shadney shook his head. ''Don't lie to me. I saw where your eyes went.''

Lord God, Zulu suddenly thought. What if the baby should look like Breel?

Chapter Twenty-Four

The seasonal rains left the city streets even more sodden than their wont, but they failed to keep the white folks from attending the Mardi Gras Balls. Even Shadney spent less time with Zulu during that week of feverish activity before the solemn fast days fell over New Orleans.

"It's not right," Zulu complained to Yvonne. "There's only a month or so more that I can attend the ball and public places, and so what happens? Shad's too busy escorting his wife to parties to take me anywhere and as soon as this week's over there won't be anything until Easter. By then nothing will fit me and I'll be waddling around like a cow!"

Yvonne shrugged. "Your time will be on you before you even realize it and then you can go everywhere again."

"But I want to go everywhere now!" Zulu stood in front of her mirror and surveyed her small waist critically. "Maybe I'll be left inches bigger and nothing will ever fit again."

"Not unless you eat too much and stretch yourself." Yvonne stood to leave. "Why don't you accompany me tonight to watch the white folks arrive at their great houses for the parties? This is the last day they can dance and I heard there's to be a masquarade at the Lastelle's. It's amusing to watch them parade around in their costumes."

"I don't want to watch others enjoy themselves," Zulu said petulantly. "That's what I've done most my life. I want to be the one having the fun."

"It's always that way when one is with child," Yvonne said tolerantly. "Things seem out of proportion. It's to be expected."

After Yvonne had left, Zulu continued to study her reflection and the rebellious mood was still with her when she sat down to eat the red beans that Annette had insisted must be eaten on Shrove Tuesday.

She could hear the sound of music and drums. It was close enough to be in Congo Square.

"Letty," she said, "Find out what's happening."

When Letty returned it was with sparkling eyes and she did a little dance step as she came through the door, skirts held ankle high.

"It's a parade," she told her mistress, "the biggest parade I ever see. They'se all goin' to parties and makin' a parade on the way."

Maybe Yvonne was right. It might even do her good to go out and watch. She could wear her new red gown—only Ferne and her dressmaker had seen it—and with the domino mask she'd worn the week before who was there to recognize her? Why she might even be able to join in—no one knew who anyone else was. She could be with them right up to the doors of the houses—and who would know what party she was to attend?

She shoved back her plate. "Stop prancing around and lay out my new red gown," she told Letty. She ran her hand over her flat stomach. Just this one last bit of fun—even Shad couldn't blame her!

She arranged a high comb in her hair and over it she draped a black mantilla to hide the tawny masses of her hair. She left the domino in her reticule, not to be donned until she was far from Rampart Street.

Letty poked her head out the door to make certain the street was clear, then she nodded to her mistress.

"Jus' you hav fun, Miss Zulu," she chuckled. "No one know you ain't one of dem!"

Zulu nodded, grateful that Annette was busy in the kitchen. She hurried down the steps and out into the darkness. Several blocks away she put on her mask and went in the direction of the drums, toward the glare of torches.

It was almost like daylight on Royal Street. There was a bedlam of dancing devils, painted Indians, Pierrots and Harlequins. Fine Colonial ladies and Spanish senoritas leaned out of carriages, and many of them danced in the streets with their escorts. The *banquettes* strained under the weight of the crowd and streams of paper floated through the air.

Oh Lord God, there must be a way. Just this once to attend a white people's ball. Just once to be treated like a lady. And what a joke it would be on them!

Her eyes roved over the celebrants, sorting out possibilities. Her attention lingered on a young man who was trying to read a bit of notepaper in the unsteady light. Everything about him indicated a stranger and that he was lost. But he was dressed for an evening out.

She moved into the stream of the crowd until she stood behind him. The note had the Lastelle crest. He crumbled the paper into his pocket and started to cross the street.

That was the wrong direction. He would never find the place that way, but maybe . . .

She ran after him and threw her arms around his neck.

"*Mon oncle!*" she exclaimed.

He carefully removed her arms and turned, the color was high in his cheeks.

"*Vous trompez,*" he said in faltering French.

So she was mistaken, was she? Zulu laughed.

"Oh M'sieur! What an embarrassment! I have lost my uncle somewhere in this madness and he has our invitation to the Lastelle ball. From your back, I thought—"

The stranger swept off his hat and Zulu saw that he was very young. Wavy brown hair was brushed back from a high, smooth forehead, and in the torchlight his face looked sensitive, his mouth almost girlishly soft. Yet he was handsome with regular features and clear hazel eyes.

"May I introduce myself?" he asked. "I'm Renny Langford of Virginia. Madame Lastelle heard I was staying at the St. Charles and she sent me an invitation." He laughed nervously. "My sister attended school with Madeline Lastelle. Maybe I can help you?"

Zulu hesitated. "I would only have to take off my domino, but then everyone would know me and the fun would be spoiled . . . Yet, if my uncle heard . . . After all, M'sieur Langford, *nous ne sommes que des étrangers!*"

"But even strangers, under the circumstances—I can hardly leave you here unescorted."

Zulu pursed her mouth, then her face brightened. "M'sieur you've tempted me! I'll go with you if you promise not to tell anyone who I am."

He laughed. "My Aunt was invited but she's indisposed. I could say you're Aunt Tess."

"Do I look like an Aunt Tess?" she demanded. Had he no tact?

He laughed harder. "Not in the least. Not like my Aunt Tess, anyway."

"Then perhaps we'd better start in the right direction? You'll never arrive at the Lastelle's if you continue this way."

There was no difficulty at the Lastelle house. Even the doorman had abandoned attempts to check the invitations closely. Renny's note sufficed. The Lastelle family had long since been swept away from the entrance and the ball was in full swing. Zulu waltzed around the huge ballroom in Renny's arms, their laughter merging with the sound of gaiety all about them.

How different from the dignified stateliness of the Quadroon Ball! Nor was it like Elmside. Even in the abandonment to the occasion there still was a certain elegance and sophistication.

"Why should this happen the night before I leave?" Renny asked. "Why couldn't I have met you last week?"

"You leave tomorrow?" How providential!

He nodded. "I inherited an interest in a steamboat and I came to dispose of it. But I missed the man I was to see—he left for a visit to France a few days before I got here." He looked at her thoughtfully. "He'll be back in the Fall, late August or September, and I've made arrangements to be here then. Isn't there someway I can arrange for an introduction at that time? Someway we can meet?"

Zulu smiled. "Who knows?"

The music stopped and he led her to the buffet. The predominant aroma of steaming shellfish gave her a queasy turn that she firmly reminded herself must be ignored. What a time to be reminded of her condition!

"I'll fix you a plate . . ." Renny was saying. "Is . . . something wrong?"

Zulu didn't dare reply. Standing at the punch table was Shadney Randolph, filling two glasses. His attention was centered on the ladle and Zulu caught Renny's arm, pulling him away.

"My uncle!" she whispered. "He mustn't see me with you."

Renny glanced back curiously. "Your uncle? Shadney Randolph?"

Out of all New Orleans did he have to know Shadney? "You're a friend?" she asked, grateful for the domino she wore.

"Not really. I thought he might take the boat off my hands. It was three days before I could get an appointment with him."

"I've got to leave." She was pulling him urgently toward the doorway. "He'll be furious if he finds I took up with a man I met in the streets."

"But won't he be relieved to see you arrived safely?"

"No. He would have expected me to return to our house. It wasn't far from where we were separated."

"At least you'll let me see you safely home?"

"I'll be safe. They're still dancing and parading. I know my way and it would be worse if a strange man brought me home."

"But to lose you like this! When I come back how will I find you?"

Zulu hesitated. By then she'd have had the baby. What harm was there in taking a small chance? It was so exhilarating to be treated as a white lady. Maybe they could meet secretly and he need never know . . .

"My Letty has a friend who works at the coffee docks. A big, black fellow they call Trojan. Maybe, if you left word with him—" She smiled and hurried out the door.

She glanced back just as she came to the great iron gates and he was still standing on the steps.

Outside, in the streets, she wondered if perhaps she shouldn't have let him walk a little of the way with her. The crowd no longer consisted of wealthy Creoles on their way to parties, now it had deteriorated into drunken rivermen and the coarser element. She tried to move inconspicuously down the darkening banquette when a man caught her by the waist and tried to pull her to the middle of the street where some were still dancing to discordant music.

She struggled to pull away, but he only laughed. For a second she thought he would pick her up and carry her to the dancers, but someone pushed in between them.

"The lady doesn't want to dance," a soft voice said.

and Zulu felt the drunk's grip loosen.

"Don' wanna make trouble," he muttered. "Jus wanna have fun . . ."

He moved back and a woman left the dancers, her hair disheveled and her mask awry. She caught him and pulled him out into the street.

"I guess that takes care of that," the stranger chuckled. It was a rich, deep sound that held no rancour.

Zulu pushed the mantilla out of her eyes and looked up at him. His accent had been cultured, almost northern in its lack of a drawl and she expected to see a white man. His skin was no darker than that of some of the quadroons she knew, and his features were, if anything, finer cut than her own, still she knew almost instantly that he was not white. He was magnificently built, broad of shoulder, flat of stomach and lean of hip. One sensed his strength, but it was more than a strength of just muscle and sinew.

"Where do you live?" he asked. "I'll see you home."

"There's no need. I can find my way."

"All the same I'll go with you." He indicated that she precede him, and she knew it would be useless to argue.

When they reached the corner of Rampart Street she was aware of his quick scrutiny, but he didn't speak until she had paused in front of her door.

"You live here?"

She nodded and lowered her domino. "You're not from New Orleans. What were you doing outside the Lastelle house?"

"My master was in there," he replied simply. "I was given the night, but with the cutthroats and drunks out I didn't want him in the streets alone."

Zulu looked at the rough, workman's clothes he wore. She would have thought him a free negro from the docks had it not been for his voice. There were many of them, mulattos, metzos and quadroons who had never known slavery.

He touched his plaid shirt. "I borrowed these from a porter," he explained, "when I set out to see the city. Mostly I wanted to see the cypress swamps."

"You were running away?" Zulu asked, torn between alarm and admiration.

He laughed. "What good could I do, hiding out in the swamps? It's not when we run and hide that the white man should fear us. It's when we stay and work."

"Running back and forth like a puppy for your master? Helping him into his coat and pulling off his muddy boots?" Zulu spat. All the memory of Rosalie's tyranny stood fresh in her mind.

"No. Teaching the children in the quarters to read. Teaching their pa to think. Teaching their women that before God they're as much woman as the mistress in the big house."

"You talk that way and you'll do better to stay in the swamps," Zulu warned. "You could be hung."

"So could you for passing yourself as white." There was no malice in his tone. He spoke simply, as if this very thing should better enable her to understand. "I don't talk that way in front of the folks at the house. I don't even talk that way to the men I've helped go north."

"Then why talk this way to me?"

He spread his hands. "Maybe because it wouldn't matter enough for you to make me trouble. And maybe because I see something in you we need. Like strength and intelligence." He shrugged. "But I can also see that causes aren't a thing to concern you."

"Would you expect they should?"

He looked at the cottage looming higher than any of the others on the quiet street.

"No, I suppose not." He started to leave, but paused. "My name's Jules," he said, and then continued on his way.

A warning sounded deep in her mind. Somewhere, somehow, there was an echo. As if words has been said that she'd heard before.

She pushed away the uneasiness. Being pregnant certainly did fill a woman with strange fancies . . .

Chapter Twenty-Five

If Rosalie had shown as soon there never would have been a question of her riding that mare, Zulu thought in disgust. She glared at the armoire stuffed with gowns she doubted she'd ever again fit. Only five months and already she was in a *blouse volante* and had been for weeks. Shad acted as if it were a modern miracle, but Breel on visits that grew more and more infrequent, found it quite humorous.

"I should think you'd have some feeling about the matter," she told him.

"Those kind of feelings are kept quite busy elsewhere at the moment," he replied. "I think you chose a very inconvenient time to start breeding."

"Why should a woman have to look like this and a man go free?"

"You should be damned thankful. How would you explain it if Shadney kept his waistline and I started to waddle?"

"Lord God, but you're revolting!" She glanced down at the dress that fell loosely from her breasts. "I'll be glad when this is over!"

Breel picked up his walking stick. "So will I," he assured her fervently.

It wasn't just the clumsiness of her figure that made the months of her confinement so unbearable. It was the boredom. To ride in a carriage without a white person was not permitted, so attending the theater was out of the question. Even leading Annette to the market was frowned upon. Very few of her neighbors accepted her invitations anymore. Their refusals were always polite and almost convincing, but the fact remained that they were refusals and had been ever since she'd moved into Naida's house. She was certain that Ferne had kept her silence. Gossip was beneath Ferne's dignity. Yet she may as well be the carrier of some loathsome disease.

By her eighth month she was so starved for company other than Shad or Yvonne, that she almost welcomed the sound of a crashing chair after midnight in her sitting room. She climbed out of her bed and lit a candle.

It's Breel and he's drunk, she told herself. Probably he had been to a party and maybe at least he could enliven her mood with a bit of gossip or the latest scandal. All Shad and Yvonne ever talked about was the baby.

She didn't bother to throw on a robe, but carried the candle into the outer room, still in a night dress.

She could see the figure slumped in Shad's chair as she lit the table lamp.

"Everyone up and down the street must have heard you stumbling in. Haven't you the decency to go home when you're in that condition?"

"I am home," a man's voice said, and Zulu gripped the table for support as she stared into Ramon Vauregard's ravaged face. His eyes seemed huge and unnaturally bright and there was an untidy growth of beard around his mouth and on his jaw.

"I thought you were still abroad. . . ." she whispered.

"We've been back a week." His voice was dull. "Everyone has been very thoughtful—no word about this. It seems it was very important that I enjoy my honeymoon. My lawyers disposed of this house, they

191

even made arrangements for my son." He laughed. "I was supposed to be grateful when they told me."

She was staring at the long duelling pistol he held loosely on his knee.

"Why did you come here?" She tried to keep her voice steady.

"I wanted to see if you slept. I thought you might lie awake at night and think about Naida with her wrists cut."

"You're the one who should think about that."

"Do you imagine I could forget? Or forget the person who told her?" He glared at Zulu. "There was a letter, you know. But you made certain to tell her before it was delivered."

"And you think a letter would have made a difference?"

"Yes. I told her how I had no choice. How only she and our son mattered. I had to go on a wedding trip—it was a gift from my wife's father. But I told her things would be as they always had been when I got back. That was all Naida asked. It would have been all right if she'd lived long enough to get my letter."

Zulu couldn't bring herself to meet the torment in his eyes. He was wrong, of course, she assured herself. They all were wrong when they blamed her. How could she live with her own guilt if she thought otherwise?

"You blame me because you didn't send the letter soon enough? If I hadn't told her someone else would have."

"Would they?" he laughed unpleasantly. "Who else wanted this house? Oh, I know about that! I've heard stories."

"You're drunk and out of your mind. The only thing I did was ask Shadney to buy this house after Naida was gone. People will make up stories about anything."

"You explain that to Naida!" he exclaimed and held up his duelling pistol in an unsteady hand.

Zulu shrieked and yanked the lace scarf out from

under the lamp. The pistol exploded as the lamp shattered to the floor, flames darting up from the rug.

Letty ran into the room and beat at the fire with a pillow from the divan, but Zulu was unable to move as she faced Ramon, waiting for another shot.

Letty had the fire out and she lit another lamp. Ramon was staring at the hole in the wall, his face white and sober. Suddenly he threw down the pistol.

"I can't kill you," he said, shaken. "I can't even kill myself."

He stood there for a moment, swaying slightly. "You've got the house you wanted. I wonder how much happiness you can have in it."

He strode out of the room and a moment later she heard the front door slam after him.

It was easier to explain the damaged rug and furniture than she had thought. Shadney had only concern for her when he visited the next day.

"He was drunk and when he saw me instead of Naida—" she improvised, but Shadney hushed her. "In your condition it's better not to think about those things. As for Vauregard—he's been drunk ever since he returned. He's not even worth calling out."

Zulu nodded, thankful she'd had the foresight to cover the bullet hole with a picture. Thankful, also, that it was Saturday and Shadney would leave early. The encounter with Ramon had left her shaken and unwell, but she knew better than to tell Shad. He would have insisted on lingering and she felt a need to rest and be alone.

It was also a consolation to know the next day would be hers, and there was no reason she couldn't spend it in bed. Shad never called on Sundays. Once she'd mentioned this to Yvonne whose Creole attuned mind had a logical explanation.

"But of course. I have heard he always accompanies Madame to the Cathedral on Sundays when they are in town, and to Church when they are at their place in the

193

Bayou. Would you expect him to come to you after going to church?''

"Lord God, what hypocrisy!" Zulu had exclaimed.

But Yvonne had only shaken her head. "You don't understand. It is the propriety."

Whatever the propriety, it never bothered Breel, and until the last few weeks he usually availed himself of Shadney's Sunday custom.

She looked at her bulging figure with distaste after Shadney left. Any man was in his right mind to stay away. Or, as was probably Breel's case, find somebody else for the next month.

She called Letty to help her into her nightclothes.

"I'm going to stay in bed tomorrow," she announced.

"Annette say the baby gittin' mighty low, Miz Zulu," Letty approved.

"It's got at least three weeks," Zulu reminded her, but as she moved to climb into bed, her increasing discomfort suddenly became a sharp pain.

Shad had arranged for a midwife to come and stay with her in a week. It had to wait until then! She couldn't possibly go into labor now.

She held still, afraid to move, aware of Letty's anxious eyes watching. Then there was a warm gush.

"De water!" Letty screamed. "Oh Lawd, you's ready to birth!"

The pain passed and Zulu pushed Letty away.

"This can happen any time," she said. "Quit your whimpering and get me dry clothes!"

But when she was finally lying in bed, fairly comfortable, the pain came again. A violent, tearing thing, moving and surging inside her abdomen.

"False labor," she told herself firmly when it had passed.

"Miz Zulu, you jus lay there and I run git Eulalie."

"No! You stay where you are."

But the next time the pain hit her there was no hiding

it. She screamed.

"I git Annette," Letty was almost hysterical, "Den I run fer Eulalie."

"Not Annette!" Anyone but Annette.

Letty nodded. They shared a mutual distrust of the Santo Domingan.

"I git Eulalie right away, Miz Zulu."

This time Zulu did not dispute the need, gripped again by the pain of the surging life within. She dug her nails into the mattress. If the first pains could hurt like this, what would the birthing be?

It seemed hours passed before Letty returned, followed by Yvonne.

"Letty came for me," Yvonne explained. "Eulalie's not at her house."

Zulu looked at Letty in panic. "You must know what to do. You've seen babies born."

Letty shook her head. "Miz Zulu, please don' ask me. I neber see a birthin'. I afraid I hurt you bad."

Zulu looked at Yvonne and the octoroon paled. "I'll do what I can," she said, "but I can only guess. Can't I call Annette?"

Zulu pulled herself up on an arm. "I won't have Annette near me. Send her to Eulalie's house. She can wait for her to come home. I won't have it until then."

But with the next pain a thousand times worse and more weakening than the last, she realized she might not have a choice.

"There's that Dr. Antone on Royal Street," Yvonne ventured weakly.

"Shad'd have a fit if a man touched me," Zulu said. Things were bad enough!

Yvonne stayed with her through the night and by morning the pains were constant, twisting and ripping. I'm going to die! Zulu thought. I know I'm going to die! The room grew dark and light again and the blinds danced in front of her eyes. She gripped the bed linen and heard it tear under her nails as she thrashed her body against the pushing and pulling that seemed to be rending her apart.

It was past noon when through the haze she thought she heard Breel's voice. He sounded angry.

"God Almighty, is Eulalie the only midwife in New Orleans? Use your head, Madame. Go ask one of the women around here who has a child. She'll know where you can find someone!"

Why hadn't they thought of that? Zulu focussed her eyes on him, but she could only see the top of his head as he bent over her.

"God Almighty!" he muttered again and rolled up his sleeves. "Why the hell did you have to wait for me to get here?"

She didn't remember much after that. There was a strange woman's face that appeared from somewhere, and it was connected with the hand that gave her a cord to grip.

"Pull!" a voice told her "Push down!"

She screamed with a new pain that made all the others seem inconsequential. The cord in her hand snapped, and there was a sudden relief. She lay back, panting and sore as the haze cleared. Faces once again became clear.

It's over, she thought, and I'm still alive. She closed her eyes and fell into an exhausted sleep.

When she awakened, Breel was sitting beside her, filling the room with smoke from one of Shad's pipes. His sleeves were unrolled but he still had his coat off and there was a blood stain on his shirt.

"You had a girl," he said. He frowned thoughtfully. "You know, Zulu, somehow as I looked at her I found myself thinking about Rosalie."

"She'd be half sister to Rosalie's baby." Zulu couldn't keep the triumph out of her voice.

Breel set aside the pipe and she was aware of his eyes searching into her own.

"How you must have hated her," he said. "I can almost feel sorry for Ramon Vauregard. When I think—"

Zulu turned her head. "Go away. Can't you see I'm sick?"

Letty rushed in on them. "Mr. Shad's at the door!" she gasped.

On Sunday? Lord God, Breel had finally done it!

Breel put away the pipe and moved indolently across the room. When Shadney came through the door he was putting on his coat.

Randolph made a sudden, sharp sound, then he stood still, his face an unhealthy, grayish shade.

"I couldn't put Vauregard out of mind," he said. "I hear he's almost insane. I stopped by to see about changing the locks. I hardly expected—"

Breel carefully adjusted his cravat, and his white teeth flashed engagingly.

"Permit me to offer congratulations, Randolph. It's a daughter."

"Sir?" Shadney appeared in a stupor.

"Fortunately," Breel continued, "I was passing on my way to visit—er a friend when I heard the commotion. The midwife you engaged was away and they didn't know what to do."

"And you?" Shadney was beginning to regain his composure, but there was a dangerous edge to his voice.

Breel shrugged. "I've often assisted with my best mares. I felt qualified to offer some advice."

"Where's Annette?" Shadney demanded of Zulu. "Why wasn't she here to help?"

"I sent her to wait for Eulalie." In her weakness it was easy to permit the tears to flood her eyes. "Please, Shad, I had a terrible time."

Yvonne appeared in the doorway. "M'sieur Randolph," she said, "Madame Randolph would have perished but for M'sieur Luton."

The grimness left Shadney's tight lips. "You were here, Yvonne?" There was something pathetic in his eagerness for reassurance, and Zulu found herself wondering whether Yvonne's lie had not been for Shadney rather than to spare Breel and herself.

"But of course. I was frightened. I cannot stand the sight of blood and poor Letty was frantic. M'sieur got us a midwife, but even she needed help."

Randolph eased himself into a chair, his hand was still at his chest, as if he found it hard to breathe. "There was a midwife?"

Yvonne nodded. "She had no time for a meal so Letty has her eating out in the kitchen now."

"You haven't even asked to see our daughter," Zulu said petulantly. "And I almost died having her."

She was aware of Breel's odd, amused glance, then she realized Shad wasn't the only one who hadn't asked to see the baby. She examined her own feelings curiously. She only felt sore and unburdened. Where was this sudden gush of maternal love everyone talked about?

Shadney's expression softened and he followed Yvonne to the cradle that had been waiting in the corner.

"She's beautiful!" he said in an awed voice. "The first really beautiful baby I've ever seen."

"They're all like monkeys at that age," Zulu said from the bed.

He looked at her, astonished. "How can you say that? Look at those perfect fingers. Her hand's like a tiny, ivory fan." He chuckled. "That's what we'll call her. Fannette."

He turned to face Breel, "I apologize. I realize I should be grateful to you."

The mocking smile was still on Breel's lips.

"You've no idea." He bowed and left.

"Could I hold her?" Shadney asked Yvonne, and the octoroon smiled as she lay the blanket wrapped bundle into his arms. Then she went out of the room, leaving the three of them alone.

Shadney carried the baby to the bed and pulled away

the covers so she could see the tiny, perfect face.

"Why she is beautiful!" she gasped, astonished. She reached out an experimental finger and touched the soft, ivory white cheek.

"I'll visit my attorneys tomorrow and increase your legacy," Shad told her. "At the same time I'll set up a separate fund for Fannette. She'll never have to worry."

Zulu smiled. Now that the worst of the pain was over she could see it had all been worth while. Now there was nothing that could sever the hold she had on Shadney.

Shadney gently placed the baby back in her cradle and disappeared out into the sitting room. He returned with a bottle and glasses.

"Champagne. One of the better vintages. I've had it set by."

When he finally left in the late evening it was the only time Zulu had ever seen him the worse for liquor. He kept starting out the door only to return to be assured the baby had no immediate needs. Finally, with great dignity he strode down the banquette toward Orleans Street and Zulu could hear him whistling as he passed her window.

The next morning one of the Randolph coachmen called with a note. Letty brought it to Zulu who lay in bed visiting with Yvonne. She glanced at the flowing writing, then broke the seal.

"Shad's ill," she told Yvonne after scanning the note. "I guess he had too much to drink last night."

"He looked very unwell when he saw M'sieur Luton."

"He was fine later. He drank a bottle of champagne to the baby."

Yvonne nodded her approval.

Zulu had Letty bring her a quill and some paper and she propped herself up to write. Then she lay back and read her reply aloud.

"Shad, beloved:

199

We haven't heard from Eulalie yet and I know you arranged for a wet nurse through her. We must have one at once. My darling, you know how I've looked forward to nursing our baby, but I'm afraid it's not to be. You must find a wet nurse at once.

I can't bear to think of you ill. Do hurry and get well!

My love,
Your Zulu"

"You can't nurse her?" Yvonne's eyes filled with sympathy. "*Quel dommage!*"

Zulu shrugged. "I could nurse a whole litter. But why should I go around with my breasts bound and swollen? I'm no cow."

"I'll never understand you," Yvonne murmured.

"How many of the white ladies nurse their babies?"

"But that's different. They lack our feeling for children."

"If a white lady's too fine to suckle her child, why should I be any coarser? I can be delicate, too. Besides, once my milk dries up maybe I can get into my gowns again."

The baby had begun to cry and Yvonne brought her to Zulu to be fed. "You have so much to be thankful for—why is it you can't find joy?"

"There'd have been a wet nurse waiting if I'd been Shad's wife."

"But there was. It wasn't M'sieur Randolph's fault you were so early." Yvonne smiled down at the suckling baby. "So happy a mite! She'll not be fighting the world, that one."

Zulu glanced at her child with curiosity. Was that why she didn't really feel as if it belonged to her?

Chapter Twenty-Six

Zulu was pleased by her reflection in the mirror. Nobody'd guess I'd given birth only three weeks ago, she told herself. In fact there was hardly a time when she could remember looking better. Not even a stretch mark!

Letty burst into the room, excitement in her eyes.

"Miz Zulu," she whispered, "Der's a quality lady to see you. She come in a cah'age!"

A white woman? Zulu looked out the window and saw a landau drawn up by the gate.

"Tell her I'll be out directly." She turned back to the mirror and brushed her tawny hair. She bound her curls with a green ribbon that matched the robe she wore, and paused again to study her reflection. Her waist would soon be as slim as ever, she decided, and even if her breasts remained a bit fuller it would only add to the voluptuousness of her curves. She put a touch of color high on her cheekbones and lifted her chin.

This was her house. No white lady could lord it over her here. Still, some of the old fear swept over her as she went into the sitting room.

The woman stood with her back to the doorway. She was tall and slender and her wide skirted black taffeta dress was trimmed with ivory lace. A black lace scarf concealed her hair and one small, glove encased hand rested on the lamp table.

Zulu resisted the impulse to lower her eyes and she forced authority into her voice.

"You wished to see me?"

The woman turned. The straight, slim back had led Zulu to believe she would be youthful, but she saw now that her visitor was past middle age. Her luxuriant hair was silver white, but her pale skin was almost without a wrinkle. She had proud, dark eyes and there was the suggestion of an arch to her aristocratic nose.

Zulu drew herself up under the penetrating scrutiny of the other woman. Maybe she couldn't sit in her own chair without the white lady's permission, but there was no law that forbade her to meet the other's direct gaze.

The visitor spoke, then. Zulu had addressed her in English, but the reply was in a soft, melodious French.

"Yes," she said. "It was necessary I see you. You are Zulu?"

Zulu nodded.

"You're very beautiful. Even more beautiful than I had expected."

"Madame has the advantage. I do not seem to recall—"

A shadow passed over the woman's sensitive face. Then it was gone.

"I am sorry to intrude. But I had to talk to you about my husband. I am Madame Randolph."

"This is an honor I hardly expected." Zulu hoped her voice sounded detached, but she clenched her hands into fists to keep them from trembling.

Madame Randolph appeared faintly embarrassed. "Please understand that I am not a jealous wife. I understand about these things and I never would have come for myself. It's for my husband."

Zulu narrowed her eyes. "I'd find it difficult to believe Shad sent you. I've every reason to know he's satisfied."

"My husband is neither young nor well. His heart is not as sound as it should be and this last year it has become worse. His physician is concerned. He cannot continue to live this way."

Shad had never told her his health wasn't good! Yet, there had been times . . . the tiredness . . . that greyish pallor. Still, there was no reason to let his wife know

202

she'd been ignorant. Zulu shrugged.

"He's happy. I know how to keep a man happy. Would you take that from him?"

Madame Randolph was obviously having difficulty controlling her distress. She moved restlessly to the mantel and touched an ivory book marker Shad had left there.

"I'm willing to pay you generously to leave New Orleans."

Lord God, the woman was all but begging! Momentarily a dizzing sense of power dulled her mind like a drunkeness.

"How generously?" Let the mouse savor a chance of freedom. Let Madame Randolph hope!

". . . . *You'd never believe it, but I had Pa get me your papers. Then I thought about it . . . .*"

Madame Randolph opened her reticule, her fingers trembling.

"I didn't say I would. I just asked how generously."

Their gaze met and locked. The long golden eyes with their mocking light, and the dark ones, still proud for all the beseeching.

"I will give you far more than you'll need to be comfortable for the rest of your life. All I ask is that you leave the city."

"Shad has already provided for me. Money means nothing."

Madame Randolph's lips thinned in a useless attempt to control her anger. "You enjoy this! Don't you have any feelings?"

"Maybe if someone had asked that a long time ago it would be different now. Yes, I am enjoying this."

Then why was she trembling?

"I see." Madame Randolph's voice was soft. "You are very nearly white, *n'est ce pas?* Eight parts or more, I think. Perhaps in your place I might feel a bitterness also. But is it worth it? Do you want blood on your hands?"

Zulu looked at her hands and laughed. First Breel holding Rosalie's ghost to batter at her conscience and now this woman blaming her because Shad had too much champagne a few weeks before! Would they never quit blaming her?

In the nursery Fannette cried for her feeding and there was the soft voice of the woman Shad had bought to tend his daughter. Madame Randolph looked toward the sound and then back at Zulu.

"That isn't—? It can't be—?"

For the first time in months Zulu was aware of the *loa* stone against her breast. Aware of the power it brought.

"Letty," she said, "Fetch Fannette and her nurse." She smiled at her guest. "You would like to see Shad's daughter?"

Madame Randolph put her lace handkerchief to her lips. For a second Zulu thought she was going to faint, but when the nurse entered the room, she swept over to them and stared down at the child.

When she turned away she seemed to have suddenly aged. She sank into a chair, her hands over her face. Zulu motioned for Letty and the nurse to leave.

"I'm the one who was barren. Then it was my fault . . ." She looked up, seeming to regain some of her dignity. She went to the nursery door and watched the baby feeding, then she turned back to Zulu.

"If you will let me raise her there is so much I can offer. I'd school her in France. I'd even arrange for a marriage there when she's of the right age. She has so little black blood no one need know—and in Europe it wouldn't even be of consequence."

"Do you think I'm a complete fool?"

"Is a mother a fool to give her child a chance in life?"

"As if you're thinking of Fannette! You know as well as I what a hold she will always be on Shad. Bear your own children if you must have them, but Fannette belongs to me."

"You know that's impossible. But still I'm more of a

mother than you in my heart. Doesn't the child's happiness matter at all?"

"I've been cheated by white folks before. I'll not be cheated again."

"The worst tragedy," Madame Randolph said, "is when one cheats oneself."

When Breel stopped by, Zulu told him of the encounter, but he was not amused.

"You know," he told her, "it would have been for the best."

"Why? Shad's already said he'd have her educated in France and arrange for her. What more could his wife do for her?"

"She could give her a name." He pulled Zulu down into his lap. "Not that such a detail would ever worry you."

"You just don't understand how a mother feels. . . ."

"Neither do you, my love. As far as I can figure, there's just one thing you do understand!"

While she waited for Shadney to call that evening, Zulu pondered the possibilities of the situation. Surely there was some way she could use the encounter with his wife to her advantage. But how best to assure herself of his sympathy?

It was the humiliation, she finally decided. Surely he couldn't help but realize how humiliating it had been!

When he finally arrived she greeted him with a touch of coldness. After he had kissed her, she turned to rearrange some flowers instead of following him into the nursery. She waited until he returned and put his arms around her shoulders.

"Aren't you feeling well?" His voice was concerned.

"I feel well enough. It's not that."

"You've been shut in too much lately," he decided. "I'll arrange with Ferne for her to accompany you to the theater. And maybe by another week you will be up to a waltz?"

Zulu pulled herself free. "Do you think that settles everything? Am I like Fannette? When she cries we give her a sugar tit and she's happy. Why should it matter that I have been humiliated? A play or the ball and I'll forget it. No, Shad, it's not so easy."

He pulled her down onto the stool beside her chair and took her hands into his own.

"Now tell me what's upset you."

Zulu looked down. "Hasn't she told you?"

Shadney remained silent. Waiting.

Zulu yanked her hands free and paced across the floor. No longer was there the need to assume anger. Indignation swelled up inside her and sharpened her voice.

"Your wife was here. She tried to pay me to leave. Lord God, I might as well have been some creature from Gallatin Street!"

"My God!" Deep trouble lines creased the corners of Shadney's mouth. His hand was unsteady as he poured himself a drink. "I had hoped she'd never know. I thought I was being careful."

"Don't you think a woman would know? After all, Shad, you've stayed through the night more than once. How could she help but know?"

He nodded. "Of course. But she's always so busy I didn't think she'd notice—and I used to spend a lot of time at the club. Her bedroom's down the hall from mine."

"She wanted to take Fannette."

Shadney dropped his glass and clutched at the side of his chair. "Good God!" he exclaimed, suddenly angry, "Wasn't she spared anything?"

Zulu stared at him. She'd expected his concern would be for her. This was not her doting protector. This was a man defending his wife against an intruder. It gave her a bereft feeling, with it was the realization that the security she had thought hers was no more than a gossamer thing.

Yet, she should have known. She should have remembered the way he had looked back at the Orleans Cathedral. Remembered the occasional shadow that crossed his face unexpectedly when there was no reason for a shadow.

"Maybe I should have accepted. I refused because I thought you loved me."

"I do love you, Zulu. I don't think I could have endured it if you had left. But I didn't want her hurt. My God, don't you realize there's more than one way to love?"

Zulu turned her head away. "I only know I've been insulted and all you can think of is her."

"I'm sorry. More sorry than you realize." He pulled a jeweler's box from a vest pocket and smiled at her, though his face was still strained and his eyes sober. "I was going to give you this after dinner," he told her.

"A sugar tit?" she asked bitterly.

Shadney regarded her steadily for a minute. Then he put the box back into his pocket. Zulu caught his arm.

"I didn't mean that." Her voice was muffled. She tore open the wrappings and undid the catch. An emerald brooch set in heavy gold glittered against the satin lined box.

"I bought that for the mother of my daughter. The most perfect stone I could find."

Zulu went into his arms, her cheek resting against his chest. "I'm sorry," she whispered. "I didn't mean anything I said."

He stroked her hair. "You did mean it. Every word of it. And perhaps you were right—just as she was right. But I can't let you go, *ma belle*, Not now or ever."

A mosquito buzzed near her ear and she jerked her head.

"Annette's left the lattice open again in the kitchen," she said impatiently. "I keep after her about that." She pulled free. "I'll have to speak to her."

Shadney went back to his chair. He picked up a pipe

and turned it over in his hand.

"Don't blame them on her. August is always a bad month for mosquitos."

August? Zulu paused, her hand on the kitchen door. August. Wasn't that when Renny Langford expected to be back in the city?

Lord God, there was trouble enough. She'd have to forget about that.

Chapter Twenty-Seven

The boom of cannon fire awakened Zulu the next morning, and she ran to the window, throwing it open. Outside the air was deadly still and heavy with the acrid smell of burning tar. She quickly closed the window against the choking miasma that enveloped everything.

Lord God, she thought, has New Orleans been attacked and they're burning it?

Letty came into the room and helped her pull the curtains.

"Ain't nothin' out dere fit to see," she said.

"What's happening?" Zulu demanded. "Are we at war?" Thoughts of the rebellion of the Santo Domingo slaves flashed through her mind. Where would she be in such a case? Would the little black blood in her veins save her?

Letty shook her head. "De way I hears it we'd be better if we was in a fight." The cannon blasted again, shaking the house. "Dat and de smoke is to clean de air and drive out de fever."

"Clean the air?" Zulu repeated, choking. "Between

the smoke from the cannons and the tar it's all a person can do to draw a breath!''

"Annette say dat's what dey always do—de big men of de city gits de cannons and tar put out soon as dere's sickness. Some year, way back, she say, it drive out de plague and de fever.''

"That's not all it should drive out,'' Zulu muttered.

Toward evening the cannons were fired with greater frequency, and the smoke from the burning tar made the still air a yellowish, unreal color. Even the courtyard offered no escape, it held the stifling atmosphere in its hollow, both greenery and flowers took on a poisonous, eerie hue.

Zulu paced restlessly through the cottage. Shad was still ill, a note he'd sent the day before warned her it might be a week before his doctor permitted him to leave his bed. Ferne had refused her request to chaperon her to the theater, and then Letty added the last straw.

"Annette say she too sick to cook. She say I gotta cook and I ain't neber even boil water 'cept I burn de pot—''

Zulu started toward the kitchen to put an end to the nonsense, when Breel walked through the doorway.

Zulu ran to him. "I've never been so happy to see anyone!'' she exclaimed. "Shad's still sick and Annette's in the kitchen wailing about a bellyache. I'm going to put on my new dress and you're going to take me to dinner!''

"This is a surprise,'' he said, setting down his hat and loosening his coat. "I'd planned a cozy evening with you.''

"I'm going to get out of this house if it kills me!''

"And it just might. Don't you realize folks are dying all over the town? Hasn't anyone told you what that out there means? And where could we go without Randolph hearing of it?''

"You'd know a place. I'll go out of my mind if I'm shut in here another minute.''

"Come, Zulu," Breel chided, his eyes mocking her, "have I lost my manly appeal? I don't come here to take you out."

Neither had seen Shad enter the room, but they both turned at the sound of his voice.

"And just what do you come here for if I may ask?"

Zulu had never heard him use that tone of voice before. It was as if she were listening to a stranger.

Not even by a flicker did Breel's face betray discomfort. "Now that," he said, "is a well put question." He stood and extended his hand. "Glad to see you better, Randolph."

Had the man no nerves? Couldn't he read danger in the very set of Shad's mouth?

"I asked a question."

"I could say I stopped to see the child I helped into the world." The two edged meaning didn't escape Shadney, and Zulu bit her lip in dismay, as she saw him stiffen.

"No doubt you've seen her by this time. May I suggest you leave?"

"It's your privilege." Breel straightened his cravat and picked up his walking stick. He bowed to Zulu, nodded at Shadney and started toward the door.

"A friend will call on you this evening. Perhaps by then you will have selected your second to make the arrangements."

Breel turned abruptly, and Zulu realized it was one of the few times she'd ever seen him taken off guard.

"Surely, Randolph, you don't mean the Oaks? Not over her?"

"The Oaks or St. Anthony's Gardens. It's your choice."

"God Almighty, man, I didn't seduce her any more than a hound seduces a bitch in heat!"

Shad's face drained of what little color it still had. He snatched off a glove and whipped it across Breel's face. For a second Zulu thought Breel would leap at him, but

210

he held himself in restraint, his fist still drawn back, his eyes black and dangerous.

"I presume you'll fight over that?" Shadney's voice was even.

"Yes," Breel said. "I'll fight over that. And I'll kill you." He went out the door, slamming it behind him.

Zulu stared at the door, afraid to face Shadney. Finally his voice came to her, barely more than a whisper.

"Come here, *ma belle*."

She turned, defiant, ready to disclaim Breel's implications, but she found him bent over in a chair, his hand to his chest, his breath harsh and uneven. She knelt beside him and loosened his clothing. Finally he leaned back, some of his color returning.

"Shad," she begged, "you don't believe him? Tell me you don't believe what he said!"

He shook his head, but his eyes did not condemn her. "I think I knew from the first that you couldn't stay away from him. I tried to blind myself, but all of the time I knew."

"Shad! You must believe me! I don't love him."

"I know you don't." He lifted her chin and looked down at her. "Strange, I thought it would be different, but I don't feel violence. I'm just tired—and sorry for you." He paused, his eyes gentle as they searched her face. "You've given me happiness, that's more than I've given you. Have you ever really known happiness, *ma belle*?"

Outside the cannons fired and Shadney drew himself up, the far away look leaving his face. "That's why I came here. You must pack your things and tomorrow—afterwards—I'll have my agent find a place in the country for you. Haven't you realized that they're firing the cannons more often? And the tar? I've never noticed that either were very effective, but they're supposed to purify the air. Fever and plague are all over the town."

Breel had said almost the same thing earlier, but for some reason Shadney's words carried greater implications . . .

The memory of a moonlit night in Alabama returned. Of Breel describing the dead in the gutters for Norman Peltier's benefit.

"Oh no!" she whispered. That had been only a ghastly story, not something that might be as near as her kitchen. "Shad, Annette said she was sick. I didn't pay much attention—"

He got to his feet. "Stay here," he ordered. "I'll see her."

Zulu rushed after him. Annette was slumped over the table, her eyes glazed and her skin no longer a shiny ebony. There was a black filth on the floor around her.

"*Moin yin-yin*," she whimpered. Then, without warning, she slipped off her chair and onto the tile floor.

Shadney caught Zulu by the arm and pulled her back into the hallway. "Thank God I brought my carriage," he muttered. Letty had joined them and he turned to her. "Get Henri in here. He can carry her to her room."

Zulu stood back numbly as Shadney's big black Domingan coachmen went into the kitchen. A second later Letty came running out, sobs shaking her.

"Miz Zulu," she cried. "Oh Miz Zulu!"

Henri was close behind, his eyes wide and white. "Dead, Maitre," he explained to Randolph.

Dead? Zulu felt a churning in the pit of her abdomen. Only a few hours before she had thought Annette was shamming!

"That's the way it is," Shadney told her gently. "Don't any of you go in there. I'll send someone to get her body and I'll arrange for a woman to take her place." He breathed deeply. "I'll miss Annette."

Then he gave his attention to Zulu. "We'll have a talk after I meet Luton."

Zulu caught his arm, Shad, Annette, the plague—all forgotten—in the foreboding that gripped her. "What

212

are you going to do? You don't have to believe Breel. If only you'll listen to me it can be just like it was before. Shad, you've got to listen to me!"

He shook his head. "It wouldn't make any difference," he said.

She could never remember the rest of that evening in detail. A cart drew up and some men took Annette out by the back of the house. Shortly afterwards Henri brought a woman who might almost have been Annette.

She pointed to her chest and grinned with a friendliness never displayed by her predecessor. "Celeste, Maitresse," she announced. Then she went into the kitchen and Zulu could hear her scrubbing.

Shad would see to her comfort, but it was over. Even the legacy could be changed. I'll be like Eugenie, she thought, with nothing left but to run a rooming house. No more glittering ballrooms. No more theater and extravagant gowns.

She untied the bag that covered her *pierre loa* and let the stone roll onto her palm. Ferne was right. There was no happiness in what that pebble brought. It only tantalized with a taste of what might be, then snatched it back. She clenched her fingers tightly around it. There must be something she could do. She couldn't just stand here and watch everything tumble at her feet.

She called Letty. "Fetch Yvonne," she instructed. "Tell her there's trouble and I need her."

She moved impatiently back and forth about the room, waiting, but Letty returned alone.

"I look in de window," Letty explained. "Miz Yvonne, she busy."

Zulu turned unbelieving eyes onn her maid. "A man?" she asked incredulously.

Letty nodded. For a second she forgot Annette and a broad grin spread over her face. "Dey by de window when I start up de path."

Yvonne who pretended to be so chaste? She would have to see this for herself! Zulu threw a scarf over her shoulder and ran across the path between the houses. There was no one by the window as she went up the steps, so she knocked on the door.

Yvonne answered, though Zulu had expected the maid. Her eyes were swollen with tears, but there was a new happiness in her face. She stepped back for Zulu to enter.

"I'm so glad you called," she said. She swept across the room and into the arms of the man who stood by the hearth. It was as if she couldn't bear to be free of those arms, even for a minute. Zulu felt a pang of envy. "You've laughed at me so often, Zulu, but you see my prayers have been answered."

"M'sieur LeSieur? He's come back to stay?"

"We are leaving for France the day after tomorrow."

"We?" Zulu wasn't certain she heard right.

"Such a little black blood, Zulu. In France it doesn't matter at all. His uncle has set him up in a business and we'll be married there."

Yvonne who would have been content with being a *placee* so long as her lover was near. Why should this come to one who really didn't care?

LeSieur laughed. "Yvonne, you forget your manners. You have as yet to make introductions. My affianced must do better than that."

Yvonne's laughter matched his, but she observed the formalities, and Zulu watched with a new wonder. She couldn't remember ever hearing Yvonne laugh. She seemed completely transformed, as if she'd only been a shell before.

"But I'm even further forgetting my manners," Yvonne said. "I haven't asked what brought you here."

Zulu returned to reality. "Annette took the sickness. The cart's already come for her."

Yvonne blanched and LeSieur's mouth tightened. "We're not leaving any too soon. I'd like it better if we were on a boat that had already left port."

"But that isn't why I came." Zulu hesitated. "Where

214

can I learn where a duel is to be held?"

"Duel?" Yvonne echoed.

"Shad called this evening. I wasn't expecting him."

"Sacre Nom! M'sieur Luton wasn't—?"

LeSieur's eyes sparkled with interest. "So Luton's still at it? Things haven't changed much!" He glanced down at Yvonne. "It used to be a pleasure to watch Randolph use a rapier. I'd like to be there. *Que désirez-vous*?"

She nodded.

LeSieur turned to Zulu. "Madame, I'll find out where it is to be," he assured her. "Be ready an hour before dawn. Yvonne and I will take you in my father's landau."

As it evolved, Zulu was waiting by the landau when they came down the stairs. Yvonne's eyes were sleep heavy, but the glow was still in her face. When they had settled in the seat, LeSieur put his arm about her, and she nestled back against him.

"I had trouble awakening this one," he explained.

Zulu was aware of Yvonne's questioning look. "For whom are you praying?" she finally ventured.

"I don't know," Zulu said.

LeSieur's landau reached the Oaks none too soon. Randolph and Breel were already facing each other in their shirt sleeves. The dim dawn light cast an unreal haze over the field.

The oaks with their great spreading boughs were the painted backdrop to a play. Only the cascades of Spanish moss stirred to the morning breeze. The grass was still and lush. A little beyond the grove the lushness grew rank.

The traditional salute over, one of the seconds called out a command. Then steel glittered and crashed. Shadney dodged a parry, his own blade flashing through the air. Zulu held her breath as Breel leaped aside, but a bright splotch grew on his left shoulder.

LeSieur leaned forward, his eyes bright. "Randolph's

still a swordsman!" he exclaimed. "*Mon Dieu! Regardez-vous!*"

Shadney's sword had drawn blood again. The side of Breel's face was slashed and a crimson stream spurted from it. His thrusts were wild and Shadney avoided them with ease. It would be over soon. Randolph could finish it any time he wished.

She never remembered clearly what happened next. Just confused pictures of LeSieur catching her arm, trying to hold her back as she jumped to the ground. His sharp voice.

"You'll distract them. Stay here!"

There was a smile on Shadney's face as he parried about Breel, thrusting at him occasionally, a cat poking at its intended prey.

Then she was running across the field, shouting about Fannette. It was her voice, but somehow she couldn't remember consciously planning the act or the words. It was as if she came back to herself with the echo still in the air.

"Shad! Fannette's sick!"

It was then that she tripped on her skirt and fell. As she pulled herself up onto her elbow full awareness was hers once again. That and the horror of what she had caused. Shadney had dropped his sword, his face contorted as he clutched at his chest. He tried to speak but there was not enough breath for words.

Breel's blade flashed a quick streak and plunged through Shadney's fingers to pierce his heart. Shadney's knees doubled and he rolled over as he struck the ground.

The surgeon bent over him. He motioned to the seconds and then, slowly, he unfolded a handkerchief, covering Shadney's face. He rose to his feet and went to Breel.

Before he had his bag open, Breel brushed past him and started unsteadily across the field.

"Let him go," someone said. "Just pray he bleeds to

death.''

LeSieur and Yvonne stood over Zulu, and LeSieur jerked her to her feet, his lips white. Suddenly he slapped her across the face.

Zulu's eyes blazed. ''Why blame me? He was in no condition to duel.''

''We heard you,'' Yvonne said. ''You knew what it would be like if he thought Fannette had the fever.''

''It was Breel who killed him, you saw it.''

''With a foul!'' LeSieur spat. ''There's no one in New Orleans who'll receive Luton once this gets about.'' He helped Yvonne into the carriage, but left Zulu to climb in by herself.

Yvonne leaned forward. ''Perhaps you do love M'sieur Luton? If it was to save him because you love him—that I can understand.''

''If you used a trick like that to save me, I'd kill you,'' LeSieur muttered.

Zulu faced the two of them knowing that a measure of justification had been offered, but for some unfathomable reason, she could not accept it.

''I've never loved Breel,'' she said. ''I've never even imagined I did.''

LeSieur's glance almost held some respect. ''At least,'' he granted, ''you are honest.''

It wasn't until she was alone in the cottage that she was able to think. She looked about her, at Shad's pipes, his tobacco pouch, his robe, his slippers in the bedroom, and she felt an overwhelming sense of loss. Fannette cried once, and she brushed the wet nurse aside so she could snatch up her daughter and hold her against her own breast in an unreasoning passion of possessiveness. But it was no good. Fannette was more accustomed to the nurse and she only cried the louder.

She went into her own bedroom and stripped off her dress. There was mud on the skirt and a seam had torn where she had fallen on it. She rolled it into a bundle and tossed it into a heap. As if that way she could rid herself of a reminder.

The *pierre-loa* was in its bag resting between her breasts. She snapped the chain and the bag joined her dress. Then she stood over the pile, at war with herself.

If I throw it away, she thought, I'm putting the blame on it. I'll be like Ferne, muttering about *loas* and good and evil. She picked up the bag and relinked the chain. After all, this was her only heritage. The only thing to prove she hadn't just evolved.

Still, just in case, there was no need to wear it. To have it would be sufficient. She dropped it into her jewel case and closed the lid.

She put on a fresh gown and as she fastened the hooks it occurred to her that Letty hadn't appeared. Lord God! Could she have taken the sickness too? She hurried into the kitchen and found Celeste kneeling on the floor telling her beads, while Letty was weeping and praying in intermittent gasps.

"Miz Zulu," Letty sobbed, "We's all goin' die."

Outside a cannon boomed as if to punctuate the maid's words, and for the first time Zulu realized that there had been few carriages on the streets and almost no one afoot. She had been too preoccupied with her own problem to notice that the cannons were now blasting at shorter intervals.

"We're not going to die!" she snapped. "Unless Celeste stays on her knees and we all starve to death."

Celeste pulled herself up and lumbered to her pots. Zulu left the kitchen, and in the sitting room she looked out the window. Some men were starting fire to a barrel of tar only two doors down. There'll be no place here for me once talk starts, she reflected. At least not for a while. First thing in the morning she'd see Shadney's lawyers and arrange for money. Then she'd take Fannette and leave town.

She was sitting down to the belated meal Celeste had served, when there was a banging on the jalouise. Letty started for the door, but Zulu waved her back. There was money in the cottage and also her jewels. Was it possible there were already looters in the city? She went to the desk and drew out the pistol Ramon had left that terrible night before Fannette's birth.

She opened the door, ready for anything but what she saw.

"Breel!" she gasped.

He leaned against the jamb, his face flushed with fever. Somewhere he'd found a sling for his left arm, but the side of his face was a mass of congealed blood.

He moved toward her, swayed and fell on his face. Fresh blood spurted from his shoulder, drenching the carpet.

Zulu shrieked for Letty and Celeste, then she knelt beside him, trying to staunch the bright crimson flow. She packed the wound with towels the maids brought her and the three of them worked to move him onto the divan.

"Clean his face as well as you can," she told them, then stood back to evaluate the situation.

Of all the places in New Orleans he might have gone, why did he have to choose her cottage? Had he done it as a deliberate act of malice? A final tribute to Rosalie? Scandal there was bound to be, but this was the finishing touch!.

Somehow, someway she had to get him to his own house, but she didn't even know where it was located. And it was certain she'd need a carriage which was out of the question. She glanced doubtfully at Letty and Celeste and finally at the wet nurse who was watching from the nursery doorway. No, this was not something she could trust to a third party. She'd have to go by herself.

She put on a cloak and paused by the couch. "Stay by him," she instructed Letty. "If he wakes try to feed him some of the soup."

She drew on her gloves and went out into the tar-smoke filled air. Perhaps Ferne would know where to find the Luton residence. It was the first time she had realized how little she knew of Shad and Breel's life away from Rampart Street.

Eugenie shook her head when Zulu asked for Ferne.

"She's away and I do not know how to find the Luton house. Docie would know. She goes out there to do Madame Luton's hair."

It was not difficult to find the shop of the *coiffeur*. She was a mulattress with a plump, amiable face, and she nodded her head violently.

"*Certainement*," she said. "I go there often. She is an angel, that Madame Luton."

Making no effort to mask her impatience, Zulu interrupted, "I don't care what she is, I want to know where!"

Docie immediately became suspicious. "I would not have harm come to her. Why do you wish to know?"

"It's a matter of importance to her," Zulu explained. "I've got to find her at once."

Docie, hesitated, then she shrugged. "She lives on Esplanade Publique. M'sieur Moulton, her father, built the house. He was from Santo Domingo, you know, *sans doute!*"

"Is there a name outside? How will I know the house?"

"You will see a house that is built like a castle on the same side of the street. On the next *ilet* you will find the Moulton—the Luton residence. It has an iron fence, much taller than you, and by the gate is *un grand lion*." She paused. "You are certain this is not harm for Madame? You—"

But Zulu was out the door before the mulattress had finished. She breathed deeply and almost choked on the air. She set out for Esplanade Publique damning the white man's law that forbade her to ride in a carriage alone. It would be a long walk and anything could be happening at the cottage.

She was tired and breathless by the time she reached

the house. She stared at the iron lion that reclined behind a grilled fence in a semi-tropical garden. A fountain spurted to the side of the path and twin palm trees swayed near the gates.

The house itself was of plaster covered bricks, a bluish shade, and it was in the shape of a huge "L". On the second floor a balcony with wrought iron grillwork circled the otherwise plain walls. On the third floor there was a covered gallery, and the lacework of iron grilling formed the monogram "M".

Breel never let on he lived in a place like this! she thought. Her courage almost deserted her as she opened the gates and went up the walk to the door.

As she brought down the knocker she had a memory of the elegant, assured woman who had sat at Breel's side that night at the theater. This was no Rosalie she was about to face. Suppose she wanted no part of Breel? But no, white folks were quick to hide their own scandals, no matter their feelings.

A sable skinned Santo Domingan butler opened the door. He waited for her to speak.

"I've come to see Madame Luton," Zulu said. Her respect for Breel mounted. What an elegant negro!

"A qui est-ce que je parle?" he asked politely, but still effectively barring the door with his bulk.

"It doesn't matter who I am," Zulu retorted. "Tell Madame Luton it concerns her husband."

The butler looked at her steadily a minute, then he stood aside so she could enter the foyer. He led the way into a drawing room and motioned for her to take a seat. He drew the double doors together when he left the room, and Zulu felt free to take in her surroundings.

A huge crystal candelabrum hung from the ceiling and a fireplace of black Italian marble was set in the far wall. The furnishings reflected taste and money.

Elmside was a cabin compared to this, she reflected. No wonder Breel hadn't been overly anxious to marry Rosalie!

She moved across the high piled rugs and examined the intricately carved clock that ticked on an exquisite little table. There was no sound to warn her of the door opening, or of Donna Luton's prescence, until a soft, cultured voice addressed her in English.

"Madame?"

Donna Luton was much younger than she had appeared at the theater. Her face was pale, and her fine white hands were clenched at her sides. Still, despite her obvious tension, everything about her proclaimed her gentility.

"André says you have news of my husband?" There was something close to desperation in her words, and unexpectedly Donna Luton caught up her heavy, wine colored skirts and ran across the room to Zulu. There was no awareness of black and white nor of wife and mistress. Only a great, overwhelming anxiety.

"He was injured! Is it very bad? Can I reach him quickly?"

She's warm and alive, Zulu thought, surprised. Breel means as much to her as Ramon meant to Naida. And she's a white woman. It was confusing. Set values of herself as a woman of color and of all white women tottered.

This wasn't a sheltered, shallow Rosalie. Why did Breel come to her cottage? This woman could have given him all the warmth a man might desire.

Yet he had come to the cottage on Rampart Street. What had twisted his mind? Did Rosalie stand between him and this woman as well? Did he blame his wife even as he blamed her?

"Is he dead?" It was barely a whisper. "Please, he isn't dead?"

Zulu shook her head. "He's alive. He's at my cottage."

"Thank God!"

"You'll have to send a carriage for him. He's very weak."

"I read the account of the duel." Donna hesitated. "Please forgive me, but I must ask. Was it you?"

Zulu nodded. "Did the accounts mention he killed my protector with a foul?"

"My husband would have purposely killed no one. Let alone with a foul!" She turned her face away. "What's the use of pretending to you? You know Breel as well as I do."

She moved to a satin covered rope and pulled it. After a minute the butler came into the room.

"André," she said, "Send for Dr. Ballard. Tell him to go to the ramparts—which is your house, Madame?"

Zulu told her.

"And have the carriage ready for me. Tell Velma I'll need a wrap."

"You're not going!" Zulu exclaimed.

Donna looked at her in surprise. "My husband needs me," she replied simply.

"But it's not proper for a white lady—"

"You live there. Are you a savage?" Donna's lips curved in a faint smile. "I'm sorry if I intrude, but it's my place to go to him."

"Is it?" Zulu felt a sudden rush of anger. "Is it, after the way he treats you?"

"My husband has always been good to me," Donna replied, but the knuckles of her closed hands whitened.

"Pride doesn't make a very convincing lie."

Donna's eyes flashed. "You call me a liar?"

"Breel Luton's not capable of being good to any woman."

"Pride..." Donna said softly. "By the second week of my marriage I had not a particle of pride left." Her eyes searched into Zulu's face, "It seems strange I should say these things to you and I don't expect you to understand, but I love my husband very much."

Lord God, Zulu thought, disgusted with herself, why should the first woman I ever liked have to be white?

Chapter Twenty-Eight

Breel was stil unconscious when they arrived. Donna tossed off her cloak and knelt beside the couch.

"Quick!" she exclaimed. "Have you any spirits?"

Zulu took a bottle out of Shadney's liquor cabinet and poured some brandy into a glass. Donna lifted Breel's head on her arm and let a little of the liquid slide between his lips. He choked and opened his eyes.

"Ah," he said after a minute, "my good and dutiful wife."

Zulu clutched the bottle surpressing a desire to throw it into that mocking, blood clotted face, but Donna smiled.

"Thank God," she whispered. "For a moment I thought—" She caught sight of Letty watching from the hallway. "Bring me towels and warm water. Quickly, s'il vous plait!"

Letty jumped to obey and Zulu looked at Donna with respect. For all of her gentleness, she was a firm person. When she commanded it was in the tone of one who expected to be obeyed.

Letty returned with a steaming basin and Donna placed it on the floor at her side. With steady, gentle hands she bathed her husband's wounds. Zulu tried to watch, but the dangling bits of flesh upset her stomach.

"How do you stand it?" she finally asked. "Why don't you let the doctor take care of him when he gets here?"

Donna looked up and Zulu saw tears in her eyes. "It'll be such a terrible scar," she said. "Breel's always been so handsome."

The wet nurse came out of the nursery and passed by on her way to the kitchen. Clearly, through the open door, they heard Fannette cry.

Donna rose to her feet. She motioned for Letty to take the basin and soiled towels. She waited until they were alone, then she moved toward the nursery. She stood on the threshold looking at the baby. Finally she turned to Zulu, her eyes asking the question she could not speak.

"I was Shadney Randolph's *placee*," Zulu evaded.

"May I go in?"

Zulu nodded, following.

Donna reached down and took a tiny hand. Abruptly Fannette stopped crying. Her wide set eyes regarded the two as if even she sensed the strangeness of the situation.

"She's a beautiful *minet*," Donna said. "Her eyes are like Breel's and so are her lips." She turned away. "I've a small son, you know."

Breel had a son? For the second time that day she found herself startled by a relationship in which she could know a man so well and yet so little.

In the main room Letty had opened the door to the doctor, and Donna hurried out to greet him. He was a lean, gray little man, and his face was sallow from lack of sleep.

He looked at Donna with unconcealed anxiety. "I was afraid it might be you, Madame Luton. Are you feeling better?"

Donna's color heightened a little. "Better than I've a right to expect. It's Breel who needs you."

"I read about that in *L'Abeille*," he said bluntly. "I'd have been here sooner, except—"

"La fièvre?"

He nodded. "At least a hundred cases—all in different sections of the city—and like before, there's plague as well. Does one bring on the other or is it a coincidence? If only we knew—"

225

Donna's faced had whitened. "I've never been really frightened before. But it's different when one has a child."

The doctor patted her hand, then he went to where Breel lay on the divan, his eyes half closed. He inspected the facial wound and lifted the towel off the gash in Breel's chest.

"Tell your maid to bring me water and take Madame Luton away."

"But I want to help!" Donna exclaimed.

"The maid will do well enough. We'll all do better with you out of the room."

Donna unwillingly followed Zulu into the kitchen, where she sank into a chair, resting her head against the back. Outside the cannons boomed again.

"I was hoping this time the sickness wouldn't be so bad. I'll never forget the time when I was a little girl. My father took me and my nurse and a few of the house servants to the plantation, Bijou, out in the country. He cut all communications with the city. Did Breel ever tell you about Bijou?"

"Breel never told me anything," Zulu said sullenly.

"It's a sugar plantation and it's almost entirely surrounded by swamp and marshland. There's only one road in and my father had it closed." She drew a deep breath, remembering. "You've no idea how lonely I felt there. My father loved Bijou—it reminded him of the plantation in Santo Domingo where he grew up. And I guess Bijou is beautiful, but I found it—frightening. The tall cane—the slaves my father brought with him from Santo Domingo. And the constant fight against Voodoo."

"Is that so different from New Orleans?" Zulu asked. "You don't have to look far here to find a *gris-gris* or hear of a meeting."

"It was different at Bijou. To wake up in the night and see a great fire burning beyond the cane fields and to hear the drums. It still chills me to remember, even

226

though my father put an end to it while I was still very young. But this time I felt trapped there. He even sent back the driver and carriage that brought us—"

The cannons fired again, and Zulu closed the windows. "Celeste is as bad as Annette about letting in the mosquitos," she remarked.

"At night we could hear those cannons," Donna said. "Then they finally stopped. Still, it was a long while before my father dared take us back to the city." She looked down. "I'll never forget the smell when they opened the doors to the town house. My father went in alone, and when he came out he set fire to the house with his own hands. I remember I cried because he wouldn't let me rescue my favorite doll."

"Was it as big as the house you have now?"

"Bigger. It was one of the fine old houses, but years later my father told me how it was. Everyone was dead. They lay in the halls, on the beds and in the courtyards. Not a soul was alive. I still have dreams of that house burning with all its dead inside."

Dr. Ballard appeared in the doorway, and Donna motioned for him to enter.

"We moved your husband into the bedroom," he said. "I think he'll be all right, but it's going to take time."

Donna rose to her feet. "I've everything packed for Bijou. I'll send to the house for them to follow us. We should be able to leave immediately."

The doctor shook his head.

"But surely, with the fever in the city, it would be safer to take him to the country?"

"He can't even be moved across the city without danger. He's lost far too much blood to risk breaking open the wounds. You take the boy to Bijou, Madame. I'll arrange for a woman to come here and nurse him."

Donna interrupted, flushing with embarrassment. "You forget. We're intruders here. But no matter what, I'll stay with him."

227

For the first time Dr. Ballard turned his attention to Zulu.

"Surely you wouldn't turn him out? Madame Luton will pay you well for your troubles."

"Pay me!" Zulu exclaimed, the old anger hot inside her. "You white folks think you can pay for anything."

"I'm sorry," Donna said, "we're already so much in your debt."

"Not so much that you have to treat me as an equal. I'd thank you not to forget I was born a slave." Zulu went out of the kitchen, closing the door, but their voices carried to her.

"She's a strange person. She spits like a *minou* that's afraid of being kicked."

"Strange?" The doctor grunted. "I could give you a better word. Donna Luton, it's none of my affair, but I've known you long enough to feel a responsibility. Remember, I warned you against marrying Breel."

"I'd marry him again, this very minute, knowing everything."

"Even if you knew about her?"

Donna's voice was weary. "I knew before I married him there would always be other women. Only—when I saw her—" her voice faltered, "it was the first time I despaired. But why blame her? I know that Breel never loved me."

"Are you certain?" The doctor patted Donna's hand and picked up his bag. "I'll be back when I can," he said as he left. "God knows when that will be."

It was Donna who ventured out in her carriage with Celeste, and they returned with kegs of solid food.

"We can buy our vegetables from the street vendors," she explained, "and with all this none of us need leave the house." She shuddered. "Outside you can feel death all around. It's in the very air."

"That and tar smoke," Zulu muttered. "There must be a better way to drive it away."

Donna watched Celeste and her coachman carry the

228

foodstuff into the kitchen, her eyes thoughtful.

"Some call it God's judgment for the evil in this city," she said, "but I can't believe God could be that cruel."

Each time Dr. Ballard called to tend Breel, his face was more haggard. He shook his head when Donna told him about the provisions.

"Maybe it'll help not to go outside," he said, "but as many who haven't been exposed come down with the fever as those who are nursing the sick."

"In that case," Zulu announced, "it's time I called on Shad's solicitors and made arrangements. I'm getting away from here as soon as I can." She caught sight of Donna's startled expression and added, "I'll leave Celeste and you have the woman Dr. Ballard brought. You can stay as long as you want to."

"You'll have trouble getting on a boat," the doctor said. "Folks are fighting to board anything that floats."

"I'll get on."

Her confidence ebbed the next day. Her visit with the solicitors was simple enough. Shadney had arranged that well. Yet, there were disappointments. For one thing she could only draw a little of Fannette's money at a time and only at given periods. Still, all in all, he had left her more than she had dared hope.

The rioting mobs she encountered on the docks filled her with a despair of ever leaving the city. In-coming steamboats no longer pulled up to the piers but anchored out in the river. Twice she almost stumbled over a corpse sprawled out of a doorway in the poorer section of town. Then she realized with horror that they had been left there to await the cart that passed daily with its grisly load.

Now that I've freedom and money I'm trapped, she thought. I'll never get away!

And worse, still, when she finally pushed her way through the thickening tar smoke to her cottage, it was to be greeted by a fully conscious Breel. From where he lay on her bed he had a full view into the sitting room.

He watched her as she stood by the table, stripping off her gloves, then his eyes flickered to Donna who, after smiling at Zulu, had returned to her knitting.

"I see," he said to his wife, "that you've met my playmate." The uninjured side of his mouth turned up in a smile. "No doubt you've found her charming?"

Donna met his look with calm eyes. "I've found Zulu more than charming. I've found her both generous and considerate."

"Oh? Indeed?" He cleared his throat. "And I'm also indebted to Zulu. I trust Fannette is better?"

"She never was sick," Zulu snapped. "And I'd thank you not to feel indebted to me. For all I care, Shad could have killed you."

Breel laughed. "Hardly! You might have lost your precious legacy."

"Breel!" Donna exclaimed.

Zulu whirled on her. "But it's true! Breel knows!"

"Bravo!" Breel exclaimed. "At least you've never been a hypocrite." He patted the space by his side. "This bed has fond memories for both of us, why are you staying so far from it now? Is my wound that disfiguring?"

Donna set down her work and went into the kitchen.

Zulu shrugged. A woman foolish enough to love Breel probably got what she deserved.

Breel lay silent, his eyes closed. Where was the handsome stranger who had raced a winded horse up the avenue of elms? It was hard to see in this scarred, unshaven face the lazy, careless charm that had enraptured Rosalie.

"It might have saved a lot of trouble if you'd been as solicitous of Rosalie," Breel observed bitterly.

He's back at Elmside, too, Zulu thought. It's Elmside we have together.

"When you look at Donna don't you realize it should be Rosalie?" He pulled himself up a little on his elbow.

230

"Doesn't it worry you that you changed what should have been?"

"If you'd married Rosalie you'd have been sick of her in a month! You lost a pretty plaything and you're taking it out on Donna!"

"You wouldn't understand."

Zulu laughed. "It didn't take much to persuade you to leave Rosalie. Nor much for her to turn to Norman."

Breel made an attempt to sit up. "Get out of here!" he roared. "Get out of here before I kill you!"

Zulu yawned and paused before the mirror to pat her hair into place.

"Lie still," she cautioned. "I don't want you to break open your wounds—and have to stay longer."

Breel had regained his calm, but there was a restrained fury in his voice. "We'll talk about this some other time," he promised, "and I won't be helpless then."

Donna was sitting by the kitchen table. She looked tired and ill.

"I heard you fighting with Breel. I'd prefer you let me take care of myself."

"It had nothing to do with you. It was about what happened in Alabama."

"But that was just before we were married! If you knew him there, maybe you could explain—?"

"There's nothing to explain," Zulu interrupted. "I don't talk about Alabama any more than Breel does."

When Dr. Ballard called that afternoon, Zulu was in the kitchen instructing Celeste about dinner. He had already left when she returned to the front of the house. Donna was standing by the door, her face blanched.

"My baby has the fever," she said. "I've sent for the carriage so I can go to him."

"Aren't you afraid of catching it?" Zulu exclaimed.

"Don't you understand? It's my baby. I've got to go to him."

"What about Breel?"

"I don't know. He's getting better, and there's Marie to see to him. And you—?"

"I've already told Letty to see to my packing. I thought you'd be here to close the house and instruct Celeste."

Donna started out the door, her hands together. "I don't know what to do. I don't want to leave Breel while he needs me, but I've got to go to my baby." She turned to Zulu. "It's such a big thing to ask, but maybe it'll only be a few days. The fever doesn't take long and—my baby is so little..."

"You've just said there was Marie and Celeste."

"But if the sickness gets worse—they're liable to lose their heads and run away. What can I do, Zulu?"

There's no reason I should help her, Zulu thought indignantly. It's her worry. Yet... could a few days make so much difference? Maybe it would be quieter at the docks and maybe she still might hear from Renny Langford...

"I'll see Breel's fed, but I've been expecting a message. If it comes, I'll—"

"I'll have to take that chance," Donna said. "I was selfish not to have taken my baby to Bijou." She sat down and rested her head. Her face was sallow from lack of sleep and there were dark smudges under her eyes.

"You see, I'm carrying again. As a mother I should have considered them both. I wonder, Zulu, if it's a very bad sin for a woman to love her husband more than her children?"

"I don't know about it being a sin," Zulu replied, "but it's damn foolishness when the husband's Breel."

Lord God, she thought, Breel didn't just sit around those last two months I carried Fannette!

Soon after Donna's carriage rolled away, another drew up to the house. Letty opened the door to Shadney Randolph's widow.

"May I come in?" Madame Randolph asked. Black

232

accentuated the clear pallor of her skin and when she lifted her veil her eyes held determination.

Zulu moved forward to greet her, grateful that the bedroom door was closed. Madame Randolph took a chair by the table and leaned forward.

"I want to take that child to the country with me," she announced bluntly. "With my husband dead I have no one, and the child is part of him. If she stays here she's sure to take the fever."

"Others have lived through it."

"Can't you see this would be best for her?"

"You want Fannette so I can't touch her legacy." Still, Zulu thought, this could be an answer. Both for herself and for Fannette. If Renny's note did come, and, somehow, she was certain it would, how could she explain her child?

"Money!" Madame Randolph made a contemptuous gesture. "I've more of that than I'll ever need. I promise that after the sickness I'll bring the child back to you."

"Why should I believe you?"

Madame Randolph spoke slowly, her voice reflective. "I want to do this thing for my husband. It was my fault he looked to someone like you. I—I lost sight of the purpose of a marriage and it became a round of entertaining. In a left handed sort of way, I'm responsible for that child."

"You expect me to believe this?"

"Yes. Yes, I do."

"I'm no fool."

"You refuse, then?"

Zulu nodded.

Madame Randolph arose and started toward the hall. She paused.

"*Tres bien.* You realize, of course, I can invoke the law against leaving money to a mistress? Since there was no secret about the relationship, this should be a matter of ease."

Zulu stared at her. "You wouldn't do that!" she

exclaimed.

"*Non?* I am going now to see the lawyers."

"If I let you take Fannette will you sign a paper that you'll return her when I ask? And that you'll never question the legacies?"

"I have promised you that."

Zulu sat down at her escritoire and wrote hastily on a piece of note paper."

"You have a beautiful handwriting," Madame Randolph commented as she signed the paper. Then she dropped the pen. "Now where is she? I want to start for the country at once."

Zulu dropped the document into a drawer, locked it and dropped the key into a pocket. She called the wet nurse and ordered her to pack the baby's and her own belongings.

When everything necessary was in a basket, Zulu took Fannette into her arms. The baby made a happy gurgle and touched her cheek with a tiny hand. Zulu was aware of a strange, smothered feeling. I've been listening to Donna too much, she thought. Zulu held the child out to Madame Randolph.

She watched at the window until the carriage disappeared around the corner of Orleans Street. Breel called out.

He was half sitting, half reclining when she opened the bedroom door.

He said, "Madame Randolph has always been an unusual woman. Taking Fannette is the sort of thing Rosalie might have done."

"Rosalie was a fool, but not that big a one!" Zulu looked toward the empty nursery.

"I didn't call you to discuss Fannette," Breel went on. "Where did Donna go? She kissed me and ran out with a handkerchief to her nose."

"You son has the fever."

Breel lay back. His voice sounded strange when he spoke.

"When did this happen?"

"Dr. Ballard told her when he stopped in to see you."

Outside a cannon boomed in Congo Square, a few blocks away, another echoed it. A wagon rattled by and Zulu glanced out the window.

"Lord God!" she exclaimed. "Oh Lord God!"

Breel propped himself up again. "Do you have to scream?" he demanded.

Zulu turned. "Breel," she whispered, "that wagon. It was like they said. It was loaded with bodies. They were dead. All of them were dead and just flopped on top of each other."

She tried to move from the window, but the fascination was too great.

"Dead," she repeated, "and dumped in a cart like garbage."

She thought of the fresh smell of growing things at Elmside. She drew a deep breath and the tar smoke almost choked her.

"Damn you, Breel! Why couldn't you have gotten killed on the field, or at least have had the decency to crawl to your own house? If I stay here much longer, I'll go crazy!"

Breel's mouth curved in a twisted grin.

"Cheer up, Zulu. Maybe tomorrow you'll be in that cart, and then all your worries will be over."

Chapter Twenty-Nine

The Luton carriage drove up late the next day. Donna mounted the stairs slowly and brushed past Zulu. She paused in front of the bedroom door and a shudder ran through her slim frame.

"Zulu," she whispered, "I can't face him."

The cannon fire shook the cottage. It was coming from all parts of the city now, and a constant rain dribbled against the window. The heavy air held the tar smoke low.

Donna started to tremble. "The baby died," she said. Her soft voice was devoid of expression. She turned away from the door and moved toward the fireplace and Zulu could see now that her face was ashen.

"He didn't even look like my baby. His veins were swollen and his face mottled. I knew he couldn't live as soon as I saw him."

"Give me your cape," Zulu said. She paused to slap a mosquito that fed on Donna's wrist.

"I went to the church, but the priests were all at the cemetery. I carried him to the graveyard myself... There wasn't a casket left but the Father made one of wood for me. My baby didn't need a very big box..."

She looked at the swelling mosquito welt. "The priest said that he had been at the cemetery all day and still there wasn't time to give service to all."

She swayed and Zulu took her arm, forcing her to sit down. She stared straight ahead.

"The wind blew terrible smells. Carts kept rattling over the shells and dumping bodies. I had cleaned my baby and burned his clothes, but most of the others lying there still had the black vomit. Some were already decaying..."

There was a noise behind them. Zulu looked around and saw that Breel was leaning against the bedroom door.

"The boy is dead?"

"I think all the town is dying." Long shudders rippled through Donna's frame. "I've always been at Bijou during the other sicknesses. I never realized... The priest said they've lost all count."

Tears started to roll down her cheeks and she turned

away. "My baby reached for me," she whispered, her voice muffled, "and there was nothing I could do."

Breel made his way across the room and hesitated over her. Then he turned abruptly and sat on the ottoman. He rested his elbows on his knees and hid his face in his hands...

Zulu left them there. She went into the nursery and looked at Fannette's empty cradle. Glancing up she caught her reflection in the mirror and it startled her. Her hair was untidy, her face streaked and she wore a *blouse-volante*.

"I came to New Orleans to be a great lady," she said to the mirror, "and instead, maybe Breel's right and I'll be in a cart tomorrow."

The doctor stopped by that evening. "I want you to try this quinine," he said to Donna. "I don't know if its effective with the plague but they've found it seems to help with fever where they used it in the West Indies."

"Why give it to me?" Donna demanded. "Why didn't you give it to my baby?"

"I did. But maybe if you take it now it might help. We don't know much about it."

"I bathed my baby and I held him to me. If one can catch it that way—"

"That doesn't seem to mean a thing," the doctor said heavily. "It's mostly strangers who get the worst cases. If it weren't for your condition—"

He looked at Breel who was sitting in Shad's chair, still weak and pale. "In a few days you'll be able to travel. But get back in bed now."

"Go to Bijou?" Donna asked. "What difference does it make now? We're probably safer here than riding through the streets with—" she shuddered.

Dr. Ballard bent over Donna and looked into her eyes. He scowled. "I want you to lie down. Unless you want to lose your new baby, too, you're going to have to rest."

Donna shook her head. "I've got to keep busy," she

said. "I can't stand to think."

Together, Donna and Zulu walked Breel to the bed. "My women," he remarked, "take good care of me." He patted the mattress. "One of you can sleep on each side." Somehow his words fell short of the mockery intended and Zulu looked at him closely. Breel's hurting, too, she thought, surprised, but he'd die before he'd let on.

"I haven't heard Fannette," Donna said. "She's all right?"

"Madame Randolph took her to the country."

"I was afraid. I keep thinking..." Donna swayed and Zulu put a steadying arm around her waist.

"The doctor's right. You've got to rest."

"Send for the carriage tomorrow and we'll go back to the house," Breel said.

"No! Not the house! I couldn't go back there now!" Donna exclaimed.

Breel scowled. "Believe me, for once I was trying to be helpful. To Bijou, then."

"Stay here for all I care," Zulu interrupted. "But I'm leaving on the first boat. I'm through with the stink of death!"

"Bravo!" Breel applauded.

"I can live like a lady now, and that's just what I intend to do."

"A lady of color, remember that."

"Breel, will you stop it." Donna said sharply. Suddenly she burst into tears. She threw herself down on the bed, her face against his chest.

Breel stared over her head. His hand trembled as he smoothed her hair.

Chapter Thirty

The next morning Zulu sent Letty to the docks to make arrangements. At noon the girl returned, her customarily good natured face dejected and close to tears.

Everywhere, it seemed, were people pushing carts loaded with belongings, people with only a portmanteau and people with no baggage at all, filling the area by the wharfs. Fighting and begging for passage even on the river barges. Some had been waiting for days and some had even died while waiting. Constantly the carts rolled up to drag away corpses. The gutters were clogged and the mosquitos and flies thick.

"It's all my fault," Donna said. "Maybe you could have gotten a boat a few days ago."

Zulu tied a scarf around her head. "I'll find someway . . ."

"You don't know what it's like out in the city," Donna told her. "At least let me send for my carriage."

"You'd have to go with me, then, and from what Letty says it would never get near the dock."

"You could come to Bijou with us."

"I'd stay in New Orleans first!"

Zulu felt as if she were walking through some horrible sort of a fantasy as she made her way down Orleans Street. In the shops a few of the Creole merchants were still plying their trade, contemptuous of *la fievre* that was mostly reserved for the *Kaintuck*. Even they, she thought, must be choked by the horrible stench of rot and sewage. Carriages slopped through the mud on their way out of town. She almost stepped on the outflung hand of a dead man who lay in an alley.

As she neared the levee she passed more of the dead awaiting the cart. She moved on the outside of the banquette and tried not to look where the flies were the thickest. A cart slushed by and the smell told her what it was before she looked. She clung to a wall, sick and weak.

By the docks it was all that Letty had said, and worse. One glance was enough to realize it was hopeless. She turned back toward Rampart Street.

What a long stretch from the triumphant trip she'd planned up the Mississippi. She resisted a hysterical impulse to laugh.

Breel was fully dressed when she opened the door. He was leaning against the wall, drawing on one of Shad's pipes.

"Decent of him to leave me these," he remarked.

Zulu ignored him and looked at Donna. "It's impossible," she said. Then she paused, noting the yellowish hue of Donna's complexion and the unnatural brightness of her eyes. "You don't look very well," she added.

"If only I hadn't kept you!" Donna closed her eyes tightly. *"Je ferai tout mon possible pour vous aider."* She spoke with an effort, falling back on the more familiar French. She stood up and then clung dizzily to a chair. Suddenly her nose started to bleed and before either Breel or Zulu could help her to the divan the hemorrhage of the mouth had started.

"Go find a doctor!" Zulu shouted to Celeste. Then she caught sight of Letty huddled in a corner. "Get Madame Vievra!"

"It's no use," Breel muttered.

"C'est la fievre!" Celeste moaned.

Lord God! Zulu thought. Why Donna?

Outside her door the *jalouise* banged and her knocker crashed.

Zulu straightened up from Donna and moved slowly across the room. She opened the door.

"Trojan!" Letty gasped from behind her.

He was a huge, fine looking man, and he grinned over Zulu's shoulder at her maid.

"Get back to Madame Luton!" Zulu snapped. This was about the last straw!

"Since when," she demanded, "have you been received at my front door?"

Trojan's grin widened. He handed her a note.

Zulu stared at it, knowing what it would be. She looked at Donna who was convulsed with nausea, and she felt a strange reluctance to break the seal.

"He want an answer." Trojan said.

No one would be a fool for me! Zulu told herself and ripped open the envelope.

She glanced once again at Donna, who lay quiet and spent, then she held the note to the light.

> "My dear Miss Randolph:
> I've completed my business and am anxious to leave. The town is in such a state I find it impossible to meet you through the channels I'd anticipated. However, I cannot bring myself to leave without first offering my services if there should be any way in which I can help in this time of stress. I'm on *The Muse* which will pull out this evening.
> Faithfully,
R. Langford
> P.S. If I can't meet you now I'll be back as soon as possible."

Donna moaned softly and Zulu felt Breel watching her. This was the chance she'd despaired of happening. In the confusion of the plague ridden city there'd be no one to question, no one to interfere. What good would it do Donna for her to stay? There was Marie, Celeste and Breel—and the doctor, if they ever got him. There was absolutely nothing she could do that would alter whether Donna lived or not.

But her entire future was opening out in front of her.

She sat down at the escritoire and took up the plume.

"My dear Mr. Langford:

How can I thank you for your gallant offer
at a time of sore perplexity! Can you help me
to board *The Muse*? I'll explain when I see
you. In two hours I will be in front of the
Cabildo with my maid and baggage. Believe
me, I shall ever be most grateful.

I remain,
L'etrangere"

She gave Trojan the note. "If he asks where I live,"
she said, "just shake your head."

Trojan nodded and grinned widely. Zulu wondered
just how much Letty told him on those Sundays they
met to dance in Congo Square.

"So you're leaving," Breel said. "I didn't think
you'd stay." He bent painfully to try to ease Donna into
a more comfortable position.

Zulu called out orders to Letty, ignoring him and
trying not to look at Donna.

But as she started to follow her maid out of the door
later, she felt an unfamiliar reluctance.

"Don't think you're rid of me," Breel called after
her. "We've still a score to settle, and by God when the
time comes I'll find you, wherever you are!"

"I hope he catches the fever!" she muttered as she
hurried down the stairs after her maid.

Chapter Thirty-one

The reluctance to leave with Donna ill, oppressed Zulu
so strongly that she stopped at the corner and told Letty
to set down the bags.

"I want you to go on ahead," she said. "You'll meet Mr. Langford in front of the Cabildo and tell him I'll join him as soon as possible. When he sees you, he'll wait for me."

Letty shook her head violently, and Zulu saw that she was terrified at the prospect of going through the city alone.

"If you don't do what I tell you," Zulu warned her, "Mr. Langford will leave New Orleans without us and we'll be here for all the sickness."

Letty picked up the bags and started down the street. She moved slowly, glancing back hopefully every few steps.

Zulu waited until she was out of sight, and then went to Eugenie's house.

To chance missing the boat didn't make sense. Yet she felt a compulsion drawing her.

Ferne showed no surprise when she opened her door. She stood aside and waited for Zulu to enter the room.

"I read about M'sieur Randolph in the *Picayune*," she said. "If you've come to ask me to be your chaperon again—"

Zulu shook her head. "I'm going on a trip," she explained, "and I don't want anything to go wrong."

"Go to Madame Dédé!" Ferne snapped. "She'll wrap a mess of bad smelling leaves together and sell them to you."

"I don't want a bag thrown at me like the one Yvonne took. That isn't what I came for."

Ferne licked her lips uneasily. She moved to the other end of the room and back again. "What do you want me to say? No good'll come of this trip or any other you take."

She opened the door to a room no bigger than a pantry. "*Cela ne vaut vraiment pas la peine*," she muttered. She beckoned to Zulu to enter and then closed the door. In the darkness Zulu could hear her moving objects, then a light flamed as a candle was lit.

243

It was a black candle and she placed it on an altar in front of two stuffed cats. Zulu had an uneasy memory of that night with Yvonne when the voodoo fires had driven her out into the open air.

Ferne opened a basket and pulled out the gleaming length of a snake. She stroked it and it lay in stunned stillness.

"This is no ordinary candle," she said. In the flickering light her eyes were strange. The pupils dialated as she stared steadily at the flame.

"It's made of many strange things. I'll expect a generous offering for what I have to burn of it."

The snake started to writhe. It swayed its head back and forth and its forked tongue darted out. It seemed to Zulu that rather than threatening Ferne with its poison, it seemed to be trying to lick at her face like an affectionate kitten, and Ferne swayed in unison with it.

"Ou poco bliê'm..." she droned. It wasn't the pure French she usually spoke, but a dialect that reminded Zulu of Annette.

"Chongé'm..." Her voice stumbled on, over strange words. Occassionally Zulu distinguished a phrase.

"Adie. . . Moune arroyo. . ." Her voice stopped and she turned to Zulu. Her eyes glittered and pierced.

"Mine's not the bastard voodoo of New Orleans. My mother was of Santo Domingo and she had the power. I can't be exorcised, Le Grand Zombi holds his own. I was conceived in the sight of the snake and when I was born it crawled across my lips..."

"The candle's burning," Zulu exclaimed, "you'll be taking my money for listening to your story."

I've got to get out of here! she thought. She felt the strangeness slithering over her like a smothering weight.

Dimly she could see that fire again. She could feel its warmth in the room. It was growing in the candle, it was enveloping the cats, it was climbing to the ceiling, and now, again, it soared over the tree tops.

"There's a song about your soul," Ferne's voice was

244

saying, "it has captured you, and you're compelled to live to its pattern. You don't need a *gris-gris*. You don't need your *pierre-loa*. The song will bring what you ask. At first."

The room was blazing red now, with fire. She wondered why Ferne didn't see it. Ferne was standing in its very midst, yet she seemed unaware.

...And the trees were swaying against the night sky. The serpent writhed out of Ferne's hand and was crawling to her as it had crawled at the voodoo meeting. In another minute it would be on her skirts...

"The song," Ferne continued, "will bring you what you want ...until it reaches its climax." Her voice sank to a whisper. "Then there'll be no *gris-gris*, no *loa* powerful enough to help you against its descent."

At her feet the snake was twisting and turning. She could hear its body flop on the boards.

"The song was stilled... but now you've freed it again. You can't always run, Zulu. Sometime you'll have to stop and pay."

The fire was dying down again. She could see the tree-tops and the black sky above them. A shudder rippled through the snake.

"There's a chance to still the song before it reaches its crescendo," Ferne said softly, "but..."

The snake lay belly up, limp and the candle went out. Ferne threw open the door, permitting light to shine into the closet, then she picked up the snake, but it sagged lifeless in her hand. She stared at it in mounting horror.

"Get out of here!" she screamed to Zulu. "Feed that song! Its happiness can only be maintained by a full diet. But don't come back to me!"

Zulu reached into her reticule and took out the first coins that came to her fingers and gave them to Ferne.

Slowly and deliberately, Ferne moved over to her bed and dropped the money into her chamber pot.

Zulu stood still a minute, anger fighting with pride.

"Soon as I leave she'll grab the money and wash it

off," she consoled herself.

Letty and Renny Langford were waiting in front of the Cabildo. He was standing with his feet apart and a worried frown on his face.

He looks a little like Norman Peltier, she thought, disturbed. But then, again, it made everything more fitting.

He swept off his hat when he caught sight of her. She took his hand.

"How can I ever thank you!" she gasped.

"I heard of your uncle's death," he said.

Lord God, how much had he heard?

"Mort sur le champ d'honneur..." he said, quoting the newspapers. "You must be proud he died defending his honor. And not a young man, either."

He didn't know the details! Zulu felt a gratitude for the epidemic that had reduced all gossip to ill-bred frivolity.

She drew a weary breath. "I had to see to his funeral. I'm to meet a cousin at Baton Rouge, but when I tried to board a boat—"

"I never saw such a sight," he agreed. *"The Muse* wasn't taking on any passengers, and I had to insist you were the exception." He smiled. "After all, I'm still an owner until the papers are filed."

"Merci," Zulu murmured. *"Merci beaucoup, M'sieur."* How long, she wondered, would she have to continue inserting French? Sooner or later her accent was bound to give her away.

"My arm?" He smiled down at her. "When we're on board I'll have my aunt make the introductions." His eyes grew serious. "You'll never know how highly I value the trust you've placed in me."

The captain helped her up the ladder to the deck. He was a thin, worried looking man and he glanced nervously over his shoulder.

"This must seem a queer way to take on passengers, Ma'am," he apologized. "but you realize, of course, the

246

circumstances warrant it." He cleared his throat. "To be frank, I'm a bit uneasy about—"

"I'll keep to myself as much as possible until you're certain there's no danger of the fever," she promised.

"Very sensible," he approved. "Your name, ma'am? And how far are you taking passage?"

"Miss Randolph," she replied, "and my maid, Letty." She looked over her shoulder for Renny, but he had kept his promise and removed himself from her presence.

"How far did you say?" the captain persisted. "You know the difficulties of navigating up river makes the cost of passage higher than down. It's $16.00 to Baton Rouge and $30.00 to Natchez."

Zulu opened her reticule and gave him $30.00

"Coming back, it's only $15.00 from Natchez," he said. "Now if you wish, I'll show you to the ladies' quarters."

He moved down the deck in advance of her. Zulu's eyes were caught and held by a deckhand who stood back, holding a length of rope. He stared fixedly at her out of his one good eye while a muscle in his cheek twitched.

His body was slim and well porportioned, its clean lines a contrast to his ravaged face, with its flattened nose, empty eye socket and broken cheekbone. There was a scar on his head that parted his sun bleached hair by several inches.

Zulu frowned. Something in the way he held himself, something in the way he planted his feet firmly on the deck. There was a familiarity she could not place.

She turned her head away, but she felt the malevolent one eye follow her.

The captain led her below deck and stood aside so she could enter a huge, beautifully furnished cabin.

"I hope you'll find your quarters comfortable," he said and closed the door behind her. She heard his feet move away.

She looked about the room. There were about twenty beds each with a curtained port hole. Crisp red material partitioned off each section and the flowered material of the counterpanes bulged over fine feather mattresses. Great gilt mirrors hung on the bulkheads. There were sofas set against the wall.

Her feet sank into a thick, fawn colored rug as she approached the only person in the cabin, an elderly woman who sat at a writing desk.

"Pardon me, Madame," Zulu said hesitantly, "but which one of the beds is not taken?" It was the first time she'd ever addressed a white woman as an equal.

The woman took off her spectacles and wiped them as her eyes traveled from Zulu's head to her feet and then back to her face again.

It's no use, Zulu thought in panic. I can't get away with it. White folks are bound to know.

"So you're the girl my nephew has been raving about?"

Zulu couldn't trust her voice. When she was excited it was always husky. And why was the woman looking at her hair so intently? Had she noticed that tendency to curl too tightly in the hair that fell against her throat? Or was it the faint hint of gold in her skin? Lord God, she should have known better!

"You've got nice hair," the woman decided. "I always did say Renny was partial to a good head of hair." She sighed. "We can blame it on that if we all come down with the fever."

"I'm indebted to your nephew." Zulu smiled her brightest.

"I should think you would be," the lady agreed. She dipped her fingers into a gilted little box and lifted them daintily to her nostrils. She inhaled the snuff and sneezed violently.

"That's a sure way to keep from getting a sickness," she explained. She snapped the lid of the box. "Speak up, miss! What's your name?"

Zulu looked down. "Zulu Randolph."

"Zulu!" The woman snorted. "Isn't that the name of some sort of savage? The names people give their children!"

Zulu said quickly, "Not Zulu, Zula.'"

"Oh." The woman took another pinch of snuff. She sneezed again, violently, then she nodded. "I'll call you Zula," she decided. "No reason to stand on formality. "I'm Tessa Langford. My nephew insists I cultivate you so an introduction is possible. Why are you traveling without a guardian or chaperon?"

"My cousin is expecting to meet me in Baton Rouge," Zulu explained. "My uncle died last week. He was my guardian."

"Oh my dear child." But her eyes were on the grey traveling suit.

"There wasn't time to visit my modiste," Zulu said softly. "And in times of *la fievre*—"

"Your uncle died of the fever?"

Zulu looked at the carpet. "No," she replied, "it was on the field of honor."

"Oh," Miss Langford was obviously favorably impressed. "I've heard of the duels you Creoles indulge in." Her voice lowered to an eager whisper. "I hope it wasn't over one of those dreadful quadroons?"

"My aunt," Zulu retorted with dignity, "said it was a gentleman's honorable dispute."

"Oh." Miss Langford was clearly disappointed. "Your aunt was unable to chaperon you?"

"Friends took her to the country place. She wasn't up to travel but she wanted me as far as possible away from the sickness."

Miss Langford looked down at the note she had been writing. "You must forgive my questions, child, but it concerns me to see you without protection. The world's not safe for a young, pretty girl."

Young, pretty girl! Zulu thought. She means for her precious nephew!

She ran her hand over her forehead imitating the gesture Donna used when distracted. "You must pardon me," she murmured, "but I'm afraid I still haven't recovered from my uncle's death. If my answers seem confused—"

"Not a bit of it," Miss Langford grunted. "I suggest you sit on that sofa and relax. This trip should do you good."

Zulu sank down, grateful not to be under the scrutiny of those sharp, piercing eyes. Her heart was beating heavily, and she felt very much as if she were drowning in a high sea...

After a minute she summoned the courage to speak again.

"Lor—My, but this is a beautiful boat!"

Miss Langford stared at her.

"This? Why child, it's one of the oldest on the river! That's why I urged my nephew to sell his interest."

"Oh." Zulu decided in the future to let the white folk start the conversations. Apparently there was much to learn. Evidently a lady could complain, but must, under no circumstances, be caught admiring accommodations.

She rested her head back and listened to the roar of the engine.

"We're leaving!" she exclaimed.

"About time," Miss Langford sniffed. Her pen scratched a minute more, then she got up. "I must watch this from the deck," she decided, "I must describe every bit of it in my Journal."

Zulu started to follow, but Miss Langford shook her head.

"Best you stay below until later. The passengers were told no one would be taken on at New Orleans. Wait until dinner to show yourself."

Zulu tried to rest, once she was alone in the cabin. But somehow she kept seeing the deck hand.

Chapter Thirty-Two

I'm a white lady! she thought as she prepared to dress for dinner. Letty brought her the freshly pressed red taffeta and she reluctantly shook her head. Of all the times to have to be in mourning!

She was reconciled when she observed how her black velvet stood out against the bright colored ballgowns the other ladies were wearing. She pinned a black lace scarf over her curls and stood back to admire her reflection. The other women looked insipid in contrast to her warmly glowing skin and the delicate black lace added a sultry, exotic air.

She lingered a few minutes after the others had left, fighting a surge of panic.

"What an extraordinary beauty," she had heard one of the women whisper as they left. "When did she get on the boat?"

That certainly should have reassured her. Yet, this was a daring step and she knew it.

She stepped out into the companionway to find herself facing the one eyed deckhand. He stared at her and she was aware that his fists were clenched as if in anticipation. There was the sound of approaching voices and he darted away. Zulu remained still a minute, her knees weak.

The captain had arranged for her to sit at his table. As she took her seat she noted that the people on either side of her had been set apart at a little more than the ordinary distance. The captain nodded reassuringly and she inclined her head.

She glanced down the table and her eyes were caught by Renny. He nodded, but didn't speak.

Miss Langford sat on her right and she leaned closer to Zulu.

"I'll introduce you later," she whispered. "My nephew's fit to explode!"

Never, not even at Elmside's biggest banquets had Zulu ever seen food such as was set in front of her. She watched Miss Langford to make certain she took the correct amounts of each course, but before the meal was half over, she felt uncomfortably full. Miss Tessa Langford beamed.

"It's a joy to find a young girl with a healthy appetite," she approved. "I declare, you've kept pace with me and Renny says I eat like a horse!"

Zulu noticed then that Miss Langford was helping herself to twice as much as anyone else, but it was too late to change her tactics. She had to continue eating while those sharp eyes watched.

When finally the last course was over, she felt she'd pop if she drew a deep breath. She wanted nothing more than to have her corset loosened and to forget food.

"My nephew will be waiting in the saloon," Miss Langford said.

"If you don't mind . . ." Zulu murmured. "I'm not up to it."

"How thoughtless of me. I completely forgot what you've been through. You poor child, do you want me to go below with you?"

Zulu shook her head mutely. Lord God! What a time to feel sick.

The captain saw her leaving and he beamed at her.

She remembered the deckhand suddenly. "Miss Langford," she said, "if you'd help me find the cabin?"

Once in bed she scowled her misery at the port hole. Upstairs she could hear the music and the sound of laughter. Out on deck a roustabout was singing. She pounded her pillow.

As the night wore on the women began to come

below. Assisted by their maids they prepared for bed and finally the lights were dimmed.

Zulu began to drift into the drowsy state preceeding sleep when there was a sudden crash, then a splintering sound. The boat shuddered from stem to stern and above, on deck, there was the sound of running feet and voices shouting out commands.

Zulu remembered the steamboat she'd seen explode and she jumped from her bunk. The other women were doing the same. A few of them pulled on robes and went to the door. One of them put her head out and spoke to someone.

"We're in no danger, ladies," she assured the others. "We've struck a log and it's done some damage to the wheel."

The boat lay at anchor the remainder of the night. Occasionally a light flashed by the porthole on the starboard side, illuminating the cabin. They could hear men shouting and cursing. Once there were jeers from a riverboat that glided past in the night. Several times there was a rending, tearing sound.

Zulu buried her face in her pillow and tried to sleep. Ferne's words ran through her mind, and she tossed uneasily. Then she thought of Donna. Donna was probably dead by now. She closed her eyes tightly and tried to shut out the picture of Donna sprawled in a gutter, and of the cart clattering to a stop so that she could be tossed on top of the heap of bodies.

She fell asleep, finally only to dream of the deckhand. In her sleep she knew who he was.

The morning sun fell across her face and she opened her eyes. She lay still, trying to recall her dream. After all, it was just a dream. The sort of dream to be expected after eating a heavy meal.

She drank in the luxury of her surroundings as she sat up. She smiled and stretched. If only Prissy back at Elmside could see her now!

Miss Langford stuck her head around from the next

bunk. Her hair was in rags, sticking out like multiple horns.

"Renny was fit to be tied when I told him you'd gone below. Now he's twice as anxious to meet you." She gave Zulu a knowing look.

Lord God, Zulu thought, she thinks I did it to be coy!

"I didn't want to offend him after all his kindness," she said, "but I just wasn't myself."

She lowered her lashes and tried to look unhappy, but it was difficult to keep the glow out of her eyes and the excitement out of her voice. This was living!

Miss Langford's steady gaze did not waver from her face.

They dressed and went up to breakfast. The captain nodded at Zulu.

"You're looking mighty fit today, Miss Randolph," he told her "I don't think we need worry about you carrying the fever."

Zulu smiled. "I don't see how I could," she told him. "I wasn't exposed to it." The picture of Donna's head lolling back as she helped Breel carry his wife to the divan, flitted across her mind. She repressed the desire to laugh in the pompous little man's face.

Miss Langford nudged her.

"Are you ill? You've hardly eaten a bite."

With a sinking sensation, Zulu realized the reputation she had to uphold. She reached for more. If I keep eating like last night, she thought, none of my dresses will fit.

She put down her fork and smiled at Miss Langford. "I only eat like that when I'm nervous," she explained. "And in the morning I'm just never hungry."

Miss Langford grunted.

They went out on deck after breakfast. Renny Langford followed like an eager puppy.

"Lord love me," his aunt said, "I might as well introduce you! Miss Randolph, may I present my nephew, Renny Langford? There. Thank the Lord that's over! Now I can take my turn on the deck."

Renny smiled. If he really were a puppy he'd be wagging his tail, Zulu thought.

He helped her into a chair by the rail, and after he'd made certain that she was comfortable, he settled in the seat beside her.

He pointed out the lawns that sloped to the river from the big houses they passed, and to the cabins nestled here and there along the bank.

"I like our Virginia plantation houses better," he told her "They may not have all that fancy iron work, but they look more durable and peaceful. I suppose that's because I grew up in them."

Zulu nodded, but though she tried to listen, her mind was busy with the problem of Baton Rouge. How would she explain it when no one met her?

Miss Langford returned. She paused to take a pinch of snuff, but refused Renny's offer of a chair.

"The captain's a very sensible man," she said. "He tells me he was challenged to a race and he refused. Besides, we need some new fittings on one of the wheels damaged last night. It can't be repaired until we dock."

Renny grinned. "I swear you're carrying on a flirtation with the captain, Aunt Tess."

Miss Langford appeared pleased. "Nonsense!" She snorted. "I have to find out about these things to make my Journal complete." She gathered her dignity about her and disappeared around a cabin.

Zulu looked down. "An aunt like that must be very helpful with one's children," she ventured. "Your wife must find her invaluable."

Renny reddened. "I wouldn't know," he stammered. "I don't have a wife or children."

He made a motion as if to reach for her hand, but lost courage.

"There isn't much time between here and Baton Rouge," he said, his color deepening still. "If only you had your guardian with you. I would like to assure him

255

of the honor of my intentions."

"I might not leave the boat at Baton Rouge," Zulu told him softly. "If my cousin has finished his business, we'll stay on until Natchez."

Renny's face brightened.

The captain announced the boat would remain docked a day in Baton Rouge while repairs were made. Most of the passengers disembarked to see the town. Miss Langford was very anxious to join the group, Journal in hand, but Renny hesitated by Zulu. She stood near the rail with Letty, baggage piled around them.

"Shouldn't your cousin be here by now? Are you certain you'll be all right?"

Zulu managed a worried nod.

"Maybe I should stay here with you until he comes?"

Lord God, she'd overdone it!

"No!" she exclaimed in real alarm. "He'd never understand if he saw me with a stranger! Like my uncle, he's very quick tempered. Why already, he has—"

"I don't want to set him against me," Renny agreed hastily. "I only hope he's ready to continue upriver."

As soon as the group had disappeared, Zulu had Letty take their bags back into the women's cabin and she remained there until she heard the passengers returning in the late afternoon.

When Miss Langford came below to freshen up, she found Zulu reclining on the couch and Letty hovering over her with smelling salts.

"We heard you hadn't disembarked and my nephew's been searching the boat. Why . . . is something wrong?"

Zulu nodded, handkerchief to nose. "My cousin's dead. He died on the boat on the way up here. I couldn't even learn if he was buried decently!" She sobbed. "I don't know where to go. Not back to New Orleans until the epidemic's over. . . . But where else?"

Miss Langford inhaled her snuff, sneezed and

frowned.

"This is a fix," she finally muttered. "Where had you and your cousin planned to go when you arrived in Natchez?"

Zulu thought quickly. "My aunt said it was a long trip from Natchez. He'd bought the property just before he came to New Orleans on a business trip. He said his wife would be happy to have me stay with them and so I planned to meet him up here. I couldn't leave when he did . . . my uncle . . . I couldn't leave until after the funeral and I knew my aunt would be all right. . . ."

"This is dreadful," Miss Langford muttered. "Dreadful."

"I'll go as far as Natchez, then take a boat back to New Orleans," Zulu sniffled.

"New Orleans!" Miss Langford repeated, horrified.

"What else can I do?" Zulu renewed her sobbing as Letty watched with an admiring eye.

"But child, if your aunt is in the country—Oh, of course, you'll find a carriage to take you to her. Or are there friends?"

"My friends are all in the country and there aren't any carriages for hire—they're using everything for the dead. In Baton Rouge they say they aren't even using vaults. They're just dumping them into pits, then they cover them like a trench full of potatoes. I couldn't even be certain the slaves haven't run off and left the house in town empty—"

Miss Langford paced across the cabin. She opened her snuff box and snapped it shut.

"I'll have to talk to Renny," she decided.

When the door closed behind her, Zulu sat back to wait. Letty grinned. "You do mighty fine, Miz Zulu," she said.

Eventually Miss Langford returned with a tight lipped look.

"We decided there's only one thing to do. We'll write your aunt and tell her of your cousin, and that we've

257

invited you to come to Virginia with us and wait at Nollgrove until the sickness is over.''

Zulu hesitated. "I don't know—I couldn't impose—"

"Nonsense!" Miss Langford snapped. "I'll write the letter now and we can get it off before we leave port.''

"My aunt is rather eccentric,'' Zulu said doubtfully. "It would be better if I wrote.'' She smiled through her tears. "How can I ever thank you?''

"Don't bother.'' There was something too close to suspicion in Tess Langford's eyes to please Zulu.

She pursed her lips. "I certainly insist on enclosing a note with your letter, child. Undoubtedly your aunt has faith in you, but I'm certain a note from me will make her rest easier. Besides, I have to let her know where to write when she can send for you.''

She sat down at the desk and started to write. She tore up her first efforts and started again.

Zulu watched awhile and found herself yawning. She turned it into a sob and dabbed at her eyes. With a muffled apology, she went up on deck.

Renny found her at once. He caught her hand and carried it to his lips.

"If there is anything I can do?''

Zulu smiled wanly. This being a bereaved lady was beginning to wear on her nerves.

"During time of *la fievre*,'' she said bravely, "we expect anything. I remember. . . .'' and she told him the story Donna had told her.

His face was pale when she finished. "Ghastly!'' he whispered. "That you—''

Zulu looked down. "*C'est la fievre*,'' she murmured.

"I only hope,'' Renny ventured shyly, "that someday I may have the honor to make up to you for all the unhappiness.''

A muffled sound, suspiciously like a laugh startled both of them. Zulu turned and saw the one-eyed deckhand moving a chair for an elderly passenger. He had dropped the chair and was apparently caught in a coughing fit.

Miss Langford joined them. She proudly displayed a sealed note.

"Here's your letter. Now go below and write that note to your poor aunt."

Below, in the cabin, Zulu's first move was to break the seal and open the note. She read it and then tore it into tiny shreds. She opened a porthole and dropped the scraps into the river.

Back at the desk she folded blank paper into the envelope. She sealed it and addressed it to Madame Shadney Randolph on the Bayou St. John.

On deck, in Miss Langford's hearing, she gave her letter to the captain for posting.

"It certainly didn't take you long," Miss Langford observed when she joined them.

"I knew what I had to say." She parted her lips to add more, but she stopped, appalled.

A tall, broad shouldered man was standing behind Renny, holding a coat. In the torchlight of New Orleans that Mardi Gras evening she had been aware of the virility Jules exuded, but now she could see clearly the penetrating intelligence in his dark eyes as they flashed over her. There was no change in his expression, but she knew he recognized her.

I should have realized, she thought. It all came together. Renny, a stranger in town and Jules waiting to see he came to no harm.

"There's a wind coming up, Mister Renny," Jules said. His voice was as soft and compelling as she had remembered.

"Thank you, Jules." Renny was obviously embarrassed at being pampered in front of Zulu. "I catch a chill easily," he explained.

Jules eyes swept over her again as he moved to leave and it was like a physical impact.

"Jules treats me as if I were a baby!" Renny laughed.

259

"He doesn't talk like a darky. Except for his skin, he could be white," Zulu said, trying to sound casual.

"He is a handsome fellow, isn't he? His mother was almost white and his father—You know how those things are. But Jules is smart. Sometimes I think he'd be a lot happier if he wasn't so smart."

And Zulu knew that suddenly everything wasn't going to be as easy as it had seemed.

Chapter Thirty-Three

Though the music in the main saloon made her tingle to dance, Zulu realized that as a recently bereaved lady she must content herself with sitting on the moonlit deck listening to Renny talk. However, she enjoyed watching the twinkling lights of grand houses and cabins on the bank, and Renny droned on endlessly.

"Watching the shore at night always makes me want to write poetry," he told her. Then he confided shyly, "I used to compose poems when I felt in the mood."

"How wonderful!" she said automatically.

He appeared pleased and embarrassed at the same time and changed the subject. "I know you'll like Nollgrove. I think it's the most beautiful place in the world."

"Your aunt said you were the owner," Zulu said carefully. "Are you an orphan, too?"

He nodded. "My mother died when Reginia was a baby. My father was killed by some runaway slaves a few months later."

"Reginia?" Zulu repeated. She hadn't reckoned on a sister.

"The prettiest girl in the county!" Renny told her proudly.

Zulu's frown deepened. "Is she like—like you?"

Renny laughed. "Wait till you meet her."

One of the roustabouts was singing softly on the deck above

    "Pauv' piti Mom'zelle Zizi!

    Pauv' piti Mom'zelle Zizi

    Li gaignain bobo, bobo

    Dans so piti tchoeur. . . ."

Renny moved a little closer and his eyes were warm and adoring as he looked down at her. Zulu smiled back.

What else does he need? she wondered. There was that rich, mellow voice crooning above them, a full moon and the soft lapping of the water.

She raised her face and their eyes met. If he's half a man he'll kiss me, she thought. And once he kisses me . . .

There was a sound near them and Renny glanced up. She followed the direction of his gaze and saw that the one-eyed deckhand was moving chairs back into the shelter of an overhang. He was humming under his breath and the song sent a chill through her. She knew he was humming the tune deliberately and that it should mean something to her. She shivered.

The black roustabout on the upper deck moved away and his lament for Mom'zelle Zizi followed him. Zulu looked up at Renny and saw that the spell was broken.

"I'm tired," she said. "Will you see me to the cabin?"

Miss Langford was waiting for her in her nightdress.

"I saw you and Renny mooning by the rail," she said. "He's inclined to be impetuous. If he gets out of hand you tell me and I'll see to him."

"Don't worry," Zulu muttered, "he's a perfect gentleman."

Miss Langford looked up quickly.

Zulu smiled. "You don't have to worry."

"I don't know," Miss Langford said. "He's fretting about whether you'll like Nollgrove and whether our darkies are up to those fine Creole niggers, and all the time I think he'd do better to wonder how you and our fine Reginia are going to get along."

"If she's like her brother—"

"That's just it!" Zulu wondered if there wasn't a slightly malicious note in Miss Langford's voice. "She isn't. She isn't like anyone but Reginia. And Renny's her whole life."

Zulu sat on the sofa and picked up a magazine. She turned up a lamp that had been arranged so one could read without disturbing those who were in their bunks asleep.

"Aren't you going to send for your maid to get you ready for bed?" Miss Langford inquired.

"I can't sleep," Zulu told her. "Maybe if I read awhile—"

Zulu waited until Tessa Langford's gentle snores merged with the others. She went to the bunk and whispered softly.

"Miss Langford. . . ."

There was no response. She went to her bunk and opened her portmanteau. She took a cape out of it and dropped Ramon's gun into the pocket.

She hesitated, almost out into the companionway. But there was no turning away. She had to find who the deckhand was. She couldn't rest easy until she knew.

She moved stealthily up onto the deserted deck. She felt certain he would be waiting. That he knew she wouldn't dare not to meet his challenge.

He was leaning back against the rail, smoking. He turned around at the sound of her feet.

"Why have you been watching me?" she whispered.

He laughed. "You mean you haven't recognized me?"

"Should I?" But fear had her reaching into her

pocket for her gun. With a quick movement he caught her arm and the pistol clattered to the deck.

"You made a fool out of me once, but you won't again," he said, his voice low and tense. "Maybe you didn't recognize me. You never stayed long enough to find out how I looked when Gram got through."

"Oh Lord God," she whispered. "Bill!"

"Didn't expect me to be alive, did you?" He touched the scar on his head. "Got this broken open for me, didn't you, and you made a sick looking mess out of me, but you didn't get me killed."

'It was Gram. Gram did it."

"Sure it was Gram. That's why my money's gone. That's why my wife left when she heard the fight was over a woman."

"I didn't mean any of that to happen to you. I needed the money. Needed it more than you. I can repay you now."

"Repay me? Not ever! Not with money." In the darkness a knife gleamed in his hand. "You know what I'm going to do? I'm going to slash that pretty, lying face of yours and when I finish I'll be a beauty, next to you. Then you can try baiting your white man. Then you can separate a man from his wife. Go on, scream! I'll tell them what you are."

There was no freeing herself. He moved closer, still holding her arm with his left hand, the knife in his right.

It can't end like this, she thought terrified, but there was no mercy in that one eye.

Suddenly he seemed to fly backwards. She fell against the railing as he whirled around and struck out at the shadow that had pulled him from her.

The shadow lurched forward and there was the thumping of fists striking flesh. Bill fell to the deck, but he sprang up again. In that brief moment, Zulu saw Jules' face in the moonlight.

How much had he heard?

"You damned nigger," Bill snarled, "you'll hang for

263

this. The both of you!"

Jules' grin flashed.

Bill struck out wildly, his breath made a loud, hissing sound, but Jules breathed easily, as if he were barely exerting himself. He side stepped and his fist crashed into Bill's chin. Bill staggered, but kept his feet. He sprang at Jules.

Why didn't Jules kill him? Couldn't he see Bill had to be killed?

Bill thudded to the deck and lay still. Jules bent over him.

"Get some rope so I can tie him," he said.

Zulu swooped down and caught up the pistol. She held it by the barrel and brought it down on Bill's head. She heard a crunching sound and knew she was going to be sick. She dropped the pistol and leaned over the rail.

After a few minutes she looked up weakly. Jules was standing in back of her and he held the gun loosely in his hand.

"You didn't have to do that," he said.

Zulu shook her head. "I didn't mean to hit the thin place where his head had been broken. I just wanted to be sure no one would believe anything he might say for a few days. Don't you understand? If he told the truth it would be a colored man fighting a white for a colored woman. You know what they would do to you."

"It was a life," he said.

Zulu brushed past him, once again in control of her emotions. She screamed as loudly as she could, and then again. There was the sound of rushing feet. Someone held her steadying her and the captain pushed his way through the gathering spectators. He looked down at Bill.

"Who did this?" he asked.

Jules came forward with the gun still in his hand.

I've got to faint, Zulu thought. I've got to faint so there'll be time to think!

She gave a low moan and collapsed against the man

who held her.

"It's Miss Randolph!" someone exclaimed, and the next thing she knew Renny was shouldering his way to her.

The captain's attention was centered on Jules, "God damnit, don't just stand there holding that gun!" he raged.

"It's a nigger. A God damn nigger!" Someone shrieked. "Killed a white man!"

"Who owns this man?" the captain demanded. "Speak up, whose nigger is this?"

Renny looked up from Zulu. "He's mine and if Jules killed that man there must have been a right good reason."

An angry muttering greeted his reply.

If I keep quiet long enough, Zulu thought, no one will know about me. But she knew she couldn't. No matter the consequence, she couldn't.

"It's plain enough," a man said, "this nigger was attacking the lady and that poor man tried to save her."

Zulu realized that unless she interfered there was nothing Renny could do to save Jules. If he were white they might have waited for her story. As it was, they'd pull over the first possible place and leave him on a tree.

She moaned and hid her face. "It was horrible. . . ." she whispered.

"Captain!" Renny exclaimed, "Miss Randolph has regained her senses. She'll tell you it wasn't Jules. Wait till you hear what she has to say!"

"No need to put her through that," the captain retorted. "It's plain to see."

"No!" Zulu exclaimed. "I came up for air and that man there sprang out at me! Look, there's his knife on the deck. The gun was mine, he took it from me. I—I thought—but then that man," she pointed at Jules, "he saved me. He hit him," she pointed at Bill's body, "with my gun. He had a bad place on his head and it—" It wasn't difficult to sob wildly at this point.

265

The captain stared down at the body. "Maybe he wasn't pretty with that gouged eye, but he always did his work. He seemed an upstanding sort. I can't understand it."

Zulu felt Jules' eyes on her. She looked away.

Renny took her below to the cabin and cautioned his aunt not to question her until she'd recovered from the shock.

As Miss Langford helped her to bed, Zulu had the feeling she approved of her even less than before.

But Renny would never forget she'd saved Jules. Then she opened her eyes wide. But why did I do it? He knows. Yet she was aware that from the beginning there was no other way she could have acted.

Chapter Thirty-Four

Renny watched Zulu eagerly as the carriage turned up the avenue that led to Nollgrove.

"The lawn's never very good this time of year," he said anxiously.

Zulu smiled at him and looked toward the columned verandas. There was an air of leisureliness about the rambling, matured lines of the white house. Something comfortable and permanent in the way the roses twisted around the pillars and prowled up the walls.

Then she looked at the slaves who lined the avenue, laughing and waving. It could almost be Elmside. Only at Elmside she'd stood beside the road, too.

Renny helped her down from the carriage. As if by accident, his hand brushed her wrist and he blushed.

Their eyes met. "I love Nollgrove already," she whispered.

A tall, slender girl came out on the gallery. She wore a pale green gown, flounced out by yards of crinoline. Her darkly auburn hair flew in loose curls to her shoulders and it was tied with a deep green ribbon. Her brown eyes were widely spaced and and her mouth had a haughty curve at its corners.

She descended the stairs with a quiet grace and kissed her aunt and brother. Then she turned to Zulu.

Renny took Zulu's gloved hand and gave it to his sister.

"Miss Randolph," he said, "I want you to meet Reginia."

"What a delightful surprise!" Reginia smiled. "Are you of the Georgia Randolphs? Or, perhaps, the Mississippi branch?"

Renny laughed. "She's of the New Orleans Randolphs. You'll find no complaint against that, I'll warrant."

"But I'd never take you for a Creole!" Reginia said. "You don't look a bit like Madeline Lastelle or the other Creole girls I knew at school."

Zulu widened her eyes. "No?" she asked.

"They were such pasty white creatures with big, cow-like dark eyes. Pretty enough, I guess, but no spirit. No wonder their husbands desert them for those dreadful quadroons!"

"Reginia!" Renny's face suffused with color. Miss Langford hastily inhaled some snuff.

"But you know it's true, Renny. Everyone who visits there talks about it, Why be afraid to discuss what exists?"

"My sister, I'm afraid, is very modern about some things," Renny apologized. "She doesn't mean to sound as . . . the way she does. You'll get used to it in time."

Reginia's eyes narrowed just a little. She glanced

sideways at Zulu.

"Oh? It's to be an extended visit? How delightful. I'll have the room next to mine freshened for you."

"We've persuaded Miss Randolph to stay with us until the epidemic in New Orleans is over," Renny explained.

"Of course." Reginia glanced at her brother. "We already have some guests. It'll be nice to have the house full again."

Renny frowned. "Guests?"

Reginia nodded. "Cousin Thalia. You remember she married Cousin Norman when she went to stay with Aunt Ivers in Alabama? She's been visiting around the county, but she'll be with us tonight."

Zulu dropped her fan. Renny swooped to recover it and she took it from him without remembering to murmur her thanks. No wonder Renny had reminded her of Norman!

"Norman?" Renny asked.

"Oh he was far too busy this time of the year. Besides, I think he'd be grateful to get away from those noisy twins."

"Twins?" Renny looked as if he would choke. "Not Cousin Thalia!"

Reginia nodded. "They haven't stopped squalling since they got here."

Zulu felt a profound relief. Thalia had never bothered to set eyes on Rosalie's girl. Still, this was something to consider before she was in too deeply.

"I don't want to interfere with a family reunion," she murmured.

"But I want the family to meet you. All of the family."

Reginia said, "Oh?"

Tessa Langford nodded at her niece. "Yes," she said.

Reginia bit her lip and her eyes clouded.

Chapter Thirty-Five

Zulu stood in the center of the room and looked around. Letty was unpacking, her eyes wide with appreciation.

The bay windows were curtained with a crisp, ruffled material and the bed spread a flowered taffeta. It had none of the French elegance of Rosalie's room, but a dainty femininity of its own.

Zulu leaned out the window and drew a deep breath. It was good to smell growing things again. Sewage running in the gutters under the wooden *banquettes* would never replace the rich aroma of moist soil and flowers.

She crossed the carpet and threw herself onto the bed. She stretched and rumpled her hair and tried to sort out everything that had happened since her arrival.

She dimly remembered hearing Thalia speak of Nollgrove on one of those warm afternoons when she had lingered in Rosalie's room to listen to the leisurely talk on the front gallery.

I'm not going to think about it, she told herself. I'll never go back to Alabama, and it's just to show off she's not an old maid that brought Thalia here.

"You gonna git yerself married?" Letty asked from the wardrobe corner.

For all her planning, she hadn't permitted herself to pause and consider what marriage to a white man would imply. Was it really worth the tremendous risk involved?

"I used to pray de Lawd make me a white nigger," Letty elaborated.

Zulu turned over and rested her chin in her hands.

"I don't know," she said slowly. "I could get into a lot of trouble if they ever found out."

"Lawd! To be mistress of this whole house!"

From Miss Rosalie's body servant to mistress of a Virginia plantation. It was a temptation.

She climbed down off the bed and went to the mirror. She took her hair in each hand and swept it to the top of her hair in a crown. "It would make me look different, wouldn't it?" she asked Letty.

"Makes you right elegant," the maid agreed.

Thalia returned too late for dinner. Though she knew there was nothing to fear, Zulu still felt relief. She had just about decided the meeting would be postponed till the next morning when the carriage rolled up the avenue.

She had a moment of panic when she heard the door open. Renny caught her hand and drew her to her feet.

"I haven't seen Cousin Thalia since she went to stay with the Peltiers over four years ago," he said. Then he added with a grin, "I could never picture her married to Cousin Norman."

Thalia's voice, a little more monotonous and not a bit as self-effacing, carried in from the hallway.

"Now Nordelia, you take the babies right on up to their bed. You simply must stop whimpering, we're all tired. I declare, Nordelia, if you wasn't kin, I wouldn't put up with your laziness!"

"Our cousin has become a bit uppity," Renny remarked to his sister.

Reginia nodded. "For heavens sakes, Renny, aren't you going out to welcome them? She's been looking forward to seeing you."

"I'll stay in here," Zulu said. "You'll have a lot to talk about after all those years."

Renny took her hand. "I would think it an honor if you came with me." He glanced upward from where screams of protest could be heard in the old nursery.

"She's leaving tomorrow to visit her mother's folks north of here," Reginia reassured him. "She won't be back until just before she leaves for Alabama."

"Thank the Lord for his mercies," Tessa Langford murmured.

There was no getting out of it any longer, Zulu thought. If she was going to be white she had to stop this panic every time she was about to be introduced.

Thalia came through the door just before Renny reached the entrance hall.

"We wanted to be sure you had everything settled before we bothered you," he said. "It's a pleasure to have you with us, Cousin."

She glanced upward, the clamor had reached an even higher pitch. "I told Cousin Norman Nordelia would never do," she said.

Cousin! Zulu thought. She would still refer to him as Cousin! She repressed the desire to giggle and suddenly she was no longer nervous.

Miss Langford came out into the hall and kissed Thalia on the cheek. "What a welcome home!" she said. "Why we'd have taken a different boat if we'd known you were here waiting for us!"

Thalia parted her teeth in what could pass for a smile and nodded her head.

"I almost gave up waiting for you to get back before I went to stay at Aunt Rose's! But I knew you'd want to see the twins."

She still looks like an old maid, Zulu thought.

Renny led Zulu forward. "Cousin Thalia," he said, "it's my pleasure to introduce you to Miss Randolph of Louisiana."

Thalia held out her hand. Lord God, Zulu thought, that this could ever happen!

"I guess I'll have to see to things," Thalia said plaintively as the uproar in the nursery showed no sign of abating. "The Thatchers were going to travel back to Alabama with me when I leave for home, and now

271

they say their plans have changed. Cousin Norman has just got to send me out more help."

She lifted her skirts slightly to climb up the stairs.

"I'll be able to visit in the morning," she promised.

Reginia and Miss Langford returned to the sitting room, but Renny lingered by the doorway.

"I want you to see the gardens in the moonlight," he told Zulu and led her out onto the gallery and down a side path.

Zulu shrugged her shoulders so her gown would slide a little lower and they paused by the rose garden. "I love Nollgrove and Virginia," she whispered.

"Zula—I have your permission to call you Zula? I would like to have your aunt's address. I have something very important to ask her."

"Tell me first what it is," she begged.

He smiled. "I can't until I have her permission to court you."

"But it might take months for a letter to reach her in the confusion. It might not even get to her."

"But I've got to state my intentions!"

Zulu laughed softly up at him. "After all we've been through together, are formalities so important?"

"Zula," he whispered, "you don't know what you're saying. . . ."

She put a hand on each of his shoulders and raised her face so her lips were close to his.

"I know what I'm saying," she told him softly.

His mouth crushed down on hers and she felt his rising passion against her. If he didn't think I was a lady, she thought, he'd have me down on the grass!

He raised his head and held her away from his body. "You do love me, don't you?' he begged.

"Would I have allowed you to kiss me if I didn't?"

He was down on his knees before she realized his intention. "Zula," he said formally, "will you do me the honor of becoming my wife soon as I get your aunt's permission?"

She shook her head. "You'll never get my aunt's permission. That's why I don't want you to write her."

He stood up slowly, shaken.

"But I can offer you a good name, a comfortable home and Nollgrove . . ."

"It isn't that," she said, choosing her words as she spoke. "In Louisiana we have early betrothals." She brought her lace handkerchief to her nose. "Don't you understand, Renny? She'd never consent!"

"Do you mean you're promised?"

"I've never even met him," she wailed. "Oh, Renny! Renny. . . ."

He took her into his arms again, and she buried her face against his chest. "He's at school in France, I never want to meet him. I want to marry you, Renny. I don't care about my aunt or anyone else, this'll be my family. It's all I need."

"But we can't just run off and get married. We've got to consider others."

"If you love me enough," she said passionately, "nothing else would matter!"

She turned and ran up the garden path, through the front door and up the stairs to her room.

She sank down into a satin upholstered chair and fanned herself.

I'm into it now, she thought. There's no turning-back!

She heard the curtains rustle and she turned to the open windows. She'd forgotten that like Elmside, Nollgrove had an upper gallery crossing the back end of the house.

Jules came into the room and he regarded her steadily a moment before speaking.

"I saw you out in the garden."

Zulu clung to the back of the chair.

"Leave Mister Renny alone," he said.

Zulu's eyes traveled over his well proportioned body, wishing that Renny had as much ability to stir thoughts she knew must be repressed.

"You'd get it for sure if anyone knew you climbed into my room," she told him. "You'd better get out before I scream."

Jules' eyes were disdainful. "Maybe," he agreed. "But they might just as easily believe what I'd have to tell them."

"I could have let them hang you back on the boat."

"You didn't. I never thought for a moment that you would."

"Well then you knew more than I did," she retorted. "I thought about it."

"I knew you thought about it, but I knew you wouldn't do it anymore than I think you realized what you were doing when you hit that man."

"I wouldn't be bad for Renny," she said. "He needs a strong woman. He'd be marrying me, not a race."

"My mother was as white as you and my father was a white man. How would you explain a child with a skin like mine?"

"I'd say you raped me!" she snapped.

He nodded gravely. "I have no doubt. Me or some other poor devil. You're not Mister Renny's kind of woman. I'd think that even if you were white."

"I could keep him happy."

Jules shook his head. "He wouldn't be happy and neither would you."

"Don't be a fool!" Zulu exclaimed, impatient. "Will you get out of here so I can go to bed, or—" her voice took on a taunting tone, "would you prefer to stay?"

He grinned. "You'd let me stay just so you could say I'd attacked you. That might be a clever way of getting rid of me."

Zulu yawned. "I thought so." Then she added, "but as you said—they just might believe you."

He strode across the room and rook her bare shoulders in his powerful hands.

"I could break you," he said, "with just a little

wrench of the wrists. And there's something inside that says I'd be doing a good thing."

"But you wouldn't, Jules." She looked down and he saw where her eyes were. The color surged into his face.

"Yes," he admitted. "I want you. I've wanted you since that first night. That's why I was glad when I saw where you lived. Once we would have been good for each other. Once, a long time ago."

Even Breel's most intimate touch had never made her feel the way she felt with Jules' hands on her shoulders. I could live with Jules and never want another man, she thought, surprised.

She touched him lightly and felt him shudder.

"You wouldn't want me to go away," she said.

He took his hands off her shoulders and looked at them as if they were to blame. Then he turned and went out of the window.

With light fingers Zulu stroked her shoulders where the marks of Jules' grip still remained.

There was a light knock on her door and Letty came in a little unsteadily. Zulu, remembering Elmside, suspected she'd been helping the butler empty the wine glasses.

"There's to be no drinking," she said. "I know you nipped at what Shad left in his glass and in New Orleans it didn't matter. But here I can't take the chance you might get muddled and say something."

"Not eber. Not me." Letty protested.

Zulu studied her a minute.

"Don' look at me dat way! You send chills down my back."

Zulu shrugged and glanced away. "Has Jules got a woman?" she asked.

Letty shook her head. "Not dat man. He don' even talk to no one 'cept to learn some of the ninnies to read." She touched her forehead significantly.

Breakfast the next morning was a hurried affair so Thalia could get an early start. Renny left as soon as courtesy permitted, for a talk with the overseer.

In the din created by the twins who did not want to spend another day in the carriage, Zulu escaped to the gardens.

Her curiosity about Jules increased, it seemed, with every breath she drew. I've got to get him out of my head, she told herself. I'm going to live here and be mistress and Renny's wife. I can't be thinking about my husband's body servant.

She sat on a bench under a shade tree for a while, until driven by the unrest inside herself she wandered by the neat row of cabins in the quarters and finally to the kitchen house. The door was ajar and she pushed to look inside.

The sight of Jules standing with one leg on a chair brought her to a standstill, then she realized he was talking to the cluster of kitchen and house help who stood around him.

"That makes you grumble," he was telling them in his resonant voice. "I wouldn't want to be called willfully ignorant, either. But it is willful and it is your own fault! Everyone in this room knows I'm teaching the children and will teach anyone who will trouble himself to come up to my room. Someday you'll be glad you learned to write and to read. Someday everyone here might be free. If you stay the way you are it'd be better for you to remain slaves."

Jules held up his hand against the protests.

"There's no reason you should live like a vegetable just because you're black. I know there's a law against learning to read, but if Mister Renny is willing to look the other way, you should be willing to take advantage of it!"

He took his foot off the chair and pushed toward the door. He stopped when he saw Zulu standing outside.

She laughed. "You're wasting your time on them," she said.

Jules followed her until they were out of sight of

either the kitchen house or the gallery, then he caught her arm and swung her around to face him.

"You're free! There's so much you could do. And you laughed."

"I was just remembering," Zulu said, "something I heard a long time ago."

"A little freedom," Thalia had said, "goes to a darky's head. There's the boy my uncle bought for my cousin. His father was a white man, a professor . . ."

"I should think," Zulu went on, "you'd remember what abolitionist talk did to your father."

"I'm not talking abolition, though I think it'll come, someday. Can't you see it's up to the few of us with an education to help the others?"

"You think I could throw away everything I've fought to get for a few niggers that are happy where they are?"

"While those 'niggers' are happy to be slaves you'll never get beyond the closed door to the white man's world. Not unless you lie and cheat like now."

"It's worked."

"Has it? If the *gens de couleur* took half as much effort to establish their own society as they do to imitate the white man, they could be a productive world of their own. They could prepare a place for others when the day comes."

"Forget it," Zulu said. "Do you think any of us—except maybe a few like you—could care? We've enough trouble finding our own way."

"I could buy my freedom," Jules told her, "but I've never considered it because I can reach the others as a slave where it would be different if I were free." He looked down into her face. "I would buy my freedom for you, Zulu. We could leave here and no one would know it was together."

Zulu stared at him, hardly believing what she heard. "You'd give up everything—all that back there?"

"I wouldn't give it up. I couldn't. But we could work

together for our own people. What a miserable segment we are—lording it over the full black and kow-towing to the white man. We could teach our own kind to respect themselves and they, in turn could help those in that kitchen house and others like them."

"How would we live when folks found out what we were doing? In ditches?"

He took her into his arms and she clung to him, hating the desire she felt for him. He kissed her and her body hungered as it had never hungered before. She moaned softly, limp against him.

He released her then and it was a moment before he could speak.

"That's how we would live. And it wouldn't matter where."

She shook her head. "I'm going to marry Renny. I'm going to live here, at Nollgrove. And you're not going to stop me."

"If you hurt Renny," he said softly, "I'll kill you."

Chapter Twenty-Six

The sooner she got Renny to marry her, the safer she would be, Zulu decided. Jules wouldn't dare approach her once she was Nollgrove's mistress, and she would have too much to lose to even be tempted.

After dinner that night she made certain Renny caught a glimpse of her skirt as she went through the door. She settled herself in a corner of the moon drenched gallery, half concealed by the shadow of the climbing rose vines.

She heard Renny coming through the door and then there was the pattering of smaller feet.

"Brother Renny, please wait. I want to talk to you."

Renny sounded a little impatient. "Couldn't we talk later, Reginia?"

"No." Her voice was firm. "I know you're chasing out after her and that's why I want to talk to you."

"Yes?"

There was a slight rustle of material as Reginia placed her hand on her brother's arm. "Believe me, all I care about is your happiness. I'm certain that woman is an adventuress."

"Reginia," Renny said, "you've not been yourself since Miss Randolph came. In fact, several times you were close to being downright rude. I know you're upset at an outsider coming into our circle, but don't you think that's my business?"

Reginia was quiet a minute. "I always thought when you married it would be a nice Virginia girl—like Betsy or Mavis—but it isn't just that. Renny, we know so terribly little about Miss Randolph!"

Renny laughed. "So that's it! But her uncle is one of the most prominent business men in New Orleans. Her aunt comes of one of the old Creole families. You couldn't ask for anything better!"

"After all, you met her in a most peculiar way. She might be—anything. You've no proof but her word."

"I wouldn't ask for a better proof."

"If nothing I can say will stop you . . . oh, Renny, please, I don't want you to do anything foolish!" She hesitated. "Would you make me a promise?"

"What sort of a promise?"

"Of course I know you're not likely to, anyway, but would you promise you'll wait at least a month before you plan a wedding?"

A month! Zulu could plainly see the purpose. Within a month an explanation would be expected as to why she hadn't heard from her aunt.

"You're certain she'll even have me?" Renny sounded amused. "A month would be reasonable enough."

"She'll have you, all right," Reginia said bitterly. "Randolph or not, Renny—there's something wrong."

"Couldn't it be that you're a little jealous, Reginia? I know how you love Nollgrove and that you can't be too happy to know someone will take over from you. But isn't it time you thought about a home of your own?"

Zulu slipped off the gallery and stood by the garden path. Renny came through the door and stood at the top of the stairs looking for her.

"Zula?" he asked as she moved out of the shadows. He descended the stairs and joined her. "You've been avoiding me all day," he said.

"I've had such a lot to think about. Of course you're right. We can't just get married without thinking of the others. You'll have to write my aunt. I know she'll send after me and we'll never see each other again . . . and I love you so much, Renny."

"Reginia knows how I feel about you. I told her we would wait a month. By then maybe everything will be different."

"It will be different, all right," Zulu spoke a little more bitterly than she had intended. "Renny, either we go to Richmond tomorrow and come back married or—or it'll never happen."

"I can't go through life without you!" he exclaimed. "But, Zula, I gave my word. You wouldn't want to marry a man who had no regard for his honor?"

She wrenched her hand out of his. "Honor?" she repeated. She managed a sob. "Of course, Renny."

"I've got to go down to the gatehouse right now," he told her, "there's some things I want to be certain the overseer has done tomorrow. Will you wait here for me till I come back?"

"No!" she exclaimed. "No!" She ran into the house. With the door closed behind her, Zulu threw her fan across the room and pulled her hair free. She whirled around and fell on the bed. She laughed until the lacings on her corset hurt.

So it's honor, is it? she thought. She'd fight Reginia with her own weapon. She untied the straps of her slippers and kicked them off. One upset a vase of flowers on a small table.

When Letty came through the door, Zulu was standing in front of the mirror with a perfume vial in her hand.

"Ain't no one spect you'd birthed a baby," Letty told her appreciately.

"Lord God!" Zulu snapped. "How thick do you think these walls are? I'd like you to remember that's Reginia's room right next door."

She handed Letty the vial. "Rub this over my back. Down there, a little more between my shoulders. That's it."

She put the stopper in the bottle and she motioned for Letty to bring her the cerise colored satin robe that she'd flung over the bed. Letty started to get her a night dress as well, but she shook her head. "I won't need that tonight," she said.

She pulled he robe around her tightly, the shimmering lines revealed the curve of thigh and fell low over the roundness of her breasts. She nodded for Letty to leave.

She waited by the door until finally she heard Renny coming up the stairs. She put her hand on the knob and at the same time she heard movement in the next room. So Reginia had been watching for Renny, too. But what did that matter.

Renny's footsteps were outside her door, when she threw it open.

"Oh!" she gasped drawing back and pulling her robe closer, "I thought it was Miss Langford. I can't get my window open."

"Which window?" Renny asked and she could see he was having trouble keeping his eyes averted.

Zulu pointed to the one furthest across the room and as he went toward it, she eased the door shut.

"This one?" Renny asked, and Zulu heard movement again in the next room. Well, Miss Reginia, she thought, I'll bet you're wondering!

She came alongside him. "No," she said, "that one." She pointed, then hastily snatched at her robe as it fell apart.

Renny colored, trying to look away, but Zulu moved closer and put out her free hand to him.

"I'm sorry I was angry with you earlier. I thought you felt the same way I feel about our getting married."

"Zula, you're so innocent, damn it! Don't you think, Zula, I wish we were married right now, so . . . But can't you see, Reginia's right. People will . . ."

"Don't look at me that way. . . ." she whispered and swayed against him.

"Oh God, Zula—if you only understood how it is with a man . . ." Her arms went around him and he was holding her, whispering her name over and over. Suddenly he became aware that her robe had parted and he buried his head in her breasts with something like a sob. She lay back in the cushions, her arms still around his neck.

It had been so long. . . .

The heat that had been building within her since Jules had taken her into his arms, soared into a frenzy of need. She closed her eyes and it was Jules she was straining against, Jules' hands she was guiding. It was his flesh she was stroking. Caught up in the pulsating demand of her hunger she was only dimly aware that she could again hear Reginia in the room next door, but nothing mattered.

Then, slowly she came back to sanity, but her body still called out for an ecstacy she hadn't quite obtained in Renny's arms. She lay still until the throbbing eased and her breath slowed to normal. Lord God, she thought, I planned to have Renny seduce me and I all but raped him! She raised herself up on the cushions, trying to think.

Renny knelt beside her and hid his face against her.

"Oh God, Zula," he was sobbing, "Oh God, I didn't mean to. Forgive me—" He caught her hands to his mouth, looking up at her. "A guest in my house, a woman I honor and—"

For a minute Zulu was too astonished to speak, but only for a moment. She cradled his head to her. "I couldn't fight you. I love you so much—"

"After what I did, you can still say that?"

She looked down, as if ashamed to meet his eyes. "How could I help but love you . . . now? But Renny, how can I face people, knowing—"

"You'll be my wife as soon as we can get married," he promised.

"But your promise? You're honor-bound."

"What honor would I have if I didn't marry you first thing?" He kissed her gently. "You're sure you're all right?"

She looked away. "I—I hurt a little—but—"

He pulled her tightly to him.

"I'll go get Jules to pack right now," he finally said.

"Oh no!" She choked back her words and looked down again. "We don't want anyone to know. We'll get our own things together and leave a note."

He smiled, humoring her. "If that's what you want." He glanced out the window. "But we'll wake the whole house. It'll be light before we're started."

She looked out at the sky. How long had they lain in the window seat together? She'd lost track of time. Renny was right, it was too late to get away now.

"We'll wait until tonight," she told him. "You can tell them you have to go up to Richmond on business and I'll pack this afternoon."

"You're so cool," he said admiringly.

"I've got to be," she told him. "You're so impetuous and . . . Well, I've just got to keep my head."

283

He started to take her back into his arms, but she shook her head. "We can't trust ourselves," she murmured, "and you've got to get back to your room before everyone is awake."

"Oh God!" he exclaimed. "If anyone saw me!"

She closed the door after him and climbed up onto the bed. In the next room she was again aware of movement. Had Reginia listened all that time? She shrugged. What if she had?

She curled up her knees, cradled her head on her arm and in a very few minute she was asleep.

It was early afternoon before Zulu dressed and went downstairs. She met Reginia on the landing. The girl looked tired and pale.

Zulu smiled. "Good morning, I hope it isn't rude to get up so late—but I hardly slept last night."

Reginia's mouth tightened. "Aunt Tess and I had breakfast alone. Renny just came down a little while ago."

"Oh?" Zulu said.

Reginia flushed and looked away.

After her lunch, Zulu called Letty up to her room to pack. She tried not to think of what marrying Renny involved.

Was it worth the risk of triumph over a ghost? Deep inside she realized this was what she was doing. Somehow her thoughts kept reverting to Ferne with her guttering candles and a snake limp in her hand.

"There's a chance to still the song before it reaches its crescendo . . .

"No *gris-gris* or *loa* can protect you against its descent. . . "

Zulu took her *pierre-loa* out of the jewelry case and dropped it into her reticule.

Chapter Thirty-Seven

They were married the next afternoon and three weeks later they returned to Nollgrove.

Zulu reclined back against the cushioned seat of the carriage, counting each mile that brought her closer. She hardly listened to Renny, though he was talking earnestly in his soft, persuasive voice.

"I wish you'd reconsider," he was saying, "as soon as danger of the epidemic is over, it's our duty to go to New Orleans and call on your aunt."

"How many slaves do we have at Nollgrove?" Zulu asked.

"Your aunt—what? I don't know, offhand, Zula. That's not important now. Your aunt has every right to expect that courtesy."

"Did you say there were fourteen rooms or sixteen?"

"Sixteen. Then there's the—Zula, we're not discussing Nollgrove. We've got to get this settled."

Zulu concealed a yawn behind her fan. "It's settled."

He looked at her. "It—"

She shrugged. "We're not going."

"But aren't you anxious to see her? To set things right?"

She stroked his cheek playfully with her glove hand. "Renny, you just don't understand Creoles! She'll be furious. She won't even receive us. But if we wait a while—maybe a year or so—it might be different."

"I still don't like it," Renny said.

"What difference can it make? She can't stop my legacy. After all, she's not a blood relative."

"The money doesn't matter," Renny said a little sharply. "You don't need to worry about money."

"You keep trying to live other people's lives. Let me worry about my aunt. You'll find it's trouble enough living our own life."

He did not smile. "I'm discovering that."

"And I've been gentle with you," Zulu teased.

He pulled her against him. "I thought once we were married I'd get over this feeling of—of violence you arouse in me." His arm tightened. "But I haven't. Right now I could crush you till you screamed. I have to fight myself to remember to be gentle with you!"

"A woman wants to be loved by her husband," Zulu said.

"A woman like you wouldn't understand what I'm trying to say. I heard grandpa was pretty wild. I must have inherited bad blood from him."

Zulu sat back with a sigh. If he only had a speck of bad blood maybe marriage to him might be a little more satisfying.

The house servants were assembled on the gallery and the field hands lined the drive. Zulu looked at them and felt dizzy with elation. She was mistress of all this! White folks and slaves all dependent upon her whims!

"Frightened, sweetheart?" Renny asked.

Zulu tried to appear nervous and he smiled down on her.

"Don't worry. Aunt Tess loves you already and it'll be only a matter of time till Reginia—"

A matter of eternity, she thought.

As Renny helped her down from the carriage the first person to meet her eyes was Jules. There was no expression on his face, but somehow the elation she'd felt was gone. Something else took its place, but she wasn't quite clear as to just what it was.

"You're trembling, darling," Renny whispered. "You're my wife and this is your home. No one can say anything to you. No one at all."

Tessa Langford came forward. She pulled Zulu into a tight embrace, her eyes streaming.

"I'm so glad Renny's settled down!" she sobbed.

Then it was a white faced Reginia's turn. With no attempt at a smile, she held out her hand. "I hope you are very happy, Zula," she said, then she kissed her brother. "Renny—Renny, you promised."

Renny glanced at Zulu. "Please, Reginia, this is not the right time . . ."

"Will there ever be? Renny, you promised you wouldn't."

"Sometimes things change, Reginia. I want you to try to understand."

"Oh, I understand," she said, wiping her eyes. "I quite understand."

"Zulu didn't want a lot of fuss. Don't forget she's recently lost an uncle and a cousin—"

"We could have had quiet services here, Renny."

Renny looked at Zulu. "It was better this way. We've had three weeks of just each other."

"And of Lord Tennyson, Byron and Shelley," Zulu thought bitterly, "and of museums and art galleries."

Jules had been commissioned to present her with a bouquet of flowers. She accepted it, nodding graciously to everyone, but still unable to avoid meeting his eyes. With a little shock she realized it was disappointment that she saw in his face. She was aware of a twinge of guilt.

Letty started to carry her hand baggage to the bedroom next to Reginia's, but Zulu stopped her.

"The end of the hall, Letty," she said.

Miss Tessa Langford inhaled some snuff and broke into a series of sneezes.

"Aunt Tess!" Reginia said sharply, "I wish you wouldn't use that stuff." She twisted her hands nervously.

Once in the entry hall, Zulu put her arms around Renny and kissed him full on the mouth, aware of Reginia's eyes on her and of Jules half way up the stairs with Renny's bags.

"Your brother's so impetuous," she said to Reginia. "Don't you think he looks well?"

"No," Reginia said. "No, I don't." She turned and left them.

When they were alone in the master bedroom, Renny looked at the closed door with a worried frown.

"I'm not going to stand for much more of that from my sister," he said. "She's got to understand you're the woman I chose to marry, and she's got to respect you as such."

Zulu put her hands on his shoulders. "I can't really blame her for being jealous," she told him. "I wouldn't give you up easily, either."

"You're so wonderful," he whispered. "I can't see how anyone could help loving you."

Chapter Thirty-Eight

Zulu sat on the gallery and stared at the embroidery she'd started. There was a chill in the air, and she shivered. The day, she decided, was as gloomy as her mood.

Everything had been so different when she was a guest at Nollgrove, she'd been in her element then, but her position as Renny's wife was another story.

"It's those uppity Virginia niggers," she told herself. They were courteous enough in their soft spoken way, but they always gave her the impression they couldn't wait to get out of her sight to laugh at the airs she took.

It wasn't really anything she could put a finger to. It was more a combination of little things. Such as the times she asked the butler to see that the library chairs be rearranged, and he'd looked at Tessa Langford for comfirmation before he had the orders carried out. Or the way the maids always waited for Reginia to nod her head before they brought in the last course.

She closed her eyes tightly. All those things might be bearable if only Renny didn't try to be such a gentleman! To him, making love to her was an apologetic affair that must be dispatched as soon as possible, to cause Zulu the least possible inconvenience. The result left her in a frenzy of unfulfillment.

If she tried to make her needs known, clinging to him, moving her body against his in an effort to obtain a degree of appeasement, the act would leave him white and shaken, shamed that his sensuality had stirred in her what no man had a right to arouse in his wife.

Lord God, she thought more than once as she lay rigid beside him, trying to control the undulation of loins that were left hungry and wanting, if Breel came by, I'd fall on him!

During the daylight hours she knew that those around her suffered for the torment of a ripe body stoked, but left just short of the glorious burst of pleasure. She was short tempered with the slaves and would argue over trifles with Reginia. She'd find herself caressing Renny until he nearly went out of his mind, and when ashamed of his inexplicable carnality he followed her to their room, it was only to be left in a worse state than before.

She tossed her embroidery down and moved across the gallery, nervous and tense. The door to the house opened and Tessa Langford joined her.

"I told Merribelle to fetch some lemonade," she said. "She'll be here directly."

"If I asked Merribelle to get it," Zulu thought bitterly, "I'd be lucky to have it by mid-day."

The maid hurried out onto the veranda with pitcher and glasses. She carefully poured Miss Langford's, and then sauntered over to where Zulu sat. She tripped and some of the liquid splattered on Zulu's skirt.

Zulu jumped up and slapped Merribelle's face, first with one hand and then the other. Somehow, all the repressed, throbbing desire of her body flowed into a channel that found an outlet in this burst of rage.

Tessa Langford caught Zulu's wrists. "Shame on you!" she exclaimed. "Merribelle didn't stumble on purpose!"

"Let go my wrists!" Zulu spat out. Her eyes were angry golden streaks. "Let loose and don't talk to me as if I was a child!"

Tessa glowered back at her. "I'll not let go if you're intending to punish that poor girl anymore. I'll have no beatings around me!"

"You forget," Zulu said softly, "I'm mistress here."

Tessa released her grip. "I may not be the mistress, but my nephew trusted me with running this house until you learn something about it. If there's any more of this kind of thing I'll turn over my keys. Maybe you'd like to find what a problem looking after a household like this can be?"

"What makes you think I wouldn't?" Zulu retorted, rage welling up in a blinding wave. That old maid! That poor relation! Treating her like trash!

"Do you know what you're saying?" Tessa asked.

"Just because you've got Renny thinking we can't do without you so you'll have a roof over your head doesn't mean—"

"So that's what you think!" Tessa whispered through stiff lips. She took the keys out of her pocket and slammed them onto the table.

"I can see it'd be better if I open the house in Richmond. I'd a sight rather live alone than—"

"Live with me? Aunt Tessa, you've hurt my feelings."

"It makes me shudder to think of my nephew married to you." Tessa Langford turned and strode off the gallery.

Zulu continued her pacing after a short drink of the cooling liquid in the glass Tessa left.

Renny'd have a fit, there was no doubt of that. Lately he'd been nervous and short tempered. Something like this could result in a lot of unpleasant questioning.

"It's all the fault of the black trash they've got in this house!" she told herself. "Snickering, clumsy, sly."

She caught a glimpse of a skimpy shadow trying to sneak across the avenue.

"Charlie!" she shouted.

The little shadow halted and mounted the stairs reluctantly.

"You were told to pull the fans over the table at dinner this noon. Where were you? We had to eat without a bit of air."

Charlie looked down at his brown little feet.

"This is the second time that's happened."

Charlie nodded.

"You'd have been at the fans if Miss Reginia had told you."

Charlie shook his head emphatically.

"Don't lie!" Zulu exclaimed. "You're all alike. From now on I want you to know I'm the one to obey. You'll know it if I have to beat it into every last one of you!"

She called to the surly gardener who had been trimming the hedge.

"Take the boy to the stables and see he gets a lashing he won't forget."

"Please, missy!" Charlie begged, the tears running down his cheeks. "Please, missy—"

"Get him to the stables before he has the whole house out here!" She stood very still, watching until they disappeared around the curve that led to the stable. Then she put her hands up to her head and for a minute she thought she'd shriek.

"Do you feel proud?"

She whirled around and faced Jules. He stood stiffly in the doorway.

"What business is it of yours?"

"I kept Charlie from the fans. I have him learning to read just before noon and sometimes I forget to notice the time. Charlie's a bright little boy, but he's not very strong."

"I'll speak to Mister Renny about you keeping him from his work. Now get off this porch." She started to move past him, but he caught her arm.

"You're going to the stable and watch Charlie get his beating."

She glared at him, trying to pull herself free.

"If I have to drag you all the way, you're going."

Wasn't it bad enough to feel as she did without Jules touching her? "Let go of me," she said. "I'll go."

She heard the boy's screams from outside. Jules glanced at her, then held open the door.

Charlie hadn't been touched by the whip yet, but the sight of it had him in hysterics. Zulu stood very still while the surly gardener bound his hands and put him facing a wall.

The whip was raised and slashed down on the skinny back. Charlie screamed and Zulu felt Jules looking at her.

She seized the whip before it could fall again. She turned on Jules, still holding it, her eyes flashing.

"Charlie can go," she said, "if you take his place."

Jules undid Charlie's hands and gently eased the boy's shirt over his back.

"Go up to my room," he said quietly. "After a bit I'll be up and rub some lotion on that welt." He nodded for the gardener to leave.

When they were alone Jules ripped off his shirt and threw it onto the floor. He turned to the wall, his broad back exposed to her, muscles rippling under the smooth skin.

She gripped the whip aware of the savage desire to hurt Jules, to see him wince. She closed her eyes tightly and almost she could see the great jungle fires leaping to

292

the black sky.

She drew back her arm and the whip slashed down on Jules' back. *The fire was blazing, reaching out for her, and her body throbbed and ached to feel the flames encircle it.*

She drew her arm back again and her eyes fell on the bloody strip across his smooth skin. The red haze of the jungle faded away. Her knees were weak and for a moment she thought she'd faint. She leaned against a stall, half sick.

Jules glanced around. He helped her into an old chair.

"Why?" she asked.

"Because," he said gently, "there's a hunger in you that'll never be fed until you face yourself."

"You know," she said, "because you're like me."

"But I don't beat people. I try to teach them, instead. A force like that inside a person can be used for more than oneself."

She made a movement toward him, but he backed away and picked up his shirt.

"I'd sooner pick up a burning coal than touch you," he told her.

"Someday," she said. "You won't be able to stand it any longer."

Renny was both hurt and bewildered by his aunt's sudden decision to leave Nollgrove. Zulu waited impatiently for Tessa to face him with the real reason, but as the time of departure grew closer, it became apparent nothing was going to be said.

When finally the carriage rolled through the gates, Zulu felt half delirious with relief.

She held the keys up to Renny.

"Look," she laughed. "Now I'm really the mistress here!"

He smiled and kissed her. She caught his head and drew his mouth hard against her parted lips.

"Renny," she said impatiently, "when are you going

to learn how to kiss me?''

He flushed, pleased but still embarrassed. She knew the expression well.

"You're like a child sometimes," he told her.

"A child?" she pouted, but it turned to a frown when she saw his eyes weren't on her, but on the departing carriage.

Over his shoulder she saw Reginia watching her with a cold, set face. She realized, then, that Reginia was the reason Tessa had left without speaking.

She drew away from Renny. "Now would be a good time to see about the new driver. Then we won't have to keep dinner waiting."

After Renny had ridden down to the gatehouse, Zulu sought Reginia out in the garden. It was a dead, dormant spot, she noticed. Winter was setting its mark all around them.

"If I make you so unhappy," she said, "why didn't you leave with your aunt?"

"I know you'd like that, but I don't intend to desert Renny. I told Aunt Tess that this morning and I'll warn you of it now."

"You told her not to go to Renny about—about the other day?"

"It would only have made him more miserable." Reginia brushed her skirts as she stood up from the bench. "But I wouldn't feel too secure if I were you. You know what a great hand at letter writing she is."

Chapter Thirty-Nine

Zulu hurried through the gardens with a paper tucked under her arm. She paused a minute to look around.

Spring had done beautiful things to the orchard and lawn of Nollgrove. The trees were budding, the narcissus sent up their scents, the birds were nesting, and there was a feeling of the unity of male and female in the very air.

She went beyond the formal gardens, past the summer house and ventured, for the first time, into an overgrown area where she felt certain the gardeners seldom wondered.

She pushed aside the high bushes, anxious only to be well concealed so she could read the paper Jules had been studying with such interest before Renny had called him. Anything Jules did was of interest to her.

She glanced over her shoulder. She was a good distance from house quarters. She looked around for a flat rock and almost stumbled into a small pool. It was fresh, sweet water, but marshy around the edges.

This was far better than anything she'd hoped to find. There was an air here of solitude and peace. It spread through her like a balm. She moved around the edge of the pond until she found a cleared place where she could stretch out and enjoy the quiet and peace.

She sat on a rock and took off her slippers and hose and dipped her feet into the cool water. She lay back onto the soft, young grass and her eyes rested on the hollow inside a tree trunk. Unmistakably there was a blanket bundled up into a ball. So she wasn't the sole discoverer of this sanctuary! It didn't really matter. Everyone was busy with the spring planting and they wouldn't be likely to have time to laze away a day. The grass was still a little damp so she reached into the hollow and pulled out the bundle.

With the dry cotton cover under her, she put her feet back into the water, lifted her skirts to feel the sun on her skin, and stretched out. Throughout the winter months she had arrived at an uneasy peace with herself. Part of it was the realization she could never change Renny from what he was and she no longer strove for satisfaction from him, but tried to divert her energies into running the household, long walks through the woods—anything that tired her physically. She had chosen this life and it was up to her to fit into it. There were times when she almost deceived herself into thinking she had succeeded.

She wriggled her feet in the water, enjoying the caress of soft, cool mud. Reaching back, she undid her hair and shook it around her shoulders. Then she opened the paper.

It was the *Baton Rouge Gazette*, she noticed and the date was March 1, 1839—almost a month old. She knew at once what article had interested Jules, it concerned runaway slave trouble and the vigilant guard imposed on back country. She folded the paper in disgust. Everything that interested Jules was of that fiber. It was either a pamphlet by one of those fool abolitionists or some attempted uprising among the slaves. She closed her eyes and let the paper fall from her fingers as she lay still, half drowsing, half dreaming.

The cracking of a twig awakened her to find Jules standing over her, his fists clenched at his sides.

She sat up. "What're you doing here?" she demanded.

"I might ask the same," he replied. "That's my blanket and I see you even have my paper. I might have known you'd find this place."

She saw, then, that he was unable to take his eyes from her. She glanced at herself. Her skirts were above her knees and her tawny hair hung about her shoulders and down her back in a confusion of waves and ringlets.

He threw himself down beside her and roughly wound his fingers in her hair. He jerked her head back and his full, sensuous mouth caressed her throat until the tenseness left her.

His hands were seeking, caressing and she knew surrender to Jules would be more than a union of bodies. That he called to a part of herself that was deeper than sex. The part of herself she had spent a lifetime surpressing.

Though she had wanted him before, she was afraid, now. She fought him with as desperate an urgency as she'd fought Len that long ago evening in Alabama. She bit and seratched. She fought that elemental entity that had first quivered in response to Esmeralda's talk of well spirits, that had fanned to life when she held the *loa* stone and flamed to maturity at the voodoo meeting. She fought the reaching out of the swamps, the lure of home.

His flesh was moist and warm against hers and with a last, desperate burst of strength she tried to pull herself free. He whispered softly to her and the world thundered and crashed. Nothing mattered then, nothing but Jules and the glorious fulfillment of every fiber of her body.

She clung to him a long time afterwards, trying to understand the wonderful completeness of just having him hold her. She was bathed in perspiration and Jules' breath still came hard.

It had never been like this. It should never have happened. She moved against him.

Jules chuckled. He ran his hand over her. "Aren't you satisfied yet?" he asked.

"It's never been like this," she whispered.

"I know," he said.

Realization suddenly returned and she pulled herself away.

"You attacked me!" she said. "And you said you'd rather pick up a burning coal!"

He nodded. "I swore I'd never touch Mister Renny's wife. But I didn't expect to stumble on a colored wench with her feet in the mud."

She pulled on her slippers and tied back her hair, then she stood over him. "Now," she said, "it won't matter."

But as she hurried out of the thicket she reached into her pocket for the loa stone. It was gone. It had rolled into the pond while she lay in Jules' arms.

Suddenly she was frightened.

Chapter Forty

When Renny sent for Jules that night, he was nowhere to be found. He had disappeared, leaving clothing and books in his room.

"He didn't have to run away," Renny told Zulu, his eyes puzzled. "He knows he only has to ask if he wants to go somewhere. And I can't understand him leaving his books."

So this was Jules' answer to her. "He'll be back," she assured Renny with confidence.

Renny shook his head. "I don't think I'll ever understand Jules." He patted her hand, "Any more then I'll ever understand you, my dear."

"He'll be back," Zulu repeated.

It was more than a week before Jules walked into the cookhouse. His clothes were mud splattered and torn. He ate like a man who hadn't seen food in days.

When he appeared before the family he was dressed with his usual neatness, but he avoided meeting Renny's eyes. He stood before them with his hands limp at his side, looking down at his feet.

"I've been right worried about you, Jules," Renny said. "You know there was no call to run away. If there was something you had to tend to, I'd of trusted you to go."

Jules stood patiently, waiting for Renny to finish.

"You know how I feel, Jules. Damn it, I about fretted myself sick!"

"I had to go like that," Jules said. "There wasn't any other way."

After the others went into the house, Zulu left the gallery and went down to the pond. Jules was standing under the tree that shaded the still water.

"I knew you'd be back," she told him.

"I wanted to die. I tried to die. But a weakness inside me held me back. You're that weakness."

"I spoke at some meeting," he went on, after a minute. "I should have been able to do some good, but there was no fire in me. Whatever I had, it's gone."

"Come here," Zulu said softly, and held her arms out to him.

She sat back against the tree with Jules' head in her lap. She twisted her fingers in the black thick curls.

He looked up at her and smiled. "Thank you," he said simply.

"Don't try to run away again," she said.

His eyes were grave. "I'll have to, someday. But first I've got to come to terms with myself."

For the first time in her life Zulu knew what it was to be completely content. With Jules near, it was more than just a release of physical craving, it was a sharing of thoughts, of self. She enjoyed listening to him talk, even when she didn't entirely understand what he said. Even when they disagreed.

"This can't go on," he warned her repeatedly. "It's

all wrong and I'm neglecting my work."

"Does teaching a few field hands and house slaves to read mean more than me?"

"Whether you know it or not, it can be the beginning of important changes."

"No one is going to thank you for your efforts, Jules. Not the blacks and not the whites."

"Maybe not. But someday someone will finish what a few of us are starting. If I only smooth the road a little, my work will have been worthwhile."

"Worth the chance of being hung?"

Jules nodded.

Chapter Forty-One

Zulu waited by the pond for Jules. She lay back and watched the September leaves fall into the water while she planned how she would tell him about the child.

When she heard him coming through the thick shrubbery she sat up to welcome him.

"You're pale," he observed, his eyes searching into her face.

"It's no use, Jules," Zulu said, trying to sound slightly amused, "I can't keep telling myself it's something else. I'm pregnant."

He was silent for a few minutes. When he finally spoke his eyes were on the almost dry pond.

"Suppose it's mine?"

Zulu shrugged. "You've no more black blood than I have and you're not really that dark."

"Dark enough. And it could be, too. We've got to

300

think of Mister Renny."

"Renny!" Zulu snapped. "I should think you'd be a little concerned about what'll happen to me if it's dark."

"We should have both thought of that before."

Zulu moved restlessly. "Just what do you want me to do?" she demanded sullenly. "You know if it's white Renny'll go around crowing like a rooster!"

"I warned you before you married him, and you laughed."

"I'm still laughing. I planned what I'd do a long time ago."

Jules' looked at her in alarm. "You wouldn't—"

"Don't worry," she interrupted. "I'll have it. But not at Nollgrove."

"Do you think he'd let you out of his sight once he knew your condition?"

"He won't know," Zulu replied. "Not until I'm a long way from Virginia. And then I'll neglect to mention how far along I am."

Jules tossed a stone at the puddle of a pond. "I don't know," he said. "I just see too many things that could happen.

"It isn't the worst thing that's ever happened to me," Zulu replied. But she wondered.

That night when they lay in bed, Zulu told Renny the time had come to effect a reunion with her aunt.

"She hasn't even replied to my letter telling her about marrying you," she said. "Remember, I posted it from Richmond and the epidemic was over then. I've got to call on her in New Orleans and try to get her to forgive me."

"We'll go together," Renny said eagerly. "When she sees how happy we are—"

Zulu put her fingers gently on his mouth. "I wish we could do it that way," she replied. "I have to go alone. She wouldn't even receive us if we went together. But if I send a message telling her I'm alone with only my maid she can't refuse to be at home to me. She'd never let me stay alone in New Orleans!''

"It's a good plan," Renny agreed, "but I don't like the idea of you traveling alone."

"You'll see me onto the boat and as soon as I get to New Orleans I'll send word to my aunt. She'll have the carriage for me right away. Letty and I have traveled alone before.''

"You will come back as soon as possible? You'll write me as soon as you arrive? Are you certain I can't just stay in the background?''

"If we deceived her, she'd never forgive us. Trust me, Renny.''

He finally agreed and Zulu curled up to sleep. She was aware of a vague happiness at the prospect of visiting New Orleans again. She hadn't realized that she'd been homesick for the city.

She dreamed that she had the baby at the Quadroon Ball, and it was a full grown black who talked about educating the negroes and swore like Breel.

Chapter Forty-Two

Zulu stood on the dock and watched the crowds mill around her while Letty bargained with a young mulatto porter.

Nearby a flatboat was anchored and she almost expected to see Gram step from it to run up the whisky bottle on the flagpole. She smiled a little as she remembered how impressed she had been by the quality folks who drove up in carriages to board the steamboats.

She tried not to think of the terrible fight, and the even more terrible results of the fight. At the time it hadn't seemed so bad taking a money bag from someone who already had more waiting for him in his wife's keeping. Enough to buy interest in a steamboat. Maybe it would mean another trip up river—a delay of a few months at the most. She wondered if she would have done what she did had she known the brutality that was the river man's way of life.

But that was past and there was no place for it now. Regrets didn't change anything. She looked around her. There wasn't much different from that day. A few less flatboats, many more steamboats, and still the aroma of coffee, stale fish and spices, still the same mixture of black and white, poor and rich, the same clatter of different dialects.

The porter loaded her luggage into a cart and they started toward Orleans Street.

The white cottage looked exactly as she remembered leaving it, except now she saw it through clear air and not the haze of tar smoke, even the gutters smelled as bad as ever. She noticed that a window was open and a curtain rippled with the light breeze.

She unlocked the door and waited for the porter to take her trunks into the hallway. While Letty dismissed him, she moved around, touching the furniture, opening the lattices and shifting objects. Somehow, this was more a home to her than Nollgrove with all its fine rooms.

"*Qui est là?*"

A strange young negress came from out of the back of the house. She was a slim girl, with skin lighter than Letty's.

"What're you doing here?" Zulu demanded.

"What you doin' heah?" Letty echoed from behind.

The girl smiled and Zulu saw now that she was

303

probably a mulatto. When she spoke it was in the soft Creole French of a trained house servant.

"Madame Randolph, perhaps?"

"Where is Celeste?" Zulu demanded.

"*La fievre—*" The girl shrugged expressively. "Madame Luton dispatched me to take her place."

"The fever certainly seems hard on cooks," Zulu observed. She sank down into Shadney's chair and unbuttoned her cloak, then she fanned herself with her hat. She hadn't remembered how stifling the city could be.

Belatedly the implication of the girl's explanation struck her.

"Madame Luton is alive?"

The girl nodded.

"M'sieur Luton?"

"That one! It would require Le Grand Zombi himself to take that one!"

It wouldn't do to have this girl start out by taking liberties.

"I might tell Madame Luton what you said," Zulu suggested.

The girl shrugged. "The devil has taken him, that is no secret." Then she added smugly, "Madame Luton had my papers made over to you."

"We'll want to eat in about an hour," Zulu told her. "You'll have the cooking and the housework. Letty takes care of my clothes and me."

The girl nodded and Letty strutted across the room carrying Zulu's hand baggage, conscious of her red jacket and the plume in her hat. It was the same hat Zulu had worn when first she came to New Orleans.

Zulu stripped off her gloves and went to Shadney's desk. She pried out the locked drawer and took the jewel case from it.

She pulled a pin out of her hair and worked at the lock, but it was useless. When the mulatto brought in her dinner, she set aside the case, frustrated.

"Have there been any messages?" she asked.

"People have come here," the girl said, "but no one left a message."

The next day Zulu decided to call on Madame Randolph and to see Fannette. She had Letty arrange for a carriage while she waited in the lobby of the St. Louis Hotel, wearing a heavy veil. She'd get around this law about not riding in a carriage. Who'd dare challenge a white lady?

She watched the flow of people toward the platform under the great copper rotunda. A man on the platform was hammering on a table. Behind him stood four blacks, father, mother and two children.

As she watched the auction progress her mind kept going to Jules and things he had said. She turned away, disgusted with herself and went to see if Letty had made arrangements. It was time to stop being a fool over Jules.

It was nearly evening when she reached the Randolph home on the Bayou St. John. An *allée* of trees led from the bayou up to the front stairs. In the distance were the quarters and the overseer's dwelling. The main house, itself, was a gracious building with an iron grilled second balcony onto which French doors opened. Dormer windows jutted out of the sloped roof and the pillars that supported the galleries were free of vines.

There was a singular air of quiet to the place. No one ran out to meet the carriage, though she heard the dinner bell ring back in the quarters as the carriage had turned up the *allée*. She missed the usual shouts and laughter of slaves coming out of their cabins to get their meal.

She alighted from the carriage and went up to the door. After a few minutes, an elderly black butler answered.

"I wish to see Madame Randolph," Zulu said.

The butler motioned for her to follow. He led her to a reception parlor and disappeared. After a short passage of time a young man stepped into the room. He bowed over her hand.

"I'm Marc Bauzart," he announced. "Madame Randolph's nephew. What is it I can do for you?"

"You can tell your aunt that Zulu is calling."

"*Pardonnez-moi,* but that I cannot do. My Aunt has been dead for some months, now."

Zulu took Madame Randolph's note from her reticule. "I want my baby," she said.

Bauzart scowled over the letter.

"Timothy!" he called.

The butler came into the room.

"Timothy, why haven't I been told of this Fannette? Where did they send her when Madame died?"

Timothy avoided their eyes. He shuffled his feet. "Don' know bout a chile," he muttered.

"This is ridiculous!" Zulu exclaimed. "There are laws about stealing a child!"

"*Cela n'est pas vrai!*" Bauzart protested hotly. "There was no child when I arrived. It's been two months—"

"Do you think I'd have this note if there'd been no child?"

Bauzart turned on the butler. "I want the truth!" he said.

Again Timothy showed signs of agitation. "No, *maitre,*" he insisted and shook his head.

"Bring in every man and woman and child in this house!" Bauzart snapped. "*Sacre Nom!* To bè accused of child stealing!"

When the household was lined up in front of them, Bauzart paced back and forth with his hands thrust into his pockets.

First he asked them as a unit, then, when there was no reply he singled them out as individuals.

Zulu watched closely. She didn't listen to the violent denials but instead noticed the expressions that passed over their faces as they were questioned.

Bauzart turned to her, his hands outstretched, beads of moisture on his forehead.

"What is there I can do? he asked.

Zulu said quietly, "Send them all away but that yellow girl on the end."

The slaves filed out of the room. When the door was closed behind them, Zulu spoke softly.

"Why won't they tell what happened to Fannette?"

The girl shrugged. "They are afraid, Madame."

"Of what?" Zulu demanded.

"Afraid, Madame, of the devil that is in the man who came for her."

"A man came for her? Who was he?

The girl looked around. "M'sieur Luton, Madame."

"Lord God!" Zulu could not repress the exclamation. "Breel? When?"

"The day Madame died. He came in the night and broke his way into the room where *la petite* slept. All the candles went out around Madame's coffin, so the others thought he was a devil."

"I've noticed the draft from the front door," Bauzart said, "But to blame the devil!"

Zulu thanked the girl and sent her away.

"That Berthe," Bauzart observed, stroking his chin, "she has a good accent. I don't think I'll dispose of her with the others. I'm settling the estate, you know."

"I think I can handle this matter from here on. Thank you, M'sieur."

"No thanks to me, Madame. You understand the negro."

Zulu smiled. "Only the mixed bloods. I understand them well."

The next morning she set out for Breel Luton's house. As she turned down Promenade Publique she fought the resentment that filled her thoughts. It was necessary to keep her head, but would Breel never leaver her alone? What could he possibly want with Fannette?

He was a devil. Her own personal devil who always turned up just when things were going well for her.

She paused outside the gates of the Luton residence. The lions needed polish and the shrubbery was untrimmed. On the lower floor there was a window open, but the rest were boarded.

She went up the walk slowly, wondering if there would be any response to her knock, but the butler answered the door. Even he appeared to have changed. There was less of a sheen to his skin, less pride in the way he carried his head.

"I must see Madame Luton," Zulu said, and he led her into the drawing room without a word.

She drew a deep breath. It smelled musty, like a house that had long been deserted. Dusty white covers were over most the furniture and there was an emptiness.

There was a light step in the hall and Donna came through the doorway. She paled.

"Zulu!" she exclaimed. "You've got to get away from here!"

Zulu stared at her. This wasn't the proud, dark haired girl she'd first met in this very room, but a woman with the beginning of a white wing that swept from her temples back to the glossy knot at the nape of her neck. A woman whose eyes were frightened under their long lashes. The fine bones of her face pressed sharply against her almost transparent skin, and her dress fitted loosely.

"I shouldn't have expected you would want to see me," Zulu replied, but she felt a strong disappointment.

Donna crossed the room quickly and took both her hands.

"Please, I didn't intend to sound so rude! But it frightened me to see you there. I'm expecting Breel any moment."

"You know I'm not afraid of Breel. You don't have to

apologize for not wanting to see me."

"*Mais non!*" Donna exclaimed hastily. "It's that Breel's—different."

"I would have stayed with you, but I didn't think you could live."

"I understand. That isn't the question. Things are very different from when you went away. Maybe it's his scar—but I think it because of the way he killed Shadney. He drinks almost constantly." Donna looked down at her hands, "I talked to his second and he says Breel was half blind and stunned—that he really didn't know what he was doing."

"Does that give him reason to take Fannette?"

"Fannette's at Bijou," Donna replied. "But it wouldn't be safe for you to go after her."

"Breel has no right to her. She's mine!"

"If you're patient, Zulu, I'll find some way. But don't go after her. If only you could comprehend how terribly Breel's changed. Sometimes I think it's not what he drinks at all—that his mind has warped."

"Maybe you imagine—"

"I'm his wife," Donna said, "I know. I've been almost a prisoner at my own plantation since I recovered from the fever. I had my baby there, at Bijou, with only the midwife who attends the field women."

"Breel delivered Fannette."

"Blessed Virgin!" Donna bit her lip. "It wouldn't have been possible when Ted was born. Breel didn't even know he had a child until three days later. He was locked into his room and only opened the door for what little food he ate."

She stood by the window, as if she needed the fresh air. "I couldn't stand it any longer last week. I took the baby and ran away. I intended to leave Louisiana—only I couldn't do it. This morning I had word Breel's on his way. That's why you must leave."

"You're a fool to stay here and wait for him!"

Donna turned back to the room. "I can't leave him.

In my heart I know he needs me. Besides—"

"Besides?"

"There's my baby. I don't want him to face a world that looks down on him because of his father. If I left Breel everyone would know what he's become."

"But if you raise the boy in the same house—"

"Ted'll be sent away to school soon as he's old enough. I can protect him until then." She shivered, "Now please leave while you can!"

"You still love Breel. How is it possible?"

"I don't know. He has only to smile and I forget everything he's done." She looked out the window again, her agitation increasing. "He took Fannette to Bijou to trap you. Your little *Tignasse* is well taken care of. She lives in the house like one of the family and she still has her wet nurse with her." Donna smiled faintly. "She is exquisite, your Fannette."

"Growing up like family," Zulu said bitterly, "then someday someone'll tell her she can't ride in a carriage alone. That she must stand if a white woman's in the room. She'll have to forget everything she's learned. Lord God, Donna, that's what I don't want for her!"

The front door opened and slammed. Donna caught the back of a chair for support.

"Quick!" she gasped. "Get behind the drapes! You've got to believe me!"

The urgency of Donna's words was not to be ignored. Zulu stepped behind the heavy drapes and almost choked on the dust. Donna moved toward the hall, but Breel came through the doorway before she had crossed the room.

From her hiding place Zulu could see him plainly. He was still handsome, but the scar that curled a corner of his mouth gave him a slightly sinister aspect. His jowls were dark with beard stubble and his hair needed cutting. His eyes were bloodshot. Always before, even at his angriest, there had been just a little amusement in his expression, but Zulu realized there was none of that now.

He's drunk as a river man on the town, Zulu thought as she watched him stand in front of Donna, swaying a little.

"So you got tired of Bijou," he said. "You ran away."

Donna was silent.

"You know what we do to slaves that run away."

"That hardly applies to me," she replied. "I came to town to do some shopping."

"Shopping, hell!" he roared. "You ran away."

Donna moved toward him, but he pushed her aside and threw himself into a chair. The dust sprayed up around him.

"I can't run away as long as I've Ted to consider."

"The only way you'll ever escape from me is by dying. Have you ever thought of that?"

"Yes," Donna replied. "Many times."

He sniffed. "I've never known you to wear scent." He drew another breath, "Damn familiar odor." Suspicion came into his eyes. "So that's it, you met a man here and you wore scent for him."

"Breel!" Donna exclaimed, disgusted, "you're drunk!"

He glanced around and sniffed again.

"Oh!" Donna said. "Of course. Shelia Bardon was sitting there just ten minutes ago. She saw my carriage and came to call."

Breel glanced at the dust around him. "If she was," he remarked, "her gown won't look the same." He leaned back, stretching out his booted legs. "Well," he added with something almost like his old mockery, "have you finished your—shopping?"

Donna nodded.

"And you're coming back to Bijou with me?"

"Yes."

He stood up and started toward the open window, but Donna caught his arm. "If we're going, we'd better start now. It's a long ride."

Breel looked down at her. "What's the hurry, my love? Afraid some more of your friends will call? Are you ashamed of your husband?"

"It's been at least a week since you've had yourself shaved. And I think you must have slept in those clothes for a month."

He laughed. "I hope the entire stiff-necked lot of them drop in. God Almighty, but I'd enjoy parading in front of them!"

"If you want me to go with you," Donna said, "you'd better see to the carriage."

After they had left, Zulu came out from behind the drapes and leaned against the wall.

I'm not Donna, she reflected, I couldn't have my skirts soiled and remain clean.

The butler came into the room to close it up, and Zulu felt a dizziness.

"Some smelling salts, please," she said.

She inhaled deeply, coughing and choking, then slowly the room settled and became still again. She allowed him to show her out.

The gates clanged shut after her and she started for the ramparts. It would be safe enough to stay at the cottage tonight, she decided, but she'd have to make other arrangements for later. The cottage would be the first place Breel would go.

It wasn't going to be nearly as easy as she'd thought. She had known it would take every device to keep Renny from coming for her ahead of time. And now there was Breel to consider, too. She missed the feel of the *loa*. Suddenly she felt vulnerable.

Back in the cottage she sat down to think. Her eyes fell on the jewel casket. She picked it up and shook it, but there was no answering rattle.

Letty came to take her hat, but Zulu shook her head.

"I'll be back directly," she said and went out the door again.

It was easy to find a craftsman to open the lock, but when he gave her back the casket, Zulu imagined that he smiled a little strangely. She gave him his fee and hurried out of the shop.

She could barely refrain from examining the contents right on Royal Street, admidst the steady stream of promenaders, but instead she contented herself with picturing what she might expect.

Letty was waiting by the door, her eyes bright with anticipation, but Zulu moved past her to the table in the sitting room. She opened the lid and stared at the note that lay on the satin lining. A note and nothing else.

She unfolded it to find Breel's careless script scrawled over the sheet.

"Permit me to congratulate you on the exquisite collection that was in here. I've taken the liberty of having them sent to Madame Randolph. I'm certain that's as you'd wish it."

She tore the note into scraps and stamped on it. Then she slammed the casket against a wall. She couldn't go to Bauzart and demand her jewels anymore than she could go to Bijou for Fannette.

Breel had defeated her at every turn. But the time would come! She was certain the time would come when she could meet him on his own grounds.

She made arrangements to stay with Eugenie LaFrome. It was a bigger room than the one she had taken on her first day in New Orleans, and she settled herself down for the months that would stretch ahead.

On one of her walks she passed the Luton residence and she saw that it was boarded tight. She felt safe, then, to attend the theater. She avoided the Orleans where visitors were taken and went to the Theater Marigny on the Champs Elysees, which was for the colored. There was also the Theatre d'Elenes on the Rue des Grands Hommes, which showed only light French vaudeville. It was unlikely a visiting Virginian would attend there, she decided.

She wrote glowing accounts of the plays she was attending. In between the description of an opera and an imagined reception, she sandwiched news of her pregnancy.

When Renny's reply finally reached her, he sounded half hysterical. Despite her instructions to the contrary, he was preparing to come to New Orleans for her.

She should have known he could be relied upon to become difficult. She wrote him a carefully considered reply.

"My Own Darling;

The baby won't be due until late in March. There's no need for you to come rushing down here from Nollgrove when you're needed there so badly this part of the year. The doctor prefers I stay in New Orleans for the birth, and I'm well taken care of. However, I'm going to be a bit selfish and ask you get here around the last week of February or early March. Then you'll be with me when my time comes . . ."

She read back over the paragraph and smiled. The baby, of course, would arrive prematurely in January. Unless—well, in that case it would be a miscarriage and she would be on her way back in either event, before he ever left Virginia.

She saw Ferne passing through the hall one morning in late December. Ferne went on by her as if she were not standing in her path. She started to go into Eugenie's sitting room, when, unexpectedly, she turned back to face Zulu.

"I heard you were here," she said, "but up till now I've managed to avoid seeing you."

Zulu shrugged, looking down at herself. The baby was due within a few weeks and her *blouse volante* stood out in front of her.

"I'm not the most attractive sight," she agreed. She

314

lifted her hand so Ferne could see the diamonds in the ring Renny had given her.

"I've married, you know."

"I could have told you there would be a marriage."

Zulu laughed. "Anyone can say that after the thing's happened." Her eyes narrowed. "Tell me who it was I married?"

"I couldn't tell you his name," Ferne replied heavily, "but I can tell you that you're foolish. Nothing good can come of marrying a white man."

"You can't know that!" She had taken care to give the impression she was married to a wealthy *gens de couleur*.

Ferne moved closer. "The song has reached its crescendo—how long can you satisfy its hunger?" She stared ahead. "In Santo Domingo there is a saying: *'Joy yun fé tombe nans d'l'eau C'est pas jou li coulé.'* The day a leaf falls into the water, is not the day it sinks."

Chapter Forty-Three

Zulu's baby was born in the early morning of a very gloomy day in January. Eugenie delivered it and held it from Zulu's sight.

Zulu was too exhausted to ask to see the child until she awakened in the early afternoon to the reality of the birth of her second daughter. When she asked to see the baby Eugenie shook her head doubtfully.

"Wait until you're more rested," she suggested.

"I'm rested enough. Bring her to me."

Eugenie shrugged. *"Très bien,"* she assented, and

brought a bundle of blankets to Zulu. Letty tiptoed into the room and stared over Eugenie's shoulder.

Zulu lifted the cover and looked at her baby's face. She was quiet for a long time, finally she glanced up at Letty.

"Send in the wet nurse."

Letty nodded and left the room. Though she had opened her mouth twice, Eugenie had motioned her to silence.

Zulu turned her head to Eugenie. "Bring me paper, please. I've got to write to my husband."

Eugenie returned with writing material and propped Zulu up on cushions. Zulu frowned thoughtfully over the blanket sheet.

"My darling," she wrote.

I have very bad news. Today our baby girl was born prematurely and lived only a few minutes. I'm still very weak—as much from heartache as from labor. My darling, if only at this moment we might be together. As soon as I am strong enough I'll start for home. I need you so terribly! I can hardly wait, my dearest, to hear your voice again, and to tell you how sorry I am."

She set aside the note and picked up the baby. She held it close and smiled at the contrast the light copper hands made against her own golden skin.

"You're so much like Jules . . ." she whispered, and she knew, suddenly, that she was glad.

Poor little thing. No one would ever take her for white. She lay the baby at her side wondering if perhaps that wasn't better. What did being taken as white bring other than heartache?

Out in the hall Letty's voice rose shrilly. The door burst open and Renny came into the room.

Lord God, Zulu thought, this is it!

Renny's face was white and strange as he made his way to her. He dropped on his knees beside the bed.

"My God, Zula," he exclaimed, "I've almost gone

out of my mind trying to find you! And then—in this place! A boarding house for young men!"

She had pulled the cover over the baby, but was afraid to look down to make certain it was concealed. She kept her eyes on Renny's face and tried to smile.

"Renny. . . ." she whispered frantically, not able to think of anything else. If only the baby didn't decide to cry.

"Why didn't you write that your aunt had died? Why aren't you staying with friends or at a hotel?"

"I. . . .feel sick," she murmured. "Please go find Letty."

He hesitated, started for the door, then turned back.

"I've got to talk to you alone. There's a lot I need to know."

The door opened and the thin young woman Zulu had purchased as wet nurse, entered.

"You sent fo' me, Miz Zulu?"

Her way clear at last, Zulu managed a firmer smile. At the same moment little gasping cries came from the covers by her side.

Renny stared, his mouth open.

"Azure," Zulu said, "you can take your baby, now." She looked up at Renny. "It was foolish, but my arms felt so empty. I had to hold a baby—just for a little while." She gave him the note. "I—can't talk about it. I just finished this letter to you—"

He read slowly and then he put his arms around her. "We were redecorating the nursery when I left Nollgrove," he told her. "I was so excited—" He pulled her hand to his lips and she could feel the tears on his face. He tried to smile at her, "There'll be others, my dearest. We'll have a big family."

At the moment Zulu found that hardly an inducement, but she managed to look comforted.

He clung to her a minute, then he looked around the room. "I still don't understand."

She wiped his cheek with a corner of the bed linen

317

while she pieced the story together. She took his hand again and held it against her face. It took no effort to make her voice tremulous. "I felt so sick when I left the boat that I couldn't bear to think of seeing my aunt—and I didn't want to go to a hotel, I came here because Eugenie is my old nurse's sister. I felt safe with her to care for me. Then, when I felt better I sent Letty with a message for my aunt—and I found she had died. It was just then I realized I was going to have a baby."

"I couldn't even find the house at first," Renny said. "You never told me it was out of town. Why did you write me about the parties and plays, when—"

"The doctor said I wasn't to travel. I knew you'd worry if you thought I was alone. I didn't think you'd understand how safe I was here with Eugenie."

"And the house out on Bayou St. John—when I finally found it there were people from Baton Rouge staying there." He stood up and paced restlessly across the room. "They didn't know anything about you. They said they'd bought the place from a nephew and he'd gone back to France."

"Nobody knows I'm in town," Zulu said. "When my aunt got my letter she told everyone I'd died of fever on the boat. I couldn't just call on my old friends and tell them a story about being married. They'd find out I was pregnant—and you know how people think."

"Not if you'd sent for me!"

"Please, Renny," she whispered weakly.

"I couldn't remember how to find the Lastelle house—you know how confused I am in this city! Then I remembered Trojan. At least I knew where the tobacco docks were."

"Trojan brought you here?"

Renny nodded and knelt beside her again. She pulled his head down so that his face was against her shoulder.

"I'm starting a new life with you," she told him. "It's better people here don't know my aunt lied. As soon as I'm strong we'll leave for home."

"You're certain?" he asked.

"Yes. It's the only way." Then she added truthfully, "Please call Letty. I'm terribly tired."

She closed her eyes and wondered what she would call Jules' daughter.

Chapter Forty-Four

Zulu lay her head back in the deck chair and listened to the throb of the steamboat as it prepared to pull away from the dock. Overhead seagulls were screeching and diving for the praline crumbs Renny was throwing to them.

"I'd like to have seen a few plays before we left," he remarked.

"You could have gone without me."

Renny laughed. "I'd still be hearing about it. Do you realize you hardly permitted me out of your sight this last week?" He sighed. "Not that I wanted to leave you. And what cooking!"

The wheels had started thrashing and Zulu sat up to watch. She glanced at the dock in time to see a carriage pull up. Was that the Lastelle crest? But what did it matter, they were already safely headed upstream.

Yet she didn't feel safe. She felt for the *loa* in her pocket and remembered again that she no longer had it. What was wrong with her? Everything had gone better than she'd had a right to expect. Juliet was safely settled in the cottage with a wet nurse and the new cook. Eugenie had managed all of it for her.

"Letty was crying when we left," Renny said.

Zulu nodded. "She didn't want to leave Trojan. Last time she thought she'd be back in a few months, but this time she knows she'll never come back."

"I told Trojan he could come to Nollgrove. We could give them a room or one of the cabins in the quarters. I should think he'd jump at the chance of shelter and food and no work."

"If I was Letty and you Trojan would you like to live off me?"

Renny scowled. "We can hardly compare ourselves to them. Naturally, I'd feel differently about such things."

"Why? Because you're white?"

Renny stared at her. "Don't you think that alters everything?"

"Should it? Don't you think Trojan might have some self respect, too? He's a free man and he's worked all his life."

Renny laughed. "You sound as if you've been attending those abolition meetings I've heard about. Anyway, it's better he didn't come. I got the feeling he's involved in something he can't leave."

Zulu lay back, exhausted and frightened by her outburst. There were three paths, she reflected. A colored person could pretend to be subservient and be a "good nigger," they could be mean and overbearing, even "pass" if they were light enough. Or they could fight like Jules. . . .and, she suspected, Trojan. And end getting hung.

"I just feel guilty about Letty," she confessed. "Trojan wanted to buy her freedom and I set the price higher than he could pay so I wouldn't have to part with her."

Renny smiled affectionately at her. "That's your privilege."

But wasn't that just about what Rosalie had done when she held on to the Writ?

"That's the last we might ever see of New Orleans . . ." Renny was saying as the docks

320

disappeared from view.

Somehow, deep inside, she knew it wasn't.

"The day a leaf falls into the water. . . ." Why should she keep thinking of that foreign saying? Hadn't everything worked out?

I'll miss Juliet, she thought, astonished. I hardly saw her and I miss her already. I never really missed Fannette.

Renny reached over and patted her hand.

New Orleans and the cottage are in the past, she told herself firmly. I belong to Nollgrove.

"I run to de sea and de sea run dry . . .
I run to de gate but de gate shut fast . . ."

Why think of that song now?

Chapter Forty-Five

Reginia waited on the gallery to greet them when the carriage rolled up the avenue to the foot of the stairs. She kissed Zulu lightly on the cheek, but her eyes were unchanged.

Zulu glanced at the trunks that were lashed to the top of the carriage.

"Wait till you see the things I bought in New Orleans! Soon as I knew I was carrying, I had Madame Vaupont take my measurements so I'd have new clothes when I came home. I've enough gowns for years!"

Later, when the trunks were unpacked, she invited Reginia into the bedroom.

"I had this made for you by Madame Vaupont. She's the most popular modiste in New Orleans." Zulu held out an exquisite pink velvet dress that she knew Reginia would never wear.

Renny put his arm around Zulu's shoulder. "It was good of you to think of Reginia with all you had on your mind!"

Reginia took the dress. She smiled a bit stiffly. "Just what I'd choose to wear with my red hair," she said.

"I thought a few new gowns might bring the gentlemen calling," Zulu said lightly. "Afer all, we don't want our Reginia to be an old maid!"

"Oh no!" Reginia retorted. "We don't want that!" she left the room.

Renny watched her go, a thoughtful look on his face. "I'm afraid she's getting a little sensitive," he said. "It isn't that she hasn't had offers, but family means a lot to her and I think she means to select a husband in Richmond."

"She can't wait forever," Zulu said. "Maybe if she went to stay with her aunt—"

Renny kissed her. "She'll do what she wants to do in her own time. Now I've got to check with the overseer and I think you should rest. Do you want me to call Letty?"

Zulu shook her head. "I'll just sit here by the window for awhile. Letty'll have enough to do later with all this unpacking."

Renny had hardly gone down the hall before Jules came into the room. Zulu moved toward him, but he stepped back to avoid contact.

"I have to see to Mister Renny's unpacking," he said. Then he lowered his voice, his eyes anxious, "The baby was mine?"

"The baby's dead."

Jules caught her wrist so tightly that tears sprang into her eyes. "What did you do? When you saw it was mine, what—"

Zulu couldn't meet what was in his eyes. "She's

322

alive," she sobbed. "Do you think I could hurt our baby?"

Jules let go of her hand. "I'm sorry," he said, looking at the red marks on her wrist. Then he added, "I should have run away before you got back. But I had to know."

"I named her Juliet, but already they're calling her Papillotes."

"Papillotes?" Jules grinned suddenly.

"Curl papers. Her hair springs right back into tight little ringlets." Then she added defiantly, "But it's not wool. It's more like silk."

She was in his arms suddenly, and she felt an almost overwhelming desire to cry.

"I wasn't going to touch you again," he told her, stroking her hair. "I've tried to hope it wasn't mine, but all the time, underneath—"

He pulled away and picked up an arm load of Renny's clothes which he carried to the dressing room. As Zulu started after him the door opened and Reginia came into the room.

"One would think you could knock," Zulu snapped. "Or were you looking for something?"

"Your aunt's death notice, perhaps? I came in here to offer my condolences. It was thoughtful of you to spare Renny's feelings and not tell him in your letters."

Zulu sank down into a chair, fighting the temptation to call Letty and put Nollgrove as far behind her as possible.

I'm married, she thought. I can't do things like that when I'm married.

"I don't understand," she said.

Reginia smiled. "Don't you? You forget Aunt Tess has friends in New Orleans, and Thalia has relatives there. She sent a notice from the *Picayune*. It was regarding the sale of the property of the late Mrs. Shadney Randolph."

"Renny knows about my aunt's death."

"He knows now. But he didn't when I suggested you were in too delicate a condition to be away from your husband."

"You sent him to New Orleans ahead of the time we'd planned?"

"I didn't tell him about your aunt. I didn't want him to worry in case there was some explanation."

"You hoped he'd learn something—something that would hurt me."

"Yes," Reginia said. "I know there's something—and I'm going to find what it is."

She paused by the door, "And I'm not nearly as easy to deceive as my brother."

Jules came out of the dressing room, his face worried.

"I've known Miss Reginia since she was little," he said. "Generally when she sets out to do something, she does it."

Zulu turned to him. "Promise me you'll stay."

He shook his head. "Can't you see it won't work?" He glanced at the clothes. "I'll come back later when Letty's taking care of your things."

He won't go! Zulu assured herself. He can't go! But she knew he was right.

Chapter Forty-Six

When Zulu awakened the next morning, Renny was throwing the curtains open. She pulled herself up on one elbow.

"Where's Jules?" she asked.

"Reckon he got spoiled with me away so long," Renny grinned. "I've never known him to oversleep before."

A tight little knot formed inside Zulu.

"Renny, do you suppose he might have run away again?

Renny laughed. "Not Jules. He learned his lesson that other time."

"Do you think he might be sick?"

Renny frowned as he struggled with his boots. "I've a few things to tend to, then I'll go to his room. But he looked right well last night." He bent over and kissed her on the forehead while he buttoned his shirt.

"Should I have Letty come in?"

Zulu nodded.

When Zulu went to the breakfast room, Reginia was waiting, but Renny's chair was empty. They were almost through the meal when Renny came through the door.

"Jules is gone again," he said.

Zulu stopped eating. It was a minute before she could speak.

"It's not like the other time," Renny said. "He took his clothes and his books."

"You'd btter send out a searching party," Zulu said. The thought of life without Jules was something she couldn't face. This time he wouldn't come back on his own. There had been more than determination in his face when he had left her.

"I can't send out hounds and have him dragged back," Renny said. "I can't do it. Besides, I've never satisfied myself just how legal my ownership of Jules might be if it was challenged. He's only an eighth black and if it wasn't for his father running slaves, he'd never have been sold in the first place."

"But he's a valuable property." Reginia had looked up from her coffee, her eyes on her brother.

"No," Renny said. "No."

It was damp and threatening to storm, but Zulu hurried across the gardens to their place by the pond. She stood still, staring at it.

He's got to come back, she told herself over and over. But it was no use. He had stepped beyond her.

The weeks went by in a weary monotony. Zulu read all the papers that came to Nollgrove searching for rumors of black uprisings, half frantic for fear she'd find an account of Jules' death. She'd awaken at night trembling from nightmares that always ended with Jules being dragged away by an angry mob.

Her nerves grew brittle and her temper short. She flew into rages for no reason. Even Letty ran from her in tears on two different occasions.

Jules had been gone over three months when Reginia took up the argument.

"You've got to do something about Jules," she said. "The others will think they can run off too."

Her logic was unquestionable. Zulu wished she'd thought of it earlier. Renny spent the night pacing the library and before breakfast he rode into town to make arrangements.

When he came back in the early evening his face was lined with weariness. He spoke very little, even to Zulu.

"I hope he's out of Virginia by now," he said when they went up to bed. "If only I could understand why he ran away—"

Jules was picked up in Louisiana. Renny was tight lipped about the entire matter, and Zulu gave up trying to extract information from him.

"You treat me as if I were a child!" she finally exclaimed.

Renny patted her hand and went down to the stables. They were holding Jules in town and he had to call for him.

It was a bright June afternoon and Zulu waited impatiently on the veranda.

If only he needs me like he did before, she thought.

Then everything will be back the way it was. She thought of the wonderful spring and summer hours they had spent by the pond and for the first time in months she found herself smiling.

She ran down to the stables when she heard Renny drive in. She paused when she saw Jules. He was dressed in rough clothes, but his head was up and his shoulders back.

"I didn't want them to find you," Renny was saying. "I had to start the search or there'd have been trouble with the others."

"I understand." Jules' voice was deeper, more assured than Zulu remembered it, but his eyes were somber. As she came into view he closed the hand that had hung loosely at his side.

He hasn't forgotten! she thought, jubilantly.

Renny glanced at her a little oddly, and Zulu realized how fixedly she'd been staring at Jules.

"Those—those clothes," she said. "Whatever have you been doing to wear clothes like that?"

"I was in the swamps," he said. "They found me when I came to town for supplies. I hadn't heard they were looking for me so I got careless."

"Why don't you go to your room and change," Renny suggested. "I've got to ride over to Bowman's so I won't need you until tonight."

Jules turned to leave, but for a minute his eyes met Zulu's. What she saw there made her weak.

As soon as Renny had ridden away, Zulu ran down the path, through the gardens and to the pond. Jules was waiting under the tree and she threw herself into his arms.

"Jules!" she gasped. "Lord God, but I've missed you!"

He held her a little away, looked into her eyes, then he buried his face in her neck.

She felt a thrill of pride in his great strength as he picked her up and gently laid her on the ground. She put

327

her arms around his neck.

"It's been so long," she whispered.

The dinner bell clanged in the slave quarters, and she stirred in Jules' arms.

"Renny'll be coming home," she said.

Jules sat up and leaned back against the tree.

"I'm going to take a wife," he told her. "Maybe that way I can keep away from you. I've about decided on Alma."

Not if I can help it! Zulu thought.

"If it weren't for you, I'd never take a woman. Someday the blacks are going to rise up here the way they did in Santo Domingo and I'm going to be right at the front. I haven't the right to ask anyone to take the chances my family'd have to take."

"I thought you were against violence," Zulu said. This is a new Jules, she thought, a harsher, more practical man, less of a dreamer, more of a realist.

"Violence? I was against it—until Missouri." He turned his face to hers, his eyes burning. "I was the only man without my papers in the entire camp of free colored people. We had our wagons and provisions and were camped on the edge of town. We were ready to start west as soon as we found a good guide—across the plains to free country. Remember, Zulu, it wasn't a band of men—it was families, women and children. All of us minding our own business."

"What happened?" Zulu asked.

"They attacked in the night. Some fool started a rumor that we were set to raid the town. They sneaked up after dark and those they didn't kill there they hanged later. I was away looking for a guide. When I came back there was only smoke and rubbish."

He paused, "And the bodies of men and women hanging from the trees. This wasn't the work of savages or Indians. Then they write editorials that the black man is too close to the jungle to ever be civilized!"

"Lord God," Zulu exclaimed, "Do you think a field woman's the equal of Reginia?"

"Miss Reginia has generations of educated folks behind her. My father was an educated man, but my mother was like you, she had to pick up her learning where she could. After Missouri I knew I had to go back. I went to the swampland out of New Orleans where my mother grew up."

"That's where Letty's man, Trojan was raised. Back near Bijou." Bijou . . . she thought, remembering . . .

"Trojan? The big roustabout at the tobacco docks? The man Mister Renny had me bring a letter to?"

Zulu nodded. How very long ago that had been. . . .

"We have to learn to value ourselves for what we are. Not to imitate. There's no other race ashamed of what it is."

"Who makes a worse owner of slaves than a free black?"

"A poor white."

"I suppose you'd have the lot of us shipped to Liberia?"

"Were you born there?"

"Of course not!"

"Neither was I. If everyone in America was sent to their ancestor's land there'd be nothing left but Indians. And maybe even they'd have to leave."

"Fighting isn't going to change things, Jules. There's a lot more white folks here than there were in Santo Domingo."

"The fight's got to start somewhere."

Zulu stretched out on her back, her palms under her head, a half smile on her lips. "I didn't come here to talk about slaves," she said, "nor to fight."

He knelt over her and put a hand on each of her shoulders. "Trouble is close, Zulu. So close I can feel its shadow."

She laughed at his seriousness and glanced down at the open bodice of her dress.

"Button me up," she said. Then her arms went around his neck when she saw he meant to move away.

"They'll be looking for me at the house, soon," she whispered. "There isn't much time."

"I wish you'd been born with a black skin!" he exclaimed. "We could have been happy!"

"I wouldn't have been happy."

"You wouldn't have felt you had to fight the world. Fighting by yourself only makes you selfish and hard. And in the end you lose, anyway."

Zulu placed her fingers over his lips.

"I won't meet you here again," he told her. "I can't let how I feel for you destroy everything I've worked for."

She pulled him down and stopped his words with her lips. She took his hand, pushing it over her breasts.

"There's still time," she whispered.

It was then she heard the brush crackle as it swished back in place. She glanced over Jules' head and all of the passion drained out of her.

"Lord God!" she exclaimed. "Reginia!"

Jules sprang to his feet and stood above her, straightening his clothes. Zulu sat up and met Reginia's horrified gaze with a calmness she wished she felt.

"Are you happy? You've found what you've been looking for?"

Reginia's face was a strange color between white and yellow, her eyes wide with shock. She pressed her hand to her abdomen as if she were physically ill.

"Oh my God!" she gasped. "You might at least cover yourself." She turned and pushed her way blindly through the brush.

She'll run right to Renny, Zulu thought. Suddenly she started to laugh. Jules stared at her as if she'd lost her mind.

"This is what I wanted!" she exclaimed. "I've found a way to get rid of Reginia!"

"What do you mean?" Jules' voice was dangerously soft.

"Renny'll never believe her. He knows she hates me and he won't stand for what she'll say. There'll be nothing for Reginia but to go to her aunt in Richmond."

"I won't let you do that," Jules said. "I know Miss Reginia. If you leave here she'll never tell what she saw."

"Let her drive me away? Give up all of this?" She laughed again. "Lord God, Jules, I'm no fool!"

She got to her feet and started to leave, but he pulled her back.

"I said I'd kill you before I let you hurt Mister Renny, and I meant it."

"What do you care about them?" she demanded.

"Will you go away?" His eyes should have warned her.

"No!" she snapped. "And there's nothing you can do about it. Nothing!"

His strong fingers closed around her throat. She screamed and tore at his hands, then her wind was cut off. She was falling into the pit again, and the pit beneath it. Her feet were grazing the surface of a swamp and then, for no reason, she stopped falling. Someone was holding her, talking to her—

It was Renny's voice. Why did it have to be him?

"Thank God!" Renny exclaimed. "Thank God!"

She tried to talk, but her throat hurt too much. She turned her head away. It wasn't Renny she wanted to see.

"I was cutting across the woods when I heard you scream," he was telling her. "Jules got there ahead of me and he took out after whoever attacked you."

She saw, then, that she was in her bed and a strange man was standing in the corner.

"I sent after Dr. Manton. You've been unconscious

for most the night. He said you'll be feeling better tomorrow. It's Reginia that has us worried.''

"Reginia?" Zulu managed to say, her eyes on the doctor.

"Miss Reginia has always been high strung, Mrs. Langford. The attack on you seems to have unhinged her. She's in a state of shock and is confused.''

"Confused?" Zulu repeated hoarsely, almost afraid to believe.

The doctor nodded. "You mustn't pay any attention to what she might say. She won't remember any of it later.''

So Reginia tried to tell them and they thought her out of her mind! Zulu repressed a hysterical desire to laugh. Even without the *pierre-loa*, luck was with her.

She must have been asleep for several hours when a noise outside her window awakened her. The curtains were drawn back and the sun was flowing into the room. She watched the light motes, waiting for the sound to recur. Just as she'd almost drifted back to sleep, she saw Jules' face at the window.

The girl Renny had left to watch over her was dozing in a corner. Zulu called to her.

The girl blinked and hurried to the bedside. "What you say, Miz Zula?" she asked.

"Send in Letty. I won't need you anymore.''

Letty came through the door almost immediately. She started to smooth the bedding, but Zulu shook her head and sat up.

"Open the window," she said, "then go out in the hall and wait. Scratch on the door if anyone comes upstairs.''

Was it in another age when she had done that for Rosalie?

Letty threw open the window and stepped out into the hall.

Zulu waited. Finally Jules came into the room. He glanced around.

"Is it courage or did you know I couldn't try that again?"

"Both," Zulu replied. Lord God, but her throat hurt!

"I came back for you," Jules said. "I'm going to take you with me.

Zulu closed her eyes. She had a vision of living with him. Awakening in the morning with him at her side. Whispering to him in the night . . .

It was the swamp reaching out again. If she went with Jules she'd have to renounce every drop of white blood. They'd live in holes and end up with a rope around their necks. If she went with him his fight would become her fight.

"I couldn't live your kind of life."

Jules looked over the room. "Is this a life? This pretense?"

"It's what I've wanted since I can remember."

The door opened suddenly and Reginia rushed in, followed by Letty.

"I tried to keep her out, Miz Zulu. I tried!"

Reginia looked at Zulu, repulsion in her eyes. "Isn't it enough that you . . . Oh my God, I can't even say it!"

Renny had come into the room. He looked at Jules, then at his sister who wore her bed clothes.

"You were supposed to be in your room, Reginia," he said, "Now what was it you couldn't say?"

"Your wife. Lying in the grass, committing adultery. With a nigra. With your own faithful Jules! She—"

Renny slapped his sister roughly across her face. "Shut up!" he shouted. "You've always been jealous of Zula. She tried to hide it from me, but I wasn't blind. To think you'd resort to such vile lies!"

Reginia had her hands to her face, tears streaming down her cheeks. "Renny—Renny—you know how I love you. How much I want you to be happy. I even turned away admirers so I could take care of you. You know I couldn't lie to you."

"You're out of your senses! Dr. Manton said you

were to stay in bed."

"I saw her, Renny. Lying in the grass with her dress open—"

"Zula's my wife and I'm not going to let you and your crazy fancies hurt her. I'll see you're locked in your room until I can take you to Aunt Tess. I'll give orders to her to see you're locked up until you come to your senses. If you ever do."

"Mister Renny." Jules soft voice came across the room. "Mister Renny, what Miss Reginia says is true."

"Jules!" Zulu screamed. Lord God, there went everything. Everything! Didn't the fool realize what he was doing? She threw back the covers and ran into Renny. His arms closed protectively around her. "Don't believe them," she begged. "Don't believe them!"

Jules shook his head.

"It's no use," he told her. "I can't see Miss Reginia shut up like a crazy person for the rest of her life."

She looked at Renny and knew that he heard the truth in Jules' voice, even though his arms still held her tightly. Her hatred of Jules at that moment made every emotion she'd ever felt infinitesimal.

Loathing was in her tone when she was finally able to speak. "If I ever get the chance I'll make you wish you were dead!"

"I wish that now," he said simply. "Mister Renny, I've loved Zulu ever since I first met her. I took her to her house that night she left you at the Lastelle's."

"But she wouldn't let me. She said—"

Jules looked at her and Zulu knew there was nothing further he would say. What difference did it make now? Everything was over.

"I couldn't let you take me home, Renny. Not to my cottage by the ramparts. Don't you understand? I wasn't Shadney's niece. I was his *placee*." She was aware of Jules moving toward the open window, but Renny and his sister had eyes only for her.

334

"A nigra!" Reginia gasped. "You know what it means to lie to a white man and marry him. We'll turn you over to the authorities. They'll see to you!"

"Reginia! You'll still leave for Richmond tomorrow. And for your own sake, you'll keep quiet about this."

For the first time Reginia realized that the three of them were alone.

"Jules has gone, Brother!" she exclaimed. "You've got to send out after him before he gets away!"

"I saw him leave," Renny said, "and this time I'm not sending after him. I should never have had him hunted down before. None of this would have happened."

He looked down at Zulu and she saw the hurt in his eyes. She knew that shattered as her dreams were, it was nothing next to what had happened to him.

"Did it have to be Jules?" he asked.

"That was Jules' baby in New Orleans."

Renny went to the window and stared out at the bright sunlight.

"I'll see you safely on a boat," he said. There was no life in his voice.

From the past she heard Ferne's warning in her ears.

The song will bring you what you want. . . .until it reaches its climax. Then there will be no gris-gris, no loa powerful enough to help against its descent. . . .Feed the song! Its happiness can only be maintained by a full diet!

Nigger talk!

What was the use of her education if she let herself be disturbed by nigger talk? Let Ferne rave. Let the ignorant listen! Voodoo!

"I'll feed that song," she vowed. "I'll feed it so well it'll never start downward.

Renny turned. He started toward her, then stopped. He left the room.

It can't be too late, Zulu thought. It can't be.

Chapter Forty-Seven

Zulu looked around the familiar front parlor of her cottage and tried to shake off the depression that had been with her ever since the carriage had driven down the avenue at Nollgrove.

I've my life ahead, she thought. The past was best forgotten. After all, she was barely twenty. There was no reason things couldn't return to what they were after Shadney's death. No reason, even, to hide from Breel, despite Donna's fears. As Renny's wife it had been important to avoid anything that might result in scandal. But who was there to care, now? She could even find one of her old admirers to take her to the Quadroon Ball. Without the interest of a protector or the illusion of innocence to guard, there was no further need of Ferne.

But it was no use. She had lost the eagerness with which she used to face life. A defeat was a defeat now, not a challenge. And it was Jules' fault. Just as losing Nollgrove was Jules' fault.

Letty closed the door after the porter and carried the small bags into the bedroom. Just like the last time, Zulu reflected, Only this time it was different.

"Please, Miz Zulu," Letty was begging, "can I go now? I ain' goin' be long."

"Trojan?" Zulu asked. That was the way she'd felt about meeting Jules—once.

"I thought you'd forgotten him by now."

"Not dat man," Letty grinned. "Please, Miz Zulu, can I wear dat hat you was goin' toss out?"

Zulu shrugged. "It doesn't matter." She turned to Adena, the cook Donna had given her, "Has M'sieur Luton been back?" she asked.

"*Oui*," the girl nodded, "but not of late."

"No?" Zulu asked.

"He's been ill. He almost died, they say."

"Too bad he didn't," Zulu muttered. She started down the hall to the baby's room, but paused with her hand on the knob.

Why be so eager? This baby should mean even less to her than Fannette. Nothing but unhappiness could come of letting it reach out to her heart. Jules had proven that.

"Mom'selle Papillotes is sunning in the patio," Adena said.

If I just pass by her crib, Zulu thought. She went to the patio and stood in the doorway, one hand on the jamb.

The baby was propped on a blanket with a soft toy in her tiny hand. Her black hair covered her well shaped little head in the glossy ringlets Zulu had remembered, and her copper skin was no darker than Naida's had been. But the soft grave eyes that regarded Zulu were still Jules' eyes.

"She smiles so seldom, *la petite*," the cook said, looking over Zulu's shoulder. "The world is on her shoulders."

"Does she cry much?" Zulu asked. Why should she care? Why should there be this knot inside her chest? The baby belonged to the nurse who was half asleep in the sun.

"Cry? *Mais non!* Almost never."

Of course. Wasn't she Jules' daughter?

"Do you want me to get her for you, Madame? You would like to hold her?"

"No!" Zulu said shortly. She turned away.

She went into the bedroom and threw open the *armoire* and let her eyes run over the clothes. They had been aired often, nothing had mildewed, but the styles were wrong. She wished she had taken more of her new clothes from Nollgrove. She hadn't been able to think of anything, those terrible last days, but to get away. Away from the thought of Renny shut up in the library. Away from the thought of Jules and his betrayal.

"Adena!" she called, "Go to Madame Vaupont and tell her if she wants my business she's to come here at once."

"*Oui, Madame,*" it was plain that Adena was horrified at Zulu's audacity. Even white women vied for Madame's services.

Zulu smiled. This time she was no *Kaintuck*. Madame Vaupont would come. There was no better advertisement of her skill than a voluptuous body.

Zulu studied her reflection.

This time, she thought, I'll know more than Ferne could teach me—and I'll have a wardrobe that'll make the white women turn in their landaus!

But somehow, there was still that heaviness in her heart. It was almost as if one half of herself was cut from the other.

She went into the sitting room, and with all of her strength she threw Shadney's pipes into the fireplace. She jerked Renny's ring from her finger and tossed it onto the mantel.

"That's the past," she told herself.

The Orleans Ballroom was as glistening and as gay as Zulu remembered it, but there was a more fevered pursuit of excitement. It was as if everyone realized a colorful fantasy was nearing its end, and all were bent on clutching at the fragments as they drifted past.

She entered on the arm of Louis Reton, a slim young banker, and they paused by the entranceway.

"I'd like to renew the offer I made before you became Randolph's *placee*," Reton was saying. "I was inconsolable for weeks."

Zulu nodded, scarcely listening. "Who is that woman

338

with all the man around her?" she asked. "I don't remember her."

Reton shrugged. "She calls herself Madame Noir."

"But she's dark as a mulatto and has as much shape as a beanpole!"

Reton laughed. "At the moment," he said, "she's the fashion. She has most the men in New Orleans running after her."

Zulu looked to see if he were joking, but his face was serious.

"Madame Noir may be too much for the others," Zulu told herself. "But I'll take care of that."

"Walk me past her," she whispered to Reton, "I'd like a closer look."

As they passed the corner where Madame Noir held her court, Zulu dropped her fan and pretended to stumble, kicking it out of Reton's reach. It's not very original, she thought, but it will do.

There was a scampering to retrieve the fan, and Zulu smiled, embarrassed.

"It was so clumsy of me!" she exclaimed, half laughing when it was handed back to her. "M'sieur, how can I thank you?"

She felt the warm scrutiny of admiring eyes. She'd show Noir! She'd not sit back like the others!

"But Messieurs! I'm torn with curiosity!" Madame Noir exclaimed petulantly. "If no one has the intention of finishing the story, I—"

Like faithful puppies, the men smiled at Zulu and turned back to Noir.

"The dance will be over before we start it," Reton told Zulu.

She permitted him to lead her out onto the floor, but her eyes followed the other woman. There was an answer. There had to be!

"The next dance?" Reton asked when the music stopped, but Zulu shook her head.

"No more until the fifth." It'd be admitting defeat to

dance with the same partner all night.

She withdrew to the room set aside for the ladies to repair their toilette. As she closed the door she saw the room was empty except for Antoinette Soulier.

Antoinette stepped aside so Zulu could see herself in the mirror. Her hair was as luxuriant as ever, her eyes as golden. Beside her Noir was an ugly brown frog. Why, then—?

"What's wrong with me?" she demanded of Antoinette.

"You mean Madame Noir?" Antoinette shrugged her tan shoulders. "It's the duels," she said as she adjusted the necklace that glittered at her throat. "*Sacre nom*, already there have been three fought for her, and always she laughs while they fight. It makes her someone who is talked about. *Comprendez-vous?*"

"I should think it would! I'd think the men would be disgusted."

"Does it look that way?" Antoinette spread her hands. "It makes them feel wicked. Daring." She looked at Zulu. "You've been away too long. It's no longer the innocent the men look to, it's the flame that sears them."

The music had started again when Zulu returned to the ballroom. Her eyes were caught by a man who had pushed to her side.

"M'sieur LaFruge!" Hadn't he taken a *placée* yet?

"What a surprise!" he exclaimed. Behind his huge spectacles his eyes were as worshipping as ever. "You will give me this dance?"

Zulu nodded. Why insult him? Noir had left her few enough men. As she danced she watched the woman whenever the chance arose.

Of course. There was always a way!

She looked up into LaFruge's face. "It's so sad for me—not to see M'sieur Randolph waiting for the dance to end."

340

"That shame!" LaFruge exclaimed. "Luton's still in disgrace."

"M'sieur Luton in disgrace? But how stupid." She sighed. "There was a man, M'sieur. A man who would fight for what he wanted. If he were in New Orleans now, I'd have no difficulty deciding upon a friend."

LaFruge almost tripped over his feet. "You're going to take a protector?" he asked excitedly.

Zulu lowered her lashes. "I'd only consider a man who is willing to fight for what he wants. Now, M'sieur Luton—"

"M'sieur Luton!" LaFruge scoffed. "I'd have done the same thing if I'd had the chance. I'd meet anyone in this room for you!"

"You would?" Zulu smiled up at him. "But you're flattering me!"

"Just give me the opportunity."

"But you've forced me, M'sieur." She hesitated. "I've promised the fifth dance to M'sieur Reton. Do you want it, instead?"

It had to work. LaFruge was made to order.

"M'sieur Reton, do you think—Would he understand?"

Zulu came to a standstill. "So it was just talk! Go back to your cradle!"

He followed her across the floor, trying to get her to listen to his pleas, finally she stopped and turned to him.

"There's only one dance I'll have with you," she said, "and that's the fifth." She took the arm of one of Shadney's friends and turned her back on LaFruge.

At the end of the fourth dance, Reton claimed her.

"I don't see why you limit me to two dances," he said petulantly. "After all, I'm your escort."

"Perhaps," Zulu suggested, "it was to allow you time for Madame Noir.

"You don't see me following her, do you?" he grimaced. "No one in this room would even look at her

341

except for two young idiots who, if they'd been sober, wouldn't have been seen with her, who got themselves in a drunken brawl that ended on the field.''

"They wanted her enough to fight over her," Zulu reminded him.

"*Le Bon Dieu* knows why! Out on the field the wine she'd been drinking set her into laughing hysterics as one of the fools killed the other. The story got out and pouff—she was *La femme fatale*."

"But not to you?"

"I was second to the man who was killed. And the only sober person there."

She had been watching LaFruge approach and she smiled up at Reton. "You made me an offer when we came here tonight. Do you still feel the same?"

"You're joking?"

"If you really mean it, you'll hurry me out to the dance floor. I'll be *placee* to the man I dance this waltz with."

LaFruge caught Zulu's arm as Reton started to lead her away.

"*S'il vous plait, Madame*," he said shakily. "This dance?"

"I beg your pardon," Reton said, "This dance is taken."

"But I insist! I'm certain Madame will tell you she has changed her mind!"

Reton's dark eyes flashed. "Really, M'sieur," he started, but Zulu put her finger lightly on his lips.

"Messieurs, this is hardly the place to settle an argument."

"I don't fancy boys as dueling opponnents," Reton said.

"Boys!" LaFruge raged. He ripped off his glove and slashed Reton across the face.

Reton whitened. "We'll find out," he said, "at dawn." He turned to Zulu. "Meanwhile I'll have what's left of this dance."

Now was her time. Zulu knew that excitement stained her cheeks and that her eyes were bright. She extended one hand to each of the men and smiled.

"Messieurs," she murmured, "how can I dance with either of you? Tomorrow I'll make my choice. Tomorrow just after dawn."

Then she added louder, so others could hear. "The man I make my protector will be the one still standing under the Oaks."

She saw, then, that Madame Noir was standing alone in the center of the room. The malice in her gaze would have shriveled Zulu had she been vulnerable.

Zulu laughed. "Meanwhile, M'sieur Reton and M'sieur LaFruge, I'm hungry—and it's a long wait till dawn. I refuse to accept even a glass of wine from either of you alone until tomorrow. So you will both see to me until then."

There was a murmur in the group who had gathered around them. Zulu didn't realize it, but she was setting a style that was to scandalize polite society. The rivals and their lady dining and drinking together until the first light of dawn found one a victor—and the other, possibly, a corpse.

The Oaks with their long streamers of moss were unchanged. The field was hazy and unreal—and beyond was still the rank growth of grass. Nothing was different—but the men.

Last time, Zulu thought, I cared.

The swords flashed in the dim light. LaFruge smiled as he side stepped a parry. There was sweat on his forehead and a sleeve ripped open.

Suddenly it was over. Reton's sword plunged into LaFruge and came out dripping. LaFruge's left arm was nearly severed and he fell unconscious under the Oaks.

This is the answer! Zulu thought hysterically. Food for the song! She ripped a bit of lace from her gown and passed LaFruge without a glance. With the tip of her tongue she moistened the lace and wiped the blood away

343

from a scratch on Reton's face. He put his arm around her and led her off the field.

She rode back into town with her head on his shoulder and overcome with a sense of shame. To be another Madame Noir took more than she had thought. Once, maybe, but no more. Out on the field a young scion of an old Creole family might have lost an arm.

She closed her eyes and tried to think of what she really wanted and she knew it was not this.

Reton saw her to her door. He made a move to follow her inside, but she shook her head.

"I'm tired," she said. "The excitement—" She smiled up at him, "I'll see you this evening, M'sieur?"

She had no premonition as she stepped across the threshold and closed the door behind her.

Chapter Forty-Eight

The smile was still on Zulu's face as she turned away from the door and started to undo her wrap. She stopped with her fingers still on the button.

"Breel!" she exclaimed. Then, with an attempt at calmness, she put aside her wrap and managed a smile.

He nodded his head in acknowledgement. His dark eyes darted over her burgandy moire gown, the diamond pendants in her ears and the large diamond set in a golden teardrop that caught the light on her breast.

"Rather formal for early morning, isn't it?" he asked. He was thinner than she remembered him, and well dressed. He looked very different from the man she'd seen in Donna's drawing room. He wore a small mustache that partially concealed the scar at the corner of his mouth, and his skin was pale.

It's as if no time has passed since we stood like this before, she thought. Nothing else was real. But Jules was real. Jules and that terrible scene at Nollgrove when he had ruined everything for her.

"What do you want?" she asked.

"I've come to take you to Bijou."

Zulu laughed. "Still the same Breel! Your audacity is unbelievable."

He nodded. "Quite. You've assumed a pretty polish, Zulu, but I'm willing to bet you're the same little bitch I met at Elmside."

She bit back a retort, trying to keep her dignity. "What makes you think I have to take your insults?"

"Cousin Thalia regularly sends duty letter. Especially when there's scandal in another branch of the family. She heard about the terrible affair (heavily underlined, by the way) that had happened to dear Cousin Renny at Nollgrove."

There was no way he could connect that with her, Zulu thought in desperation. She had been so careful—

"It wasn't difficult to piece it out when I heard the woman's name was Zula. Especially as you left Renny's note on the table when you left Donna and me here in your cottage." He smiled thoughtfully. "You were lucky Cousin Norman didn't come to see Thalia home."

"You'd have known there was no chance of that if you'd heard her twins," Zulu muttered.

"So you admit it, Mrs. Langford? Of course, by law—"

"Even if you reported me, Renny would never prosecute."

"Renny, my dear, is dead. I imagine his sister feels differently."

Dead? She didn't dare ask. She didn't want to know.

Breel's mouth twisted in disgust. "God Almighty that was a rotten mess. However, it puts you in a position I find very desirable. You are coming to Bijou, you know. And without protest."

He pulled her to him and pushed back her curls with a rough hand. "I may not be gentle, but I'm gentler than a lynching mob."

The outside jalouise slammed and the knocker crashed down. Zulu stood with Breel's arms still around her as Letty hurried in from the kitchen to open the door. Donna Luton pushed past Letty. She stopped when she saw Breel.

"Mother of God!" she exclaimed.

"Surprised?" Breel smiled. "This time you had no chance to warn Zulu."

"I tried," Donna said to Zulu. "As soon as I knew you were in town."

"My dear," Breel interrupted. "You remember Cousin Thalia's letter? Let me have the pleasure of introducing you to Mrs. Renny Langford of Nollgrove."

"I don't think that is very humorous, Breel," Donna said.

"It's not humorous," Zulu agreed, "but you may as well know he's telling the truth."

Donna stared at her a moment, then some of the shock left her eyes. She went to Zulu and took her hand. "I think I can understand," she said. "You couldn't have known what would happen."

"What about the nigger involved?" Breel asked pleasantly.

"I understood he was a man of color," Donna said. "Breel—we don't know anything but what that scandal loving cousin of yours said. We can't forget the debt we owe Zulu. She took you in when you were hurt. She helped us when the baby died. She turned her cottage over to us."

"And now," Breel said, "we're going to return her hospitality."

"You can't do that!" Donna exclaimed. "You can't

346

force her to come to Bijou."

"You know I'd never be that crude, my dear. I merely extended an invitation that she is going to accept. Aren't you, Zulu?"

Zulu glared at him out of sullen eyes. Down the hall the baby started to cry. Breel raised an eyebrow.

"Surely, Zulu, you can't blame me for that one?"

"Juliet?" She shrugged. "Hardly."

Breel opened the liquor cabinet. "Still Randolph's stock," he observed. "I always said he had good taste."

Donna hurried across the room and caught his wrist.

"You promised, Breel! Put it back."

Breel laughed. "Wouldn't you have me drink to our guest?"

"But you've kept your word all of this time."

Breel threw a careless arm around Zulu's shoulder. "But we have Zulu, again," he exclaimed. "Don't you know she always brings out my worst instincts? That's what's so charming about her."

He moved to the hallway.

"Letty," he shouted, "get Zulu's things together." He went to the nursery door and looked in. "I think we'll take this one, too," he decided. "It interests me."

He turned, joining the two women. "Wait till you see Fannette," he said with something close to pride. "We did a good job on her."

"I'm going out to the carriage," Donna said unsteadily. "I'll wait there."

Her handkerchief fell from her fingers as she fumbled with the latch, and Zulu saw it was ripped into shreds.

She looked at Breel. He had seen the square of linen, also, and there was an odd scowl on his face.

Chapter Forty-Nine

The carriage rolled over the uneven road, bumping and pitching. On each side the swamps stretched, lush with wanton growths. White mingled with rose and here and there a carmine bloom lay like a great drop of blood that had spurted up from the dank, compelling depths.

Cypresses with their tormented knees twisting out of the water for air, grew to the road's edge on either side, and sometimes their green boughs reached out, meeting over the carriage for horror fraught seconds that left Zulu trembling. Each time it was as if the swamp had closed in on her.

And always ahead the Spanish moss trailed grey streamers from the branches, like moldering shrouds.

Yet it was beautiful. A deadly, destroying beauty that pulled at Zulu as it had pulled at her before, in those terrible nightmares.

Only now it knew. Now it was willing to wait because it knew there was no turning back, no running away.

It had been patient for a long time. . . .

She closed her eyes. This was the same as giving in to the pull of voodoo. It was only in her mind. The swamp was harmless as long as one knew the paths. It had no life. It was stupid to allow herself to become hysterical. Reaching for her! As if the swamp could come up and draw her back with it!

But something inside her could draw her to it. . . .

She was aware of Breel watching her. Donna was sitting next to him, but she hadn't spoken since they'd left the cottage. She kept her face to the window, her hands clasped tensely in her lap.

"I've never known you to be quiet for so long, Zulu," Breel observed.

Zulu pulled her eyes away from the great field of wild cane that lay ahead.

"I don't like this kind of country," she said.

"You'll get used to it," Breel assured her. "Bijou's a peninsula in the middle of the swamps. I've heard there's a path out, but the only way I know is by this road. Once the gate closes behind us—" He shrugged. "At least we don't have many slaves running off."

To have this all around her! Zulu shuddered.

Papilottes started to cry and the nurse crooned softly to her.

Breel watched, interested. "I didn't hear about a baby. For that matter, I can't believe my cousin was its father."

Zulu looked away.

It was nearly mid-day when they turned off the main road and drove up the narrow peninsula of firm ground that formed the entrance to Bijou. A colony of heron swept across their path as they came in sight of the sprawling buildings. The silence was shattered by the dogs barking and leaping at the sides of the kennel.

An old negro unlocked the cast iron gates, and Breel turned to Zulu.

"Welcome to Bijou. May your stay last as long as—your charms."

Zulu looked at the lush greenery on all sides, the gloomy buildings with their strange, foreign roofs, and at the blue-black negroes who ran down to meet the carriage.

"I hate this place already," Zulu said.

"But Bijou's beautiful!" Breel protested. "A jewel, like its name. Ask Donna, her father built it. We even spent our first few months together, here." His eyes clouded. "That must have been when Rosalie—" he shrugged. "There's not a doubt. This place fairly reeks of sentiment."

349

The carriage stopped in front of the house. It was a raised, plantation type cottage with a stilted stairway that led to the second story. Here a wide gallery with iron railings circled the building. Tall, shuttered windows jutted out of the sloped roof.

The avenue was jagged and boggy and the gardens were overgrown, but the fields that stretched on all sides were neatly tended. The cane swayed in the light breeze like waves in an ocean. Against the horizon Zulu could see a tall sugar mill, and a little beyond an abandoned shed sagged against the sky.

The quarters sprawled behind the house and outbuildings were bunched behind them. And the smell of swamp country was in the air.

There's hate here, she thought.

"I haven't decided," Breel said, "whether to put you in one of the empty cabins in the quarters or above the kitchen house."

Donna spoke for the first time since they had started the journey.

"I've put up with a lot of things, but this is too much. If Zulu won't take up for herself, I certainly shall. I forbid you do do this."

Breel looked at his wife with something close to interest in his eyes. "I'd hardly wish to cause you distress."

"Then you'll see Zulu gets back to New Orleans?"

"I'll do better. I'll see the proper authorities are advised of her arrival. And suggest they contact Nollgrove."

"You can't do that, Breel."

"Ask Zulu. It's really a surprising way for you to repay the debt you say we owe her. You understand, Donna?"

"Yes," she said. "I quite understand." Then she added quietly. "There are empty rooms in the house."

"Exactly," Breel agreed. "I just wanted the suggestion to come from you. What about the room that's closed off? The one that looks down into the swamps?''

Donna shrugged. "You'll find there's not a servant in the house who'll step over the threshold."

"Letty will," Breel said. "Voodoo may bother Letty's mistress, but not Letty."

"Voodoo?" Zulu repeated.

"It's really silly," Donna explained, "but the house servants used to hold their meetings there when I was a little girl. My father found out and had it boarded. You know how stories grow about anything that's closed up."

"It doesn't matter," Zulu said.

"I'm disappointed, Zulu," Breel told her. "I thought you'd appreciate it. Especially the view."

Donna called to a burly Santo Domingan black who stood by the pathway. She spoke to him rapidly in a dialect Zulu could barely follow.

"He'll knock down the boards and open the door," she explained as they went up the stairs. She smiled for the first time. "I know you must be anxious to see Tignasse and I think you'll be delighted. If you ever decide you don't want her—"

"Shad made provisions." Tignasse—tangled hair. That was as bad as Papillotes.

Donna opened a door. "Tignasse!" she called. "Ted!" There was a patter of feet and a girl of two ran to them, her tawny hair flying in a soft confusion of curls, her skirts swaying out behind. A blue turbaned nurse followed, guiding a small boy's toddling steps.

Donna knelt down and the children ran to her. She hugged one with each arm, then she looked up at Zulu, ruffling Fannette's hair.

Zulu moved closer. This couldn't be the baby Madame Randolph had taken away. Not this exquisite golden creature who regarded her so intently out of Breel's expressive dark eyes.

The shape of her face is mine, Zulu thought, but

there's Breel in the way she tilts her head.

"Didn't I tell you she was a treasure?" Donna asked.

Zulu nodded. There was no doubt that the combination of smoldering eyes and tawny curls was a startling one, especially when set off by a full silken mouth.

Yet, there was something more—something familiar about the girl's expression that puzzled Zulu. Something that was of neither Breel nor herself.

"What do you think of her?" Breel asked from behind them. Fannette ran to him, but the boy shrank back against Donna.

Breel took Fannette up in his arms and carried her to Zulu. He passed his son without a glance and a shadow passed over Donna's face.

"She's got our looks, but thank the Lord, neither of our dispositions." He glanced at Donna. "Of course, that might be influence. But I never observed that early influence changed your disposition, Zulu."

Lord God, would he never forget Rosalie?

"In fact," Breel continued, "there are times when Fannette reminds me very much of . . . Naida."

Zulu stared at Fannette. That was the familiarity she'd tried to place. Had Ferne and her meaningless chant robbed her of her daughter?

Breel sat the girl at Zulu's feet, but when Zulu knelt beside her, she hung back.

"Aren't you going to hug your mother?" Donna asked.

Fannette shook her head.

Zulu tried to smile. This was her child. The baby she had birthed that terrible morning. She undid her pendant and Fannette moved closer, distrust still in her eyes. Zulu lifted the heavy hair and fastened the clasp. She remembered, suddenly, the tugging she'd felt at her heart when Fannette had stroked her cheek just before Madame Randolph took her away.

"There!" she said as the pendant fell into place.

Fannette touched it, then looked up.

"*Merci*," she whispered. "*Merci bien*!"

Donna nodded approvingly.

Zulu's face darkened.

"No!" she exclaimed. "*Merci beaucoup*. Don't ever let me hear you say *merci bien*!" She drew back.

Breel regarded her oddly. "Really," he murmured, "it is correct, you know."

Zulu got to her feet and moved to the door. Out the window across the hall she could see fields stretching to the cypress borders, but in her ears was Naida's soft voice, thanking her.

"*Merci. Merci bien . . .*"

She looked at her hands, half expecting to see the orange she'd been peeling that unforgettable day.

It was no use. Everything was here waiting. Naida. Rosalie. Everything. Even the swamps. She shuddered.

Donna touched her shoulder.

"I've sent them to finish their meal. It must be very hard. Seeing your child after all of this time."

Zulu turned on her. "That isn't my child. My child was taken from me before she was born!"

"They've opened the room," Breel called to them. "You do the honors, Donna."

Donna led the way down the hall to a door that hung open on a broken bolt.

"Is that a room?" Lord God, the cobwebs must be ankle deep!

"It doesn't look very inviting," Donna admitted, "but it is by far the largest of the empty rooms, and once it's cleaned—"

The place was airless and smelled of damp and mold. Shadows darted about the walls as if in search of hiding places.

I've disturbed them, Zulu thought, and tried not to pry after them into the dark corners. She looked at the black marble fireplace and the stately bed that was hung with dusty drapery. A thick carpet rotted on the floor.

This isn't a room, she thought. It's a ghost of a room.

Donna threw open the dormer windows and the shutters. "The jalousie needs repairing," she remarked.

Zulu watched in a sort of wonderment. How could Donna appear so efficient and detatched when—

"This can't be very pleasant for you." Her own voice sounded muffled.

Donna met her eyes without an attempt at evasion. "If it wasn't you, it would be one of the house girls. That's the way men are, *n'est ce pas*? Once I hated every girl he looked at. But hating just gave me a sickness. And sometimes, Zulu, he can be so charming . . . so tender."

"A woman can forgive most things in a man if he's tender when he makes love," Zulu observed. She tried not to remember how he'd been with Rosalie . . .

Donna blushed. She started moving tables and chairs and stood back to survey the effect.

"The room has possibilities," she decided.

"Don't you realize Breel never wants what he has? Maybe we're alike, that way. Someday, Donna, you'll see him the way I do. Then you won't want any part of him."

Again their glances met, but this time Zulu saw the deep distress in Donna's eyes.

"Please," she said, "it would be a favor if we didn't talk about him." Her voice faltered. "Not this way." She went to the door. "I'll send help—and Letty."

Zulu watched Donna's skirts swish over the threshold, then she looked out the window. Underneath there was a soft, lush growth of grass, and just beyond it the cypress thicket. Almost, it seemed, all of it was out there waiting to creep into the room. A snake slithered under her feet. A harmless snake and Zulu picked it up to toss it out the window.

Letty screamed from the doorway.

"Lord God!" Zulu snapped. "Close your mouth!"

She stepped past the girl to face the burly house servant who waited in the hall.

"Get in there and tear out the carpet!" she said.

His eyes were round and frightened. "*Oui, mamaloi!*" He bobbed his head, and in a few seconds he was on his knees ripping at the rug.

Donna came back. She paused to look in. "But how did you manage?" she asked. "They'd almost as soon dare Le Grand Zombi!"

Zulu looked at the snake she still held. She threw it out the window.

"Almost," she agreed. "But not quite."

Breel's voice carried down the hall and it was followed by a girl's giggle. Donna frowned and looked in the direction of the sound.

"Neeta!" She spoke a little sharply.

A young mulattress moved toward them. Her hips swayed with an uninhibited grace. Impudent eyes set off a pretty, piquant face.

She smiled. "*Maitresse?*" There was an insolence in her manner that was too subtle for a reprimand.

"Antone is in the room and you can see nothing's eaten him. I want you to strip the bed and scrub and dust. When it's ready, I'll send up linens and a new *baire*. *Vitement!*"

Donna looked back at Zulu. "You've got one of them past the threshold and that should be the end of this silliness." She paused. "What was that Antone called you?"

Zulu smiled wryly. "*Mamaloi.*"

Donna laughed. "But no! Since when have you been a voodoo priestess? One should take care when they pick up a snake!" Her face grew serious. "There are so many things I have to see to."

But was it the snake? Zulu wondered.

Neeta touched her arm after Donna had left. "You not like Bijou, *oui*? You want me to show you the path?"

355

Zulu saw the jealousy in the girl's eyes. "Any path you showed me would most likely end in the deepest bog. Get back to work."

Zulu found Donna preparing a room for Papilottes and her nurse.

"I hope Neeta is behaving. I think I'll have to send her to the quarters."

"Breel?" Zulu asked.

Donna pretended she hadn't heard.

Chapter Fifty

When Zulu returned to the room after the evening meal, the carpets had been ripped out and the floor scrubbed until it gleamed. Donna had scattered throw rugs where they were needed, and there were clean curtains at the window. The bed linens smelled fresh and the new mosquito *baire* was spotless. On the surface everything should have looked inviting.

But underneath, nothing was different. Zulu still had the feeling of invading—disturbing what should not have been disturbed.

Letty threw the other window open and the swamp noises came up into the room. The croaking of a bull frog, the murmur of a night singing bird, the wail of a swamp animal. And, over it all, the tinkling bell-like music of the tree frogs.

She could not bring herself to go through the newly repaired door. She moved down the hall until she found an exit leading to the gallery that circled the house. She found a chair and lay back trying to think. But she was tired. Too tired to fight.

She was awakened by the sound of voices and realized there was light in the room behind her.

"Why?" Donna was saying. "I've failed you somewhere, Breel. But where?"

"Most women are damn glad not to have to put up with their husbands," Breel replied.

"Why did you have to awaken my need for you, those first few months? Couldn't you have left me unresponsive? It would have been so much easier, Breel."

"Where's that Moulton pride?"

"Should there be pride between a husband and wife? Sometimes I feel you do these things to hurt me. Then I think maybe there's hope."

Breel slammed a drawer.

"Sometimes," Donna continued, "it's as if you're trying to punish yourself, and hurting me is one of the ways." She laughed. "That's senseless, of course. *Tres bien*, if my lack of shame troubles you, I promise not to embarrass you again."

Zulu moved out of the chair as quietly as she could and went into the house. It was not pleasant to hear Donna talk, stripped of pride.

She entered the room at the end of the hall reluctantly, and was relieved to find Letty there, waiting to prepare her for bed. It was with mingled emotions she permitted herself to be helped into a nightdress. While Letty brushed her hair she rested her head back trying to think—to plan. But it was as it had been since Nollgrove. There was only confusion in her mind. A hatred of Jules—and an unwillingness to face life without him.

Breel came into the room and motioned for Letty to leave. Where was the thrill his nearness used to bring? The fear?

"I haven't finished with her yet, Breel."

"You're through with her for the night." He stood

over her and their eyes met in a silent battle. "I told you the next time we discussed Rosalie I wouldn't be helpless."

Oh Lord God, she'd all but forgotten his promise. So much had happened that was more real. For the first time she saw the emptiness of his threats. He's clinging to a memory, she thought, and he knows the meaning behind it has faded.

"That isn't why you came in here," she said.

He moved restlessly across the room and when he turned to her again his eyes had lost some of their purpose.

"I've dreamed of you. Night after night I dreamed I was about to tear you apart. But when I touched you, it was like this."

She lay down on the bed and stretched. She waited until he stood over her, then she took his hand and put it at her throat.

"Another man tried to strangle me. Do you think you would have that much nerve? Think of Rosalie and how much she means to you—now."

He was trembling, fists clenched at his side. Suddenly he tore off her nightdress and his body was on hers, pressing her into the feather mattress.

"You little whore!" He reached over to put out the lamp. In the darkness she felt herself clutching at him, moving with him, but it was a purely physical thing. Always before she had striven for an ecstatic blending in his embrace, but she knew now she would never find it with him.

When he finally rolled away she felt relaxed and lethargic, but there was no joyful crashing of the stars.

Jules spoiled me for other men, she thought.

Breel raised himself on an elbow, his breath still uneven.

"What was wrong?" he asked. "God Almighty, I may as well have made love to a statue!"

How had he known? Her body had responded to his.

It had never been more than physical, in any case.

He continued to look down at her, then he laughed. "Two can play at a game," he told her.

The swamp noises were loud about them. She got up and slammed a window shut.

Chapter Fifty-One

After breakfast the next morning, Zulu found a copy of the *Picayune*. She took it up to her room to search out accounts of local trouble with bands of runaway slaves.

If only she knew where Jules was hiding. She had guessed his intention was to come back to the cypress swamps, and where once she had feared to read of his capture, now she looked eagerly for it. What a triumph it would be to turn him over to the hounds and men who searched the swamps. Let him pay for Nollgrove! Let him pay for the indignities she was suffering right here at Bijou.

Yes, and let him pay for Renny. She had tried not to think of Renny. How he had trusted her and how secure he had felt, certain of her love. Yes, she had loved him. Not as a man, but more as a child who adored her. He had been kind and he had been gentle and Jules had done this to him.

Jules and herself.

She became aware of Letty singing as she worked with the clothes in the *armoire*.

"Pauv' piti Mom'zelle Zizi
Pauv' piti Mom'zelle Zizi!

Li gaignain bobo, bobo
Dans so piti tchoeur

"Pauv' piti Mom'zelle Zizi
Li gaignain bobo, bobo
Li gaignain in maladie
Dans so piti tchoeur à li."

Wasn't that the song the roustabout had been singing
on the upper deck that evening she and Renny had stood
by the rail together? It had been so long ago . . .

"Pity poor Mom'zelle Zizi
Pity poor Mom'zelle Zizi!
She's sad as sad can be
In her little heart

"Pity poor Mom'zelle Zizi
She's sad as sad can be
Sick and tired of life is she
And her heart aches bitterly—"

She looked up with the sudden realization that it
couldn't be Letty singing. Letty wasn't even able to
speak gumbo! She put aside the paper and went to the
armoire corner. Neeta met her eyes with a wide grin.

"You like my song, *oui*?"

"What are you doing with those dresses on your
arm?" Zulu demanded. "That's Letty's work."

Neeta shrugged. "M'sieur Le Maitre say for Neeta to
get herself *les belles robes*. Always Neeta obey Le
Maitre."

"Put those back and get out of here!" Zulu
exclaimed.

"I told her she could take them." Breel lounged lazily
against the wall. "Don't you think she deserves better
than that house uniform?"

"If you want to dress her, buy the clothes yourself. I
paid good money for those."

"Randolph's or Langford's?" Breel murmured.
"Don't you think you're unreasonable? It's hardly right

to use Donna's money for Neeta's clothes. Of course, if you object—"

"Take them!" Zulu exclaimed. "Take everything!"

"Not everything," Breel protested. "Just a few." His voice sharpened. "Put some of those back, Neeta. You're overdoing it."

She bobbed her head. "*Oui.*" She smiled and left all but three in a heap on the floor. She paused in the doorway to grin at Zulu, then she went on down the hall, singing.

> "Calalou porté madrasse
> Li porté jipon garni
> Calalou porté la soie
> Li porté belles belles
>
> "Pauv' piti Mom'zelle Zizi
> Li gaignain in maladie
> Li gaignain bobo, bobo
> Dans so piti tchoeur. . . ."

Furious at both Breel and Neeta, Zulu found herself attempting to translate

> "Calalou wears madras rare
> Little coats of silken ware
> Calalou wears rich brocade
> Jewels made of finest jade
>
> "Pity poor Mon'zelle Zizi
> Sick and tired of life is she
> She's sad as sad can be
> In her little heart. . . ."

"Not very sutble, is she?" Breel remarked. He led Zulu to the window. "See that cabin up near the house? I've had it furnished for her."

"Why tell me? Do you expect I'd be jealous?"

There was something in his answering smile that made her feel uneasy. They both turned at the sound of Donna hurrying down the hall.

"Roc sent word they're getting a search party

together. "They'll stop by for you and the hounds."

"That band of maroons?" Breel asked.

Donna nodded. "They've been making raids for food." She looked inquiringly at Breel. "Is it true we've lost some hands?"

"Someone in the band knows the paths around here. Damn it! I had other plans for tonight."

Donna watched him leave. "I keep remembering the stories of the insurrection in Santo Domingo. It frightens me."

"When first I came to New Orleans everyone was talking insurrection. But they caught Squire's gang and hanged all of them."

"That didn't stop anything." Donna moved restlessly to the window. "The cypress swamps are full of them again."

Breel rode away after dinner. Zulu watched him leave from her room. "I hope they hang every one of them," she said. Thinking of Jules.

Letty's full lips moved in a prayer.

It was late when Breel returned. Zulu heard him pass her door and she turned in her bed. The moon was shining thrugh the lattices and she could feel the uneasy presence of others in the room. Malign . . . Alien . . . Eyes that were gouged out like Bill's, watched her. She pulled the covers over her head. Only shadows, she thought, but another part of her whispered, "It's the Will of the Wisp that's come for you." Or Feig? Feig sick for home?

She waited for Breel to return, almost welcoming him, but later she heard him go out of the house and there was a light in the cabin.

Breel opened her door as she was getting ready for bed the next evening. She sent Letty away.

"You're not so aloof tonight," he observed.

"Anything's better than sleeping alone in this place," Zulu said, shuddering. She got into bed, waiting for him.

He pulled back the covers and removed her nightdress. His lips caressed her, traveling over her body until her breasts rose and fell with her quickened breathing.

He looked down at her, raising himself on his elbows. "You purr and bridle like some golden animal," he told her. "And you've about as much shame.

She watched him through half closed eyes that reflected the heat mounting within her.

"Lord God, Breel, put out the lamp. . . ." she whispered. "I'll catch cold lying like this."

"That's about the last thing you'll catch right now," he told her. He put on his robe and went out the door.

"Have a good sleep," he added, just before pulling it shut.

Zulu sat up in bed. It was impossible! But she heard him go down the stairs and she knew he was crossing to the cabin. She ran to the window in time to see his silhouette. A few minutes later there was only darkness where a lamp had glowed before.

The night air was heavy with the fertile, earthy smell of vegetation. In the swamps a bird called its mate.

He's not going to bring down my pride! She pounded the pillow with each word. She'd never have even been at Bijou if it wasn't for Jules! It was all Jules' fault.

Breel took her for a walk in the garden the next evening.

"Exercise will do you good," he told her as they approached a trail that led a little way past the cane fields toward the swamps. "Of course, if it makes you nervous . . ."

Zulu choked back the knot in her chest. "Why should I be?" she asked, moving closer to him.

He continued up the path until they reached a place where nothing lay in front of them but still waters overgrown with great blooms, exotic and strange in the moonlight. Zulu turned her head away, but Breel drew her roughly to him.

Then—it was the same as before. He drew away from her just short of culmination.

"I can't keep Neeta waiting," he said.

She jumped to her feet and ran after him.

"You can't leave me out here!" She screamed, almost in hysteria. "Don't leave me alone, Breel."

Neeta was waiting at the cabin door. She grinned at Zulu and then turned to follow Breel inside.

Zulu ran into Papilotte's room, and only the memory of Fannette's screams that time she had clutched her in a spasm of insecurity, kept her from snatching up Jules' sleeping child. The wet nurse watched curiously as Zulu leaned over the cradle, half sobbing.

"Go get Letty," she said.

A short while later the nurse returned. "Ain't nobudy dere," she said.

Letty not in her room? What could she find at Bijou to keep her out at this hour?

She moved slowly down the hall and climbed into her bed. She drew the covers over her head again, but this time the thing that waited by the window, came across the room and sat in her dreams.

Chapter Fifty-Two

Zulu sat in her robe by the open window and listened to the voodoo drums throb in the night. Each pulsation struck a cord in her body, stirring the hunger Breel had awakened before a party of planters rode through the gates to enlist him on another search for the band of fugitive blacks.

At least she though, with scant satisfaction, this time he's no better off than me!

The great fire blazed up beyond the cane and the smoke hid some of the stars, but the moon shone full and round through the haze.

She could hear chanting in the distance and it was difficult to keep her body from undulating to the sensuous rhythm.

She put her hands over her ears, but it was no use. That steady throb . . . throb . . .

She climbed up onto the bed and lay very still. The drums beat up to a frenzy of passion, then slowed again, only to work up to another pitch of ecstasy. Her body became a part of it. A craving, lusting medium of the primeval urge that pulsated through the air.

Her mind dulled, conscious only of the hypnotic boom . . . boom . . . that grew and absorbed. And possessed.

. . . .*The night closed about her, the vibrations were her own heartbeat and she was home. She moved slowly, swaying to the rhythm and the rank grass brushed against her as it had at Elmside so many years before. . . .*

She picked a flower and put it over her ear as she continued steadily toward the place where the trail ended. Ahead of her were floating clumps of water lilies and cypress knees. She moved from branch to branch, aware only of the steady throbbing that drew her onward.

Soon the soothing water would fold around her. She'd find coolness there. She'd find. . . .

Suddenly the drums stopped.

Lord God, what was she doing out here? She clung to a cypress knee, trembling. Finally she mustered the strength to climb back the way she'd come, until she was once again on solid ground.

She ran up the path to the house, afraid to look back or even sideways. She had to be clear of the place before the drums started again. Before it was too late.

She stopped at the edge of the clearing. Someone was coming up from the fields. Then Donna came into sight with a great whip in her hands. A large house servant followed her holding a lantern above their heads.

That was the reason the drums had quieted. Donna had gone down into the cane brakes and broken up the meeting. Another second and it would have been too late.

Zulu closed her eyes tightly tried to reason it out.

As long as Neeta was at Bijou, Breel would torment her, and as long as this restless hunger stirred in her, she was in danger. There was only one answer.

The whip lay on the porch where Donna had left it. Zulu picked it up and went to the cabin near the house.

Neeta heard her and opened the door. The eagerness left her face when she saw it was Zulu and her eyes widened when they rested on the whip Zulu held.

"*Oui?*"

"Get on your clothes," Zulu said.

"M'sieur Le Maitre—" Neeta started.

"Get your clothes on!"

When the girl had pulled on the plain dress of a house servant, Zulu pointed out the door. They moved silently through the unkept gardens, across the avenue, and finally they were at the edge of the swamp. Zulu pointed ahead.

"You said you knew the path. Take it and get out of here. If you come back, I'll kill you."

Neeta tossed her head defiantly. "M'sieur Le Maitre loves me, *oui*? Is that a reason to kill me? Is it my fault?"

Zulu laughed. "You mean as much to him as one of his dogs." She pulled off the opal ring Shadney had given her. "When you get to New Orleans you can sell that. I'll pay Donna your price. You won't be hunted."

Neeta stared at the ring and then raised frightened eyes to Zulu. "But I don't know the way out!" she

366

screamed, "I don't know it!"

Zulu lifted the whip. "Leave while you can still walk!"

The moon had been obscured by a cloud that drifted away and for a moment the full light flashed in Zulu's eyes.

Neeta back away, terrified.

"*Mamaloi*!" she screamed and turned to run into the darkness. The branches broke and the leaves rustled, then were still again.

Zulu started back toward the house when she heard Neeta start to scream.

Lord God, had that stupid woman lied about the path?

She turned and ran to where she had left the girl. Little by little she made her way to the edge of solid ground and the moon showed Neeta struggling. Zulu threw out the whip and the lash fell within Neeta's reach.

"Catch it," Zulu screamed. "Hang on to it and I'll pull."

She pulled with all the strength she could muster, hanging onto a cypress knee when she found her own feet slipping. Trying to thrust out the picture of the mud drawing . . . claiming . . .

She knew it was no use. But she pulled until she fell on the ground, exhausted. Still she tried to pull.

Then the whip was out of her hands and Breel was standing over her, shouting instructions to the girl. The sweat stood out on his forehead and she heard his breath hiss in gasps. Then there was a dragging, floundering sound and a mud caked swamp thing lay sobbing on the bank.

Breel helped Neeta to her feet. "Get someone to go to the well with you," he said. "Have them slush you off. Tomorrow you move back into the quarters."

When the girl staggered away toward the shadow of the house, Breel looked at Zulu, distaste swept across his face. "I suppose it should be a consolation to know that no matter how low I might sink, I could never reach your level."

"She said she knew the path!"

"And you believed her? Did you really believe her, Zulu?"

Why fight him? Why protest? Nothing she said would matter.

"When I came back tonight I intended sending her back to the quarters. She was a lesson you had to learn, but I guess I taught you too well."

"There were voodoo drums tonight," Zulu said. "Donna stopped them. She went out in her night clothes with just this whip and one of the house servants."

He scowled. "They wouldn't have dared except they knew I was away. They know too many things. I'm beginning to think all the trouble we've been having is centered around Bijou."

Zulu slept uneasily that night. In her dreams it was she, and not Neeta who floundered in the swamp. There was a rank growth of irises and *graines-a-volée* all around her. And mixed up with them was Bill's gouged out eye. His split head. Shadney, reaching for her. Ferne laughing and jeering. Renny—Renny wasn't there. But Naida was. Stupid, trusting Naida.

"*Merci. Merci bien.*"

Chapter Fifty-Three

She heard Ferne's laughter often in the months that went by. She had only to close her eyes to hear it.

It's a conjur, she told herself. I know there's

nothing to a conjur but the person, herself.

What good did it do to know what she couldn't believe? It didn't stop Ferne from laughing in her dreams, it didn't dry up the swamps, and knowing didn't remove the heavy feeling of apprehension that grew with each day.

She even went so far as to try to talk about it to Donna's priest on one of his infrequent calls at the plantation.

"You expect me to fight magic with magic," he told her. "You look on religion as another superstition. As long as you look on the Church that way, it can't help you."

"It couldn't anyway," Zulu said.

"It's difficult to be without faith."

"Faith?" Zulu laughed. "You say there's no such thing as a conjur, then you talk about faith. Have I any more proof of what you talk about, than I have of a conjur? If there's one, why can't there be the other?"

"I wish," he said sadly, "that I could help you."

"If what Ferne said was true neither you nor all your faith can help."

After he left, Zulu went to her room and sat by the window, trying to clear out her mind. Letty came through the door and started to sort underclothes. Zulu watched absently as her maid opened a drawer to the *armoire*. For the first time she realized Letty looked different. Tired and unwell. Even her clothes fit wrong. Then she understood.

"Lord God, Letty!" she exclaimed. "Are you pregnant?" She frowned. "You can't be more than three months or I'd have noticed before. You've been away from New Orleans longer than that." She started to laugh. "What will your man, Trojan say? You running around getting yourself fixed up while he saves to get what I'm asking for you!"

Letty set her mouth, and her eyes flashed.

"So Trojan's the only man you'd look at!" Zulu

taunted. "Someone changed your mind for sure!"

"Der ain' no man but Trojan!" Letty blurted. She appealed to Zulu, her fingers interlaced. "Please, Miz Zulu, don' you devil me about him."

"You mean you're carrying Trojan's baby?"

Letty nodded. Pride was in her eyes.

"But how do you see him? Where?"

"In dat old shack back of de mill," Letty answered. "He wuz raised hereabout, but he made me promise—"

"Made you promise?" Zulu repeated, "but if he knows the path—"

"Please," Letty begged, "I swear befor' Jesus I couldn't tell you. Trojan, he—"

Zulu's eyes narrowed. "Are you trying to tell me he's with that gang of maroons? He's a free man."

Letty nodded. "He ain' de only one dat's free."

"Lord God, Breel would kill him on sight!"

"Dey doin' great things. Teachin' and' sendin' folks up north. Dey—"

Zulu took hold of Letty's arm.

"Who's leading that gang?" she demanded, her eyes glinting.

Letty rolled her apron into a knot. "I ain' knowin'," she sobbed. "Fore Jesus, I ain' knowin'!"

"It's Jules! Lord God, I might have known it!"

"He don' know you heah, Miz Zulu. I ain' nebeh let on to Trojan dat I knows him."

"I'm going to write a note," Zulu said. "And I want you to see that Trojan gets it to Jules."

Letty shook her head. "Trojan kill me if I bring dat man any harm."

"If Trojan takes my note to Jules I'll give you your papers. He won't need to worry about buying you." She paused. "I going to ask him to meet me in the shack. I promise you this time he will be safe."

But not the next, she thought. Let him feel secure. Let him trust her. The next time she'd see Breel was waiting.

She wrote rapidly. "If you would like to see your

370

daughter I'll have her with me tomorrow night. Trojan will know where."

Papilottes was the one bait Jules would not be able to resist. Of that she was certain.

To meet Jules at night wasn't going to be as simple as she had made it sound in the note. There were so many things to consider . . . Yet, Letty had been going out there by night all these months and no one had known. . . .

She couldn't fall into that line of reasoning. Breel didn't make it a practice to spend the night with Letty, for one thing. And who really cared what she did? A black slave who didn't even belong to Bijou?

Her head spun with the effort to think sanely. This was her chance. She couldn't afford to make an error.

Of course. She was sick. Too sick to see anyone.

She took to her room shortly after the mid-day meal, and it wasn't difficult to feign illness. She actually did feel unwell. The thought of seeing Jules again left her shaking with a fear she couldn't analyze.

When Breel stopped by that night, Letty barred the door with her body.

"Miz Zulu sick," she said. "She too sick to see anyone."

Zulu held her breath until she heard Breel move away. At one time he would have been harder to convince, she thought. Lately there had been a change. Something she couldn't quite put her finger to—maybe it was that he never mentioned Rosalie anymore. Maybe it had to do with the way she caught him looking at Donna when he didn't know he was being observed.

But that was their problem. She had enough of her own.

Donna knocked and came into the room with a hot *tisane*, and a worried expression.

"It's nothing to fret over," Zulu assured her. "Just a headache."

If only she could tell her! But she knew Donna would

371

never approve.

It was very late in the night, and long after Zulu felt certain everyone was asleep, before Letty indicated it was safe to go to the nursery where Papilottes slept. The wet nurse was easy to arouse and they both stood by while she dressed the baby.

Zulu found herself studying her daughter, trying to see her as Jules would see her. She was pretty, but it was with a quaint loveliness, quite unlike Fannette's startling beauty. Awakened out of a sound sleep, she was still happy, and she made a gurgling noise when the nurse put her into her mother's arms.

"She's like Jules," Zulu whispered to Letty, and the baby snuggled closer.

It seemed forever, moving through the dark house, praying the baby would remain silent. Then, finally, they reached the door. Letty opened it, letting them out. Zulu leaned against the closed door, afraid to go down the long outside staircase. She knew Letty would be waiting to let her back in, but still it was as if she'd cut herself away from everything that meant even the shaky security represented by Bijou.

The moon was almost full. She forced back her fears and descended the stairs to the path. The light shone on her as she crossed the avenue and started toward the edge of the field, but she found herself looking back over her shoulder. It was as if she were being watched, followed, and it alarmed her, even though she knew it was only moonbeams casting reflections of light and dark on objects along the way.

At last the deserted outbuilding came into sight. It was then she realized it was all wrong. Everything she had planned and thought all those months was only a cover for what she did not want to admit.

I can't face him, she thought. Not like this. Memories of Jules flooded over her and she felt weak. It was no use. She had to turn back.

It was too late. Jules stepped out of the shadows, and

it was almost like the pond at Nollgrove. She wanted to throw herself into his arms, but she knew she couldn't.

She moved slowly toward him. It was as if a magnet were tugging at her.

When she was close enough she held the baby between them. Anything but to have him touch her. He looked at her a long minute, then he took his child and buried his face in the soft black ringlets.

"I've lived on hating you," she said. Somehow there was a need to tell him, to hope he would understand.

He looked up at her again, his chin still against Papilottes' head.

"I know."

"This was to be a trap."

"I wondered, but I had to come here."

The injustice of it all still rankled. She tried to bite it back, but she couldn't.

"You did all of that to us because of Renny. And now Breel tells me that Renny's dead."

Jules shook his head. "Breel didn't tell you the truth. I get word from Virginia when I can. Renny put his aunt over Nollgrove and he left. For the west, I guess. He always was interested in stories about the west."

Zulu was aware of a lessening of guilt. Jules set the baby in its blanket against a bush and took Zulu into his arms. They clung together, content just to feel the nearness of the other.

"Trojan and the others are back in the brakes," he told her. "I want you to come with us."

She held tighter to him. "I can't," she whispered. "Jules, I want to, but I'm afraid."

"That's a child's fear, Zulu. You're a woman now. And we'll be together." His lips were on hers again and for the moment there was nothing in the world but the two of them.

The baby cried suddenly and Jules raised his head. She felt his arms stiffen protectively around her.

"That's enough," Breel said. "In fact, that's more

than enough.''

She turned and saw Breel standing close to the baby in the moonlight, a pistol leveled at Jules and Neeta by his elbow.

Breel saw her staring at Neeta and he jerked his head in the girl's direction.

''She saw you crossing the road with the baby in your arms. She knew you were up to something and she came right to me.''

He moved his eyes back to Jules. ''So you're the one who has been making monkeys of all the planters around here? I guess we'll all have to thank Zulu for trapping you.''

She hadn't arranged the trap, but she may as well have done it. Jules put his arms around her again, reassuringly.

Breel said something in a low voice to Neeta and she ran toward the gatehouse.

''I told her to get the overseer up here and to see the dogs are let loose. I'm sending out word and we'll have a party together before dawn. I can't believe you came alone.''

The song ran through her mind . . .

''I run to de sea, but de sea run dry . . .

I run to de gate, but de gate shut fast. . . .''

Not as long as she could help.

''I have to get the baby,'' she said to Breel. She moved past him and tripped on something that wasn't there. She fell heavily against Breel, knocking the gun out of his hand.

''Run!'' she screamed.

Breel had the gun again and he swore as he shot into the field of tall cane.

He turned to Zulu after a minute.

''I'll see him hang if it's the last thing I ever do!'' he told her. He stuck the gun into his belt. ''If I have my way there won't be a damned runaway nigger in this entire parish by morning!''

Chapter Forty-Four

Zulu huddled in a chair on the gallery listening to the sound of the hunt. Occasionally there was the firing of a gun in the distance, and over it all, the yelping of the dogs in the swamps and the answering barking of hounds still held in the kennels.

Donna brought her a cup of coffee.

"I went to find Letty for you, but she's gone."

"She must have left to warn Trojan when Neeta came to the house . . ."

"I tried to stop Breel," Donna said, "but nothing could have stopped him." She was silent a minute, then she looked over her cup at Zulu, frowning slightly.

"Is it because of that man—because of him that Papilottes always meant more to you than Fannette?"

"He's Papilottes' father, if that's what you mean."

"You must love him very much.

Zulu was silent.

"Breel wouldn't—" Donna started uncertainly.

"Don't be a fool!" Zulu snapped. "He certainly would."

The yelping had grown closer. Zulu rushed to the edge of the gallery and looked down. There was the flash of a torch at the end of the field, and the kennel keeper was driving his dogs back into the run.

"They've caught him," Zulu said.

Donna gripped the railing until her knuckles were white.

I can't just stand here, Zulu thought. But what was there she could do? She tried to see through the mists. It was past dawn and already the light was pushing back darkness. Someone put out the torch and then the air cleared enough for her to see them standing under the live oak that had once been the center of the slanting lawns.

She could barely see Jules' figure in the background at first, then he was clear to her eyes, his hands bound behind his back and his legs bound together at the ankles. She tried to remember why the scene was so familiar, then she realized it was like a drawing an artist had sketched of Squire's hanging.

There was only Breel and the overseer. The kennel keeper locked the pens and walked over to them. The planters' party was still out after the band of maroons.

She had to try. She had to try something. But first it was important to think of those who would be left. She ran into the library and snatched writing material out of a drawer. Donna joined her and she held out the note.

"This is for Shad's lawyers, so they'll know you can act for me. I want Letty to have her freedom. You know it's been arranged that Fannette be sent to France when she's ready. But everything I have is to go to Papilottes. I don't want her to be like I was."

"What are you going to do?" Donna asked, then she watched Zulu open the case that held the Moulton dueling pistols. Donna waited until Zulu stood, holding one in her hand, before she spoke again.

"Give me that, Zulu."

Zulu drew back, but Donna still held out her hand.

"Do you really think I'd have let that—" Donna glanced over her shoulder, "happen?"

"Don't stand in front of me!" Zulu exclaimed. "There's no time!"

"What can you do with an empty gun?" Donna took the pistol from Zulu and opened a box of amunition. "Don't you realize they'd kill you before they let him go?" There was quiet authority in Donna's voice. "But they can't hurt me. I'm the owner of Bijou. Don't you see?"

There was a look on her face that reminded Zulu of

376

the night she had come from the cane brakes with the long whip in her hand.

They moved rapidly down the stairs and across the overgrown lawn. It was all Zulu could do to restrict herself to Donna's steady pace. Any moment could be too late. Any moment!

The overseer and kennel keeper saw them before Breel did. He was intent on tying the noose.

Donna came up on him quietly. "Drop that, Breel," she said.

Breel swung around. His eyes widened in disbelief.

"God Almighty, Donna!" he exclaimed. But he dropped the noose.

"Zulu's going to cut him free," Donna went on, indicating the knife that lay beside the rope. "I intend to shoot anyone who tries to stop her. That includes you, Breel."

"By God," Breel said slowly, "I believe you would." There was something close to admiration in his voice, and Zulu knew that both she and Jules were forgotten as he stared at his wife.

"I don't believe I've ever seen you before."

"Does it matter?" Donna asked.

"Yes," he said.

Zulu finished cutting the rope at his ankles, but Jules still stood in front of her.

"You're coming with me?"

Zulu shook her head, but still Jules did not move.

"Hurry!" She exclaimed. "There isn't time to waste!"

He turned and moved slowly toward the hazy brush that marked the start of the marshes. Zulu watched the greenery fold about him, knowing the heaviness she felt was with her to stay.

"Is he gone?" Donna asked, her eyes steady on Breel over the barrel of the pistol.

"Yes," Zulu replied.

"Then why are you still here? Am I doing this for

nothing? For someone who cares so little?"

"It doesn't matter," Breel said. "Hell, Donna, they can have the carriage for all I care!"

"So they can be picked up when the rest come back with their dogs?"

"Don't you understand, Donna? All these years I've lived for something that wasn't really there. But it's going to be different."

"Is it?" she asked. She lowered the pistol. "Maybe. Someday. But all I feel inside now is a sickness . . ."

Zulu moved toward the edge of the field. The ground was beginning to grow soggy.

. . . .The song has a last verse, Rosalie had said. Yes. She remembered now. It did.

"He casts out none dat come by faith. . . ."

But that was Rosalie's song. Her own was different.

Jules was waiting.

"Go back!" he called. "Everyone's scattered. They might never find us and I don't know how to reach the path without Trojan."

"You know the hiding places around here?"

"Yes, but not the way out. You've got to go back."

"There's not much time. Once the others get to Bijou there's nothing Donna or Breel can do to stop them from hunting us. We've got to run!"

But she couldn't run at first. She could only look at Jules and try not to feel what was all around her.

. . . .The grasses bent toward her . . . A dark pool reflected her shadow. . . .

Then she felt the wild, savage beauty sweep through her, clutching at something inside her being. Something locked and sealed away, a long time ago at Elmside.

She looked at Jules and let the pride flow through her as she had let the pride of her white heritage flow through her that morning in Alabama.

This is my place, she thought. This is me! And she knew that was the important thing, even though she could hear the song swelling to its finish.